LIKE A BLUNT DAGGER AIMED AT THE
HEART OF BRITAIN, THE WEDGE OF
LUFTWAFFE BOMBERS CAME ACROSS
THE CHANNEL. . . .

There were flights of Messerschmitt 109s close in
on both sides of the Heinkels, Mike Browning
reckoned, and more high above—poised to drop
like lethal darts onto the defending Spitfires.

Coming in at well above 350 m.p.h., he took the
leader. The frontal silhouette grew rapidly as the
closing speed approached 600 m.p.h. . . .

Center dot steady. . . . Hold it! Hold until your
judgment tells you that you *will*, not maybe, crash
head on. . . .

Then, with the Heinkel filling his sight,
Mike at last squeezed the gun button. . . .

THE FIGHT
OF THE FEW

A STIRRING SAGA OF THE R.A.F.
AND ITS FINEST HOURS

THE FIGHT
OF THE FEW

Richard Hough

A DELL BOOK

Published by
Dell Publishing Co., Inc.
1 Dag Hammarskjold Plaza
New York, New York 10017

Originally published in Great Britain in 1979
by Cassell Ltd.

Dell ® TM 681510, Dell Publishing Co., Inc.

ISBN: 0-440-12771-8

Reprinted by arrangement with
William Morrow and Company, Inc.

Printed in the United States of America

First Dell printing—July 1981

To the ground crews of
195 and 197 Squadrons R.A.F.

CONTENTS

1

THE NEW FACE

For the first second of consciousness, Keith knew that he was dead. He knew it for certain. So often since 10 May had he been close to the final violence of war, and so filled with sound had his life become, that the silence of 0445 hours was the silence of total unconsciousness. Then the stale overnight taste of whisky told him he was alive, and suffering a ferocious hangover. It had been a no-bloody-reason party, as the C.O. called them. No one had gone missing all day. No one had as much as damaged an enemy aircraft. Someone—it might have been that tough, foulmouthed Australian, Range Powell—had said, 'It's time we had a bloody party,' and no one had said No. And there was a party. A few bruises and minor cuts, a few broken chairs, a few smashed bottles of Haig. No more.

And now this unfamiliar silence in the dispersal hut with the emergency beds. Not a single Merlin engine warming up, not a single Browning machine-gun firing, not a single cry of instruction, warning or information on the R/T. None of the preliminary sounds of battle, nor the aftermath, nor the tearing, urgent row of battle itself, pounded Keith's ears. Running his tongue round his unappetizing mouth, he told himself with a grimace, 'Never heard a sound like it.'

When the telephone rang ten feet from his bed, his body twitched like a dying rabbit's, and he turned and had his feet in his boots before the orderly had raised the telephone. Range Powell always woke himself up by rolling onto the floor. The little sergeant, Bill Watson, had to be hit on the head with a flying boot, party or no party the night before. Christopher 'Flynn' Marston would arise, swing down like a seaman from his hammock, further confirmation that this good-looking pilot with the long hair justified his nickname, derived from his similarity to film star Errol Flynn in *Captain Blood*.

All this painful activity occurred in total darkness while the orderly spoke. 'Yes, sir . . . Right, sir . . . I'll do that at once, sir. Of course, right away.' There was a pause while Keith zipped up his Irvin, slipped into his Mae West and began feeling for the gauntlets he always kept beside his boots. Then the orderly replaced the telephone and, in a mock world-weary cockney voice, said, 'N.A.A.F.I.'ll be up in ten minutes.' Pause. 'Sirs.'

From the four pilots there came groans. A few boots were thrown in the direction of the orderly's table. Sergeant Watson released a string of invective he had acquired during four years as a Halton boy apprentice. Pilot Officer Marston was heard to say, 'You'll do this once too often, Aircraftman Godfrey.'

'Sorry, sir. Only trying to keep you hinformed.'

There was a creak of springs as the pilots lay back on their beds. The orderly began removing the blackout screens from the windows, revealing in turn squares of dark grey sky. Keith got up and made for the door, keen for the pre-dawn air, less to clear his whisky-ruined head than for the sight of trees and hedges taking shape, and the smell of the rye growing in the field behind the dispersal, ripe for the reaper. Country bred, an only child, Keith Steward needed moments of solitude and reminders of the Leicestershire landscape in which he had grown up. He needed them more than ever now, and much more than the whisky, though that was becoming important.

Keith stood on the edge of the grass watching R.A.F. Savile Farm coming alive around him as the light from the east revealed first shapes and then shades, all of them familiar, the nearest the most familiar of all, the sleek yet sturdy configuration of his Hurricane C-Charlie in its blast pen, pointing outwards for quick take-off, cockpit canopy closed against the summer dew.

Beyond was the winding strip of the perimeter track leading, like an artery, to the beating heart of the aerodrome, the squat watch office set forward of the three great square hangars, and beyond, the tall parachute store like a chapel to salvation, the soaring R/T tower—the 'drome's voice—the brick messes, admin blocks, the M.T. garage and fire station. All Keith could see of the spitfire squadron which shared the aerodrome was the silhouette of their pens and their dispersal huts. It was still too dark for the definition of the dainty little single-seat fighters themselves.

Savile Farm. Keith had first been stationed here more than a year ago and it had never before struck him how inappropriate was the name. No doubt it had once been a real farm here, bordering what were now the south-western suburbs of London, a farm like all farms dedicated to production instead of destruction. The only thing a fighter station had in common with a farm was a concern for the weather, which with this heavy dew, a faint east wind teasing the wind sock and the dying stars in the sky, indicated late summer sun. And that in turn would mean flying—perhaps four or five sorties—shooting and killing. Jerries, that was this farm's harvest, not rye.

Keith lit a cigarette, stamped the match into the grass and wandered towards the aerodrome's boundary, away from the stench of oil and glycol that hung over the hard-standing, past the pit where the fitter threw the old tins, the armourers the discarded ammunition boxes, and everybody else what they had no further use for.

Barbed wire in three rolls, then a ten-foot wire fence, marked the perimeter. Beyond was the rye, rustling very faintly in the breeze, a reassuring sound that would soon be overwhelmed as Savile Farm faced another hard day at full stretch. The wind was right, too, bringing the scent of the crop, sharp and dry.

'Nice morning, sir.' The army guard from the emergency defence company was a dozen yards away. Tin hat, khaki to the neck, puttees, a belt with spare cartridges, a heavy Great War Lee-Enfield rifle, and gasmask with tin helmet strapped over it.

Hatless, Keith nodded to return the salute. 'Yes. Another busy day.'

'Rather you than me, sir.' Keith offered him a cigarette, and he lit it and smoked like most rankers, hand cupped round it for concealment, taking long, greedy drags and letting the smoke out of the corner of his mouth.

From the far side of the field a Spitfire's engine crashed into life.

'Well, we're in business,' said Keith, crushing out his cigarette and walking back to the dispersal. He could see the hooded lights of the N.A.A.F.I. van moving along the perimeter track, carrying its urn of hot, strong, sweet tea and penny buns and rolls. Keith felt marginally recovered. The tea would complete the cure.

Then the outside telephone bell rang a few feet away, and Keith started as he had before. There would be no second reprieve. He knew that. As day follows night—and it had not yet done so—this would be a scramble. Sod Jerry. Didn't he ever have a hangover? Wouldn't he ever let up?

The dispersal hut door opened before he reached it and Range Powell was out, the big, lusty Australian swearing like the rest of them—except Marston of course—as they raced for their machines, maps sticking out of their boots, clutching gauntlets and inners.

'That bloody N.A.A.F.I.'s got a private line to Field Marshal bloody Goering,' Range shouted. 'You can see it in that sheila's bloody eyes.' Then the first detonations from the nearest Merlin cut off the Australian's harsh voice, and Keith collided with Marston in the doorway.

'Frightfully sorry,' said the pilot officer. Mike had commented only yesterday that Marston, goddam it, would apologize to a Jerry as he shot him down in flames, if he ever did, and then recite 'The Waste Land' all the way back to the 'drome.

13

Keith still found it painful to run and his machine had been parked in the nearest bay to compensate. He reached it just as his fitter started the engine, jumping out of the cockpit like a jack-in-the-box to make room for him. They had got the scramble routine down to a slick co-operative technique after these weeks of fighting so that there were no more corners to be cut. Parachute on the tailplane, straps lying so that Keith could grab them and throw them over his shoulder, securing the clips into the quick-release box against his chest. Leg straps too. Eight seconds.

Up onto the port wing, down into the seat. Preadjusted straps of the Sutton harness ready for pinning. On with the helmet and goggles hanging on the reflector gun-sight. The fitter clipped in the oxygen nozzle, Keith plugged in the R/T. Twelve seconds.

The rigger handed him inners and gauntlets, and both airmen jumped clear as Keith waved away the chocks and at once released the brake. Four more seconds. Cockpit drill as he taxied, fast and swinging left, right on the wheel-brakes—hiss of hydraulics—to see ahead where Range and Bill Watson were already clear of their pens and lining up for take-off. Fuel, trim, rad., magneto drop . . . Perfunctory cockpit drill. It would have you thrown off the course in training command. But they all did it now. 'The harsh necessities of war . . . the harsh necessities . . .'

Keith found himself humming it over and over to the tune of 'Begin the Beguine' as he tucked in beside Range with Marston on his right, his number two. Range raised his right hand momentarily and Keith pushed the throttle steadily forward, feeling the pressure of the seat in his back and checking his sight for brightness.

The section of four Hurricanes accelerated across the grass aerodrome in the half-light of dawn in loose formation, wheels bumping slightly, then scarcely touching. Tails up. 60 m.p.h., but no one was looking, as his A.S.I. Range was clear, then Keith, undercart already folding inwards and tucking into the wings . . . One minute 55 from the scramble call.

'Sandbag Red One, this is Nestegg, are you receiving me?'

'Yeah!' snapped Range, never one to waste words on the R/T.

'Sandbag Red One, Patrol base angels one-zero. I have trade for you.'

'I'll bet you bloody have.'

Keith tried to throw the tune from his head but it persisted as he slid shut the canopy, tightened his helmet strap, switched on oxygen and glanced down at his instruments. 'The harsh necessities of war.' So they had been. Harsh, I mean. But worse for Jenny.

✻

August 1940. Except for a brief break after escaping from France, scarcely a clear day had passed since the German attack on France and the Low Countries on 10 May, when Keith had not flown. He had collected a deep flesh wound, bailed out, and the five swastikas on the fuselage of his Hurricane were evidence of much ferocious fighting from the Meuse in France to the Kent and Sussex countryside.

Keith had been ill-equipped as a fighter pilot in two respects, two critical respects. First, his shooting was weak. And second, he had once suffered from a

15

lingering conscience about the business. In Leicester-shire where his adopted father, Sir Richard Barrett, was a landowner and had a big shoot, Keith had been brought up with the gun and the rod, and of course the hunt. But something always held him back from the full enjoyment of shooting. No matter how much Barrett instructed and chided him, Keith never improved during his boyhood, and he had always been glad of an excuse not to go out with the guns.

Keith had regarded this reluctance as a flaw in his character, and worried how he would face up to the life-or-death need to kill the enemy, at close range, in the air. By now, in August, with the struggle for the survival of his country at stake, with his own life in the balance, with daily injections of the adrenalin of fear and anger, and daily improvements in his skill and accuracy, he thought the last of his old squeamishness had disappeared, had faded from the sky like vapour trails after a high altitude dogfight.

It could not have happened without Jenny. Jenny had achieved the impossible, at once hardening and softening him, filling him with a tenderness he had never experienced before, and sharpening his resolve. 'Killing is your business and I like efficient people,' briskly spoken just after he got back from France. And a few days later she had nearly been killed herself.

He *must* see her soon. It was another necessity of war, and the need was like the pain of a burn that only the balm of her face and voice could soothe away. He could keep on flying for ever, perhaps starting a bit when the phone rang, hands shaking a little when lighting a cigarette, but he would be O.K., he would survive and fight well if he could just be with her from time to time.

They were in the sun. They had cheated and made their own sunrise up here, while below blacked-out England was still experiencing the last of the night. The familiar indentations and points of the south coast traced their way east, out sharply at Beachy Head, again at Dungeness, and far distantly the sudden reversal at North Foreland, the end of England.

Flying into this low sun, Keith felt safe, but without conscious intention he glanced in the mirror, turned left and looked up and down, turned right, aileroned his machine momentarily to look below, in the eternal vigil of the fighter pilot on patrol.

Once, not long ago but a lifetime of experience ago, he could be beguiled into the belief that there could be no enemy, no war or evil intentions, in a world of fairy-tale cumulo-nimbus cloud and brilliant sun, with glimpses of meadowland far below. Now he trusted nothing. In mist and fog, in days of wonderful clarity, at dawn or dusk or with the summer sun direct and blindingly above, Keith remained as alert and distrustful as game in lion country. He had seen too often the consequences of momentary relaxation.

Range Powell had his canopy open in order to see better and was giving special attention to the coastline east of Brighton. 'Angels one-zero, Sandbag Red One out,' he transmitted as the four Hurricanes levelled off and Keith drew back throttle and mixture and adjusted the trim of his machine.

'Sandbag Red One, vector zero-eight-five. Zero-eight-five. Many bandits in Garden area, angels one-minus.'

Keith glanced at his code card of the day and read off Dover against Garden. They would be early morning free-ranging 109s beating up the coastal towns and provoking reaction in order to get as many fighter squadrons airborne as they could. The first big raids of the day would follow when the Hurricanes and Spitfires were on the ground refuelling. That was the Hun plan. They would not succeed, and the inflexibility of German tactics was extraordinary. But these small groups of low, fast 109s were the devil to deal with. Faster and more heavily armed than the Hurricane, quicker in the climb, quicker in the dive. A superior machine in almost every respect—as, week after week, the new faces on 140 Squadron attested.

A flash of flame, and then another, far ahead and below, gave them a better guiding point than even the R.D.F. could offer. Playing silly buggers with the balloons, as the C.O. described it last week. And Rowbotham had got a 109 on the job. The protective balloons over Dover harbour were an irresistible temptation to roaming low-flying German fighters, and they were at it again. Red Section was too far away to see the ack-ack, but the gunners would be pumping up Bofors and Oerlikon fire and generally helping to keep the population's nerves on edge.

Range closed his hood and put his two sections into a shallow dive. 320 A.S.I., with the sun dead ahead and touching the horizon again in a temporary sunset. There was more definition to the countryside below, the smudge of Ashford, the straight line of the Tonbridge railway which they were following.

Give Flynn Marston his due, he made as good a look-out as Captain Blood himself. 'Bandits 2 o'clock

18

below, steering 180,' he transmitted, and Range at once turned sharply to starboard, Keith and his number two slipping under him to assume station on his port side. He could still see nothing, and they were down to 3,000 feet and at full boost with 360 on the clock before he picked out the last of the Messerschmitt 109s, a small, dark, T-shape darting south just above the fields. There were more ahead of him—two, three, nine—a whole *Staffel* of ten or eleven, on their way home in a hurry, no doubt with the intention of shooting up the Rye C.H. (Chain Home) R.D.F. station on the way out.

The Hun had eyes in the back of his head. Keith knew that they would be spotted within a few seconds. They might get in one burst before they lost their advantage of height and speed. It had better be a good burst. He slipped over the safety shield on his button and, with both hands firm on the spade grip of his stick, waited for the camouflaged shape of the 109 to fill the range bars of his reflector sight.

*

Mike Browning's head had time to recover before he arrived at the B Flight dispersal, hitching a ride in the C.O.'s Hillman. Like the rest of the Flight, he had been at 30 minutes' Readiness and had snatched a quick breakfast.

'What have Met. got to say, sir?' he asked.

Squadron Leader Rowbotham was burly, balding, fair, a cheerful extrovert with a broken nose—probably several times broken, judging by his enthusiasm at mess parties and his record in the R.A.F. rugger team. He told Mike not to ask fool questions so early in the morning. 'Just raise that Yankee nose,

19

sniff and look up. Hot, dry, unlimited visibility, un-limited ops.' He slammed shut the car door behind him and strode to his office.

Mike asked Chiefy, 'When did they scramble?'

The Flight Sergeant said, 'Just before five, sir. Gets earlier every day.'

'Cheer up, I guess the nights are getting longer.'

'Then it'll be night-flying, sir. Take my word for it.' The Flight Sergeant could not be cheered up that easily.

It was the implacability of the German onslaught that was hardest to take. On another hot summer, ten years ago on Long Island, Mike and a buddy had wanted to clear an area of the beach to erect a hut, a secret place cut off by shrubs and dunes. Working with shovels through a long, sunny day, they had made almost no impression on the soft sand which had come pouring down on them, in a never-ending torrent, as they dug. Just like the goddam Luftwaffe. Every day you went up, maybe five sorties, fought till the sweat poured off you, picked up a few shells or bullets getting through to the Dorniers and Heinkels, and perhaps got a quick burst before the 109s were all around you like stirred up wasps.

So you did break up the formation. Maybe on a good day a dozen or more bombers went down and more than that number went home crippled, dead men on board. The Spit boys on the other side of the field got five 109s a few days ago. But, as one of them remarked bitterly (and drunkenly) in the mess, 'There were twice as many the next day, like a many-headed Medusa, or whatever the bitch was called.' Meanwhile, and increasingly, faces disappeared from the mess, sometimes temporarily while the pilot made his way back from some field in Kent or the mud of the Thames Estuary, or damper still and much the worse for wear, by courtesy of the Royal Navy. Sometimes permanently.

Once or twice a week, the C.O. would call for his car after dinner and settle down to the miserable job of writing to parents or wives. Mike imagined them. 'It is with a very heavy heart that . . . a really wizard member of the squadron, like by all . . . you can be proud . . .'

Mike Browning, cheerful, bouncy, an adventuring scion of a New York banking family, had suffered a great many surprises since he had joined the R.A.F. on an impulse before the war. The close-knittedness of the service was one, the class barriers another, the way they could be circumvented (more easily in some ways than American money barriers) a third. The backs-to-the-wall grit he had witnessed in the Norwegian campaign was less of a surprise because he had been brought up to believe that the British were at their best on the brink of catastrophe with everything, including their own incompetence, loaded against them. Falling in love had been a surprise, too. He had planned to leave that sort of nonsense until the war was over. But Eileen, only daughter of Keith's adopted parents, had knocked the idea to angels five-zero. But why doesn't she write me?

More serious still (because it might lead to his never seeing Eileen again) was the power, and strength, and the remorseless character of the Luftwaffe's assault, growing from attacks on coastal shipping and ports in July to this day-after-day attack on

R.A.F. Fighter Command, its bases, its R.D.F. warning chain, its factories and the fighters themselves, in the air and on the ground. All this, while the invasion forces built up in the newly-captured ports in France, Belgium and Holland, in numbers and strength unequalled since Napoleon's Grand Army stood poised to strike nearly a century and a half ago. Nelson had fixed that. Now they had to fix this.

As Mike waited on the edge of the perimeter track by the B Flight dispersal, anxiously alert for the sound of Merlin engines, he wondered again about the odd strokes of fate which had brought him here—an R.A.F. fighter pilot in the heat of the biggest air battle in history, with a leg that still ached from a flying injury, and with a score of five Huns, like Keith. Here, crazily, he was at the beginning of another day of highly lethal combat, instead of starting his third year at Harvard or working in Wall Street with his own 812 Cord convertible and a party every night. 'Well, I guess I've got the parties, and ol' J-Johnnie in the hangar's faster and more fun.' Then, as often before, he thought about his ancestors, who had fought at Yorktown: what would old Morris Browning have to say about his direct descendant, Michael, flying alongside the British?

Rowbotham emerged from his office at the first sound of aircraft. Not a man at Savile Farm could confuse a Merlin with a Daimler-Benz now. Three Hurricanes came out of the early morning sun at five hundred feet above the suburban semis of Sutton, Surrey. 140 Squadron had long given up any fancy flying after combat. Tight formation spelt death. A victory roll, in a machine that might unknowingly be damaged, could lead to a court martial. All anyone wanted nowadays was to get down unscathed, light a cigarette, then go to sleep and wake up to a triple whisky.

The broken gun patches and black stains from the gun ports were the first confirmatory signs that they had all been in action. The three Hurricanes, hoods open, undercarriages and flaps extending, open gun ports whistling as if in glee, flew in a vic on the downwind leg. Range was all right and leading them, and another was T-Toc, Watson's machine, the little sergeant's head low in the cockpit. For a moment he obscured the third aircraft. Then as they turned, Mike caught a glimpse of the letter C. So Keith was O.K. again. 'Thank the good Christ!' he muttered, and at once wondered why he had especially minded this time when he had awaited Keith's return so often.

That meant Flynn was probably down somewhere. He might turn up, but in fifteen minutes he'd be out of gas. Maybe they'd have news. Pilot Officer Christopher Flynn Marston had come (with his library) two months before to replace the irrepressible (until July 4th) Buffer Davies, now being patched up by McIndoe. Flynn was a steady safe pilot with the eyes of a hawk. But he never seemed to score.

Mike watched Keith taxi-ing in fast, braking and turning through 180 degrees just outside his pen, his straps thrown off before the prop stopped turning and jumping down, parachute over his shoulder. His corn-coloured hair was plastered with sweat and the oxygen-mask had marked a circle about his mouth and across his nose. The C.O. and Mike and two other pilots walked in with him.

23

'He's O.K., sir,' said Keith, his voice hoarse from breathing oxygen. 'Unless he got shot up after he landed.' It had been known to happen during these twitchy days when a parachute could mean a paratrooper—a German paratrooper.

Mike gave him a lighted cigarette, and Keith glanced at him and smiled, wiping his face with the back of his sleeve. 'Thanks. But for God's sake some-one give me some tea. Two hours on an empty belly after last night!'

The Intelligence Officer had engineered four mugs of hot tea and four bath buns for them in his office, and when the other two arrived he began taking down their report.

Range said, through a mouthful of bun, 'Yeah—bounced about a dozen Huns south of bloody Ash-ford. Couldn't bloody miss. Keith here and I put down one. A right flamer, eh, cobber?'

Keith nodded, and Mike could imagine the instant ball of flame as if they had touched a fuse. Then a scattering of metal and human fragments over a hop field. No more. Well, that was how Archie Lemon had gone two days ago, wasn't it?

'Bill got one—didn't you?' Range turned to the tough little lined sergeant. (He had not shaved for three days and was due for a roasting from Row-botham again for his appearance. Even now there were limits.) Watson nodded and scratched his arm-pits.

The reporting was soon over. Two months ago ev-ery detail would have been noted and double-checked. But now it was just the bare facts, with a mention of any identification of enemy aircraft—

insignia, camouflage, numerals. Confirmation of claims might come later, from the police, the Army or the Observer Corps, or from the Navy if it happened over the sea.

Flynn had in turn been jumped by a laggard 109 far behind the others, had dragged his Hurricane streaming smoke and glycol to a thousand feet and got out. 'His 'chute opened O.K.,' said Keith, 'and the Jerry turned to give him a squirt. Then he saw me.'

'He hooked his bloody bait all right then,' added Range Powell. 'Twenty bloody boost and black smoke all the way to frogland.'

*

The Spitfire squadron was scrambled twice that August morning, and 140's Hurricanes were sent up to deal with a heavy raid on the Portsmouth-Southampton area. Everyone fired their guns, and there were claims and losses. The Spitfires lost a flight commander, and 140's A Flight had a sergeant-pilot killed in a head-on collision with a Dornier 17. By noon each squadron had one flight on 30 minutes Readiness, and the bar in the officers' mess began to fill up.

Savile Farm was a peace-time station and the mess was a grand one built in the Georgian style with double glass doors, now criss-crossed with tape against bomb blast and splinters, leading from the bar onto a grass terrace. Here, in the 1930s, smart regular officers would chat about their cars and their popsies over a noggin before lunch within sight of the line-up of gleaming Siskins and Bulldogs.

War had not at once changed the scene. There had been the early alarms, and then, except for the black-out, the gas exercises, and the increasing number of W.A.A.F.s about the station, life had sunk into a winter of apathy and disillusion. The last of the biplane Gladiators were replaced by Mark 1 Hurricanes, there were patrols and exercises, but it was hard to believe there was a war on.

Mike remembered Savile Farm in September 1939, before they had been sent up to Scotland, and his own exasperation with the British. He had joined the R.A.F. to fight the evil of Nazism, hadn't he? Then it seemed that half the country didn't want the war after all. There had been strikes, talk of a negotiated peace, anti-war speeches in Parliament. They sang 'We're going to hang out the washing on the Siegfried Line' on the radio, but no one appeared to have the intention of doing any such thing, least of all the French, who had the only army that could have done it.

The contrast with the scene then and this August luncheon time hit Mike again as he walked into the bar. The room was packed like the common room at his old school, Andover, after a particularly important, fierce and victorious football game. But here the game was even rougher, the odds a great deal higher. Formality had slipped over the past weeks as the fighting had increased in intensity. Pilots wore flying boots, maps still tucked inside. Several were in shirt sleeves and still wearing their yellow Mae Wests which had become almost an integral part of their uniform. Two spitfire pilots sported their pre-war white flying overalls, none too clean now. The Wing Commander Flying, who had been in the watch office since 0430, was unshaven and wore a white polo-neck jersey as he put back his first pint. Only some of the

Penguins—the 'wingless wonders', the admin. officers, the two M.O.s and others whose work was on the ground—were properly dressed.

The air was thick with smoke in spite of the open doors, the temperature stifling, the noise cacophonous. As Mike waded towards the bar, the talk of battle struck him in waves—'I thought Charlie had had it . . .', 'The Hun just put his nose down and beat it . . .', 'Not much of a press-on type, clueless if you ask me . . .', 'So I gave him two seconds with quarter deflection and his port engine . . .', 'Biggin was pranged again—saw the smoke from Eastbourne . . .'

Mike saw Range at the bar. He was on double Scotches (strongly frowned on at lunch by the C.O.) but liquor seemed to have no effect on Range except to make him randier. He winked at Mike but couldn't get near him for the crush. Mike took his pint of bitter and fought his way back, anxious for air and peace. He was nearly at the glass doors when he spotted the pilot officer. Mike, who still tended to use American rather than R.A.F. slang, could not help reacting with the word 'sprog' to the sight of the one pilot in the bar properly dressed. The figure—forlorn, lost and nervous—was the personification of the epithet. He was standing, without even a drink or a cigarette in his hand, looking about him in bewilderment.

The poor guy! Mike squeezed his way to him, and on an impulse thrust the pint mug into his hand. 'Here, take this. I'll get another. Then I guess we can do the introductions.'

Mike returned from his second sortie to the bar, and led the pilot officer through the doors onto the grass terrace. 'My name's Mike. Mike Browning. From the

27

USA, as you might guess.' He looked at the solemn young man—short red hair, grey eyes, less frightened now, a nice mouth, a chin not yet hardened to regular shaving, about Mike's height of five foot eight—and the blue uniform stiff with newness.

'My name's Mackay. I'm new here.' He smiled when Mike laughed.

'Yeah, I can see that. But cheer up, we're used to new faces. What my Pop would call, in Wall Street language, a steady turnover. Are you for 140 or the Spits?'

At this moment, Squadron Leader Rowbotham came up and said, 'Ah, Mike, good show. You've introduced yourselves, eh? Mackay's for B Flight. Will you show him the form? I want him passed out for ops as soon as possible.' He turned to the newcomer, who was standing to attention. Rowbotham put him at ease. 'No formality in the mess. Not much anywhere just now. Too busy. Mike'll take you up this afternoon unless there's more flap.' He turned to go inside, adding, 'He drives on the left being a Yank, so watch it.'

Pilot Officer Mackay laughed nervously, then held up his mug to Mike. 'Cheers. Thanks very much.'

They lunched early, before the worst of the rush, and Mike learned more about Mackay, some of it with dismay. For instance, he had done only twelve hours on Hurricanes; his Operational Training Unit course had been cut in half, and cut in half again; he had only twice fired the guns, and only once at a towed drogue, which he had failed to hit. 'Our instructors kept being posted away so that those who were left were flying all hours. Mine used to go to sleep in the rear cockpit of the Master and tell me to get on with it.'

Mike had heard that the shortage of pilots was even more acute than the shortage of aircraft, that light bomber pilots were being taken off Battles and Blenheims and given a quick conversion course, that escaped air force officers from Poland, Czechoslovakia, Norway, Belgium and France were being pressed into service in spite of language problems, and that the Fleet Air Arm had been asked for volunteers. He had not realized that they were so near the bottom of the barrel that they were now getting young sprogs like Mackay—'Ginger' Mackay as he shyly let it be known.

It was a policy of accelerating deterioration that had been forced on High Command. Every experienced veteran, like the Spitfire flight commander that morning, was replaced either by someone new to single-seat fighters or wet-behind-the-ears guys like this nice Mackay. And each one had to be worked into the squadron, meaning more flying for tired pilots (like Mike himself this afternoon). And each one, by the law of averages, was more likely to be shot down than the pilot he replaced. As Mike pushed aside his plate and drained his glass, he judged that calculations like these were best left unspoken. But they still nagged away at you in the brief moments of leisure, or just before you sank thankfully to sleep, or woke up with the shrill sound of the telephone in your ears.

As they left the mess, they were greeted at the bottom of the steps with the surprising sight of a Rolls-Royce car which had just drawn up. There was a chauffeur at the wheel, who got out and opened the back door. A large bundle of white silk parachute emerged through it, which the chauffeur attempted to hold, though most of it spilled onto the footpath, trailing lengths of silk cord.

Flynn Marston then emerged, still wearing his Mae West, his uniform torn and mud-stained. Catching sight of Mike, he called him down and introduced him to his fellow passenger, an elderly woman wearing a large hat.

'Lady Duncaster, may I introduce a fellow pilot of mine, Michael Browning? From the United States.'

Mike put his head into the back of the Rolls-Royce and shook a hand that was jagged with rings. 'Glad to know you, Lady Duncaster. And thank you for bringing Christopher home.'

'It was a pleasure. Such good company. He recited such a lot of poetry as we drove along in the motor. Some of it rather strange but he told me it was modern. I so much wanted him to stay at my place to rest after the gamekeepers brought him in.'

Mike said, 'Well, it's sure good to have him back safely, Lady Duncaster.'

The Rolls-Royce slipped away and Marston said with a trace of bitterness, 'Yes, the gamekeepers brought me in all right, as if I was a poacher, with twelve-bores into my back and another unpleasant fellow with a pitchfork.'

Ginger Mackay, who had been an astonished witness to all this, could no longer restrain himself. 'You mean they threatened you after you landed?'

Marston turned to the new pilot and said precisely and rather disdainfully, 'Well, you see, to them it is all rather like Auden—you know:

Thought I heard the thunder rumbling in the sky;
It was Hitler over Europe, saying 'They must die.'

'What he's telling us is that anything at the end of a parachute is assumed to be Hun,' added Mike. 'And you've got to be quick convincing them you're not.'

Marston ordered a couple of passing airmen to take his parachute to the store for repacking, and left them for the mess. A voice on the Tannoy, echoing off the walls of the nearby buildings, was calling out, 'Orange alert! Orange alert! Fifty plus heading this way. Pilots on thirty minutes to immediate state. A Flight Beacham Squadron scramble . . . A Flight Beacham scramble.'

As the message was repeated, Mike saw the new pilot eyeing him anxiously. He said, 'Does that mean we take cover?'

Mike shouted back, 'No. We wait for a red alert for that. This means "Finish your noggin just in case." '

They made their way to the bus that would take them down to the dispersal. 78 Squadron's Spitfires were already lined up for take-off. The planes accelerated quickly on their arrow ballerina-like undercarriages and lifted off and passed overhead at fifty feet, six of them in line abreast, wheels tucking in, more slowly than the hydraulically-operated Hurricanes', the roar of their Merlins fading as they bore away south over Sutton.

'You've arrived on a busy day,' Mike remarked laconically. 'Though it hasn't been what you could call quiet for a long while.'

The bus picked them up, and Mike noticed a Bofors gun crew in tin helmets, just by the perimeter fence, swinging the gun's barrel onto a south-easterly setting. There was ready ammunition packed along the insides of the sandbag blast walls of the gun pit.

A Flight's Hurricanes were scrambled before the bus reached the dispersal. Mike caught a glimpse of the pilots sprawled on the grass and the chairs outside the hut. It was an inanimate scene viewed distantly through the bus's windows. Then it suddenly sprang to life, figures ran towards the Hurricanes in the blast pens, and before the bus had reached the B Flight dispersal the machines were rolling across the grass and turning for take-off.

With the fading sound of the Hurricanes' engines they could hear the distant, deep and uneven throb of a large bomber formation. Mike, with Pilot Officer Mackay standing close beside him, stared up into the hot sky. The sun, only just past its meridian, was blindingly bright from the direction of the bombers' approach. He could see nothing.

Mackay said, 'Aren't we going to scramble, too?'

'Not now. Too late. They're afraid that the bombers'll catch us on the ground. And the 109s often come in low to strafe and we'd be sitting ducks.' He gave up staring into the sun and pointed towards a zig-zag slit trench beside the dispersal hut. 'That's where you go if things get hot.'

A second after he spoke, the Tannoy crackled and a voice called out, crisply, calmly, 'Take cover! Take cover! This is a red alert. All personnel take cover!'

Mike strolled over towards the slit trench. Airmen in blue overalls, airmen in shirt sleeves, arms black with grease, Aircraftman Godfrey who ran like a rabbit from the hut, a pilot holding a puppy—all were dropping into the trench and putting on their tin hats.

Mike, conscious that he might be thought to be showing off and aware of Mackay's anxiety, fell into a trot. 'In you go,' he told him, but himself remained on the edge of the trench. He could just see the bombers now, about sixty of them in their usual stepped-up vics of five, very tight in order to get the best from their co-ordinated defensive fire as well as their co-ordinated bombing. They were at around 15,000 feet, Mike calculated, and heading straight for Savile Farm on their first visit. Behind them was a dissolving pattern of ack-ack bursts, but no fresh ones, and Mike could guess why.

He could just make out the tiny shapes of the fighters in a head-on attack at a closing speed of more than 500 m.p.h. They would be Hurricanes, probably 111 and 615 Squadrons from Kenley, and, as Mike knew, their head-on attack made the greatest of all demands on nerves and reactions. But it was also terrifying for the bomber crews.

The first wave of Hurricanes had already broken off their attack and were scattering, gaining height for a second attack, and the neat bomber pattern had begun to break up before the sound of the firing reached them. It came in short bursts that sometimes overlapped and was like far-away massed drum riffles.

A voice at Mike's feet called up. 'Come in 'ere, sir. Plenty of room.'

He looked down and saw the cheerful face of Peters, armourer corporal. 'O.K., Reg. Be right with you.'

He glanced up into the bright sky again. The

bombers were almost directly overhead but their formation had been shattered by the second head-on wave of Hurricanes, and two of the Heinkels were trailing smoke and losing height.

Mike hopped down beside the corporal and looked along the trench. Mackay was sitting on a bench with the same shy, self-effacing expression that Mike had recognized in the bar. He felt a stab of compassion for the boy. Was this, the poor son-of-a-bitch, a man of war? A warrior of the 1940s?

Mike winked and Mackay smiled back. 'This is going to be nothing—nix,' he told him. Then, in the mock-English voice he sometimes assumed, 'Our brave boys in blue have once again hurled themselves victoriously against the full might of the Luftwaffe and smashed it.'

The sound of the first bombs proclaimed the denial of Mike's claim. There was a scream, louder on a descending note, then a whoomph. A blast of air shot the length of the trench and dry soil spilled from between the planked walls.

More screams followed, overlapping, but the first bomb was the nearest to them, and distant explosions confirmed that the bombing pattern from the surviving aircraft was ragged and scattered. There would be deaths and injuries in Sutton and Cheam, little houses made into rubble, but this was nothing like some of the raids that had reduced Biggin Hill and Manston to a shambles.

When Mike climbed out of the trench the dust from hits on the airfield was drifting to the west, and there was smoke and more dust rising from explosions among the buildings. He could hear the fire engine's bell and the sound of distant raised voices. The first bomb had landed in the field of rye behind the hut, its crater spewing fine dust like an active volcano.

Mackay said, 'Do you think we'll get any flying after this?' Someone had put a tin hat on his head and he looked like the juvenile lead in some old war film.

'Oh, sure,' said Mike. 'Nothing to it.'

❋

They finally got off the ground at 6 p.m., delayed by trouble with the R/T in Mackay's machine. Everyone in A Flight had got back safely but made no claims. Both Kenley and Biggin Hill had taken a pasting again.

Mike's Hurricane was still being patched up in the hangar after a cannon hit two days before and he borrowed Keith's C-Charlie.

'Just take it easy,' he had told Mackay. 'This isn't much more than a sector recce, but I want you to stick to my tail when I tell you, and later I'll try bouncing you. O.K.?'

The take-off was not too bad. Mike opened the throttle slowly, giving Mackay plenty of time to adjust his station. When he lifted off, the new boy was trailing about ten yards behind. But not bad, not bad at all. At 8,000 feet Mike transmitted, 'O.K., spread out. Have a good look around you. The weather's not always like this. Correction: very rarely like this. So spot your landmarks. That's the Thames at Hampton Court to the north. See how it kinks round from southwest to north-west. You're nearly into the barrage balloons there, but it's a handy guide. And remember, that goddam river twists all over and doubles back on itself.'

Mike turned in his cockpit and pointed due east. 'That's Epsom Downs. It's where you have your Derby.' He pronounced it 'Durby'. 'And right below us now is Leatherhead.'

Control chipped in, 'Sandbag Red One, there's trade building up again Garden area. Will keep you informed. Over.'

'Just keep it clear of us, Nestegg. For once I ain't interested.'

He switched channel briefly to Sector and heard the chatter of imminent combat far away down at Manston.

'O.K., Red Two, line astern, line astern—go.' Mike saw Mackay holding a hand to his right headphone, and he repeated the order. This time the Hurricane dropped behind him. At once Mike went into a series of violent evolutions, throwing the forgiving, responsive machine into sudden climbing turns, a slow roll to the right, then a roll off the top, and two flick rolls in succession which finally threw him off. Mike flew straight and level and waited for the Hurricane to resume station astern, now at 15,000 feet.

'O.K. Red Two, line abreast, line abreast—go.' Mackay remained behind him, and Mike repeated the order, checking that he was on the right channel. Then he tried Sector channel but that was crammed with urgent chatter. He rocked his wings and throttled back but still the Hurricane stuck to his tail. 'He must know he's got a dud R/T by now. Why doesn't the sap use his nut?'

As a last expedient, Mike was just beginning to Morse with his belly identification light when Nestegg came through warning of bandits to the south over Horsham.

'O.K. Returning to base,' Mike replied crossly. Just his luck to be burdened with this deaf sprog at this of all times. He banked and began turning to port, but before his wing obstructed the sky to the south he saw, much nearer than they should have been, a formation of hostile aircraft—Ju.88s he identified them at once—on a northerly course and 2,000 feet below. Not many. A single *Staffel* of about 15. And then, predictably and 5,000 feet above, a swarm of 109s as top cover. It was time to go, fast. It was like being caught in a riot pushing a pram.

Mike opened the throttle wide and put his nose straight down, at the same time transmitting to Nestegg. He could see in his mirror that Mackay was hard behind him, no doubt alarmed at the sudden turn of events. Or had he seen the Huns? That would make an interesting examination question after they landed.

Mike reckoned afterwards that they were at about 9,000 feet and doing about 370 A.S.I. when the tracer started sweeping past his wingtips. Some sharp-eyed 109 pilot had spotted them, in spite of their camouflage against the English countryside. And they had come down very fast, at least five of them. Mike could count five in his mirror. And he knew how much faster in the dive they were. He ruddered to throw them off their aim, pulled out so sharply that he blacked out, and dragged back the stick hard again to get into a tight defensive circle.

'Hold onto me like crazy,' he transmitted. 'Just hold on, Red Two.' Perhaps Mackay's R/T fault had rectified itself. It was worth a try, but there was no way of telling.

'Red Two, get on my tail!' The innocent exercise had suddenly turned into fearsome reality. The boy with twelve hours on Hurricanes, who had never hit the drogue, was in close combat, and with everything loaded against him.

Mike could see him trailing, trailing far behind. There were three of them on him, and the boy was doing nothing—sweet nothing. It was murder!

Mike blacked out again trying to pull his tail round. Safety shield off, sight on, lift the nose. Far out of range. 600 yards at least. And there was another almost on his own tail. Mike gave a short burst hoping it might distract the Huns.

But nothing in the world was going to disturb them. They must have known they were onto the greenest of greenhorns, a ripe pretty sitting duck.

They carved him up in turn. Mike saw the whole thing and wished he had not. Three stern attacks did the trick. Bits fell off Mackay's machine, then his tail was shattered. Not shattered, shot off—clean sodding off. Glycol, then smoke, then flames poured from the engine. The boy with the grey eyes never got out. Mike prayed he was dead before the flames engulfed him.

He saw no more. He was too busy looking after himself. A quick climbing roll to the right failed to throw off his pursuer. So he stall-turned, and the unexpectedness of this evolution upset his foe. He hung in the sky for a second, ruddered hard when he had regained speed, pulled the stick in with both hands and at last was free. He saw the 109, dark jazzy camouflage, black crosses, swastikas and all, not fifty yards ahead and gave it a full deflection one second burst. And missed.

Mike did not curse much as a rule. When he did it helped. He shouted 'Shit!' into his mask and followed the 109 down when it dived almost vertically. He knew its low fuel capacity precluded it from engaging in a prolonged dogfight so far from home. It wanted to be away—and, my God, it was going. It shot down towards the Downs above Dorking far beyond Mike's diving speed. But Mike had other ideas. He was now hell-bent on revenge, which was all that he could offer in atonement for allowing that poor, nice, hopelessly inadequate kid to get killed.

Mike went south in a much shallower dive, due south at full open throttle, pulling out the emergency boost knob. He had lost the 109, but it had to come out somewhere. It had to cross the South Downs before the coast. Mike aileroned gently left and right as he went down to give himself maximum visibility. Ten seconds later he picked up the little plane, alone and right down on the deck and almost on top of its own shadow streaking across the fields—a harvested cornfield, a grazing meadow with the cows scattering in panic, under some high tension cables towards a village.

The 109 had lost the speed advantage of its dive. Mike had not. At 2,000 feet he was still well above him. He was catching him up fast, and was travelling faster still when he steepened his dive and came in for a half-deflection shot.

Hold it, buddy. Cool. Everything's going for you for once. 400 yards, 300. Ease back the throttle. 200. That was the range at which he and Keith had harmonized their guns.

Mike Browning, who had even impressed Keith's adopted father at Rising Hall with his shooting, held the red centre dot of the sight steadily on the cockpit of the 109, pulled it through half the ring, and fired.

He caught the wing root with the first one second sighting burst. Then, surprised that the pilot took no counter-action, fired again, a longer burst, and saw the De Wilde bullets pumping like white darts into the cockpit. It was a killing burst. Fragments of canopy, and strips of metal streamed back against the tailplane and disappeared like ashes of the dead in the slipstream.

It was as if the recoil of the eight Brownings had violently braked the Hurricane. The Messerchmitt, still flying dead straight and level pulled rapidly ahead, while Mike's machine lost the false speed advantage of its dive. He gave one more burst almost from astern, saw a scattering of strikes around the cross on the side of the fuselage, then it was out of range, now spewing glycol like a thin pencil line in the air.

But he *must* have killed the pilot, he told himself. No one could have survived that concentrated pattern of some 250 bullets, especially as the German fighters, unlike the British, had no armour plate behind the seat. And yet this indestructible plane flew up, still at around 200 feet, flashing over treetops and country tracks, farmhouses and cottages, a winding country lane.

Maddened by his failure to shoot the 109 into the

ground, Mike could do no more than follow it at an ever-greater distance, and swear at the R.A.F. for giving him a machine that was 50 m.p.h. too slow.

A mile ahead were the South Downs, rolling grassland four or five hundred feet high. On the other side was the sea, and fifteen minutes later, at this speed, the coast of France. It was outrageous, impossible that his adversary should elude him. But that's what he was doing.

The 109 streaked on, as straight and steady as ever, over the fields that arose at first gently and then gave way to the open grassland. There was a copse of beech trees at the summit, Chanctonbury Ring. The 109 did not lift with the contours. It went straight on. Mike saw its shadow racing over the grass, rapidly closing with the wings and fuselage of the fighter like embracing twins, until they met in an explosive holocaust fifty feet below the trees.

Mike had been watching so intently that the white splash left its mark on the retina of his eyes, and he had to pull up until it faded. When he looked down, circling the point of impact, he saw no more than a small tangled mass of wreckage, a stain of black over a wider area, the contrasting white of the crater dug into the chalk, and a column of smoke rising and slowly drifting west. Southdown sheep, which had scattered far, were returning, already reconciled to the presence of this hot metal scattered across their grazing land.

*

'I guess the guy just froze on the controls,' said Mike. 'Not the first time. But he had me fooled for a while.'

The squadron Intelligence Officer—'the Spy' Flying Officer Willy Williams—was writing on his report sheet. The C.O. was in the office, too. With pilots critically short, Group would be asking searching questions about the loss of a pilot even before he had been passed out for operations. He had heard a detailed account from Mike and had reassured him that he was in no way to blame. But the wireless mechanic was to be put under open arrest and there could be a court martial later.

The telephone range and Rowbotham reached for it, snapping 'Yes', into the mouthpiece. Mike could hear the voice at the other end and guessed what he was saying before the C.O. thanked him briefly and slammed it back onto its cradle.

'They found the poor sod. A field south of Dorking. Not much left, of course. It'll be another bricks-in-the-coffin funeral. And what the hell am I going to tell his parents?'

'Let me add a note, will you, sir? I'm about the only guy who ever spoke to him except you.' Mike had not the least idea what he could say but it might be some sort of relief for his guilt.

It was 9 o'clock and almost dark before he got to the mess. He glanced at the baize letter-board and saw, with a final shot of utter dejection, that there was still no letter from Eileen. More than two weeks now. No letter. No telephone call. Nothing.

Keith came out of the dining-room looking grey after the long day and three ops. He walked over to Mike and said, 'I hear they got that new boy. I never even saw him. Twenty minutes—that must be a record.'

42

'Quit that, Keith, will you,' Mike said sharply.

Keith looked at him in surprise. Most tempers were getting short but Keith had thought his friend's nerves were bearing up better than most. 'Come and have a drink,' he said. 'I could do with a few till my eyes drop in about thirty seconds.'

'O.K., bud—sorry. But I was flying with him and we were bounced. And there's still nothing from Eileen. Gee, are we engaged or not? I'm worried, Keith.'

The bar was even more crowded than at lunchtime, and the smoke and noise hit them as they opened the swing doors. Once they had known every face, every name. Not now. 78 Squadron had lost its C.O. and now both flight commanders. There were three pilots in A Flight Mike had never even spoken to. At least he had spoken to 'Ginger' Mackay. And at least that pale, nervous, nice boy had died in battle. Yes, defending his country in her hour of need and all that jazz. That's what he would have to tell his parents.

'Say, Keith. I don't think I care for a drink after all. I've got a letter to write.'

Keith said, 'Suits me.' He let the doors swing shut, closing off the din, and they walked in the last of the twilight to the officers' sleeping quarters.

43

2

A BIT MORE THAN
SIX TO ONE

Keith's awakening the following morning was for once a gentle one, and he was relieved that he was still able to regain consciousness without a jerk. He could see low grey clouds streaming across the sky from south-west to north-east, and the rain was beating in gusts against the window. To some, he reflected, the summation of delight and relaxtion might be a sandy beach, the steady lap of waves, and a sunny sky above. For himself, he would make do with this bed, that lovely dark turbulent sky, and rain, everlasting rain. 10/10ths. Harry clampers. Flying hours nil. Ops nil.

There was a knock on the door. His batman appeared with a pot of tea to complete the idyll. 'Good morning, sir,' he said. 'Very wet morning, sir. The Squadron Leader asked me to tell you that B Flight is stood down.' He put the tray on the bedside table and poured out a dense black brew. 'And I am told, sir, that you have twenty-four hours' leave.'

'Repeat that slowly,' ordered Keith, stretching between the sheets and settling his head firmly on the pillow. A.C.2 Clark from Clapham, a young man of neutral appearance and character, sometimes appeared to derive a fleeting moment of pleasure from life with his early morning bulletins—what he inevitably called the 'ace gen'.

Keith sipped his tea and contemplated the twenty-four hours of freedom as if a life sentence had been commuted. First, last and for as much of the time as he was allowed, he would be with Jenny. Her leg had been badly crushed in the bombing of her C.H. station, and he had heard last week that she had been moved from Folkestone to St. Thomas's Hospital in London. Then perhaps dinner with Tom and Moira, and the last train back. Buffer Davies, through his burn bandages at East Grinstead, had sent word that Keith had the use of his monstrous and monstrously vulgar Bentley Special, 'Garbo'. But it was one thing to share the joke with Buffer, quite another to be publicly identified as the owner of such a contraption. To say nothing of its nine miles per gallon.

The lovely rain was still teeming down when Keith took the fast train to Waterloo. There was little to be seen in suburbia to distinguish this day from any peace-time wet August morning, only a 3.7 ack-ack battery in one park, the guns and rangefinders and sound detector covered and no khaki figures in sight; several balloon sites on open ground, the great silver swollen sausages tightly held down by sandbags beside the winch lorry, airmen and W.A.A.F.s on duty wearing capes; and the prominent 'S' signs indicating the numerous air raid shelters which had not so far been needed.

All quiet on the home front. But for how much longer? Like all 140 Squadron's survivors, he could see no end to the relentless pressure of the Luftwaffe,

And, once the last reserves of pilots had gone, once total control of the skies was in the hands of Goering's boys, the war would no longer be limited to bombs on a few coastal towns and exchanges of fire at 20,000 feet. They had all seen Intelligence photographs of the massed invasion barges in the ports across the Channel. Keith had recently witnessed the dissolution of the French army in the face of the German onslaught. Mike, who had escaped from Norway in May, had seen the overwhelming of that country, too.

Last week, the station commander at Savile Farm had addressed everyone on the loudspeaker Tannoys— 'The Government expects an invasion, probably within the next two or three weeks. In that event, this aerodrome will become a fort, and every officer, noncommissioned officer and airman will become a frontline soldier . . .'

Outside Waterloo the mid-day edition of *The Star* was on sale. 'Yesterday's score,' ran the placard, 'Jerry 34 R.A.F. 9 (4 pilots safe).' It might have been the third test match. Evacuee children were tumbling out of a bus which had drawn up outside the main entrance. They had safety-pinned labels, square cardboard box gas-masks slung round their shoulders, and faced the new world to which they were to be despatched with awful unease.

Keith put his head into the wind and rain and walked as fast as his old injury would allow to the hospital.

They had given Jenny a private room overlooking the river and right opposite the Houses of Parliament. She lay with her right leg outside the bed in plaster. Her face appeared thinner and she looked as tired as

46

she had on that evening he had taken her out from Swingham, dead beat from overtime in the R hut during Dunkirk.

Keith dropped his soaking mackintosh and hat, gloves and gasmask on the floor and bent down, his wet face against hers. Her arms were round his neck pressing him so tightly he worried about bruising her. She was repeating, 'Oh, Keith, darling Keith!' And he whispered into her ear just, 'Jenny, my poor Jenny!'

At length she released him and he sat on the chair holding her hand. 'You *are* in a bad way, my sweet.' The tears were coursing down her cheeks ruining the makeup she had put on for him. She smiled the slightly uneven smile which had attracted him so desperately when they had first met.

She reached under her pillow for a handkerchief. 'I'm sorry. What a rotten, selfish way to greet you! It's just that I'm so weak here. Weak and helpless. And so crushingly worried about you, every day and every night.'

Keith recalled Section Officer Jennifer Simpson, very brisk, very determined and efficient. No love nonsense until the war was over. Then before that, divorcée Miss Simpson with the smart bijou flat in Half Moon Street and a worldly knowledge of the better class of night club. And now so dispirited and beaten. 'Poor Jenny,' Keith said again. 'Does it still hurt a lot?'

'Oh, bother the leg. Yes, it hurts. But no, it's not that. I was really doing something useful at Swingham, and there are not many people who can supervise the operating of C.H. sets, and I was good at it—I really was.'

'The best,' said Keith. 'And you'll soon be back on

the job.' He leant forward and kissed her for a long time and she stroked his hair, and he slipped his hand under the bedclothes and under her nightdress, gently caressing her.

She finished the kiss and said, half groaning, 'Oh, don't do that. It's bad enough longing for you so much when you're away.'

Keith smiled down at her. 'I shall drug the night nurse's cocoa, and seduce you right here in this bed. Never mind the plaster. You just watch.'

She laughed her deep laugh that he had not heard for weeks. 'I remember just before the first time you made love to me. Do you remember? There were street lights then, and the light came through the window so that I could see your face and your fair hair and your expression as you looked at me.'

A nurse came in, quick to sense the passion and complicity, and gave Jenny a medicine glass of white liquid. Jenny made a face and swallowed it quickly.

The nurse said sharply to Keith, 'You can't stay all day, you know.'

'Just till dusk,' said Keith lightly.

When the door had shut behind her, Jenny said, 'Ugh! To think I once used to have a glass of Amontillado at this time of day.'

'This is better for you,' said Keith, taking a half bottle of Haig out of his raincoat pocket. 'The panacea for all complaints, medical and spiritual. Especially after nasty medicine, or a day of ops.' He mixed a generous tot with water in her toothmug, and she sipped it with a sigh.

Later she said, 'They're getting me onto crutches

48

this afternoon. Just for a trial. I'll need more of that stuff to give me the nerve and strength.'

Keith held her hand again and said, 'Listen, I've been thinking. They'll soon be sending you away to convalesce. Why not come to Rising Hall? My parents would love it. They're feeling frustrated up there doing nothing for the war. Mrs. Ewhurst could help you—she was a V.A.D. in the Great War.'

Jenny shook her head. 'I couldn't, darling. I've never even met them. What would they think—this broken, wanton brunette landing up on their doorstep?'

'Well, that's fine. That's fixed,' Keith said. 'I've already spoken to them and they're longing for you to come. And I'm longing for some leave to coincide.'

*

Keith said to Moira and Tom, 'No, it's going to be the Savoy Grill, and it's on me. I haven't been able to spend any money for weeks. And anyway, I want a decent meal.'

After a second visit to Jenny, Keith had made his way to the bed-sitting room in Bloomsbury where Tom Mathers and Moira Singleton lived—'excitingly in sin' as Moira would confess with a good-natured laugh. Both were from Market Rising and friends of Keith since infant school. Tom—lean, hungry looking and highly strung—was in his third year as a medical student at the Middlesex Hospital. Moira, soon becoming bored stiff and sad at Market Rising, had come to London to look after him and add minutely to his pittance of a grant by working in a bookshop. Tom had refused to marry her until he could earn enough to keep her, and until the war was over. Never an op-

49

timist, he knew the destruction of London was imminent.

Moira said to Tom, 'Let's say "yes". You can pay him back when you're a famous knighted surgeon.' Moira liked her food. She was a tall, buxom girl, full of energy and appetite for everything, fun, food, and (Keith imagined) bed.

Tom, always a stickler for order, tidied away the books he had been studying before Keith had surprised them by his arrival. 'It's very good of you, Keith. You ought to be living it up at Hatchetts with a marvellous girl instead of with boring old us.'

As they filed down the narrow stairs, smelling of curry and cabbage on successive floors, Keith explained that the only marvellous girl he wanted to dance with at Hatchetts was unable to dance for a while. And in the taxi he told them about Jenny, as he did so undoing his shirt buttons and pulling out his two identity discs. Secured to them was the battered cap badge which had been found in the rubble near her, and which she had given to him as a good luck token.

Their comments were marvellously characteristic. Tom, leaning forward in his seat and with lines of anxiety on his brow, said earnestly, 'I'll go and see her tomorrow. And her physiotherapist. They're not bad in the orthopaedic ward at Tommy's, but I'd like to be satisfied.' His long fingers—future surgeon's fingers—were nervously clasping and unclasping about the handle of his umbrella.

'Bags I come too,' said Moira eagerly, holding Keith's arm. 'Oh, I bet she's lovely. I bet you were great dancing together, before she was wounded—in battle. Tell us more. Do you sleep together all the time?'

'Really, Moira,' broke in Tom. 'Not everyone's got your standard of morals.'

They were in Kingsway, and the taxi swung round into the Strand. The sandbags about the entrance to the air raid shelters and public buildings were beginning to leak and collapse with age. The war was almost a year old, and although Keith had been in the heat of it for much of the time, he felt curiously detached from it all with these old friends in the centre of a London which had changed so little. Couples in long dresses and dinner jackets were stepping out of taxis and cars to go to the theatre. Keith saw the sign outside the Strand Theatre—*Women Aren't Angels*. 'One is,' he told himself, smiling at his sentimentality.

The Savoy Grill had lost little of its peace-time atmosphere of luxury and pretentiousness, the menu a shade more austere, but not much. Keith was offered a table by the wall, and when they sat down the place was already nearly full.

'Talking of legs, how's yours?' Tom asked. The last time he had seen it was after Keith's return from France, and Tom had been outraged that he had been ordered back onto flying so soon and before the wound had properly healed.

Keith reassured him, and hoped that they were not going to ask him what he had been doing. They did not. Tom knew that he would want to blot out for one evening the memory of the past frantic and dangerous weeks. And Moira, a girl who spoke her mind and could babble away unthinkingly for hours, also possessed a woman's instinctive feeling for what men liked. So she talked about her customers, the poor students, the surviving Bloomsbury intellectuals who had not taken themselves off to the country, or out of the country, sad servicemen searching out poetry and her company. And Tom was always ready to talk medicine, its past, his own work, and the future.

They were eating Scottish smoked salmon that dissolved in the mouth when Keith noticed a large naval party being shown to a reserved table at the opposite end of the room. There was a lot of brass and several W.R.N.S. officers of stately bearing, a very senior bunch from the Admirality, he surmised.

Tom was describing an especially difficult brain operation he had witnessed a few days earlier when Keith observed out of the corner of his eye another naval couple, perhaps younger than the others, making their way to the same table. Blackout time had come, the heavy curtains had been drawn across the windows and the lights of the restaurant dimmed. Moira had chosen poached halibut, and Keith was relishing the pleasure of watching her enjoy her food, as well as taking delight in his own saddle of lamb.

It was almost 11.30 by the time Moira had finished her pudding, her angels on horseback, drunk three cups of coffee and was sipping an Armagnac. Tom, by contrast, had had soup and one course, rapidly consumed, and an apple. Keith said, 'I'm going to miss my last train. Will you put me up for the night? *And* get me out of bed at five?'

Tom rebuked Moira for her gluttony and warmly agreed to the suggestion. Keith was beginning to feel sleepy from the wine and a succession of short nights. The grill room was thinning out, and the naval party was standing up and filtering towards the door, the young couple again last. Suddenly Keith recognized across the dimly-lit room that the girl was Eileen. She had her back to him, and was walking slowly, her arm in the arm of the tall officer who had escorted her in. For a fleeting second he dismissed the idea from his mind. Not Eileen. If she were in London she would have got in touch with Mike. She wouldn't . . .

But the tilt of her head, the movement of her shoulders as she looked up at the officer, even at this distance in this light, were unquestionably Eileen's. They were almost at the door when Keith quickly got up, pushing aside the table and apologizing to Moira, 'Be right back—sorry!'

He caught Eileen up just outside the entrance in Savoy Street. There was a faint glow in the blackout from the hooded headlamps of the cars and taxis swinging in and out of the narrow cul de sac. Two admirals and their wives were getting into a big Daimler, other officers into a taxi, and the tall officer escorting Eileen was telling the commissionaire he wanted a cab.

Keith put his hand on Eileen's shoulder and noticed, for the first time, that she was in officer's uniform. She turned and recognized him, momentarily nonplussed. Then she said, with no great warmth, 'Keith, what are you doing here?'

'And you? I suppose we were both hungry. Why didn't you let us know—?'

'But the Savoy? You at the Savoy?' she persisted.

'Well, I suppose—' Again he was not allowed to say more. The officer had returned and was offering his arm to her again. He was taller than Keith, and as far

as Keith could see in the dim light, very dark and
good looking. He could just make out two rings on his
sleeve and the small pair of wings above: a lieutenant
R.N., and Fleet Air Arm. He took no notice whatever
of Keith until Eileen said, 'Darling, this is a friend of
mine, Keith Stewart.' She was already edging towards
the cab. 'This is Arthur Winston-Greville.'

The officer nodded and turned away.

Suddenly aroused by the extraordinary turn of
events, Keith said, 'But, Eileen, don't rush off! What
have you been doing? What about Mike? And me for
that matter? Where can we get in touch with you?'

She was inside now and settling herself in her seat,
and the lieutenant was indicating to the driver to
leave.

Eileen said, as if it were a small duty to be borne,
'I'll write to Mike soon. I'm on the First Sea Lord's
Staff and very, very busy.'

The taxi was beginning to move but Keith persisted.
'At the Admiralty!' he exclaimed. 'And an officer now!
Eileen, how did it all happen . . . ?'

'Now don't be common, Keith, don't be pushy,' she
said. 'Yes, a proper officer.'

They were her last words, leaving Keith stunned.
His Eileen, the Eileen he had virtually grown up with,
the beloved only daughter of his own adopted parents, snubbing him like this and on such close terms
with that naval officer when she was engaged to
Mike! Perhaps they aren't after all—perhaps 'Women
Aren't Angels'. Or some of them. But Eileen!

'Mind your back, please, sir,' the commissionaire
was telling him, and Keith made his way slowly to
rejoin the others. What would Tom and Moira say

when he told them? He wanted time to think, and he did not feel prepared to reveal what had happened until he had more evidence of her infidelity, or found some excuse for her behaviour to him, and, worse still, to Mike. She was often inclined to fall into a mock cockney accent, and was rather good at it. But this time it had not been intended lightly. It had been intended as a snub. And 'Don't be common!' The old class business again. Why did he mind so much? But then how could she say such a thing in front of someone he did not even know?

Moira said, 'What was all that about?'

'So sorry—I thought I saw someone I knew. Let's go home.'

'Now I really am full,' she said in a voice of total satisfaction. 'That was grand!'

*

There was a camouflage-painted car with F/11 on the back at the station, a ravishing red-headed W.A.A.F. driver at the wheel. Keith knew her well. She was Dorothy, was cheerful and cheeky and no respecter of rank. 'I'm waiting for Groupy and Adj.,' she called out to Keith. 'Come on, beautiful, I'll take you, too.'

Keith laughed and looked at his watch. 'No thanks, Dot. I've got an hour to spare and need the exercise.'

She made a face at him and went back to her *Daily Mirror*.

The overnight rain had cleared, and at 7 o'clock it was obvious that it was going to be a fine day, though there could be showers later. After the break yesterday, they were going to be busy again.

What was he going to say to Mike? Was he going to say anything? But what excuse would he have for not telling him if she did write and say that she had seen him? He knew that Mike would be completely thrown by the news of her defection, and would very likely get himself killed. He remembered a pair of twins, pilots briefly on the squadron in the middle of July. Good pilots. Then, when one was shot down, his brother was so shattered that he lost the keen edge of self-preservation while taking needless risks in revenge. He lasted four more days.

Keith had still not resolved the problem when the sirens went. He was almost back at Savile Farm, and the main gates and guard room were in sight at the end of the long suburban road. The sound of engines starting up came to him on the wind, blending with the mournful rise and fall of the siren's note. A milkman delivering bottles, three in each hand, winked at Keith as he passed. 'Old Adolf's up with the lark.'

The staff car went past at high speed, and Keith caught a glimpse of the W.A.A.F.'s red hair under her hat. Like the milkman, Keith felt no need to take cover. He was enjoying the walk, and he would hear and probably see any enemy planes well before there was danger.

Then, as the last note of the siren died, Keith realized he had been tricked. They had all been tricked. This was not a high level raid. It was low level, very low, probably coming in under the R.D.F., with only Observer Corps warning at the coast. The thunder of the Dornier 17s was as sudden and loud as an express train emerging flat out from a tunnel. Mike saw them before he heard them, but only by the fraction of a second as they raced towards the aerodrome at a hundred feet, climbing to conform with the contours of the hill upon which Savile Farm lay. He recognized them at once by their heavy bulbous noses. Their bomb doors were open and flashes from the nose told of machine-gun fire. They were half-way across the field before the Bofors and Oerlikons opened up, and then an alert airman triggered off the P.A.C., the rockets streaming up with their cables all round the perimeter of the airfield.

The 17s, jinking and banking evasively, came on in untidy vics of three, some higher than others, but all heading for the buildings adjoining the road. Keith saw the first bombs falling and turning over in the air, then threw himself into the gutter with his arms over his head.

He was remotely aware of his body being crushed and then pounded against the stone setts of the gutter, of his ears being assaulted, and a hurricane-force wind tearing at him, intent on stripping off first his clothes and then his skin. His mouth was jammed with dust and rubble.

With the passing of the bombers, the silence seemed at first to be total. But after another half minute without moving, Keith realized that it was relative and was caused by the stunning of his ear-drums.

There *were* sounds. They crept back as his ear-drums recovered. There was the sound of voices shouting, many times louder than last time; the crackling sound of flames, the rumble of falling masonry, the distant mutter of guns, the roar of a plane taking off—how could anything have survived? And nearby, the faint whistle as a P.A.C. parachute slowly fell and gently lowered its cable across the road as if indicating 'the fireworks are over'.

Keith picked himself up, recovered his hat several yards away, dusted himself down and watched the figure of the milkman emerge from under his van. Sparrows and tits Keith had seen feeding from a bird-table in a garden were twittering and flying in circles and colliding, like an aerial combat gone berserk. The milkman looked at him and said shakily, 'A bit nearer that time, mate.' He had lost his hat, too, and his striped apron was grey with dust.

The worst flames were coming from the remains of number one hangar and stores, and some of the blocks had been levelled to the ground, the wind progressively revealing the extent of the devastation as it blew away the dust and smoke. Keith could see a corner of the field. It was peppered with craters. Then he began running.

The staff car had reached the guard room at the gate when the bombs had fallen. Keith could imagine the scene, the corporal guard in white blancoed belt raising the barrier to the Group Captain and standing back to give his stiffest salute, receiving in return a perfunctory acknowledgement from the senior officer and a surreptitious wink from saucy Dot.

Perhaps at that very second of exchange, the 250 kg bomb (the crater was just too large for a 100 kg and much too small for a 500 kg) had struck the base of the station flagstaff, symbolically pulverizing the staff and blue R.A.F. flag, scattering concrete like shrapnel, lifting up the Hillman and hurling it against the brick guard room. The W.A.A.F. driver lay spread awkwardly on the grass a dozen yards away, her skirt around her waist revealing black service-issue knickers, suspenders and stockings in a final, dusty, grotesque gesture of provocativeness. Poor harmless Dot!

The Group Captain and Adjutant were not in the shell of the car, nor was there any sign of the guard; the negative reality of being blown to pieces. And then he saw some of the pieces and turned away. He put his head inside the smashed window-frame, through which identity cards and passes had been checked, and saw through the settling brick dust only a scattering of papers, the rifle rack and rifles snapped like twigs for a bonfire, and by contrast, in one corner on an intact table, a kettle for the early morning brew still singing.

The rescue squads were out, forming up into the groups that had exercised together regularly, some on heavy rescue working at the piles of rubble marking airmen's quarters on one side of the road and the W.A.A.F. quarters, 'the waffery' on the other. Limp, dusty, crushed bodies were already being laid out on the pavement, and survivors—how *could* there be any? Keith asked himself—were being supported on the difficult passage over the brick and concrete rubble. Keith heard low moaning, a chorus of pain, punctuated by intermittent screams, as he passed. His duty was to reach B Flight dispersal as quickly as possible, and seeing an undamaged bicycle, he seized it and began pedalling through the centre of the station towards the perimeter track. The heat of the flames from the stores fire reached him from a hundred yards. Oxygen bottles were popping off, a mocking echo of the bomb explosions which had started it all. The hydrant was working and the firemen were playing four jets on the flames. There was a lot of shouting from this quarter, and Keith heard shrill words of warning and watched one wall collapse in a cloud of rising sparks.

Station Headquarters had taken a direct hit and paper and files were drifting about on the barrack square in vast quantities. Keith steered round one mountain of buff paper—mostly service records—and the wind turned over some of them, revealing companionably, side by side, the boots and woollen socks of an airman's ankle and feet, and the black issue shoes and lisle stockings of a W.A.A.F. They had been caught in the open as they walked side by side. He leapt off his bicycle and burrowed away at the paper, and soon wished that he had left the task to the professionals. Both had been struck full in the face and chest by splinters.

Keith sat down for a moment on the loose heaped paper, his eye caught by, '1772389 A/C 2 Saunders, A.K.,' then date of commencement of service, postings, misdemeanours, reports, leaves. Hundreds of lives on paper, living records concealing two deaths, two final entries. 'Buried in bumf', the term of abuse against an overworked clerk. And now, reflected Keith, this battered pair had suffered that indignity.

'There're two here,' he shouted harshly to an orderly in a passing ambulance.

The bar of the officers' mess had been punched in— that would lead to some doom-laden comments. Keith punctured both tyres of his bicycle on broken glass, and pedalled on more slowly. Airmen and some W.A.A.F.s with red flags were working across the airfield in a line searching for and marking the small holes and protuberances in the grass which told of delayed action bombs. Another party under an officer was attempting to mark out a runway across the pockmarked grass with yellow flags. Already, half an hour after the bombs had fallen, Savile Farm was painfully coming alive again.

One Hurricane blast pen had taken a direct hit from a light bomb, and the engine a hundred yards away was the only recognizable evidence that a machine had been standing there. The rest of 140's aircraft appeared intact, and the airmen were checking them over for minor splinter or machine-gun damage. The only other casualty was a petrol bowser which had been hurled from a hard-standing to a semiconcealed position behind a blast wall, and was surrounded by bustling figures of airmen with cans and tins and even milk bottles, recovering the leaking fuel with desperate eagerness and an eye on the empty tanks of their cars and motorbikes. Keith pretended he had not noticed, dumped his bicycle outside the hut, and went in.

Apart from the loss of a few panes of glass, the hut was undamaged, and the interior presented its usual appearance of casual informality, as if, a mile from the worst devastation, no one had heard of the raid. B Flight pilots were sprawled in the cane bucket and wooden armchairs, or on the iron beds at the far end, reading newspapers and paperbacks. The dart-board was unused, but two sergeant-pilots were playing shove-ha'penny. There were mugs of tea lying around on the arms of the chairs or the floor, and Aircraftman Godfrey was attempting to clear the place up with every sign of reluctance. The weather board showed

'Fine. Wind North-West Force 2', the flight had seven aircraft available, and they were at Immediate Readiness. It was all in curious contrast with the scenes of death and destruction, for once a reversal of roles between those who fought and risked their lives and the non-combatants on the ground.

Mike looked up from a copy of *Life*, assuming what he imagined was his 'English' voice. 'You missed a bit of fun just now, ol' boy, ol' boy. Top hole to see you, all the same.'

'Not by much I missed it. In fact I nearly bought it with the Station Commander.'

This caught the attention of everyone in the hut, with exclamations of dismay, for the Group Captain had been a popular figure who had survived two years as a scout pilot in the Great War, which was regarded as impossible.

'Ain't that the bloody luck,' exclaimed Range Powell.

A cheer from outside heralded the arrival of the N.A.A.F.I. van. Its windscreen had gone but the tea urn, upon which the squadron, in times of extreme stress, seemed sometimes to depend for its morale, was intact, and there were buns and even some corned-beef sandwiches this morning.

Rowbotham arrived a few minutes later on a motor bicycle, his car having gone up with much of the M.T. from a direct hit. As always, he was admirable in crisis, solemn instead of breezy, economical in explanation and briefing rather than the practical joking, wisecracking Rowbotham of more relaxed times off duty.

Pilots and ground crew assembled around him outside in the early morning sun. Behind him the smoke was still rising from the stores and hangar, and the ringing of ambulance and fire engine bells was a continuous background chorus. Rowbotham, cap off and the last of his wispy ginger hair floating in the breeze, confirmed that the Group Captain was dead, and ninety or so more—'there could be well over a hundred'—had been found, fifteen of them W.A.A.F.s.

There was a stir when the girls were mentioned. High Command had wanted to withdraw them from dangerous areas, but had been beaten down by the righteous indignation of the senior W.A.A.F. officers, who correctly reflected the views of the ranks everywhere. But the death of a W.A.A.F. aroused special outrage and brought such strong new resolve to resist and keep the airfields operational that their contribution did not end with their death.

Rowbotham completed his speech as briskly as he had begun it, turning as he spoke so that he addressed them all with equal emphasis. 'Signals will be running new phone wires as soon as they can. There'll be a runway of sorts open soon. A red Very will mean scramble, instructions as you get airborne. Flight,' he ordered the crusty Flight-sergeant, 'if we scramble, I want two-thirds of your men out with the rest with shovels filling craters. A lorry'll be here in a minute. That's all.'

Walking fast, with head thrust forward as if getting down into the scrum at Cranwell, Rowbotham made for his office through the crowd that backed aside for him silently.

For two more hours, as the sun climbed and sent waves of shimmering heat across the grass and the

grouped figures slaving away in shirt sleeves to repair
the grass surface, Savile Farm was left in peace. Soon
after 10 a.m. the sirens went again. There was no station alert, but there had not been last time, and the
airmen were called off the machines and assembled
informally near the shelters and slit trenches. The
nearest Bofors crew had their gun trained at low elevation towards the south-east.

Mike and Keith stood behind the hut. The wind
had risen and was rustling the rye, and there was no
other sound until they both heard the faint off-beat
note of a very high-flying enemy. They strained their
eyes but it was Flynn Marston, as usual, who first
picked up the tiny speck of a reconnaissance machine.

'There she is, chaps. An 88—"bird thou never
wert." ' It made a short vapour trail for a few seconds,
and then must have rapidly changed altitude a few
hundred feet to cast off this tell-tale mark in the sky.
No Spitfire could get that high in the time, if at all,
and the target was far beyond the range of the guns.

'They'll be taking pretty pics to slobber over,' Mike
remarked laconically. 'Can't you hear them. "Alles
zerstört! Schauen Sie mal an! Nichts mehr zu tun."
Then off to the mess for some of that Bavarian piss.
"Gott strafe England! Sieg Heil!" '

'Yank boils over. Bitter bitte! Get it. Bitter beer.'
Mike groaned, and then said sharply, 'Here we go.'

A red Very arched up into the sky from the watch
tower, and a few seconds later as the sound of the
first—a pop rather than an explosion—reached them, a
second flare shot up, indicating that 78 Squadron's
spitfires were to scramble, too.

The Wing Commander Flying himself was on the

R/T as they taxied out, directing the Spitfires first to the beginning of the runway marked out with flags across the grass, just wide enough between the craters for pairs to take off. It was a slow and awkward business by contrast with the squadrons' simultaneous take-off, but the Spitfires were away in five minutes, and Rowbotham at once led off 140 with Sergeant Pilot Watson as number two. A minute later, with Mike at his number two, Keith opened wide the throttle of C-Charlie and the two Hurricanes accelerated close together between the yellow marker flags, over several bumpy grey-white patches of filled-in craters, and lifted off as one.

Keith loved flying with Mike. It was as if a special silent R/T of sympathetic comprehension linked their two machines, with Keith marginally the better pilot and tactician, Mike the better shot. They climbed in tight formation, then spread out to form up as the second pair on 'Kiwi' Robinson, the New Zealand B Flight commander. It was angels 15 again, fifty plus heading for Tangmere, and as usual they would be taking the bombers, the Spitfires with their greater speed and better height performance dealing, as best they could, with the escort.

Rowbotham took them due north to gain height, a lesson they had learned weeks ago after being jumped out of the sun before gaining enough altitude. At 9,000 feet he turned through 180 degrees and soon they were flying over their own base, the smoke still drifting south-east from the fire and the devastation to the buildings clearly evident. As to the field itself, it appeared from this height impossible that they could have found a straight line long enough to become airborne from its pock-marked surface.

The German reconnaissance photos taken at 35,000 feet would take no account of the grit of the W.A.A.F.s and airmen, the quality of leadership, the ability to extemporize services such as telephone, catering and water, the determination to keep the aerodrome open, nor even that enough craters had been filled in by the time the recce plane came over for flying to start again.

During the brief comparatively safe period of climbing to operational altitude, with the enemy still over the Channel, the three sections of four each Hurricanes, nose up, striving for height, Keith glanced round from machine to machine. There were the few other survivors from the Savile Farm days in September 1939 when what was happening now had been hourly expected and did not come. And the semi-veterans who had replaced the first casualties and the decimation of the Norwegian campaign. Then the three pilots, in N-Nuts, F-Freddie and Y-Yorker, who had been with them for only a few days. Those were the ones who would need watching and protecting if it came to a scrap. Green as new-sown grass.

Two machines away was the Yorkshireman, Polo Satterthwaite, one of the most experienced, who had gone through training school with Mike and Keith—likeably slapdash on the ground, an anti-disciplinarian, and flouting every rule right now, the smoke from his evil-smelling pipe visibly streaming back from the half-open hood. Rowbotham would roar. Polo would continue to smoke below oxygen height. 'Aye, if I've got a reet nasty one in the range bars, I'll maybe take it out,' he was once heard to confess.

And to Keith's starboard, Mike, hood pushed right back, helmet off for keeping his head cool—his special eccentricity and a highly risky one—brown hair streaming back, and glancing across frequently to Keith in order to keep station.

'Red Three, order your number two to put on his helmet,' Rowbotham's voice snapped out.

Keith tapped his own helmet and thumbed in the direction of the squadron commander. With a rueful grimace, Mike, stick between his knees, used both hands to slip on the helmet but still did not secure the strap under his chin.

Keith recalled Mike helmetless after their first combat up in Scotland last November, on Keith's own twenty-first birthday. And some party it had been! Mike pie-eyed the night before his final check-out at training school when he knew he was going to fail. Mike back from the Spanish Civil War, wretchedly sad for Europe and its dictatorships, and suddenly determined to do something about it.

And Mike with Eileen, at first affronting Keith with his ardour. And then Keith reconciled and happy for them. And now this. The end. What was he to do? Perhaps Mike would get pranged today, and he would never have to tell him. But, oh no, not that. Pray to God not that . . .

There had been a lot of R/T chatter, distant but urgent. 78 Squadron Spitfires had already made contact and would now be wading into the 109s and twin-engined 110s, the bombers' escort and top cover.

Then, very much louder, the familiar voice of the

sector controller—'Sandbag leader, hullo Sandbag leader, 75-plus bandits ten miles south-east of Primrose. Vector zero-eight-eight. Zero-eight-eight. Buster. Over.'

So now there were seventy-five of them. There might be another Hurricane squadron to help. Perhaps Tangmere's 43 Squadron, now down from Northolt. And then there might not. Keith began his ritual multiplication—'twelve times one is twelve, twelve times two is twenty-four, times three is thirty-six, times four is forty-eight, times five is sixty. And we're still not there. A bit more than six to one.' Plus the fighters, and most of those would get through to them. They always did.

He checked his instruments and sight, slipped over the safety-catch, and with his left hand pulled the plug for emergency boost. All twelve Hurricanes were streaming back smoke from 9-plus boost, and the rate of climb needle advanced firmly round the dial.

As usual, Flynn Marston was the first to spot them. 'Bandits dead ahead of skipper, same height. Red Two out.'

Good old Flynn! He might waste words on his precious typewriter. But not in the air.

'Sandbag leader calling—tally ho . . .'

3

THE WORST DAY

'This,' wrote Mike in his diary, 'was the worst day of my life.'

It was the day after the bombing of Savile Farm, of the C.O.'s rebuke for not wearing his helmet, of a long and frustrating action against a mass of Dorniers and Heinkels whose cross-fire was dauntingly accurate, and nothing to show for it except a 109's cannon shell dead centre through the rudder. There was a notice on the board outside the dining-room, from the War Cabinet to the secretary of State for Air:

> 'We would be glad if you would convey to the Fighter Squadrons of the R.A.F. engaged in Thursday's brilliant action our admiration of the skill and prowess they displayed, and congratulate them upon the defeat and heavy losses inflicted upon the far more numerous enemy.'

The day started encouragingly with heavy low cloud, a protective blanket over Savile Farm and the whole of southern England. Some Dorniers from KG2 had apparently got through without escort but had failed to find their target and had scattered their loads haphazardly over villages in Kent.

While Mike was playing snooker with Range Powell after lunch, and as Range, with a characteristic stream of slang and oaths, went in off the black, he caught a glimpse through the window of blue sky. 'We're not going to finish this game,' Mike said.

Range glanced at the board. 'Bloody glad of that, cobber. I'm a flipper at this game.'

Mike, in his turn, was aiming carefully at the yellow ball when the loudspeaker voice broke in. How they had come to hate those Tannoys all round the airfield, indoors and outdoors, so that there was no escape from them! Mike made as if to hurl his ball at the wire mesh and plywood loudspeaker above the billiards-room door.

'Attention. 140 Squadron to Immediate Readiness. 140 Squadron, to Immediate Readiness. I repeat . . .'

'Wouldn't it!' Range exclaimed. 'I'm goin' to cob that dill one of these bloody days.'

There was a double-decker bus outside the damaged officers' mess, appropriated from Aldershot and District Bus Company after the loss of almost all their M.T. the previous day, and it was filling up rapidly as Mike and Range ran down the front steps, hatless and still swearing. Kiwi Robinson was just jumping on board, too, and someone was heard to ask with heavy irony if anyone had seen an Englishman anywhere. A stale, burnt smell still hung about the station buildings, and the driver had to negotiate a passage between piles of rubber and broken glass.

The pilots gathered round the heavily-built, bull-like, ever-reassuring C.O. and the tall, bowed, dark-browed Intelligence Officer. As the weeks of fighting had passed, 140's pilots had assumed more and more individual gear to suit their tastes and needs. Some were in blue or dirty white one-piece flying overalls, others in Irvin jackets or heavy sweaters, Polo Satterthwaite inevitably in the filthy once-white poloneck jersey he had worn since the beginning of the war, through the French campaign, and now these seemingly interminable hot days of summer battle. Mike and Keith both preferred the wool-lined Irvin, which kept them warm at 15,000 feet and even allowed them sometimes to dogfight with the hood open, a practice advocated by many as it reduced the risk from canopy splinters and allowed for a quick emergency exit without risk of a jammed hood slide.

'There's something fairly big building up according to Group Intelligence. We're getting signs that Luftflotten Two and Three are laying on a big show,' the C.O. began.

'What was yesterday's, sir?' a sergeant pilot interrupted. 'A skirmish?'

'Bigger than yesterday,' Rowbotham said sharply. 'The Group Commander was on the blower to me. Air Marshal Park says the Hun seems to have got the idea he knocked out Detling, Manston, Biggin, Croydon and Hornchurch yesterday, as well as us. In fact they're all serviceable except Manston. He also had a go at three R.D.F. stations and he thinks—wrongly again—he's picked out our eyes.'

He offered Williams a cigarette and tapped his own on his case before lighting it. He was relaxed and confident with his men, able to give them leeway.

'Now that he thinks we're pretty well grounded, all

the signs point to a build up against the ports. And then . . .' Rowbotham shrugged his shoulders and cast his keen blue-grey eyes over his pilots, waiting for one of them to provide the word.

'Invasion, sir,' put in Mike obediently, as if it was not the first topic of conversation throughout the country.

'Right, Yank.'

Those barges, the increase in day and night railway traffic, the rapid reforming of the German armies along the Channel, the hysterical boasts of old Adolf himself. And then, at home, the swiftly-built defensive gun emplacements and blockhouses—thousands of them in fields, on cliff tops in the streets of coastal towns; the new fortress-like transformation of England's south and east coasts—barbed wire and tank traps and minefields, obstructions against landing gliders and troop carriers; removal of all road and railway signs, the formation of Local Defence Volunteers, now renamed Home Guard, armed with any weapons they could lay their hands on, instructions in newspapers and magazines on making—and. *throwing*—Molotov cocktail petrol bombs at tanks . . .

They were approaching the critical climax of the danger to this island which Mike had recognized on his return from Spain in 1937. And after Great Britain, no doubt with the Japanese joining the Germans and Italians, the preparations for another and even greater invasion. Of his own country. So, it had better be stopped right here, was Mike's reasoning. But how was he to know it was going to be like this, unremittingly day after day after day? No glamour stuff. Not now. No 'our boys in blue' heroism rubbish. Just the two s's, shooting and survival.

The C.O. was saying, 'Portsmouth, Southampton, Weymouth, Portland, Plymouth—those're the places he's likely to be going for.'

The emergency field telephone on the table beside him began its staccato ringing, and the C.O. beat Williams to it. His 'Yes' was a ferocious bark. The 'Right' that followed it seconds later was only slightly less sharp.

'Angels one-two over base,' Rowbotham called out, and began running like a scrum-half towards his plane, his own Hurricane with the seven swastikas painted just forward of the cockpit. Mike grabbed an airman's bicycle and quickly passed three pilots running along the perimeter track, and threw it down again yards from his machine.

The pilots could at once identify the controllers' voices but rarely learned their names. This one, with a marked Scottish accent, was calm and crisp, and seemed to be blessed with good clear plots, or maybe just with luck. Mike felt reassured when he heard his voice vectoring them onto two raids coming in towards the Isle of Wight. The cloud was scattered, revealing irregular patterns of the lush patchwork of Surrey, Sussex and Hampshire. The cloud thickened up near the sea so that they could not tell when they crossed the coast. Mike spotted a squadron of Spitfires to the east, probably from Ford or Westhampnett, the afternoon sun reflecting intermittent sparks from their cockpits. They were climbing steeply in old-style vics of three with a tail-end Charlie (poor devil), and probably would not level off until 25,000.

Sometimes Mike envied them their superior speed and rate of climb and dive, but if he was going to slog it out with German bombers, he was happy to have the steady gun platform and relative toughness of the old Hurricane.

There was a faint 'tally ho!' from another squadron on the R/T, and the inevitable instructions, cries of warning and glee—'I'll take him, Bunny', 'Red One break—break!' as a 109 or 110 got onto the tail of some anonymous and distant pilot, and then simply a long drawn-out, 'Wow!'.

Then that soothing Scottish voice, 'Sixty plus ten miles south of Harknott, steering due north. More trade to the east. Looks like eighty plus twenty-five miles south of Waverly, angels one-six . . .'

Mike caught a glimpse of St Catherine's Point 15,000 feet below, the ultimate south of the Isle of Wight. The C.O. was going for the first lot. It looked as if Intelligence was spot on, and Portsmouth and Southampton were going to take a pasting.

This time Mike was first with the sighting, and surely there were more than sixty of them. They looked like a solid grey shape, a science-fiction monster of the skies heading straight for them. And then, as Mike transmitted the warning cry, he began to pick out the individual machine, in tight-packed steeped-up vics of five. Steady, steel gulls they were now.

'Sandbag leader, they're eighty-sevens.' It was Flynn's voice; and there was a note of relish in the C.O.'s voice as he acknowledged. Then he added, 'We'll take them head on. Blue One, do a three sixty degree turn and come in after us. I'll take starboard.'

Kiwi Robinson at once began to take Blue Section into a steep turn to starboard, Mike conforming and slipping under the Hurricane's belly, at the same time performing his private mental routine before combat, with the unspoken counsel: calm, calm. Steady. Hold it till you count the rivets. Not too cocky. But, oh boy, you can shoot like crazy, can't you? And watch it behind, watch it . . .

As they came out of their complete turn in a steep bank, Mike saw the other two sections of four tearing into the dive bombers from slightly above. They might have been racing cars punching into a packed crowd, scattering and mauling without discrimination. The leading formation of 87s lost its cohesion and Mike could see two machines plunging down, trailing black lines of smoke, and several more were losing height and heading towards the island.

But jeepers! there was no shortage of targets when Mike began the attack, the other three pilots of Kiwi's section spreading out slightly and selecting a machine of the mass formation racing towards them. Mike took one of the wing bombers, and at about half a mile range swung into a half-roll, stick hard forward to keep the nose up, kicked the rudders to steady his sight on the target, and held the spade grip with both hands, turn-and-bank steady.

The ugly gull shape, spatted wheels of the fixed undercarriage dangling ridiculously, enlarged swiftly in his reflector sight. This was the critical instant of the most dangerous and effective form of attack, the two machines racing towards each other, pilot challenging pilot to break, their fates depending on nerve and reaction speed. Dead steady now, dead head on, the Stuka's fin central above the cockpit canopy, the prop boss central above the single big belly bomb. Two seconds firing at the most. Three seconds, and splintering annihilation.

With his straps biting into his shoulders, Mike willed himself to relax, dot dead on target, and pressed the gun button. Nothing for the first second. An impression of tracer fire racing straight at him. Then the De Wilde strikes, a dancing pattern of them all over the Stuka's nose, barely recorded in his mind before he pulled back on the stick and the sky was instantly empty, and his Hurricane was screaming down towards the crinkled grey-blue of the sea three miles below.

In the full boost climb up again Mike could see that most of the dive bomber formation was still intact. It would take more than a dozen Hurricanes to break up this lot, although more than that number of Stukas had been shot out of the sky or were limping back towards France.

He could see no sign of his target. It might have been the little heart of red flame at the end of a ten-thousand-feet smoke spiral, which was extinguished in a splash of white as Mike watched. Or it could be the distant crippled Stuka far to the west whose jettisoned bomb exploded in a great watery eruption a second later. He would never know. His business, as always, was to shoot and survive, and he was rapidly catching up with the lower echelons of the formation.

'Blue leader, Sandbag Blue Three calling . . .' Mike transmitted but failed to hear his own voice, and then realized that he had been living in a world of silence since the attack. He pressed in turn the other buttons on his set and knew at once that it was damaged. So at least one of those 7.9 mm bullets had hit him.

The second attack, a stern one from above and below, was uncoordinated and less effective, the Hurricanes coming in haphazardly and the Stukas keeping up a well-controlled and highly dangerous cross-fire, slashing the air with tracer lines. They had skill as well as guts, these Hun dive-bomber crews. Mike jinked, kicking alternate rudder until he was within 300 feet of his new target, rapidly steadied his sight, and gave a long closing burst with quarter deflection.

The counter fire suddenly ceased, and Mike caught a clear glimpse of the gunner slumped over his gun, the impotent barrel now forced into maximum elevation.

He climbed away at full boost to regain height, noting again how uncannily quiet it was without the R/T chatter that often filled his ears during a fight, and noting, too, how the silence lent a strangely peaceful and leisurely impression to an affair that was essentially noise-filled and swift. He warned himself to be especially alert now that he was deaf and dumb, and searched the sky above and behind with even greater care and frequency.

He was glad he did, too. For the battle was now directly over Portsmouth, the ack-ack bursts were thick in the air, the surviving Stukas below and to the east of him were going over onto their backs for their long, slow dives down onto their target. And the top cover was coming in at last, evidently late for their rendezvous but, as always, skilfully flown, wickedly dangerous, and fast—so much faster than the old Hurricane could ever go.

Sandwiched now between Stukas falling away and a *Staffel* of 109s racing down from 20,000-plus, Mike felt more lonely in his silence than ever before in combat, as if he, single-handed, was facing up to all the might of the Luftwaffe. There was not a Spitfire or Hurricane in sight, and the brown woolly bursts with their deadly yellow centres from the ack-ack guns seemed to be as much concerned with his own destruction as the Germans'.

There was only one defence in this situation. Mike had done it before more times than he cared to remember. As the first of the 109s came down, yellow spinner, olive drab camouflage on the upper surfaces, big black cross on each wing—even now after all these fights, the sight gave him a stab of anger—Mike threw his machine into a sharp left-hand climbing turn, the 109 tearing past and out of sight. The others came down, and for lack of adversaries, concentrated on him, making passes in turn from below while Mike tightened his circle until, with his A.S.I. showing 130 m.p.h., he resorted to the ruse of lowering fifteen degrees of flap. No single 109 could turn inside him now, but they could still wing him with a short passing deflection shot from below, or even above with luck.

Tight-rammed into his seat by 'g' [gravity], Mike held on, knowing that the 109s with their limited fuel could not stay for long, and once or twice getting a very brief deflection shot as a Messerschmitt pilot would pull out from his attack. Then, from his guns came a line of tracer. It was a warning that he was nearly out of ammunition, a trick he had picked up of

having the armourer fit tracer at the end of the ammunition belts. There was a faint rattle from the
empty breech blocks, and the last lingering fumes of
cordite in the cockpit dissolved away.

The Huns had all gone with the last of his ammunition. They had left him alone at last. Or so he thought.
The sky seemed clear. The smoke from the ack-ack
bursts to the west was rapidly fading into the blue of
the sky. Mike retracted his flaps, straightened out
with relief, for the first time was aware of the sweat
pouring off him, and began to orientate himself after
his dizzy tight circling. Near Chichester, he reckoned.
Wasn't that the tall steeple of the cathedral just visible
to the east? And there was Tangmere, recognizably
flattened, its hangars rubble, its runways a mass of
bomb craters.

Enough fuel to make it back? Mike pressed the button under the dial, and it was at that moment that the
cannon shells struck, struck pulverizingly into his machine—his tail, the length of the fuselage, two of them
clear through his instrument panel.

Out! Out quick, buddy! This machine is not going
to fly any more, no sir. The cockpit was filled with
smoke and glycol fumes, and Mike felt as if someone
had opened the door of a blast furnace straight into
his face.

Oh Christ, not burns! Fill me full of bullets, but, no,
don't let me roast. Here, suddenly, was the reality of
his worst nightmares. Even if you survived, you
wished you hadn't. Like poor old Buffer . . .

Mike had practised the rapid exit so often, his
hands moved with the speed of a cornered fencer.
Tear off helmet—that's why he never secured it under

79

his chin, his own invention. Out with the quick-release pin.

Yes, it was flames, not just heat now, but he had his machine upside down, or had it done this service for him? Always a courteous Hurricane, dear old J-Johnnie. And out he went, sucked clear by the slip-stream of his plunging fighter.

So this is what it's like to brolly-hop! Keith had done it, the C.O. twice, but it was the first time for him. Was he burnt! He snatched for the ring, pulled hard. There was a heart-stopping moment—the mind in crisis works with the speed of light, he realized la-ter—when he knew the 'chute would not open and he persuaded himself he was glad because it was better to be dashed to pieces than burned to a mask. Hang-ing for murder rather than life imprisonment . . .

But he hung by his arms instead, swinging in a great pendulum sweep, and even before looking down he tore off his gauntlets and put his hands to his face. Nose? Eyes? He could *see*, couldn't he? His mouth felt sore, but no worse. Then he looked down and saw on his legs flailed cloth, thank God, not flesh, and only slight pain. That first flash had caught his trousers and scorched them through. But no worse.

Good timing, buddy! One more fifth of one more second and your hands, too, would have been so burnt you'd be on the ground by now—in the kite or out of it. Lady luck, who had held his arms through every crisis since last November, was still at his side, bless her.

There was a lot of smoke billowing up from Ports-mouth, and he could see through it the flicker of flames down by the dockyard, the curving white wake of a small ship turning fast in the harbour. He was swinging gently, blown with the smoke and dust north-easterly on the wind, above newly-smashed houses, a street like a miniature volcano with a broken gas main spurting flame from a crater, a bolting horse dragging an overturned milkcart across a cricket field, figures running, others lying still. And the sound of bells from ambulances and fire engines, and the 'All-clear' sirens rose two thousand feet up to him as he floated down towards the holocaust he had failed to prevent. 'All clear' like hell! That lot would take some clearing, and burying.

Mike began to make calculations and to wish he could float for ever. Up here he was as devoid of responsibilities as in sleep, and he did not want to wake up. He did not want to face up to the inevitable questions, reporting, the mechanics of getting back to Savile Farm, of more reporting, medical check. And then back to the ops again.

It looked as if he would come down on the slopes of Portsdown, the spine of green north of the naval base, scarred with the defensive forts of an earlier threat to this land, and now with new camouflaged emplacements, barbed wire and the muzzles of guns still hot from the fight. There were cars parked on the hill, figures standing beside them gawping at the ruined city and docks below. Mike could even see the splash of rugs spread on the grass, and as he fell towards them he saw the children and mothers picnicking, a real family outing, some with arms pointing up towards him. He had been seen, floating down beneath his white canopy, a late survivor of the battle, playing his brief walk-on part in this free spectacular theatre production. Or would it be flying-on? Flynn would be quoting Ariel in *The Tempest*— '. . . be't to fly, to swim, to dive into the fire, to ride on the curl'd clouds . . .' Oh, but how this Ariel despised his audience!

He had been seen by others, too. He heard the crack of gunfire. The sound came from the north side of the road, where Mike saw a group of khaki figures standing beside a camouflaged truck. Half a dozen of them were on their knees, rifles pointed towards him, and firing. He grabbed the shrouds above his head and began to rock himself from side to side, and shouted at the top of his voice, 'R.A.F. . . . R.A.F. *not* German!'

More shots came, and with them the sound of shouting, drowning his own voice. He was falling fast, would land beyond the soldiers but not by far, and there were people running from the cars.

Another shot rang out when Mike was barely twenty feet up, bunching himself for the impact. He hit the ground half in a thorn bush, and rolled over scratching himself before he could punch the quick release. At once he was surrounded by Khaki figures. Two of them had fixed bayonets, and were closing in on him, others were aiming their rifles, and another had a revolver and was calling to the others.

Everyone was shouting and running. It was like the climax of a rough mess party that had got insanely out of hand. The thud of boots on turf and expletives alike pounded about him, 'Get the sod!' Thud. 'Grab him quick, Charlie!' Thud. ''e may 'ave a gun—look out!' Thud, thud.

Mike, bleeding from face and hands from thorn scratches, looked up and saw expressions of anger, hatred and the longing to kill. Real blood lust, not at all like the pink alcoholic faces of fellow officers tumbling upon him late at night. Not a wizard prang, but real murder.

Two men fell on his shoulders, another had a bayonet over his stomach, someone else was holding down his legs. And they were all shouting, a tempest of ugly sound filling the air.

Mike was screaming, 'I'm R.A.F.—can't you see?' But he could not hear his own voice.

At length there was one voice above the others, deep and commanding. 'Get back! Hold it, lads.' A man in a forage cap was thrusting the others aside. 'He wants the privilege of killing me,' Mike was thinking. 'Alone.'

''e's one of ours.' The man was a sergeant, maybe fifty years old, with 'Home Guard' stitched on the shoulders of his battle dress. Mike saw a moustache, deep blue eyes, a revolver in his right hand, Great War ribbons, many-coloured, above his left breast pocket. ''e's R.A.F.'

The deep murmurs of dissent and resentful disbelief were like a poorly rehearsed chorus in some crumby opera. But they withdrew slowly, and Mike pulled himself to his feet. Someone had undone the bow knots of his Mae West and dragged it off him. He bent down to pick it up from the branches of the thorn bush and scratched his hand again. Both hands were shaking, too, and he gave up putting it on and slung it over his shoulder.

The Home Guard sergeant was handing him a lit cigarette, and Mike drew on it thankfully. Then, as fear receded, the anger welled up in its place and he

83

began shouting at the khaki figures staring at him, some boys of barely seventeen, others older men like the sergeant.

'It's enough fighting the goddam enemy without being killed by your own side,' he shouted at them. There were civilians beyond, a sea of half-fearful, half-suspicious faces. 'For Christ's sake, we go up three, four times a day, lose our buddies, have to bail out, and what do we get?' There was silence among the Home Guard, a faint murmuring from the crowd beyond, a child's voice, shrill and demanding, 'What is 'e, Mum?'

Mike's tirade rolled on, harsh and bitter. Was it worth coming 3,000 miles to fight for these limey morons? 'God help us when Jerry does come,' he ended, 'if that's your standard of shooting. A slow-moving target at twenty feet!'

He wanted to be away from this damn place, these damn people. 'Sergeant, get your men to collect my 'chute. And I want a driver to take me back to my base.' He felt better and used his knife to cut away the flapping lengths of trouser, revealing his pink-scorched knees. It might make him look ridiculous. It also proved how steady his hands were, and that he meant business.

He walked fast towards the truck with springy, determined strides, a medium-short figure, unwiped blood on his face, open Irvin jacket revealing top button undone and the white splash of his wings on his chest: a defeated fighter pilot going back for more, and more . . .

The crowd opened up before him, lynch-mob faces, vacuous, voyeur faces, surly, frightened faces. He despised them all. They had gathered to see real blood, not scratch marks. Then, from an unidentifiable woman behind him, 'Didn't know any of you lot was around—not when you look at that mess over there.' She pointed towards the town.

And then another, louder, 'They *murdered* my Aunt Ethel—an' what did you lot do?'

And a third voice, 'Jumped out, shouldn't wonder,' and a bitter laugh.

Mike walked on, muscles taut, ashamed for them, ashamed for himself knowing that he would as soon turn and shoot into this mob as into a *Staffel* of Junkers. It was clouding over again, the wind blew gustily up here on the Downs, bringing the smell of burning with it.

He did not want to look at Portsmouth again. He wrenched open the truck's door and climbed in. The sergeant with the blue eyes was looking in through the driver's window. 'I've put your 'chute in the back. Sorry about all this, sir. The men are a bit strung up, what with all this bombing and talk of invasion.'

Mike did not answer because he knew what he would say. 'Strung up, are they? Poor guys! Gee, I'm sorry to hear that, sergeant. That's a real shame . . .'

Instead, he nodded his head.

But from that time Mike always carried his own little flat .25 Browning when on ops, deciding that you never knew where or when your real enemy might appear.

❉

'R/T U.S. 70-plus Ju.87s. Isle of Wight. Deliv'd head-on attack. Saw strikes. Followed with rear attack. Strikes again and return fire ceased. Lost sqdn. Unable transmit or receive. Returning to base attacked by five 109s. Tight turned until they left. But later jumped when straight and level, shot down over Portsmouth. Shot at again before landing by 'chute. Returned base 1730hrs.'

Mike closed his logbook and knocked on the C.O.'s office door.

'I'll take you back,' Rowbotham said. 'Feeling O.K.?'

'Oh, sure. All I want's a licence to kill Home Guards and civilians with impunity. And a new pair of pants.'

Rowbotham laughed. 'You can have a pair of mine.'

Mike looked at the rough-hewn face and the burly figure quizzically, one eyebrow raised.

'I don't want any insubordination from you, Yank,' the C.O. said. He got up and threw his Mae West onto an armchair in the corner. 'I want respect, and gratitude.' He looked about him, now snorting with embarrassment. 'I've told the Spy to raise your claim for a "damaged" to one Stuka firm today and one damaged. We've been sorting things out. The Observer Corps saw six go in, and there's no doubt one's yours.' He snorted again.

In the car, Mike said, 'So you reckon the Luftwaffe and I are evens today?'

The C.O. nodded and said, 'And we've got some reinforcements. The Navy are sending along a couple of types to swell the ranks.'

Later, after more drinks than usual in the emergency bar with Keith and Range Powell and Kiwi Robinson, discussing the day's fighting and Mike's mishap, the C.O. introduced them to Sub-Lieutenant Pomeroy, a pleasant, modest Fleet Air Arm pilot, tall and willowy with wispy fair hair almost to his collar.

86

He was destined for A Flight. He said he was quite happy to convert from Skuas to Hurricanes, which could at least keep pace with Ju.88s. He had been in the Norwegian campaign in the *Furious* when they had lost as heavily as any R.A.F. squadron. 'I'm really very keen to get at the Hun again,' he announced in an upper class voice which still amused Mike. But this one's all right, he told himself, discerning toughness as well as experience.

Mike found himself sitting at dinner next to the second F.A.A. pilot who had been temporarily seconded to the R.A.F. This Lieutenant R.N. was a different type altogether, in appearance as well as style. He was tall, dark and craggy, with heavy eyebrows and almost black eyes, full lips, square jaw, square shoulders—a heavy looking fellow but undeniably good-looking.

Mike, who after three years in England, was quick to pick up nuances of English clan and character, noticed at once that this officer seemed anxious to make an early impression of hauteur, authority and self-confidence. Mike was getting good on British accents, too, and while Pomeroy sounded authentically upper-class, his companion's 'pebble-in-mouth' accent sounded almost too good to be true. He, too, had been on Skuas in the Norwegian campaign, and had apparently taken part in the sinking of the German cruiser. She was the first ever major warship to be sunk by bombing, the lieutenant emphasized, a fact which Mike already knew very well. Nevertheless, he was now treated to a detailed minute-by-minute account of the operation, as if he were an open-mouthed schoolboy audience.

'We may have had only four machine guns firing forward in the old Skua, but by jove she packs a punch with that 500-pounder'. The King's toast had just been given, and he drew out a cigar and offered a large Havana to Mike. Dutifully, belatedly, the pilot asked Mike about 140 Squadron. 'Been having a rough time of it, I gather, old boy. I suppose that's why you've brought in the Navy.' He chuckled as he nipped off the end of his cigar and passed the cutter to Mike.

"Quite rough, I guess. Yeah, you could call it that.' He turned over his hands, revealing the long scratch marks. 'I got those defending the Royal Navy today.'

'I don't quite follow you, old boy.'

'Bailed out over Portsmouth, landed in a bush. The army had a go at me, too. But we're all buddies at heart, I guess." The irony misfired.

The port went round, but as soon as the new Station Commander had left, the lieutenant said to Mike, 'Care to come to my cabin? I've got some rather smooth Fonseca '27. You may prefer it to this—to this standard issue, what? Show you some mementoes of Norway, too, if you'd care to see 'em.'

Mike recognized that there really was no alternative without seeming churlish, although he was feeling heavy with drink and weariness.

The lieutenant's batman had been hard at it all day. There were family photographs on the walls of the 'Cabin' showing a large Georgian country mansion with grass terraces and flanked by cedars, a young man on a big hunter, an ocean racing-yacht signed 'Tommy', his own white Daimler under Admiralty Arch in London. Mike's observant eye took in the

Turkish rug on the floor, the riding boots in stretchers (Christ! does he think he's joined the cavalry?), the set of leather suitcases neatly stacked in the corner, embossed coat-of-arms pointing outwards.

'Take a pew, old boy.' The lieutenant bustled in the corner cupboard, bringing out two port glasses and a bottle. 'The journey will *not* have improved this Fonseca, but I think you'll appreciate its quality.'

After one glass, Mike desperately wanted to get away to his own room. He was on Dawn Readiness and knew he was due for an almighty hangover anyway. But the lieutenant continued implacably—photos of hunt balls (' . . . daughter of the Duke of Buccleuch and of course an ol' family friend'), coxing the first eight at Eton in his last year (photograph, 'that's me' to prove it), and his 'fairly rapid, really' promotion in the Fleet Air Arm (smiling down from the cockpit of a Swordfish).

At last, during a brief pause, Mike got up rather unsteadily and said, 'Well, gee, thanks very . . .'

His eye was caught by a silver-framed photograph on the mantelpiece, one of the few he had not been shown. He realized that his eyesight was not registering as efficiently as it had been earlier in the day, say when he was making that inverted head-on attack. But it was not, on the other hand, so clouded with alcohol that it could not recognize a face. And the photograph, which was so large that he wondered why he had not seen it earlier, was without any doubt of Eileen. Eileen as he had first known her, glorious hair to her shoulders, small delicate nose, soft mouth, her . . .

The lieutenant saw him looking at it attentively and

picked it off the matelpiece so that he could look at it more closely. 'Ah yes, quite a bird, don't you think? "Gentlemen Prefer Blondes" what? Though she's got a touch of russet. Sir Richard Barrett's daughter, y'know. He's got a nice little place in Leicestershire.' He chuckled indulgently. 'And she makes a nice lay in London—as I believe you Americans say.'

Mike's eyes turned from the photograph in its decorated silver frame to the dark, heavy man holding it, whose face expressed self-satisfaction and mock confidentiality.

Mike spat out. 'You're a liar. You're a liar, a heel and a swank.' A short two-second burst, but his thumb was on the button again. 'Eileen Barrett wouldn't look at you. She wouldn't have a low heel like you within one goddam mile of her . . .'

The lieutenant cut in, 'D'you want to know the colour of her knickers, ol' boy? Very fancy, by a little place off Jermyn Street.'

Mike sprang forward. He caught the naval officer off balance, and he staggered against the bed with its fancy linen coverlet and fell back across it, Eileen's photograph thrown to the floor, glass smashed. He was up very quickly for a big man, eyes black with danger now and a menacing smile on his lips. Fifty pounds heavier, five inches taller. Mike watched him coming, remembered those boxing bouts and lessons in self-defence at Andover, crouched and sprang to one side, but did not escape entirely as the naval officer spun round, a chair suddenly held high in his right hand.

Mike caught it on his right shoulder, felt the shaft of pain like an electric shock, and—so it's playing dirty—kicked out at the man's crotch.

The fight became very rough and very noisy after that. Some more furniture was broken, the dressing-table went over on its side, a photograph of an elderly admiral sighed 'Dudley Pound' crashed against the wall. Mike, once under the full weight of the lieutenant and being punched hard in the face, caught a glimpse of a half-smoked cigar, and the precious bottle rolling over the Turkish rug, the Fonseca '27 leaving a liquid trail, saw a hand heavy with black hair seize its neck, and suddenly recognized that his life was as much at risk as it had been under different circumstances earlier in this long, long day.

With a huge effort, he succeeded in lifting one knee to unbalance the figure spreadeagled across him, and followed this with a stabbing punch at the pit of his belly. He heard a moan, felt the weight lift from him and struggled free. The bottle had been smashed and this time the neck was in the man's big hand . . .

The noise in the room had suddenly increased, multiplied many times over. There were voices shouting, arms were seizing his shoulders, another his waist, and he was being dragged back, Turkish rug rumpled under his feet. He was being held firm against the open door, and three officers and, for some reason, the barman in white apron, were holding his antagonist. There was a confusion of smashed wood and glass between them, and Mike felt sick, dizzy, confused and, already, terribly remorseful. But not so remorseful that he could not enjoy one flash of satisfaction at the closed left eye, the blood trickling from the lieutenant's mouth, and, best of all, the long tear in his fancy pants—old fancy pants, swanky pants, seducer pants, snotty nosed Reg'lar Royal goddam Navy Fleet Hair Harm pilot.

The station adjutant was saying, 'This is a very serious matter,' and Mike wanted to reply, 'Are you kidding?' but his lips were too swollen.

Rowbotham was there, too, no longer the avuncular, jokey Rowbotham looking for a reason for a 'no-bloody-reason' party. Now he was a black-with-rage Rowbotham observing two of his pilots off ops for several days, and calling out, 'Isn't fighting the Hun enough? Christ, Yank, what's the matter with you? This is court martial stuff. D'you think time hangs heavy on my bloody hands? Get them over to the sick bay.' And off he stamped.

*

Keith said, 'For God's sake, Mike, what happened? Not like you. Even when you *are* pie-eyed.'

Mike was in his own room, lying in bed with an impressive bandage across his right eye. His lips were so swollen his voice sounded as if he were speaking through a rubber tube. But, to Keith's astonishment, he seemed cheerful, even perky.

'Gee, Keith, it was like Joe Louis against a featherweight. And I held him! I held him, Keith! Jeez, that was some scrap. And I hurt him more than he hurt me, the bastard.'

'But why, Mike? What was it all about?'

Since he had been patched up by a very bad-tempered M.O. who had been called away from his bridge, Mike had convinced himself, finally and irrevocably as he thought, that the man had been lying, that he was a phoney, that he might have met Eileen and begged a photo from her. But the idea of Eileen Barrett, his fiancée, pure as driven snow, her moral code as hard as granite, bedding down with that gorilla—it was as far beyond serious consideration as his old friend Keith being a traitor.

Mike watched Keith's expression as he told him of the pilot's claim. It was serious, and at the end he nodded. Then Keith said, 'Look, Mike, there's something I've been wanting to tell you—well, not wanting, dreading,' he began stumblingly. 'But, you know, we've been fairly busy, and . . .'

As Mike listened to Keith's account of his evening at the Savoy, of the brush-off he had suffered, of the obviously intimate terms they were on, Lieutenant Winston-Greville and Eileen, he felt again the heat of hate and grief that had arisen in him earlier in the evening and had ignited his attack.

'It isn't true. You know it's not true. Not my Eileen. Not my lovely Eileen.' His puffed-out lips made it sound like 'Peileen'. But there was nothing comic in that. There was nothing comic about anything for Mike Browning on that August night, bruised in body and self-respect, his tenderness suddenly as sharp-edged as that broken port bottle rolling about Winston-Greville's goddam cabin as if he were back in the *Furious* in a heavy sea.

Keith said, 'I know, I've been trying to convince myself, too. But I've given up. It's no good, Mike. But for God's sake don't let it affect your flying. These are tough days, things'll get better, and we want to have you around.'

'That's swell of you, Keith,' Mike muttered, and for

the first time ever there was a note of bitterness in the irony. He just didn't care any more. Yes, the worst day . . .

Mike was at the dispersal at 05.45, dead on time for first Readiness. He came on a bicycle. The C.O. saw him riding up in the dawn light, bandage gone, one eye half closed, his whole face ridiculously puffy, the scratch marks from another fight scored across his forehead. The boy's nuts, he told himself. Then he called out from the entrance to his office, 'Get back to your quarters, Flying Officer Browning. You're not fit to fly.'

But five minutes later, in face of a passionate flow of persuasion, Rowbotham had yielded, against his better judgement, and was surprised that he had been worsted. It had seemed that, to the American, it was a matter of life or death that he should be ready to fly. But, then, wasn't it always life or death just now?

4

'. . . OF 'AUGUST WEARY'

For the R.A.F. fighter pilots covering the south-east of England, if time did not actually stand still in the hot, hectic days of August, every day seemed like a lifetime of sweat and endeavour. Physically, the strain was even greater on the ground crews who often worked sixteen hours at a stretch servicing the machines, patching them up, correcting engine, gun, and radio faults; examining wings strained in desperate 500 m.p.h. dives, replacing shattered canopies, punctured landing tyres, rudders shot through.

These ground crews lived off countless pint mugs of N.A.A.F.I. tea and wads, often eaten standing up, with a fighter's tailplane as table. They would go for days without seeing their bunks or mess, sleeping down at the dispersal, dirty and unkempt, their lives all oil and tools and making-do; noise and sudden terror and kips on the grass or curled up in the bomb shelter. Endless cigarettes, and occasional pints of beer smuggled down to the flights, were their only indulgences.

At Savile Farm and Kenley, Biggin and Manston, Hawkinge and Croydon, Duxford and Hornchurch, each a tiny pocket of frantic activity on the map, airmen and officers, N.C.O.s and W.A.A.F.s, drivers and firemen, messengers and cooks, worked as they had never believed possible, in stores and ops, in messés and admin. amid the din of sirens, Tannoy announcements, engine testing and low flying aircraft and the intermittent thunder of bomb blasts.

Some stations remained untouched. The Luftwaffe bombed training fields and claimed to have wiped out a fighter station. But Manston was completely knocked out, and others so savagely damaged that squadrons moved to reserve satellite fields prepared for such a contingency. Runways were ruined and repaired, communications severed and re-connected, water supplies and sewers cut and secured.

Long 'Queen Mary' trailers transported to repair depots damaged Hurricanes and Spitfires, wrapped in tarpaulin like wounded men on stretchers. The trailer crews were ordered not to cover wrecks of German machines, which were viewed with cheer and satisfaction by the civilian population as they passed through dumps to be photographed by the Press. The least damaged were roped off in town and village squares— 6d admission in aid of the local Spitfire fund to see the downed Me109, propeller bent, holes scored along the fuselage.

For nine out of ten British people, the life-or-death struggle was no more than a distant contest of figures, an 'away fixture' which touched their lives so indirectly that it was difficult to relate the statistics and photographs in the newspapers, the broadcasts on the BBC, with anything more than a particularly important football cup tie.

Of the one in ten who caught the glimpse of the battles overhead, who sometimes heard the distant ripple of gunfire, saw shapes in the sky or the pattern of vapour trails, the Battle of Britain—as the Prime Minister, Winston Churchill, had named it—was only a little less remote. A few thousand felt it more severely, some directly and even fatally, forerunners of the thousands of dead in the night bombing to follow in the autumn.

But among those directly engaged in the battle, from seamen of coastal shipping to the Observer Corps and police and A.R.P. personnel, the men and women who manned the guns and barrage balloons, there were only a few hundred at any one time actually fighting the enemy in the sky. Earlier in the battle, the first problem had been the shortage of planes. In August it became a lack of pilots. Men like Pilot Officer Mackay rarely lasted long, and the strain on the surviving veterans became that much more intense. Almost half the Flight Commanders had been killed or seriously wounded by the end of August, and more had been promoted to fill the gaps among Squadron Commanders. Tired, decimated squadrons were taken out of the line and sent west, or north where, on 15 August, some of them had a field day against a surprise German attack from Norway which had expected no opposition.

In other cases, individual pilots who had been in action continuously for many months were given short periods of leave. On 140 Squadron, Mike refused to take his and there was another almighty row with Rowbotham, which again Mike won. Of the others given seventy-two-hour leave, Range Powell went off hellbent for his favourite sheila in Knightsbridge, Bill Watson for a mighty booze-up and any women he could find in the West End, and Keith again for one woman in particular, Jenny, repairing rapidly and due for convalescence.

Keith doubted whether the break would do him much good. There were too many anxieties related to it for that. First, there was the worry of leaving Mike behind, the bruises to his face repairing more rapidly than the injuries to his spirit and self-esteem, which really were not mending at all. Keith had not flown with him for three days, but those who had reported a new recklessness in his style of fighting. Kiwi Robinson had seen him close in alone and without any sort of evasive action on a big formation of Ju.88s, whose controlled cross-fire had been murderously accurate, and blow up the tail-end machine with a single long burst—and then turn and come in again. His machine had been damaged Cat. B as a result of that action, and he had been repeatedly hit again the next day.

Then there was the worry for Keith over what he was to do about Eileen—if anything. And what would he say to her parents? And, on a much simpler level, he was concerned about getting Jenny out of St Thomas's Hospital to Rising Hall; and how would she get on with his adopted parents? His own seventy-two hours, he decided, were going to be less straightforward than Range's.

Mike was not in the mess when Keith left. It was mid-afternoon and most of those not on Readiness were catching up on their sleep. 78 Squadron's Spitfires had been scrambled, and the boom of their take-off had just faded. Keith saw Flynn in the corner, curled up in a chair. He was not asleep. The squadron poet never seemed to sleep. He was writing in a note-book and looked up when Keith approached him.

'Sorry to disturb the muse,' Keith said. 'But I can't find Mike anywhere. Give him all my best when you see him.'

The pilot officer looked up and nodded. 'A real scrapper, that chum of yours,' he said. 'I'm trying to do a verse or two for *Horizon* on what this August is like. Not easy when it's happening all around you and never seems to end.' He uncurled in his armchair, sat up and looked keenly at Keith. 'If the Bard had not said it three hundred and fifty years ago, I'd have begun, "You sunburn'd sicklemen, of August weary . . ." and gone on from there. Blast the Bard!'

*

Lady Barrett, it was often said and with reason, had a way with her. She could persuade powerful commit-tees to reverse decisions. She could see to it that a neglected but deserving church roof was repaired, starting off the fund with a £100 cheque herself. She could arrange for the Lord Lieutenant of Leicester-shire to come as guest of honour to a certain charity ball. And she could, after a word here and there, and a telephone call to a cousin of the Deputy Chief of Air Staff, see to it that an R.A.F. ambulance collected Section Officer Jennifer Simpson from St Thomas's Hospital on the day before Keith's seventy-two-hour leave began and transported her from London to Rising Hall. It had taken her twelve minutes. She was that sort of woman.

Her well-laid plan slipped up in only one respect, and that had been beyond her control. A telegram to Keith had failed to reach him at Savile Farm due to the bombing and destruction of local telephone cables. For this reason Keith wasted several hours in London attempting to trace Jenny's whereabouts through the interstices of hospital and service bureaucracy. All his fears and forebodings, of Jenny transferred to some anonymous provincial hospital, of Jenny at an official W.A.A.F. convalescent home at Skegness, of Jenny's leg failing to heal after all and requiring amputation—all these were disposed of when he at last discovered that she was already at Rising Hall.

A taxi took him to King's Cross—'Orl right, sir, you ain't in a bleedin' Spitfire now'. The train was two hours late, a victim of the upheaval on the railway system caused by the need to send coal for the power stations south by land instead of by colliers through the Dover Straits. It was almost six o'clock, and he had lost a day before he reached Rising Hall.

Perversely, however, he told the taxi driver to stop at the main gates so that he could walk up the drive to the house, to savour again the smells and sights of his childhood. First the lodge itself, brick-built and as old as Rising Hall which it had served for 300 years, his own home until 21 February 1931, that day of tragic violence when his parents had been killed together at a hand-operated railway crossing, their old car stalled on the track. He had, minutes earlier, passed the spot in the train.

Then up the drive, winding between scattered beeches and oaks—the drive he had walked up on that same day after Sir Richard had given him the news. Nine years earlier he had walked almost to the house—there it was, coming into view in all its Jacobean glory—then diverted off into the woods, suddenly conscious of the implication behind his route, from his own humble house to the great mansion which was his only link with his parents and his past. At twelve years of age it had not been easy to bear.

And now the house was before him, splendid in its towers and turrets, the Inigo Jones porch, a miniature of Hatfield House, the roses, at their best in the four beds within the sweep of the drive up to the door.

Grand and beautiful, but not his, not Keith Stewart's. They had welcomed him here, done everything to make him feel it was his natural home, and all his years of later boyhood had been spent here. Sir Richard Barrett was the nearest Keith had to a father, Constance Barrett a kind and understanding surrogate mother. He had even been persuaded into calling them father and mother. But to Keith, as honest with himself as he was uncertain of himself, Rising Hall was still no more his home than it was to the constant stream of guests who had come every weekend before the war for shooting parties and balls, croquet on the lawn and bridge in the evening.

Home for Keith was still that humble lodge where from 1919 until he died his father had acted as estate manager and his mother had helped the housekeeper during especially busy times.

Lady Barrett, dead-heading the roses, saw him coming and ran to greet him, all-square but not overweight, fifty-ish but as vigorous as ever. 'Darling Keith.' She pulled him to her and held him tightly, and he caught the blended scent of Yardley's soap and the rose petals filling the pocket of her apron.

'What a t-t-time you've been having!' She was not much below his height—five feet eleven to his six feet two—and she looked lovingly into his eyes as she held him back at arm's length. 'And your p-p-poor leg,' she said with her slight but attractive stutter. 'I saw you limping just now.' They walked towards the house, her arm in his.

'How's Jenny?' asked Keith. 'You *are* kind to look after her. What do you think of her? Do you like her?'

Constance Barrett paused to pick up the secateurs she had thrown on the lawn. 'She's a dear, Keith. We l-l-love her. Such a nice girl.' She pronounced it 'gel.' 'So independent. I expect she told you she's on cr-cr-crutches, but she gets about like a motor.'

The truth was confirmed when Jenny emerged from the library on hearing Keith's voice. Lady Barrett said, 'I think that's the telephone ringing. So dif-difficult to hear tucked away under the stairs,' and hurried away almost before they had greeted one another across the length of the drawing-room.

'Is it safe for me to hold you like this?' asked Keith amid the clatter of wooden crutches on the parquet floor.

'Safe and nice,' said Jenny.

He carried her to a sofa and took lingering pleasure placing cushions under her head exactly to suit her comfort. 'I am *not* an invalid,' she kept saying, laughing.

'So I'll chuck these on the fire, shall I?' said Keith, picking up the crutches before putting them beside her.

They talked and laughed, Keith telling of his struggle with the admin. people at St Thomas's, Jenny of her drive up with two flirtatious medical orderlies who brought her out pints of beer whenever they stopped at a pub. Then Mrs. Ewhurst came in with sherry. She had kept house at the Barretts' place in London until Sir Richard had closed it down in May.

'Are you getting used to the quiet of the country?' Keith asked her.

'Quiet! Well, I like that, sir. Eaton Square is silent, proper silent, compared with her. The birds screaming their heads off. And those awful cocks.'

When she had gone, Jenny said, 'And I adore your father. What a darling! He's off on manoeuvres with his Home Guard company this afternoon. There's supposed to be a parachute invasion over Melton way.'

'Good. But he's *not* my father,' said Keith. 'You know very well. And this isn't my house. I still feel an interloper here every time I come back.'

Jenny tossed her head impatiently, her voice sharp. 'Don't talk such rubbish. Makes you sound silly and sorry for yourself. Eileen's quite right to tell you off about your old class chip on the shoulder.'

Keith felt the light and happiness in him fade, and the first prickles of resentment arise. How easily they came! He knew it but never seemed quite able to stamp them down. Then she grabbed his hand and ordered him to smile.

At that moment, Constance Barrett came in, dressed for dinner in a long plain black silk jersey dress.

'It's time you two changed. Shall I get Irish to give you a hand, Jenny? Keith d-d-darling, do put on a black tie. It would be so nice to see you out of that uniform, h-h-handsome though you are in it, d-d-darling boy.'

Jenny refused the offer and hitched herself onto her crutches, while Keith wondered again how and when he could explain about Eileen. Perhaps he could evade the subject altogether?

*

It was a ridiculous consideration that the subject of Eileen would not come up in the conversation: the only daughter, the only child, the object of twenty-one years of love and cherishment. In fact, Sir Richard's first question after grace and greetings at dinner was, 'Have you heard anything of Eileen?'

Keith was prepared with his white lie. 'I haven't had a letter for weeks, sir. What about you?'

Lady Barrett said, 'We're really rather worried, d-d-darling. She's usually such a good girl about writing.'

The Barretts had patriotically cut down their indoor staff to four, and Iris was helping Stokes at the table. There was turtle soup and a small saddle of lamb from the farm with fresh vegetables from the walled kitchen garden. Jenny had a chair with a cushion arranged for her leg.

'I met her once.' Jenny's interjection gave Keith time to think. 'Just for a few minutes, when I was in hospital at Folkestone. She came all the way from London to see me, and she had never even *met* me before. Don't you think that was sweet? I thought she was terribly nice. And, oh that hair! Made me wild with jealousy.'

'Yes, she's a dear girl,' said Constance Barrett, and

added with a slight laugh, 'And I expect you s-s-saw where she got her eyes when you met Richard.'

Keith recalled Eileen's eyes. He had once likened their colour to the lily leaves on the lake behind Rising Hall. Richard Barrett's eyes. And Constance Barrett's fair, sensitive complexion, small nose and sturdy chin, and her hair, too. Whenever he remembered that face he had loved through his boyhood, its innocence and eagerness, he now felt a stab of sickness. Chaste, happy, kind Eileen!

'She may be on some super hush-hush work,' Keith suggested.

'She did say she was putting in for a commission,' said Lady Barrett hopefully.

Jenny added, 'She struck me as such a responsible girl, and with her background and education, they'd almost certainly give her important work.'

Sir Richard was cleaning up his gravy with a hunk of bread. He hated waste and even managed to bring a touch of distinction to this practice of his. 'No reason why the girl shouldn't write,' he said, firmly, wiping his moustache and pushing away his plate as if disposing of the subject.

The older couple left Keith and Jenny in the library soon after coffee. Sir Richard, fifty-five and a Mauser bullet in his leg on the first day of the Somme, stomped off first, tired from a day out of doors with his Home Guard battalion and trailing cigar smoke. Lady Barrett said she was going to write some letters and would not be down again. 'Darling, put on some music for Jenny. Cheer her up.' She kissed Keith and smiled good-night to Jenny.

'The last thing I need is cheering up,' said Jenny when they were alone. 'It's so marvellous to be here.' Then she looked at Keith more seriously. 'What *has* happened to Eileen?' she asked. 'You sounded all cagey. They would have been told if she had been wounded or anything. They even told my Great-Aunt Emmy, and I suppose she is my nearest relative, when I was hurt.'

Keith realized how much he loved Jenny when he found it easy to reply spontaneously. 'She's changed. Something awful's happened. Just like that. She was engaged to Mike. When he was injured she went up to Inverness to be near him. And when he came here to recuperate, like you, she got leave and helped him to recover.' Keith lit another cigarette from the one he had been smoking, and spread his hands in despair. 'I just don't understand. It's so unlike her. Her parents approved of the engagement and they were going to get married after the war.'

He told Jenny about the meeting at the Savoy, of the naval lieutenant's arrival on the squadron, of his boasting to Mike. 'To Mike of all people—wasn't it a ghastly coincidence?'

'I hope he punched him.'

'He did.'

Then she said, 'But poor you. You loved her, didn't you?'

'Yes, in a sort of brotherly way. Not like you. But, yes. When I was younger I did sometimes dream of marrying her. But of course I knew it was out of the question, me, son of Sir Richard Barrett's ex-platoon sergeant, late estate manager. Eileen would marry

106

some Hon. or Sir or Lord or colonel in the Guards and have her picture in the Tatler . . .'

'I hate you when you talk like that.' Jenny's voice was crisp, as if rebuking a W.A.A.F. Second-class Aircraftwoman.

Keith looked at her in surprise. 'But it's true,' he said.

'It may be true. But when you say things like that in that sort of voice, you sound like a pimply clerk full of resentments. You're worth a dozen Eileen Barretts, as she's busily proving right now.' Jenny was lying stretched out on the sofa opposite Keith, her long plain beautifully-cut red dress obscuring her plaster, her face set in a determined expression as if driving a car.

Keith remembered that Eileen used to say the same sort of thing about his resentments, and this made his position even more uneasy. They could be—and probably were—quite right, both of them. But at this moment of bitterness he did not want Jenny to have anything in common with Eileen.

Suddenly, for the first time, in this comfortable study he knew so well, in a deep armchair with a whisky and soda at his side, with the light fading across the lawn and the fields and woodlands beyond—here, with this woman he wanted so passionately, Keith knew he was tired out. Whacked. Whacked out from the strain and fighting.

Jenny chose this moment to say quietly, in her slightly husky voice, 'I love you, darling Keith'.

His face was buried in her hair, her incredibly soft cheek was against his and he could feel the dampness of her tears. 'What are you crying for?' he whispered into her ear. 'We ought to be happy, just for a few hours.'

She laughed and said, half-sobbing, 'I am happy. I told you. But you looked so young, rebuked like a schoolboy, and so damned tired, Keith, I can hardly bear it. Risking your life ten times a day, week after week. It's not fair, you doing all the fighting.'

This was something Keith could cope with, and he drew back and looked into her face, the tear stains barely discernible in the last of the twilight. 'Oh, don't worry about *that*,' he said firmly, thankful that he was in command again. 'That's nothing. I'm very good at surviving—getting better every day, too.'

There was a knock at the door, and Stokes came in. 'Shall I draw the black-out curtains, sir?'

Stokes left a single light on above the desk. The heavy black velvet curtains added to the feeling of intimacy and confidentiality. Keith put some Mozart on the radiogramme and they both drank more whisky, and Keith stretched out full length on the sofa facing Jenny, and announced his utter contentment with life.

Later, he helped her onto her crutches and opened the doors leading to the old card room, now converted into a bedroom to save her the stairs. There was a basin in the corner with an old-fashioned pitcher of cold water and a copper jug of hot water. Keith took lingering delight in slowly helping her to undress and wash.

'I always thought I'd make a good nurse,' he said, gently cupping her breasts from behind as she dried her face.

'You wouldn't last long behaving like that.' She

108

laughed breathily and told him to stop, and when he didn't she stood still and let his hands run lightly from the beginning of the plaster on her thigh to her shoulder, to her face and down again over her breasts. She was breathing so fast that she did not seem able to talk and Keith spoke all the time, murmuring at the wonder of her skin and the beauty of her breasts, and the lovely squareness of her uncompromising shoulders and the sadness of her plaster.

'Keith,' she at last managed to say. 'Keith darling, I'm getting all dizzy. I'm losing my balance. It's difficult enough standing anyway . . .'

He said, 'Yes, it's always better lying down.' Then he picked her up and laid her down on the bed quite naked except for the white plaster from her right thigh down to her calf. 'We can do better still. You wait.' And he turned off the light and drew back the black-out curtains, letting in a flood of moonlight. It was not quite a full moon, but near enough for him to say, 'I laid on this full moon just for you.'

Jenny had pulled the eiderdown over her. 'This would be ridiculously romantic—very wrong but romantic—if it wasn't for my ghastly leg.'

Keith finished undressing at great speed and walked towards her. His chest and legs were still bronzed from that early summer sun in France before the collapse. He knelt down beside the bed and began to ease off the eiderdown.

'Kiss me, Keith. But I'm sorry, I can't make love. It's not practical. Anyway, you'll always think of me as the woman with the gammy leg. It's awful to be remembered like that. Crippled.'

She pushed him away when he tried to lie beside her, but not very hard, and her hands were soon on his body, and he began caressing her as before. So many months of pent-up longing and separation and being near but unable to touch. And now at last, utter, complete liberty and the shared determination that it should be utterly and completely right. In a curious way, Keith derived satisfaction from the contrast between the touch of the inanimate sheathed leg, cold and hard, and the soft, warm flesh of her left thigh; and the plaster proved no impediment when at last they sank together.

'Go on talking,' murmured Jenny. 'I like that.'

So Keith did, recalling their last love-making so long ago, until he could talk no longer.

'This is ridiculous,' said Jenny at last. 'Anyone out there could see us easily.'

They lay side by side in the narrow bed, looking across the croquet lawn to the lake and the two great yews and the wood beyond, shadows sharp in the brilliant summer moon.

'Also,' she added, 'quite improper.'

'Perfectly proper. Once in your house. And once in mine. Quite fair. And one day, every night in *our* house.'

Keith reached out for the pocket of his jacket hanging on the chair. While Jenny continued to stare sleepily out of the window, he wrote boldly at the very top of the plaster, 'I love you. Will you marry me?' Followed by 'Keith' and a large and uneven heart with an arrow through it. He had finished before she realized what he was doing. She looked down at her leg, turning her head to read by the light of the moon the up-

THE FIGHT OF THE FEW

side down words. 'Keith, you are a chump. What a way to propose! Certainly not. No time for that sort of nonsense.'

*

Twenty-four hours after Keith returned from his brief leave, the Luftwaffe knocked out Savile Farm. By 15 August, when a total of 2,000 German bombers and fighters attacked R.A.F. targets, even Fighter Command Headquarters at Bentley Priory considered this the limit of German effort, and that the Luftwaffe would not be able to continue to sustain claimed losses of up to nearly 200 aircraft in one day.

But from Lannion and Cherbourg, Orleans/Bricy and Amiens. St Omer, Calais/Marck and Antwerp, the Junkers, Heinkel and Dornier bombers and the Messerschmitt fighters continued to pour across the Channel, their numbers building up on the underground Sector and Group plotting tables, as the R.D.F. and Observer Corps reports were noted and W.A.A.F.s, in shirt sleeves, moved the counters about the table. Controllers scrambled Flight and Squadrons, ordered them onto an intersecting vector, redirected them as the height and likely target became known, striving somehow to put up at least a token presence against every raid.

Luftwaffe tactical inflexibility was a thing of the past. Every day, it seemed, the Germans were learning new tricks—feint attacks and double-bluff, high-level mixed with low-level raids, attacks on the most vital airfields, on the factory at Southampton that built the Spitfires, attacks by the fast, fierce *Zerstörer* Messerschmitt 110 twin-engine fighter equipped with bombs.

111

R.A.F. 11 Group, in the eye of the storm, was forced to withdraw from some of its forward airfields. The sustained pressure resulted in strained nerves at the highest level of command. The Commander of 12 Group, farther north and with more time to get off large formations of fighters, quarrelled with the Commander of 11 Group, who was at his wits' end to get his fighters off at all and considered he was not being supported sufficiently by his neighbouring commander. The disputes travelled fast down the line of command to Squadron Commanders. There was no time to spare for dissension but the German pressure was doing its work during those last days of August and sometimes there were hard words among the defenders.

There were sharp words over the R/T, too, which pleased the Luftwaffe command when the monitored reports came in. And it was true that the R.A.F. was beginning to crack, that control of the skies over southern England was being lost; and everyone knew that the consequences of defeat in the air would be disastrous and limitless.

Keith, with the detachment acquired by three days of absence from the battle, detected the first traces of defeatism when he got back to Savile Farm late on a Saturday evening. He walked up from the station with a couple of sergeant pilots from A Flight who were full of beer but not cheered by it. They had lost a mutual chum that afternoon in another raid on Biggin Hill, shot down by a 109 over Canterbury.

'What d'you expect—no sodding cannon and no sodding speed,' one of them exclaimed angrily. 'The Hurri's had it. Finished. Obsolete.'

Keith tried to cheer them up but became bored with their gloom and obscenities. It was not much better in the officers' mess bar. There was usually some sort of rag or party on Saturday night, but most of the officers appeared to have gone to bed early.

Keith singled out his Flight Commander. 'Mike O.K.?'

Kiwi Robinson nodded over his tankard. Like Air Marshal Park himself, the Group Commander, Kiwi was a quiet, steady but cheerful officer from Thames, North Island, who had been in the service since 1932 and was as old and experienced as the C.O. His lantern-jaw and grave, steady eyes inspired confidence. He was not a heavy drinker but had been putting it back that evening. He ordered Keith a large Scotch.

'Much doing while I've been away?' Keith asked, raising the glass.

'Nothing but flaps—dawn to dusk flaps.' The New Zealander was slurring his words and the twang of his accent was unusually pronounced. 'Ginger went for a Burton this afternoon—a flamer off Selsey, straight into the sea.' He imitated the dive with his hand vertically to the bar top and made a hissing noise. 'Soon put that fire out.'

Ginger Willoughly, a warrant officer with a D.F.M. for getting three in one day over Dunkirk. Hard to replace, and as the Flight Commander related, there would be no replacements for the two lost pilots for at least a week.

'Good to have you back, Keith. In fact, bloody necessary. Yes, thanks, I'll have one more.' He lowered his tankard, wiping off the froth with the back of his hand. 'The boss's gone to Group for the evening. Said he wanted to know the form from the mouth of god. I'd rather not know—bound to be bad.'

Keith caught a glimpse of Lieutenant Winston-Greville leaving the bar, the expression on his face hinting that this was not the sort of place and company he was accustomed to. He wondered how Mike and he were being kept apart. And he wondered about the changed condition of 140 Squadron, with only a handful of the original pilots left and its fighting fitness reduced by losses and weariness and sinking morale.

⁜

There were no half measures about this second big attack on Savile Farm. 120-plus from *Luftflotten* II and III came in from the south-east without any feint so that Control's prediction that they were heading either for Croydon, Kenley or Savile Farm proved right. 11 Group scrambled four squadrons, then three more as the raid built up in strength.

78 Squadron's Spitfires were sent off at 2.15 p.m., and 140 were held back for another ten minutes before the telephone rang and a red Very light went up from the watch tower simultaneously. It had been known for Kesselring to send in very low-flying 110s or Ju.88s a few minutes after a high-level attack to spread further chaos with incendiaries and delayed action bombs. 140 were to be held back for this contingency, and Keith, leading Red Section, with Winston-Greville as his number two, and Range Powell and Bill Watson as three and four, found himself

114

west of Horsham at 4,000 feet with orders to watch for very low bandits.

It was a clear day, no cloud at all, and the build-up was unusually fast. Far above and to the south-east, he could just make out the growing pattern of vapour trails as if a giant hand were chalking whorls and lines on the dome of sky, some straight lines marking pursuit or flight, others less steady and fading and reappearing. They were still too distant to identify machines yet, but the R/T was charged with the chatter of combat, German voices sometimes chipping in gutturally. A small and momentary orange glow was a signal wink of destruction, and another thin black vertical line marked another. A voice, louder than the rest with an American-sounding accent, shouted, 'Chrissake break, Charlie!' That would be 1 Canadian Squadron from Northolt, one Canuck in trouble.

Keith kept his hood open, looking unceasingly left and right, glancing into the mirror, then up and down. The battle had moved to the north-east and the guns had temporarily taken over. He could see the shape of the raid, four great blocks of twin-engined bombers, still too distant to identify for sure but they looked like 111s, a solid dark wedge of aircraft moving fast towards southwest London, their formation patterned by grey puffs of shellbursts.

Three minutes later control called, 'Sandbag Leader, I have trade for you at angels zero, twenty-plus steering zero-one-zero ten miles north of Well-done.'

Keith glanced at his code chart and map. They were somewhere between Chichester and Guildford, right on the deck. Control's gamble had come off—so long as they found them.

Kiwi took them east in a very fast glide, hoping for a sighting well before the target area. 'Sandbag Red Section, spread out and watch like hell,' he radioed.

The manoeuvre brought them a dream interception. The bombers with their clever mottled, dark camouflage were hard to spot against the patchwork of fields and spinneys of the Sussex-Surrey border, but Keith saw the leader as he lifted up over the plain bright green of the Hog's Back. Others streamed behind him like a string of dark pearls. He reckoned there were fifteen in all, Ju.88s and travelling flat out just 2,000 feet below them.

'Red One, take them first. We'll follow.'

Keith banked steeply to starboard, ordering Winston-Greville farther out to attack the rearmost port machine. Then he shut his hood for maximum speed and opened the throttle wide. He had always found himself struck by a special feeling of dark hatred for an enemy plane over his own land, a much stronger feeling than he had experienced when fighting in France, and he had to recite the old litany he had taught himself when his boyhood anger threatened to overcome the fine judgement essential in air fighting.

'Calm it down! Calm it down, Keith Stewart!' were the words he spoke into his oxygen mask; and at the same time he remembered that other exhortation of his training days, spoken by Randall, the foul-mouthed and scarred R.F.C. veteran. 'Wait till there's nothing but bloody Hun in the sight before you press the button. And watch that sodding temper of yours, Stewart.'

Calm it maybe. But the dark, destructive intruder trespassing on *his* land, racing with impunity over *his* English fields and cottages, sending English cattle scattering in panic, causing Englishmen and women to hurl themselves to the ground in fear, aroused fury and determination, as if he were pursuing an armed robber through his own house.

Keith shut out all other considerations from his mind, blinded his eyes to the landscape racing below and the blurred images of the other bombers ahead and to the left, giving his brain and vision one target only: *his* Ju.88, brand new twin-engined medium bomber, speed 300 m.p.h., bomb load 5,000 pounds tucked in its belly, and at this level and only minutes away from its target, a difficult machine to shoot down.

But he was going to shoot it down. There was no question of it. He was going to destroy this ugly racing murderous brute, killing the four men in it if possible. Now.

He was 500 feet above with a temporary advantage of some 50 m.p.h., and he went in on a classic three-quarters stern attack, banking left, cork-screwing right, adjusting for deflection as he came in with his wingtips close to the vertical. Check turn and bank. Then his right thumb slid over the button and pressed briefly. The smallest pressure and eight guns fired for him, each gun eighteen rounds a second. That was power, real power.

He had told his armourer to fit fifty tracer rounds at the start of each belt to intimidate the opposition.

117

Keith aimed at the rear of the greenhouse canopy that housed the crew and saw at the same time the proboscis-like gun swing round towards him. For three seconds there was a hectic exchange of tracer that Keith found blinding against the dark of the landscape and he cursed his armament decision. Every day another lesson. He saw no strikes and quickly overshot the 88, pulling up steeply and using emergency boost to offset the loss of speed advantage.

He made his second pass from dead astern. The enemy was lower than ever, skimming over meadowland and lifting over hedges, and pumping right-left-right rudder to put off Keith's aim and give the rear gunner a clear aim past the big tail fin. This time Keith came in very close, concentrating on the bomber's port engine and feeling the spasmodic knock of its slipstream. He put three seconds of fire into the dark circle of the Jumo radial engine, and before he pulled over hard to starboard in a climbing turn he saw with satisfaction the first belch of black smoke puffing back.

There was a sudden splash of yellow flame further ahead in the bomber stream—someone was shooting more successfully than he was—and he could see other Hurricanes harrying the tail end of the bombers, one mixed deep in among them with tracer arching in from three sides, and briefly and distantly another Hurricane far to the left and steering west, as if on some other urgent errand.

There was barely time for a third pass. His target was still racing along, as low and seemingly as fast as ever in spite of the smoke pouring in ever greater volume from the port engine. Very tough adversaries,

118

these 88s. Recent shot down examples had had crew
and engine armour fitted, too.

Again Keith waited until the wingtips were well
within his sight's range bars, firing first at the starboard engine, and then with special hatred at the gunner. Even Mike would have been proud of this shooting. The De Wilde bullets told of hundreds of hits, the
starboard propeller slowed so that he could see it ro-
tating no faster than a windmill's in a breeze. The 88
had been knocked out, had only seconds of life, would
blow up or crash land.

But it had not yet finished with Keith. Lumps of
metal, scraps of engine, the debris of combat, raced
towards him like shell shrapnel, and before he could
pull aside, something unidentifiable, dark and larger
than the rest, struck his prop boss and disintegrated,
momentarily blinding him and causing his Hurricane
to shudder from the shock of impact.

A whole engine must have hit him. That was Keith's
immediate response. He had survived those streams of
bullets only to be disabled by his victim's corpse, so to
speak. *Touché*, all right. And awkward. At first he
could see nothing, like the time his Merlin had suffered a major oil leak. This time again he was forced
to open his canopy, undo his straps and, with goggles
down, put his head half into the slipstream. At first he
saw no sign of damage and was able to level off at
500 feet and glance down. He was deep in suburbia.
Fields had given way to strings of houses, an arterial
road, a large common. Mitcham Common? There was
no sign of his victim, and Keith had no urge to search,
for at that moment his engine began to run roughly,

setting up violent vibrations for about five seconds, and then—silence.

His own three-blade prop was turning at the speed of the 88s, and one blade was bent back twenty degrees, another less severely. There were what looked like streams of black oil and debris all along the engine housing. It must have been engine to engine, a swift and violent embrace with fatal results.

Keith reached forward and wiped over the flat bullet-proof front of his screen with his gauntlets to clear it and settled back into his seat. He had a very short time indeed to find somewhere, to pump down his flaps, and turn off the switches and fuel cock.

He recognized the common now, a kidney-shaped area of green, trees on one side, a playground area of swings and slides on the other, a small spinney beyond giving way again to the prairie of semi-detached and terrace houses lining the network of roads. He could get in there on his belly. There was no one in sight, everyone in shelters, but the grass bristled with the usual obstruction stakes that had been erected on open land everywhere in south-east England as a defence against airborne invasion, but had so far proved more dangerous to the R.A.F. than to the Luftwaffe.

Keith banked and turned to get into wind, the controls slack with the loss of slipstream, losing height fast, scarcely conscious of the silence so hard was he concentrating on the need to touch down on just the right spot. No going round again this time. Too high. Left stick, opposite rudder and into a sloppy sideslip. All the responses dead as if the rudder and ailerons had expired with the engine. Stick forward. Now he was too fast and too high but there was nothing to be done. He would overshoot into those gardens.

There was no clear line through the vertical stakes. Some were further apart than the forty-foot wingspan of his machine, others closer. He touched down at just 65 m.p.h. almost half-way across the common, bouncing once, and while still sliding fast across the dry turf, catching a wingtip. Before his machine could swing one way his other wing smashed into another post, knocking it down but tearing off at the root when it struck another.

The Hurricane lurched to right and then to left, and the noise of tearing metal was crushing after the gentle sigh of the wind before he touched. Keith, with straps unsecured, was thrown forward, striking his head, hard but not quite hard enough to knock himself out. He felt his machine come to a halt, lurching over to one side, starboard wingtip gone and nothing on his port side.

Keith was aware of the raw smell of hot metal and a sharp and lethal compound of oil, glycol and 100 octane fuel. A sound of fast dripping came from somewhere forward. It was time to get out, very fast. He sprang to the ground and ran for fifty yards, head down, before turning.

Poor old C-Charlie. A write-off. Perhaps a few salvageable parts and no more. She had scored number eight for him that day, and he had done this to her in return. But at least she was not going up in flames after all. He returned, groggy on his feet and his head aching, to collect his parachute and helmet, and the gauntlets lying on the floor of the cockpit. These were damp from wiping the screen and he held them at arm's length to drip on the grass.

The redness of the fluid caught his eye. He studied the gauntlets more carefully, turned his eyes towards C-Charlie's nose, saw that it shone unnaturally brightly in the sun above the matt camouflage paint, told himself quickly, unconvincingly, that it was oil spill from his engine, or from the 88's engine; and in a wave of sickness was forced to accept the truth.

It was, literally, his victim's corpse. The German gunner had got him after all. The dark object that had hit him was the rear gunner himself, who had been catapulted out dead by Keith's gunfire or had thrown himself out hoping the slipstream would force open his parachute quickly and break his fall, choosing that way to go rather than the crash landing, perhaps in flames, that was so imminent.

Keith had landed a Hurricane that was streaked in blood and tissue from prop boss, where the wretched young man had first struck, along the length of nose and fuselage, and even in places on the tailplane. He threw the gauntlets back into the cockpit and walked away shakily from the scene of his crime, feeling as soiled as if he, rather than his smashed plane, was painted with the remains of his enemy.

For some minutes he remained in a closed world of horror and self-disgust, unconscious of the activity close about him, hearing none of the shouts, not the bells of fire engines and ambulances, the crackle of nearby flames, not even the wail of the all-clear siren; nor did he see the rising clouds of smoke, behind him, to left and right, and massively from a mile to the west, black here and rising in belching, oily gasps.

Still half-stunned from the blow on his head, he became aware first of his fingers, his right hand holding a cigarette which he had lit without consciousness. The next thing he saw was a dog, a big dog, a fine Great Dane. It paused, staring down blankly at him with its great black eyes, then turned and loped away, leaving in his track a trail of blood staining the grass. Another dog followed, and then another, a bitch with heavy hanging dugs and a deep wound in her side, followed by a pair of young puppies, unharmed it seemed. And then another and more—ten more, some deep brown like the first, others a shiny black, some uninjured, others dragging a leg or showing a flesh wound, all of them silently following the first, like the Hamelin rats, hell bent on achieving freedom in a canine procession of pain and fear.

Keith stared at the receding dogs, his head in his hands, his cigarette burning itself out on the ground. He was rocking to and fro, another fact of his condition that required explanation. He wiped a hand across his forehead and saw that it was streaked with blood. More blood. First German blood. Then dogs' blood. Now his own.

A voice startled him into awareness, rough and angry. 'Come on, you, give a hand!'

Keith turned on his seat. and the child's swing turned with him. A figure fifty yards away was shouting at him. 'What're you doing there? People here want help.'

He got up, half tripping over a child's tricycle. 'Sorry. Coming,' he shouted at the man, who turned and ran back towards a terrace of houses. A crater had destroyed half a dozen of them, whipped the roof off three more. Curtain rails and curtains waved from smashed windows, an Austin 7 lay on its side on the smashed wooden fencing between rear gardens and the common. There were slates and bricks scattered over the grass, thicker nearer the crater, where Keith found himself crunching glass underfoot.

It appeared hopeless to attempt to sort anything out from this scene of ruin and destruction. But there were men and women scrabbling with their hands at the pile of rubble, causing more dust to rise in the hot air.

The man who had called to Keith had seized a spade from a collapsed garden shed. He threw it at Keith. 'Come on,' he demanded roughly, 'you done this, you get 'em out.'

Keith picked up the spade, wiping his forehead again, unable to find words and still only half registering the events taking place about him. The voices were all shrill, overlapping in their cries of complaint, invective and command. One woman was crying, 'Who's let me dogs out—where're me dogs?'

'I shouted to Charlie and Eva, "Get to your Anderson", I shouted. But they never would. Hated shelters.'

'Look, 'ere's one of them wonderful boys in blue.' The voice had a harsh sarcastic note. A man in shirt sleeves and without a collar was pointing at Keith. 'Brylcreem boys, eh. That's all you're good for. But what about us? What about Mr and Mrs Barrow here?'

Other hostile voices were raised until someone called out, 'This won't get Charlie and Eva out—nor the Bakers, neither . . .'

Keith found himself picking weakly at the pile of

124

broken bricks, plaster, timber and glass until he felt a hand on his arm. An air-raid warden was at his side, black tin hat tipped back on his head, gas-mask case over his chest, his face and dark blue uniform white with dust.

'Is that your aeroplane over there, sir?'

Keith nodded.

'You'll be needing a guard on it. I'll telephone for one. And you'd better get yourself to the casualty post with that head.' He was a short man and his full moustache was rimed with sweat and dust. His eyes and voice were steady and they helped to bring Keith back to the real world. He dropped the spade and thanked the warden. 'Will you tell the guard not to touch the kite? Don't go too near it. I'll make my way back now.'

He began to walk across the common in the direction of his aerodrome, which was marked by an ever increasing cloud of black smoke. The warden called after him, 'Sorry about these people, sir. They're a bit shocked just for now . . .'

So am I, Keith said to himself. He was not a swearer but he found relief in cursing as he walked across the common. God rot them all! And he climbed with impunity over someone's fence, walked through the garden to get to the arterial road. Other bombs had fallen here, a stick of them, probably 50 kg, along the cycle track beside the road, scarring the road itself and blasting in the fronts of the houses.

Here a haunting silence prevailed as if the occupants dare not emerge from their Andersons for fear of what they might find, or had simply fled the scene for ever, like the Great Danes. Keith stood for a moment on the lip of a crater at the edge of the road, suddenly aware of how hot he was in his Irvin jacket and Mae West on this sunny August day. He took them off, automatically looked both ways before crossing the silent and empty road, and began to run, filled with the need to discover the worst about Savile Farm. It was like a repetition on a terrible scale of that morning three weeks earlier when those low-flying Dorniers had plastered the aerodrome.

When the road turned out to be a cul-de-sac he again broke through a private garden, knocking over a dustbin on the concrete path beside the house and exposing nervous faces at the entrance to the Anderson shelter in the back garden. A voice cried out, 'Is it over, mate?' And Keith called back, 'You can come out now . . .'

The bomber lay in the next street like a savaged corpse spilled from a mammoth hearse, its nose buried in a crumpled house, the twin fins and the fine tapering fuselage identifying it as a Dornier 17. Keith realized it must have been one of the high-level formation, shot down at 15,000 feet and landing within a quarter-mile of its target. He could see far up the road where it had first belly-landed, deep-scoring the tarmac, losing most of a wing on a now-shattered lamp standard and tearing a jagged scar past him and to its final point of impact. One of its engines had carried on farther, knocking off the corner of a detached house, whose front was now precariously poised over a heap of rubble. Its engine was in the next-door front garden amid smashed blooming roses. There was a red plaster gnome on its side in the middle of the road, its face gone.

Keith guessed that the plane had crashed very recently, some time after the bombing. The area was still in that vacuum-like state of shock with which he was familiar and which always prevailed after a local catastrophe, the last of the dust still falling. Several neighbours had emerged, a bald man in boots muddy from gardening and a boy who leant on his bicycle as if watching a cricket match. A woman was running with a tea pot, the panacea for all upsets.

But as Keith made his way down the road towards the scene, more people emerged, a lorry marked 'A.R.P.' approached at high speed, sounding its horn. An elderly man and woman, ashen-faced, appeared from the back of the house, stumbling over the rubble, and another called out, 'Thank God you're all right, dears.'

Keith, seeing that there were plenty of people at work, was about to leave when a man turned on him and said, 'Did you shoot this bugger down?'

He shook his head. 'Not that one.'

Then the man said, surprisingly, 'If he's alive, I'm going to kill him.'

'You can't do that,' protested Keith.

'You watch and see.' This voice spoke from behind Keith, who turned and saw a small man with a spade in his hand. He might have been gardening, but by now Keith suspected it was a weapon. He could not understand what was happening, he only knew now that the incident was rapidly becoming dangerous.

A woman called out in an ugly voice, 'You kill 'em, don't you? And they kill us.' Then sarcastically, 'Don't you know there's a war on?'

Keith hurried over to the R.S.D. (Rescue, Shoring and Demolition) squad. He spoke to a man in a tin helmet who was digging at the rubble and exposing the Dornier's long 'greenhouse' cockpit. 'They're talking about lynching,' he said. 'We can't have that, you know.'

'We'll do what we can,' said the man without turning. 'But it's getting nasty round here. They strung up a pilot over Croydon way last week.'

Another man, labouring to clear thick plaster from the bomber, looked up briefly and said, 'I'd clear off if I were you and see how your mates are. Proper old mess at your place.'

Keith clambered up over a metal girder and a smashed door and stood on some bricks above the Dornier. From here he could see the gathering throng of residents, looking like ordinary, commonplace English suburban dwellers, but evidently preparing to behave with a violence he had never expected to witness—and was going to do all that he could to prevent. He could also see, immediately below him, the emerging front end of the bomber, the smashed-in perspex nose, the crushed pilot's screen.

A big, burly man, the R.S.D. leader, had taken off his uniform jacket and tin helmet, and was brushing the dust and plaster off the length of the cockpit, kicking aside the wireless aerial which had been knocked off by the impact. It was like tearing out the net curtains from a window, destroying the privacy of the inhabitants.

Keith soon saw that it was worse than that. It was the privacy of the dead that was being swept away by vigorous strokes of that brush, the pilot crushed bloodily against the instrument panel, crouching as if in last prayer, his severed straps soaked in blood. Another crew member, probably the co-pilot/navigator, in brown overalls and ribbed life-jacket, lay on the floor of the cockpit in a posture that could only spell death; and the wireless-operator/air gunner lay across the shambles of his table, evidently shot dead in combat.

Keith turned away. He had sent machines down in flames or riddled in bullets. Only that day he had shot dead a gunner, and the rest of the crew of that Junkers were now probably lying in their hot coffin of smashed metal alloy and perspex in some Surrey field, and like these, awaiting exhumation. He had never faced the reality of defeat and death at first hand before, and when he saw a man in shirt sleeves flourishing a pick, and others armed and unarmed closing in on the wreck, he was appalled and overcome with fury.

'Keep away!' he yelled, and picked up a length of smashed timber. 'Get back! They're all dead.'

The men were making a curious animal-like sound, and the women in the road, several dozen of them now, were egging them on. One of them was even waving her fist, like some bit-actress in a French Revolution film.

'Get back!' Keith repeated, climbing onto the canopy and holding high the length of wood. The A.R.P. men had circumspectly withdrawn to their lorry and Keith was alone, a tall, fair and formidable figure with a bloody forehead and a fierce expression on his face.

'They're not dead—you're a bloody liar,' yelled the

man with the pick. This was a more affluent area than the other side of the arterial road, and he was wearing a Sunday collar and dark tie. He had probably been to church that morning, on his knees praying for victory.

'Look at him!' shouted the small man who had spoken to Keith earlier, pointing. 'We'll have *him*.'

Keith saw they were closing in on the rear of the bullet-riddled cockpit, and he saw their target for the first time, the rear gunner erect on his seat in his little turret, facing aft and clutching close to him the twin handles of his 7.9 mm machine-gun. He seemed unaware of the imminent danger to his life after alone surviving the crash, and Keith imagined he was thankfully awaiting rescue. Through the dusty perspex, he could see the canvas straps of his parachute harness, and the helmet with the goggles raised and the oxygen mask still clipped across his mouth.

Keith brought the wood down on the man as he raised the pick to smash through the perspex. He missed his head and caught his shoulder a glancing blow. The man in the dark tie took no notice. His face was set in lines of ferocity—an altered face entirely—as he brought the pick down with a mighty blow just behind the gunner's head. It pierced the perspex and sent shatter lines across the canopy. Keith advanced on the man and was pushed roughly aside by his companion with a fork. 'You mind your own bloody business,' he was told. 'We've had enough of this. We're going to string the bugger . . .'

The air was rent by gunfire. The machine-gun barrel that had faced horizontally along the bomber's fuselage had swung to the vertical, the air gunner who had been so erect had now slumped forward over the breech of his gun, his corpse impelled by the axe blow behind him, activating the firing mechanism and firing his last burst of defiance after suffering instant death at the hands of a Spitfire pilot of 78 Squadron twenty minutes earlier.

It was a long burst, too, a complete drum of bullets, every third round a tracer, now racing up into the summer sky like a contribution to some ill-timed Guy Fawkes party. The noise was shattering in the quiet suburban road, where the Sunday afternoon gathering of bank clerks and accountants and their wives was scattered, fleeing with their heads low, some throwing themselves protectively to the ground with their hands over their heads. The boy was now far-distant on his bicycle.

5

FARTHING'S 'KILL'

Mike said, 'I'd like a transfer, sir. No, for personal reasons . . . No, I'd rather not say.'

'Yank, you're getting to be what I think you Americans call a pain in the ass.' Rowbotham leaned back in the collapsible chair behind his desk and studied the tough little American—wide-apart brown eyes, brown hair uncombed as usual, the broad, furrowed forehead which normally seemed to contradict his carefree style but now accurately expressed his concern. 'You won't go on leave when you're told. You stir up trouble with your fellow officers . . .'

'Once, sir. It won't happen again.'

Rowbotham said, 'If I arrange your transfer, you mean?'

'Well, sir, it would be easier if you could.'

'Sit down, Yank.'

They were in the C.O.'s bell tent down at the dispersal on the emergency landing field to which 140 Squadron had been transferred after Savile Farm had been made unserviceable. 'It's bloody woman trouble, isn't it? We've not time for women right now. No time for anything except dealing with the Hun. There are squadrons down to four kites, no C.O. and one Flight

Commander. There are raids getting through with a four to one fighter escort which are not being touched—in or out. And now they're starting night bombing, too. We're just about at our wits' end—and you want me to go through the admin. procedure of getting you transferred because of some woman?'

Squadron Leader Rowbotham had looked played out for so long now, and the turnover of pilots was so high, that more than half the squadron had never seen the boisterous, no-bloody-reason party-throwing Rowbotham of a month earlier, who might come into the mess in his flying gear straight from a show to organize an indoor rugger match with his first drink. The unremitting pressure was changing them all, Mike realized, before answering the question: 'I guess not, sir. Sorry to have bothered you.'

Rowbotham drew a bottle of Haig out of the parachute bag at his side and laid a couple of glasses on the table. He half filled them and pushed one towards Mike. That was something else that was changing. 140 had always had a high drinking reputation in Fighter Command, but until recently the drinking was all public, convivial and in the mess or certain local pubs. Nowadays bottles appeared at the most unlikely times from the most improbable places.

The C.O. seemed inclined to confide in Mike as if anxious to defer the moment when he would have to write two more 'next-of-kin' letters and apply himself to a stack of papers.

'We're getting a few cannon through at last, though they're jamming badly, I hear. Spits and Hurris. We should get one or two next week.' Rowbotham sipped the raw spirit thoughtfully.

'That's what we really need,' said Mike. They had had a prototype four-cannon Hurricane back in June. Mike recalled the ferocious power of those 20 mm shells which could pierce any German armour plate and blow up a Heinkel with one short burst. But the machine had come to a sticky end in the hands of their previous C. O.

'You can tell the chaps. Might cheer them up.' The field telephone tinkled uncertainly at the C.O.'s elbow and he picked it up. The temporary ops room was a disused Baptist chapel in the nearby village in which the G.P.O. and R.A.F. engineers had contrived to set up a switchboard and cables to Group and Fighter Command H.Q. and this dispersal.

Rowbotham grunted into the mouthpiece and slammed down the instrument. 'You can also tell 'em to stand down. That'll cheer them up more.'

Most of B Flight's pilots were lying about on the grass or sitting in chairs from the Church Hall lent by the local vicar. There was an intense game of poker in progress. Others were playing with a mongrel dog who had recently attached himself to the squadron and been named Stuffy for his seeming likeness to the C.-in-C. Fighter Command, Air Chief Marshal Sir Hugh 'Stuffy' Dowding, whose mighty decisions had governed their lives since the beginning of the war.

Keith was lying flat on his back in his Mae West, smoking and staring up into the deepening blue of the sky, scarlet to the west where the sun had set a few minutes earlier. Flynn Marston was also lying silently on the grass, seeking inspiration from the dying day.

Pilot Officer 'Halfpenny' Farthing had been with them for three weeks, a wisp of a fellow whose name was cruelly appropriate: red hair, already receding at nineteen, an amiable face hinting gratitude that the world had not yet beaten him, a thin red moustache, slim musician's hands, very freckled, like his face. And an uncontrollable stutter which exasperated Rowbotham because it used up priceless R/T time—even to utter 'O-o-o K-k-kay, o-over'. He had been on ops almost every day but without hitting anything and was regarded as accident prone with good reason although he was a perfectly adequate pilot.

Bill Watson was now fighting with the dog over a stick, both grunting. A newly-arrived tall Canadian, Flying Officer 'Garçon' Rideau, was reading a two-month-old copy of the *Montreal Star*. A more distant figure, standing outside a blister hangar, was Winston-Greville in spotless white flying overalls. He was talking to his fitter who was standing on a pair of double steps with the port engine panel of his Hurricane removed.

Mike stood over the poker players, savouring the knowledge that by tradition the game ended with the end of Readiness. 'Who's winning?' he asked.

Range Powell pointed at a stack of chips. 'Ten bloody quid up, cobber.'

'We're stood down, you lucky guy. You owe me a double-double.'

They had been three days at Wilstead Green, and were accustoming themselves to the simpler, more primitive life. Here they were so cut off from the world that they might have been on an aircraft carrier. They even made their own power: all day and night a generator lorry in a field behind them ground out electricity for light and telephone and battery charging.

135

The nearest pub was four miles away and there were no bicycles and almost no other transport. There were no W.A.A.F.s, either, no station cinema, and recreations were self-made. All they had was a field, with camouflage hedges painted across it, just large enough for landing a Hurricane safely—no formation landings here—kitchen trailers, mobile workship, firetender, numerous tents, a large marquee for the airmen and N.C.O.s' mess, a smaller one for the officers and a bar which was a table out of doors, folded away when it rained.

But it had rained only once since they had arrived from the ruined wasteland of Savile Farm in a convoy of lorries, the pilots flying in the machines from Kenley, where they had been forced to land after the bombing. While the weather held, the informality and freedom of Wilstead Green suited most of them: 'no sodding bull' the airmen happily agreed as they worked, oily and shirtless, in the late summer sun, or in the shelter of the hastily-erected camouflaged blister hangars.

Mike and Keith shared a tent with Range Powell and, in complete contrast, Pilot Officer 'Halfpenny' Farthing. But Mike and Keith were the first to settle onto their camp beds that evening, sleepily smoking a last cigarette. Both had flown twice that day and were full of drink.

'What did the C.O. say?' asked Keith. He knew of the American's need to get away. On the morning Savile Farm was bombed there had been a letter on the officers' mess board for Winston-Greville. Eileen's round hand and the purple ink she always used were unmistakable and were like a stab wound to Mike.

The naval lieutenant remained a puzzle no one—except Mike—felt any wish to solve. There was no time for such indulgences. He flew well enough, very fancy and tight in formation which impressed nobody since they had long learned the dangers of close flying. Yes, his flying was O.K. except that no one had actually seen him close in and attack anything, and there had been several occasions when a single Hurricane had been seen leaving a combat area—as Keith had witnessed.

Winston-Greville remained politely aloof from his fellow officers, even from his fellow naval officer, the popular Pomeroy, as if he had sought friendship once, and found it wanting, which in a violent kind of way was true enough. He was seen more with the N.C.O. pilots. There was normally no service or class gulf between officer and N.C.O. pilots, but the naval lieutenant contrived to create a gap that had not previously existed in 140 Squadron, just as he somehow contrived to seek out—even here—smart 'county' young women, debs of the late 1930s, whom he collected in his Daimler which appeared to have inexhaustible supplies of petrol. All this was slightly unsettling but, again, everyone was too busy to do anything about it: in peace-time he would have been packed off back to his own service in twenty-four hours. In early September 1940 he was too badly needed on ops for any such action to be contemplated.

Leiutenant Arthur Winston-Creville R.N. seemed to be most at home with, most liked by, the airmen—the 'erks', the 'troops', the fitters and riggers and armourers and wireless mechanics and the rest—the cheerful, canny, crude-mouthed, totally loyal and dedicated (and sometimes unscrupulous) ground crew young men who kept the Hurricanes serviced and serviceable. Reflecting the style and attitudes of his aristocratic forbears, Winston-Greville gave the impression (and didn't care who saw it) that he had more in common with the less educated and rougher classes than the middle class, the grammar and minor public school officer pilots.

Not much of this was observed during the Battle of Britain, and none of it was closely analysed. All that could be said for sure was that this Fleet Air Arm pilot brought with him a faint sense of unease for everyone; and very much more for Mike Browning.

For Mike there seemed to be no comfort, even if his rival were to be shot down. It was the shock and injury of Eileen's defection and her cruel neglect of those who loved her that was so hard to bear. Mike could forget it only when flying, and he contrived to get himself onto almost every show and continued to fight with ferocious intensity.

'No go,' said Mike in answer to Keith's question. 'No time. I guess he's right. Anyway, I'd miss this bunch— or what's left of us.'

From the next tent a parrot called Goering, which someone had retrieved from the smashed waafery at Savile Farm, shrieked out its imitation of a Stuka, a sound that got on everyone's nerves, especially and ironically because these diabolical dive bombers had been so mauled by the R.A.F. that they had been withdrawn from the battle.

A sing-song had started up in the airmen's mess, and they could hear beery voices from across the field singing, 'She'll be coming round the mountain . . .'

Sure, booze helped, too. Sometimes he wondered how the erks could work for twelve hours after three hours of beer drinking the night before. And us, too! Jeez, how *did* they fly so well after half a bottle of Scotch and half a dozen pints to help it down? Or *were* they flying so well? Was his shooting as good as it had been back in July—that time he had put down a Stuka with a less than one second burst, every shot smack into the cockpit?

No way of telling. All he knew was that he needed it to steady himself in the evening, to dim out the memory of that day's fighting, and, above all, to dim out the face of Eileen . . .

'What about Jenny?' asked Mike. 'Any news?'

Keith felt uncomfortable about talking of her to Mike, for whom everything seemed to have gone wrong when everything was so right for him. 'She's having her plaster off next week. Then physiotherapy at some remedial home. Back on duty in another month, with luck.'

The other two came in together, Range very plastered on his winnings and needing Farthing's help to find his bunk. There was a good deal of cursing. Mike didn't mind. Discomforts, inconveniences, were nothing by contrast with his private pain. Another Stuka screamed from the parrot's cage. The airmen's singing was louder than ever, floating across this open country where usually the loudest sound was the snuffling of badgers and the occasional hoot of an owl. It was one of the smaller changes that had struck southern England since the Nazis had swept over Europe and were now preparing for the final assault on this island.

Garçon Rideau had acquired his nickname on his first day and at his first meal in the mess at Savile Farm. He had called for a mess waiter in French and had not been allowed to forget it. He was, in any case, a perfect target for baiting, slow and solemn and utterly good-humored. There was nothing plodding about him in the air, however. His popularity was confirmed when he proved himself an alert and determined pilot. He had been instructing in Canada and had been chafing to get on ops. He had arrived on 140 at just the right time.

But on the day after Mike had attempted to get himself transferred, Rideau was shot down, flying number two to Mike on a show off Beachy Head. Pursuing a damaged lone Dornier down to wave-top height, Mike had allowed himself to be tempted much too far south.

The Dornier still obstinately refused to go in, though trailing smoke from both engines, when Mike suddenly saw the French coast ahead, and pulled up, ordering the Canadian to follow. With his attention on the damaged Dornier, and on the sky above for any intervention by Messerchmitts, Mike also failed to spot the two German E-boats heading out to sea from Dieppe. He did not even spot them opening fire at Rideau as he turned sharply and climbed up to 500 feet.

The first indication that they were in trouble was a transmission from the Canadian, 'Green Two to Green One. I've been hit. Engine's running rough.'

Mike reduced his rate of climb and waited for the Hurricane to come up alongside. He could see the freshly punctured canvas of the painted roundel, like a fairground shooting target, behind the cockpit.

There were more holes in the tailplane, and there was a distinct trail of white vapour from the glycol header tank. Mike could also see the E-boats now, scoring the sea white with their curving wakes, as if exultantly celebrating their fine shooting.

'Oil pressure's dropping, Green One.'

A minute later, at 2,500 feet, Mike saw the Canadian's prop slow and at the same time the volume of vapour greatly increase.

'Cut your switches and turn off your fuel cock,' he transmitted. 'D'you want to bail out?'

The Canadian was already turning through 180 degrees, nose down and losing height fast. 'I guess I'll try and make it back to land. I never much cared for swimming, and I talk their language.'

Mike felt desperately remorseful that he had been responsible for Rideau being hit. Mike was his number one, should never have brought him this far, should have recognized the danger. 'Goddam it!' he exclaimed into his mask. 'Call yourself a veteran, and being made a sucker like this.'

He was going to see the Canadian down safely, that was the least he could do. He was not going to allow him to be shot out of the sky by some roving 109. 'Green Two,' he called. 'Cross in west of the town. Less ack-ack. I'll be covering you.'

'Green Two calling. I'll be O.K., Mike. You get back to base. Have a beer on me tonight. Au revoir.'

Mike remained at 3,000 feet, watching the crippled Hurricane losing height steadily towards enemy soil. Some bursts of medium ack-ack came up from the cliffs east of Dieppe, and he saw the Canadian back away from it, but refrain from further evasive action which would lose him precious height.

Luckily there was a north wind blowing and he still had plenty of height as he crossed in over the white cliffs. It was more difficult to see the Hurricane against the green of the fields of northern France, and Mike lost height to keep in contact, cork-screwing down but watching his own tail all the way. Some Oerlikon fire came up, tracer sweeping past in a broad, deadly arc, and he ruddered violently and opened throttle.

Garçon Rideau had found himself a nice clear field of corn stubble. Mike saw the Hurricane bank round into the wind and come in steeply, at a false angle without power. The hood was open and he could see straight down into the cockpit. The Canadian was nursing her carefully, touching down the plane's belly onto the chalky soil, and sending up a cloud of light grey dust. It was as clean a crash landing as he had seen, and Mike circled low while the pilot got out and began running to the edge of the field.

Mike rocked his wings, and dipped his nose down and steadied the dot of his sight onto the crippled plane at the end of its scored line in the stubble. A two-second burst sufficed. The Hurricane burst into flames, puffing up a great gout of black smoke. He watched it for a second with satisfaction and then banked away and climbed to the west. He could see Rideau beside the hedge, one arm waving good-bye.

'Oh sure!' Mike exclaimed. 'Hot shot Browning.' He was still smarting from his failure, and if he had not been so angry with himself, he would not have become so suddenly determined to do something so desperate.

He had heard of someone else who had done it at the time of the fall of France. Why not? It was a sort of double or quits gamble—two pilots lost or none. And Fighter Command could not afford to lose two experienced pilots because of his folly. He would take the chance, and win. Like Range Powell at poker.

The ground was so dry and hard that he could probably have touched down safely on the stubble. But the next field was grass, grazed by a herd of those large buff-coloured cows that you seem to see nowhere else except in France and Belgium. He hoped they were nippy on their legs.

Mike wasted no time on a fancy approach. Time, once again, was of the essence—and as to *essence,* he did not have any of that to spare either. Maybe twelve gallons. Wheels and flaps down, he approached from the south, caught a glimpse of a startled figure leading a horse and cart on a track almost under him, cut the throttle, side-slipped momentarily, and made a smooth landing, running farther than he had planned, owing to the slope which he had failed to notice from above.

The cows were running all right. And so was the Canadian. He caught up Mike before he turned and leaped up onto the port wing root.

'You're crazy!' he yelled into Mike's ear. Mike, ignoring him, was tearing off his straps, and then his parachute, which he threw out onto the grass. He climbed out of his seat onto the starboard wing, and pointed at the cockpit, his words carried away on the slipstream and on the sound of the ticking-over Merlin.

The Canadian grinned and dropped inside, and, because of the lack of a parachute under him, was at once transformed from a tall figure into a midget.

Mike leaned over and put his mouth to Rideau's ear. 'You work the damn pedals, Canuck,' he shouted, and dropped heavily onto the Canadian's lap. His head was on a line with the top of the screen, but fell several inches when Rideau lowered the seat with the handle on the right. They would have to fly with the canopy open, but it was the horizontal problem that worried Mike. His face was almost against the gun sight, and the throttle and pitch and flap controls were awkwardly far behind him. And they were not strapped in.

Neither of them saw the grey German *Personenkraftwagen* until they had brought the machine to the top of the sloping field and were turning through 180 degrees into wind. It had come to a skidding halt on the dirt road beyond the hedge. A dozen figures had leaped down from it, some were already firing with their rifles, others were racing for a gate which offered them a clearer sighting.

The Canadian saw them first. He nudged Mike and they heard the shots above the roar of the Merlin. Mike cursed himself for starting the fire which had obviously drawn the party to the spot—the Germans had dozens of damaged Hurricanes already from the French campaign, when the R.A.F. had lost nearly 500 fighters, and Rideau's old MK 1 would be of no value to the Luftwaffe.

Mike caught a glimpse of one infantryman dropping

to a knee and taking steady aim at fifty yards. Then the Hurricane was into wind and a more difficult end-on target, and Mike was pushing the throttle wide open. It was a rough, lurching take-off. Rideau seemed to be having trouble with the rudder pedals. They lurched far to the left, and with the spade grip against his stomach, Mike had difficulty both in lifting the machine off the ground and into a climbing attitude, and in keeping her laterally steady. He gained height to 200 feet mainly by using the trim tab, and succeeded in getting up the undercarriage. The cliff edge slipped below them, and with relief he re-trimmed and let the Hurricane sink down low over the sea.

'The prettiest sitting duck in all the Royal Air Force!' Mike reflected. No manoeuvrability, no ammunition, no communication, and much reduced speed.

Their situation was, in fact, worse than that, as Mike discovered a few minutes later. He had been aware of the slackness of Rideau's thighs on take-off, and now felt a dampness about his right ankle. He turned his head, and as he did so the Canadian raised a corner of Mike's helmet and shouted, 'Guess they winged me, Yank.'

So that last infantryman had scored. How could he have missed at that range?

Two people jam-packed into a small single-seat fighter cockpit travelling at 220 m.p.h. at 200 feet just off a hostile coast—these were not the ideal circumstances for carrying out a medical diagnosis and giving first aid treatment. By shifting himself to the extreme edge of the cockpit onto the Canadian's left thigh, Mike was able to peer down to the lower part of the injured leg. All he could see was a deep tear in the canvas of the flying boot, and blood—a lot of blood, dripping freely onto the floor of the cockpit.

Tourniquet. Pressure point under the knee? Or was it lower down? Mike tried to remember the one first aid class he had attended years ago at Andover—he had had none in the R.A.F. And only he could do it.

He turned and looked at the Canadian, their eyes on the same level. His grimace of pain switched momentarily to a smile, but Mike recognized at once his paleness and the seriousness of their situation. Seizing Rideau's left hand, he placed it by his own left hand on the stick. 'Just hold her steady for a while,' Mike shouted, but could not hear his own words.

Then he dragged the silk scarf from his neck and reached down blindly under his own thigh and fumblingly drew the length of silk round the Canadian's knee. With all the strength he could muster at this awkward angle, he tightened the slip knot just below the joint. He felt and noted with satisfaction the Canadian twitch with pain at the pressure, and double-knotted the silk again.

O.K. It might last. Just now there were a mighty lot of 'mights' around—like the Luftwaffe making an untimely appearance, the fuel running from the reserve tank before they hit the coast, the blood running from the bullet wound past the makeshift tourniquet before they hit the coast. . . . What a crazy situation!

It was inevitable that they should be spotted before they crossed the Channel. Three single-engined fighters came in very fast from the west just as Mike had identified the white slab of Beachy Head. His only defence, like any helpless, threatened animal, was craven submission. He pulled back the throttle, raised the Hurricane's nose to reduce speed, and reached for the undercarriage lever before the fighters arrived.

They were less than half a mile away, coming in on a three-quarter rear attack when Mike heard the thud of the wheels locking home and saw the green light come on. The fighters broke their line and formed up in suspicious company on both sides and above. They were Spitfires, one deep curved under-wing dark-painted, the other light, the letters LO denoting they were from 602 Squadron at Westhampnett, no doubt scrambled to investigate this unidentified single plot coming in low from France.

One of the pilots came in close alongside, throwing back his hood and staring in amazement at the twin-crewed Hurricane. Failing to make contact by R/T, he made the thumbs-up sign and remained alongside to give moral support.

Mike banked his machine to the left before Beachy Head, intending to follow along the coast to Shoreham, keeping an eye open for a field en route. His reserve tank was now registering zero, and their situation remained difficult. While the lowered undercarriage was increasing his fuel consumption, to raise it and make a belly landing with both of them unstrapped was certain to lead to injury. But a crash-landing with wheels down could be much worse. No parachutes. Only horns of dilemma. He had almost made it back home, but only as an inanimate object suspended in space—and that for not much longer.

The decision was taken out of Mike's hands one mile east of Seaford at 500 feet. They were above the undulating chalk cliffs of the Seven Sisters, the summit of Beachy Head behind. Then the Merlin coughed her last, and by the same blend of good and bad fortune that had taken them to France in two machines and brought them back in one, a long stretch of grass north of the town came into view. There were small figures on it, mostly in the centre, boys in shorts playing Monday afternoon cricket, deprived of the beaches by mines and barbed wire and organized into an informal match.

One of 602's Spitfires, flying very low over the boys' heads, failed to scatter them, but when Mike—pumping down his flaps as hard as he could go—banked round for the final approach, they clearly became aware of the situation and began running.

Experiencing the same deadness of the controls Keith had felt in his engine-less landing, Mike skimmed the quad and main building of the school, the clock on the bell tower, the outbuildings, then very low over the sports pavilion. No obstructions here. But no rudder controls either. He sent up a prayer of thanks, too, for the perfect manners of the Hurricane, wound back trim to the full again, jammed the stick against his stomach and kept the machine floating a few feet above the grass while it lost speed.

The Hurricane touched down at the edge of the pitch, knocking over both sets of stumps ('I guess that's what they call "all out"!') ran on for 300 yards before coming to a halt with 100 yards still to spare.

There were two men in charge of the boys. They tried to hold them back but the excitement and curiosity were too great. The air was filled with shouted enquiries and exclamations. Mike climbed onto the

148

port wing, glancing back at the now-unconscious form of Flight Sergeant Rideau.

'Crikey, how many did you get, sir?'

'Is that a captured Jerry, sir?'

A boy in thick specs with the glow of the disciple in his eyes touched his flying boot. Yes, it was real. 'How many have you shot down?'

One of the men, in open-necked white shirt and Oxford bags, was trying to apologize to Mike and clear the boys back. But only Mike himself succeeded in silencing them. Raising his hands above his head, he shouted, 'First guy to get an ambulance gets a special R.A.F. prize'.

Then, as they swarmed away towards the school buildings, one shrewd boy making for a nearby house with a telephone wire to it, Mike and the two men gently eased the big Canadian out of the cockpit and laid him down on the grass. The tourniquet had worked, as Mike noted when he loosened it and the blood started to flow again before he was able to fix the bandage and the tourniquet stick from his machine's First Aid kit. Except for covering him with his Irvin jacket, that was all they were able to do until the ambulance came racing across the grass, bells ringing and the lone boy on the running board.

Before climbing into the ambulance with Rideau, Mike picked off the threads of his wings with his knife and presented them, as if at a brief investiture. The boy was so overawed he could say nothing.

*

There was a more formal, more elaborate investiture two days later in the quadrangle at Buckingham Palace. 140 Squadron was overdue for recognition. It had drawn first blood up in Scotland early in the war when nothing was happening down in the south, and had been brought down in mid-June after suffering decimation in the Norwegian campaign. The squadron score was 44, and they had lost fourteen pilots killed and eight wounded. Now the A Flight commander had been awarded a D.F.C., an A Flight Sergeant Pilot a D.F.M. for shooting down a Heinkel 111 and severing the tail of another with his prop before bailing out. In B Flight, Mike, Keith and Range Powell were all given a D.F.C., and Rowbotham a D.S.O.

The attendance at the investitures had to be divided in order not to weaken the squadron too seriously during the few hours they would be away. Rowbotham drove Keith and Mike to London early one dour, rainy morning. The C.O. was curiously nervous about the affair, as if he would have preferred to lead 140 into odds of ten to one rather than face the praise and questions of his Sovereign.

'H.M. will deal with you first, sir,' said Keith. 'If you want to get back, we'll use the train.'

Rowbotham grunted. 'No, I'll wait. Give you lunch at the club. Looks like Harry clampers all day with any luck.' He drove as he flew as he looked, like a bull. But a champion bull, who had destroyed a dozen German toreadors, all but two after transferring to 140 Squadron. They were on the stretch of arterial road running close to the ruins of Savile Farm, and Keith noted the tarpaulined roofs and boarded-up front windows of the houses damaged by that stick of bombs. Women with shopping bags were chatting at bus stops, and he caught a fleeting glimpse of children playing on the common. He wondered how the men in their dark suits and bowler hats had greeted one another on their Monday morning train after the lynching incident.

London had been bombed badly the previous day and night, but the investiture was held outside in the quadrangle at the Palace in a drizzle that was so fine that it scarcely damped them as they awaited their turn, and provided the capital with almost certain protection from the Luftwaffe. The quadrangle was packed with men and women awaiting their awards, and the relatives or friends in the spectators' area. The Royal Standard hung limply at the flagstaff and there was a general murmur of conversation just as if this were a Palace Garden Party on a typical grey summer's day.

But this was an all-uniform occasion, from admirals heavy in gold braid and swords to khaki-clad women Mechanized Transport Corps drivers and W.A.A.F.s, dark blue-uniformed Auxiliary Fire Service members rewarded for gallantry in bombed coastal towns, army captains who had escaped from the onslaught on France, and twenty or thirty R.A.F. officers like themselves, many of them bomber crew survivors from raids on landing barges in the Channel ports.

A carpeted dais with double ramp had been erected before the tall columns on the west side of the quadrangle, and equerries in tail coats and several senior officers stood behind the King, who wore the uniform of a Marshal of the Royal Air Force.

Servicemen and women awaiting awards were moved about discreetly by Palace officials, and Keith watched Rowbotham approach the dais, a stumpy, self-conscious figure in the unusual role of subordinate, staring straight ahead as King George pinned the small cross to his chest. The two men, the Monarch and Marshal of the R.A.F. who could do no fighting and the Squadron Leader who had already done too much, talked briefly, and Rowbotham stepped back, saluted as crisply as any Station Warrant Officer, and marched down the carpeted ramp back to his place.

'I'm told you have shot down eight enemy aircraft,' the King said to Keith. He had a gentle, kindly voice which soothed and reassured. 'I expect you've had a few n-n-nasty moments.'

'One or two, sir.'

'Had to j-j-jump for it yet?'

'Yes, sir, in France. I had to brolly-hop once.'

The King smiled. 'I like that—"brolly-hop". Good luck in the future and well done.'

Later, over lunch at the Flying Club, Mike said, 'How does the man keep it up? Incredible guy. Said he knew about me through the Kennedys.'

The closed world of the club was like any R.A.F. mess, and Keith felt comfortable with his own kind. But outside in the streets, he noticed that their uniform and ribbons were catching the eyes of passersby. After the suspicion and hostility they had experienced in the Savile Farm area, where many of the local people had refused beds to the bombed-out airmen and W.A.A.F.s, it was reassuring but also discomfiting to be stared at admiringly and Keith was thankful when they reached the parked car.

'Do you mind if I come back by train later?' Mike asked. 'I'd like to look up some friends at the Embassy.'

Rowbotham dropped into the driver's seat. 'Go on then, Yank. Show off your gong.' He smiled and looked up at the low, scudding clouds. 'Clampers all day, I'd guess.'

The C.O. drove Keith back through Belgravia and Pimlico and over the river to the south. They passed two recent 'incidents', as they were euphemistically being called. A row of houses near Eaton Square had received a direct hit from a heavy bomb, revealing empty fireplaces, a patchwork of dusty wallpaper reflecting the taste of the now-dead or homeless, stairs and banisters leading from nowhere to space, and stacked rubble, glass, timber and smashed furniture that spilled onto the road. An Armstrong-Siddeley motor car lay upside down against the railings of the square.

The second bomb had fallen on humbler houses, two-storey terraced houses south of the river, and here the people who had escaped were being helped to pile up what was left of their possessions into prams. A soldier stood guard and there was a warning notice about looting.

'That's only the beginning,' was Rowbotham's comment. 'Give it another few weeks and there won't be much left of London. Our fault, too.'

'What do you mean?' Keith asked.

'For surviving. They thought they were going to break us in two weeks—that's what Park told me, according to top Intelligence. Kesselring couldn't understand how we kept coming up when their pilots' claims were higher than the whole of Fighter Command. They had it so soft in Poland and France they thought we'd just fold, too. I was told yesterday there're

153

signs they're switching their bombers to London and other cities. That's what I mean by it being our fault.'

They were on the Caterham by-pass, heading for Reigate. The cloud was still down. So were the balloons, and the guns were stood down at all the sites they passed.

'That means they won't be bombing our 'dromes,' Keith commented.

'You're darn right, Stewart. *And* in the nick of time. If only they knew how damn near they've been to finishing us off—but thank God they don't.'

There was a very boisterous no-bloody-reason party that night, involving the whole squadron, all ranks. When the moon appeared at midnight, Rowbotham, more relaxed than recently, organized an inter-flight rugger match, with rules suspended. It lasted until the last man ran out of strength. There was no score nor result. Quite like old times.

Keith woke again at 3 a.m. when Mike crawled into the tent. 'Where in the name of hell have you been?' he whispered blearily.

'Caught the midnight train to Pulborough. It stopped at every crazy station. And then seven miles walk, without a signpost, goddam it.' Mike lay on the camp bed without undressing. But Keith thought he detected elation through his weariness.

'What have you been doing? You haven't been looking up Eileen?' For a moment Keith's heart lifted at the idea of a reconciliation, of the girl's madness being cured. What other reason could there be for the note of satisfaction in Mike's voice?

'Oh gee, no. No, nothing like that.'

*

The next day came to be known in the Squadron as the day of the Messerschmitt. Again the morning was cloudy and they were put on only thirty minutes' Readiness, which was a relief for everyone. The crews went about their routine tasks after breakfast, checking and servicing the aircraft. Lacking the protection of blast bays, the Hurricanes were either covered with camouflage netting or kept under the shelter of a beech wood on the west side of the field.

Then at 10 o'clock Rowbotham issued an order through the adjutant that every pilot was to report to dispersal in ten minutes in shorts and plimsolls, for a run—five times round the field. This had happened once before in bad weather, back in early July, but it was a new experience for most of the pilots.

Rowbotham himself joined the surprised looking gathering down at A Flight dispersal, who were being openly mocked by the ground crews until the C.O.'s appearance in his car. Rowbotham had assumed an air of vigorous energy, but, slightly paunchy in his vest and shorts, appeared in greater need of the exercise than most of his pilots.

'This will work off some of last night's beer,' he told them. 'Four times round the field, with me leading you. Then a race on the last lap. Winner gets a bottle of Gordon's.'

It began to rain on the second lap, and Keith's leg ached from his old flesh wound back in May, but he kept going, fancying that bottle. He had been a good miler at school, and had won the cross-country in the last two years.

Rowbotham dropped out beside his car, shouting

breathlessly, 'Every man for himself, and a double gin. . . .'

Keith was running fifth, just ahead of Mike, with Range Powell, long-legged and muscular, in the lead. It was slippery underfoot, and two pilots had already gone down in the mud. Except for a few stragglers, they were all under the beech trees on this last lap, being cheered by the fitters and riggers working on the A Flight machines, when the Messerschmitt appeared out of the cloud.

It was a 109, flying slowly and in a steep bank at the south end of the field. Somebody behind Keith said 'Christ!' and it was this exclamation that drew his attention to it. The whole scattered pack of runners had halted under the trees, and Kiwi Robinson cried out, 'Why don't they open fire?'

The army had two Bofors and half a dozen Oerlikons to protect the field and all the gunners seemed to be asleep. One of the gunposts was only a hundred yards away, clear of the trees, and someone shouted, 'Open fire, you stupid sods!'

Seemingly unaware of how close he was to being blown out of the sky—and certainly unaware of where he was—the German pilot dropped his under-carriage and lowered flaps. For a few moments he was out of sight from them above the beeches. The machine reappeared on the final approach, very low, black crosses on wings and fuselage clearly identifiable, even the pilot himself visibly under the perspex canopy, the wheels down daintily like a Spitfire's but with the high tailplane supported by struts distinguishing it from both the Hurricane and Spitfire.

THE FIGHT OF THE FEW

Range Powell cried out, 'Stiffen the snakes, the bloody Kraut thinks he's in bloody France!'

It was a neat enough landing, and as the plane slowed down, the Bofors ahead of them began firing tracer—crack! crack! crack!— three rounds a second at lowest elevation aimed just above and in front of the fighter, as a clear warning of instant annihilation if the pilot should recognize his mistake and change his mind about remaining.

'We'll have him!' someone shouted, and began running. They all followed, weariness and breathlessness forgotten. Even the bottle of gin forgotten, for here was a bigger prize.

The lost Luftwaffe pilot was so startled by the sudden turn of events that he simply remained seated in his cockpit while outside there gathered a team of athletes in shorts and plimsolls apparently intent on lynching him.

Mike leaped up onto the port wing and released the catch that held down the hinged canopy. The pilot, a fair-haired young man with bright blue frightened eyes, had taken off his helmet.

'Guten Tag, mein Leutnant. Willkommen in England,' Mike said in his exerable German accent.

Most of the squadron's ground staff were now running out to the centre of the field as if to give the unfortunate German a hero's welcome. But Rowbotham, with the Adjutant beside him, was there before them in his car, taking command of events. He had a .38 Smith & Wesson in his hand when he got out. 'All right, chaps, let's have him,' he ordered, walking fast towards the machine. He had changed back into his uniform but was hatless, his hair blowing in the wind.

Keith, whose German was better than Mike's, called out to the pilot, 'Also, kommen Sie hier. Geben Sie bitte Ihr Luger auf. Sie sind jetzt Kriegsgefangener.'

Captured German aircrew had been treated in different ways since the beginning of the battle. Some had been roughly handled, especially after W.A.AF.s had been killed in a raid. Others were treated with cold indifference and handed over as soon as possible to the Military Police, the correct, accepted procedure. Several, especially at the beginning of the battle, had been given a jovial reception and plied with drinks at the bar. Tactics had been discussed—'Ja, Ja, zank you. Ver gut beer!'—and on one occasion at Savile Farm 140's Spy had extracted some very useful information on the German order of battle in *Luftflotte II* from a drunken Hauptmann.

Besides being the wrong time of the day for celebrations, with the cloud beginning to break and the likelihood of ops before lunch, Rowbotham preferred the perfunctory treatment of captured enemy aircrew. After accepting the young man's Luger and answering his salute, he turned him over to an armed guard.

'Get that damn thing under camouflage nets right away,' he ordered. 'If the Hun spots her there'll be hell to pay. Kiwi, get your pilots on the job. They never finished that last lap and the exercise'll do 'em good.'

'What about that bloody gin, cobber?' shouted Range Powell.

'My name's bloody sir, not bloody cobber,' snapped Rowbotham.

It was a curious business handling on the ground

the little fighter that had been their most lethal enemy in the air. It had a battle-axe insignia on its nose, indicating that it was from 3 Gruppe based south and west of Le Havre. The sight of the large and uncompromising black cross on the fuselage beside them as they pushed the trailing edge of the wings was discomfiting, and the victory stripes with roundels on the rudder indicated that the pilot had had some success, though a foul-mouthed sergeant pilot cancelled them with his pen and commented, 'Fucking line-shoot—a prick who can't even hit the right country couldn't hit one of ours.'

Later that morning, Keith saw a bowser drive round the field and fill up the tanks of the 109. Rowbotham followed in his car, and had all the camouflage netting removed again so that he could examine the machine in detail. Then, to Keith's astonishment, he saw the C.O. put on his flying gear and climb into the cockpit.

'Chaps, come and watch this,' Keith said. 'The Bull's going for a flip.'

The B Flight pilots crowded out of the dispersal tent where they had been killing time with darts, poker and newspapers until the bar opened.

Rowbotham had got the engine going and was taxiing out of the shelter of the trees. 'The bloody guns'll do their block if they see it in the air,' Range said.

The Spy was in the gathering. 'It's O.K., he's just doing a couple of circuits and bumps before the R.A.E. get their hands on it. We've told the brown jobs.'

'If I 'ad me 'ands on that kite,' Sergeant Watson threatened with relish, 'I'd fly over the bleedin' Channel and beat up everything in sight at St Omer. That'd be the hell of a donny!'

'Especially when you tried to get back home again,' Flynn Marston commented quietly.

Rowbotham was taxi-ing the 109 circumspectly to the east side of the field to take off into wind, weaving the high, steep-angled nose constantly from side to side in order to see ahead. With its narrow undercarriage and high torque and consequent swing at take-off, the 109 was believed to be a handful for a novice. Rowbotham was far from being a novice, but an accident would certainly lead to a very awkward court of enquiry.

It was said in Fighter Command that any pilot who knew the sound of a Daimler-Benz engine was condemned to immediate death because only those with a dead engine and a helpless kite ever heard it. It was an uncanny experience, then, for 140 Squadron to listen to the rising note of the Messerschmitt as their C.O. revved up and accelerated over the wet grass. Keith had to admit to himself that it looked marvellously aggressive and purposeful as its tail came up. A few seconds later, it lurched but was held and corrected, and was lifted off the grass.

Rowbotham kept her low over the boundary hedge and got her wheels up as he began to climb. Cloud had lifted but to no more than a thousand feet, and they saw the 109 bank and turn down wind, building up speed very quickly. For Mike and Keith and the others who had been in close combat so often with this machine, and even been shot down by it, the configuration of the little fighter—its square wing-tips, low symmetrical fin and rudder, high tailplane and general air of sharp compactness—the sound and sight re-primed their well-used adrenalin pumps, and they had to remind themselves that Bull Rowbotham himself was at the controls and not a German out for their blood.

The C.O. brought the Messerschmitt down low and fast dead centre across the field, rocking her wings in jubilant greeting, and from the gathered ground crew there arose a small cheer, which was abruptly cut when another machine came in from the east, back from an air test. It was a Hurricane, scraping the cloud base, and the Spy exclaimed, 'Christ—Farthing!' and tore back into the tent to wind frantically the field telephone handle.

Mike said, 'Jeez! Now watch this.'

'Farthing's got a Jerry in his sights at last,' said Flynn Marston.

The duty pilot was quick off the mark, diving into his tent and returning at once with a Very pistol. There was a light explosion and a hiss as the red flare soared up over the field.

Keith could imagine every emotion Halfpenny Farthing was experiencing, every action he was excitedly taking in the Hurricane's cockpit: the first sighting and recognition, the dumbfounded disbelief tinged with a touch of fear, the sudden flood of determination—after all the mishaps of the past—to show his own squadron, right in front of their eyes, his true mettle. Switching on the sight, slipping over the safety shield, the quick calculations . . .

Rowbotham saw the Hurricane and recognized the dangerous position he had got himself into before the warning flare was fired. He took the only action possible. At the last second, he turned into Farthing's attack, climbed steeply into cloud and disappeared. But only briefly. He dared not leave the area for fear of getting lost without maps or D/F aid, or of getting shot down and had to gamble on control warning the pilot of the real situation.

When he emerged, he had lowered wheels and flaps and was rocking his wings in the accepted gesture of surrender. Farthing was waiting for him, circling low, and at once made a pass at the 109. The whole of 140 Squadron was out now, looking up in a fever of anxiety, some of them waving, others shouting futilely, 'It's the C.O., you clot!' What a way to go, with a hundred ops behind you and the new D.S.O. on your chest! Shot down by the squadron buffoon!

But no shot rang out. No helpless 109 fell in flames. Farthing, hood open, came alongside the Messerschmitt. They could see him waving an arm to indicate that the fighter should land, and failing to recognize the C.O. through the perspex. Then Farthing took up an aggressive stance immediately behind the 109, and followed it on its final approach, ready for any tricks.

'We must keep this up for old Farthing.' It was Willy Williams's suggestion, and as soon as the 109 had taxied back to the shelter of the beech trees, and the Hurricane had landed, all the pilots ran out and surrounded it, waving their arms and cheering; and forcing him to cut his engine in the centre of the field.

The officer's freckled face was beaming with triumph. He had his helmet off and waved back from the cockpit. 'Not a shot!' he was calling down. 'Not a shot—why waste ammo?'

They carried him in shoulder high and the adjutant opened the bar five minutes early.

'You've done it at last!' 'Only old Halfpenny could *scare* him down!' 'What did you use—mesmerism?' 'Here you are, old boy, a double noggin of the best.'

The Spy said, 'I'm looking forward to writing your combat report—"I came in on a three-quarter stern attack and . . ."' Everyone was laughing and thumping the lightweight figure on the back.

When he was allowed to speak, Farthing said, 'I want to m-m-meet the pilot. Where is he? I want to g-g-g-give him a drink.'

The C. O.'s timing was perfect. With his parachute over his shoulder and his helmet and goggles in the other hand, he broke through the crowd. 'Here he is— yes, I'll have a double after that ordeal.'

The laughter broke around Pilot Officer Farthing like a storm, and he was left sitting on the edge of the bar, froth on his moustache, staring about him with a puzzled expression. 'I don't get it. I mean I . . .'

The C.O. raised his glass to him. 'Sorry, old boy. It was only me, flight testing. It came in here earlier, by mistake. Never mind, we'll credit it to you.'

Farthing climbed down off the bar, scarlet with embarrassment and disappointment amid murmurs of sympathy. 'Rotten trick to play on you.' 'You would have got him anyway.'

As un-needed proof that Pilot Officer Farthing was the nicest pilot on 140—if not the greatest shot—his reaction now to the bitter joke played on him was to smile, and then break into laughter, his characteristic high-pitched laughter. In a second he had put down his tankard, and was doubled-up in uncontrollable mirth. He had to wipe the tears from his eyes and was still laughing between deep quaffs of bitter ale five minutes later.

'Well I'm blessed,' he kept saying. 'What a boob!'

And from two tents away the frightful parrot rent the air with the screaming whine of a Stuka.

It was what they all needed to prepare them for the week that lay ahead. The reconnaissance Messerschmitt 109 with its lost and bewildered pilot was only the single forerunner of the mightiest air armadas of them all to attack England, and every other German pilot knew exactly where he was going and what he was doing.

As 140's pilots sat down to lunch that day under clearing skies, they were brought to Immediate Readiness. And at three minutes past two, the bells sounded, the telephone rang and a Very light was fired to let everyone know, without fail, that this was an emergency scramble. . . .

6

TALKED DOWN

'It was the same in "18",' said Flight Lieutenant Randall. 'Just when we thought we'd got the Hun taped—starved out by the navy, Yank army pouring into France—he hit back so hard the sods nearly got to Paris.'

'Is that w-w-when you had your gi-gi-gi-normous prang, sir?' Pilot Officer Farthing asked.

'Twenty-two years ago and here I am still at it. And only one rank better!' The veteran pilot laughed without bitterness. Jock Randall D.F.C. (the early horizontally striped ribbon) had flown in the R.F.C. in the days when Sopwiths fought Fokker 'tripe-hounds', a miracle of survival, not only of that war but of the years between when he had stunt flown at Hendon Air Displays, and even more spectacularly when no one was looking. A purple scar, clear across his forehead, dated back not to those acrobatic evolutions but to an S.E.5a crash in No Man's Land in April '18. He had taught Keith to fly, and neither his temper nor the state of his uniform had improved since.

They were discussing the new intensification of the Luftwaffe's assault which had built up in September after a lull due to bad weather. Everyone was con-

vinced that Goering had unlimited reserves and that
they were now fighting a new generation of fighter
and bomber pilots, and new machines straight from
the production lines. They had been scrambled three
times the previous day, and one section had been kept
up so late that it had had to put down at Ford with
the help of the flarepath.

Two new Hurricanes had flown in on the same day,
which made a net loss of only one. The first replace-
ment had arrived while their machines were refuelling
and rearming. It had touched down prettily twenty
yards inside the perimeter of the field, and been taxied in with great aplomb and much blipping of the
throttle. A blonde A.T.A. pilot had stepped down,
shaken out her hair from the crush of the helmet, and
walked straight to an open M.G. which was waiting
for her, ignoring the catcalls and whistles from the airmen. She had then been driven off without a glance
to right or left by a crashingly handsome male A.T.A.
pilot.

Ten minutes later Randall arrived with the second
Hurricane, this one a 4-cannon job. After circling once
to make his presence known, he did two flick rolls at
1,000 feet, dived low, inverted his machine and flew
clear across the field upside down at fifty feet, steady
as a rock until S.U. carburettor hesitancy told him to
right himself. He had later hung about Wilstead
Green, chatting with the C.O., and when they were
scrambled for the second time, tagged on behind the
formation in the Hurricane he had delivered and had
contrived to have armed, and then shot a 109 into the
sea off Worthing.

'If you mention that in your sodding report,' he was

overheard warning the Spy, 'I'll screw your bloody neck.'

He was still around twenty-four hours later, laconic and foul-mouthed when he did speak, his filthy hat crushed on one side of his head, drinking pints at ten in the morning. Rowbotham pretended he wasn't there. When it rained heavily before dawn, Flight Lieutenant Randall was seen to take off on an engine test, using the length of one of the camouflage-painted 'hedges', both for take-off and landing. When he later overheard someone accusing him of shooting a line, he barked out, 'Ignornat sprog! Haven't you learned that the tar in the sodding paint binds the grass? Stops you going arse over tit in the wet.'

Flying continuously, in war and peace, from the age of eighteen, Randall had picked up most of the tricks of the trade.

*

They moved to Southdean the next day. Returning from an abortive show south of Selsey Bill, the controller had ordered them to land there, a few miles west of Shoreham. Just like that, without notice. It had been a flying club before the war, with some hangars for the Tiger Moths and Puss Moths and veteran ex-R.A.F. surplus trainers like Avro 504s of doubtful vintage. The hangars had been bombed by a Messerschmitt 110 the previous week. But the mock Tudor club-house on the north side had somehow survived.

When they landed on the grass, an emergency mobile ground crew signalled them in. They were wearing tin hats, and had a single bowser, a lorry full of .303 ammunition, three trolley-acs, some tools, and that was about all. Some emergency rations arrived three hours later, and they were told that the rest of the squadron and their kit would be there by midnight.

At Southdean they were billeted out in cheap little holiday bungalows, abandoned by their owners since the invasion scare, and bereft of all but the basic facilities. 'Stiffen the snakes! Give me a bloody tent in a bloody field,' exclaimed Range Powell as he surveyed his empty room. There was a fireplace full of cigarette ends and a mutilated teddy bear, and the surround was of ultra-marine tiles. It was hot and stuffy with a faint smell of stale urine, and the cheap wooden window-frames proved unopenable. The Australian, exuding oaths, kicked out two panes of glass, unstrapped his camp bed, and began nailing pin-ups onto the walls.

The bungalows flanked a narrow concrete road, and beyond was a steep pebble beach strung with rolls of barbed wire and steel obstructions against landing craft. Wooden bathing huts and deck chairs, mostly broken, had been piled up to await a distant peace, and a kiosk advertising snacks and ice creams was nothing of the kind: it was a concrete gun post housing some bored Canadian soldiers who shot crap sixteen hours a day beside their ancient water-cooled Vickers machine-gun. They were the only other humans in the area, which pervaded an atmosphere of abandoned melancholy as if the Germans had already come and passed on.

From this flying club with its tattered windsock advertising Lodge plugs, where, during the previous summer chaps had arrived noisily on Saturday afternoons in their Lagondas with their popsies to give them joy rides and drink white ladies and whiskies-and-sodas in the bar—here at Southdean on the Sussex coast, 140 Squadron experienced the climactic days of the Battle of Britain.

High Command at Bentley Priory and the War Cabinet itself might argue that the German switch of target priority from aerodromes to cities was a policy of despair which admitted that the elaborate and flexible British defence system could not be broken. As further evidence that the R.A.F. was gaining the upper hand, they could point to the ever higher ratio of escorting fighters to bombers. And they viewed with satisfaction reports that the much-vaunted *Zerstören* twin-engined Messerschmitt 110s, now converted to bomb-carrying, were themselves having to be escorted by the faster, nippier 109s.

But for the front line squadrons in 11 Group like 140, the task of breaking through the swarms of 109s to get at the more vulnerable bombers was that much more difficult. Now they seemed always to be defending themselves against these single-engined machines, and there were days when they knew that their losses of fighters were heavier than the enemies'. One Hurricane squadron, given too low an altitude by control, was bounced by 109s and lost four out of nine machines in less than a minute. Hurricane pilots were always at a disadvantage against the 109. All they had in their favour were the strength of their machine and its ability to take punishment, and the moral and tactical advantages of fighting over their own land. It was a common sight in Kent and Sussex to see pilots at wayside halts and village stations waiting for a train

to take them back to their base. Most hospitals in
south-east England had at least one wounded R.A.F.
pilot brought in from his wrecked machine or found
lying beside his parachute among the hop and corn
fields.

Other pilots were shot down by the trigger-happy
navy, or in the confusion of battle by London's ack-
ack defences. There was one prolonged and bloody
duel between Hurricanes and Spitfires in which every
pilot was convinced he was fighting the enemy. The
strain told in other ways, too. Twice pilots of 140
Squadron came in from a last sortie with their undercarriage retracted, deaf to the warning klaxon in the
cockpit, blind to the red light on the instrument panel
and the red Very flare fired from the watch office.
Rowbotham fumed and fined them, but he knew that
even he might succumb to weariness and do the same
thing.

Flight Lieutenant Randall disappeared as he had
arrived, without notice. Keith guessed that his old instructor, long past his legitimate ops age, was on the
delivery business in order to sneak a sortie or two
from 11 Group fighter squadrons. Just as amateur
yachtsmen had taken unofficial part in the evacuation
from Dunkirk, the fighter airfields in the hurly-burly
of battle made tempting objects for enterprising free-
lances. A civilian test pilot, known as 'Bowler' Hampton for his distinctive headgear, was rumoured to have
been glimpsed in a dogfight off Dungeness in a
cannon-armed Spitfire without squadron markings.
An A.T.A. delivery pilot, who later claimed to have
been lost in his new and supposedly unarmed Spitfire,

was seen to be filling a Dornier's port engine with 20 mm shells over Westerham.

140 Squadron became increasingly multi-national. At a considerable bender in a Worthing pub, Rowbotham exclaimed that he was the sodding head of the sodding League of Nations instead of a British squadron commander. He turned fiercely on Halfpenny Farthing. 'You're to buy phrase books in Czech, Polish, French and Norwegian. Oh, and Australian, too.' He glared at Range Powell, head lowered like a killer at a Barcelona bull-ring challenging a picador. 'Deliver 'em to me by 0800 tomorrow. That's an order.' The C.O. was very tight.

Pilot Officer Farthing plucked up courage to ask, 'W-w-what will you d-d-d-do-do with them, sir?'

'Stick 'em round the cockpit so I can sodding *talk* to my pilots.'

They had not yet received a Norwegian or a Free French pilot, though there were many of them serving in 11 and 12 Groups, but there was a Czech in A Flight, with very primitive English, and a Pole had arrived that day. A Polish squadron of Hurricanes had been operating from Northolt for some weeks. These pilots, who had seen their nation overrun and their cities destroyed by the crushing joint strength of Russia and Germany, flew with unsurpassed passion, recklessness and hatred of the Luftwaffe.

Lieutenant Wrynkowski, believed to be the son of a count, and with only a smattering of English, had been posted to 140, however, and was undergoing a strenuous first evening at The Lion's Head. He was a pale-faced, short officer with wiry hair already turning grey and an expression of infinite melancholy in

171

his eyes. But after six pints of Tamplin's bitter he was becoming more cheerful, and before the evening was out was challenging Rowbotham to a boxing bout in the street.

The C.O. took him by the arm and they left together, mutually supportive, with Rowbotham saying, 'My good Polish friend, not only am I your commanding officer, I am also a champion boxer, and require you on ops tomorrow. . . .'

There were six of them in the party, and Keith, as the least drunken, had driven them home in the blackout. Later, he had helped Polo and Wrynkowski's jacket, and wondered at the strange turn of war-time events that had brought this young man of noble birth from Cracow on the distant River Vistula to a camp bed in a wood-and-asbestos bungalow called 'Sussex Glory'. He was already snoring, and when Keith began to pull off his grey soft leather boots he did not wake up.

Eight hours later, Keith was airborne in his new C-Charlie, leading Blue Section on standing patrol to catch early morning free chase 109s that were still getting through under the R.D.F. and beating up Worthing, Hove, Brighton and Eastbourne. He had the Pole as his number two, and Winston-Greville and Farthing as three and four. They kept radio silence and patrolled at 5,000 feet a mile out to sea. There was a faint early autumn mist, thick and like snowdrifts in the steep valleys—the deans—of the Downs, but it dissolved away as the sun got up with the promise of another hot day.

Keith flew with his hood open, the Pole on his left, the navy lieutenant and Farthing to starboard and a

172

hundred yards back. Not a very homogeneous bunch if it came to a scrap. He waved to Winston-Greville, indicating that he should keep further out and keep his eyes down: he still clung to the old peace-time practice of tight formation, almost as if he sought the comfort of close proximity. There was no sound on the R/T except a faint hum and the very distant voice of a wireless mechanic testing on the ground: ' . . . nine, eight, seven . . .'

Keith could see Eastbourne waking up behind its seafront which in any other year would later in the day be packed with children and parents, paddling, swimming and playing cricket on the sand. Now it was barbed wire thick with hidden mines, and newly-built pillboxes. He had orders to fly just out from the coast to reassure the anxious people of the town with the sight of British roundels. They had had a bad time recently, as scars among the red brick boarding houses testified. When they turned at the end of the patrol line, Keith could identify on Beachy Head the C.H.L. aerial of the R.D.F. station—low-seeing but not low-seeing enough to catch 109s at nought feet coming in from France.

When he looked left to ensure that his second pair had reformed, he noticed that the Pole in Y-Yorker had disappered from sight. He glanced above and below, and aileroned right and left to check his tail. Still there was no sign of him and Keith did not want to break radio silence. Instead, this was done for him. 'Bl-bl-blue One. T-t-tally ho! Blue Four is . . .'

A sudden yellow flash off Seaford caught Keith's eye, and he saw that the sky over the town was filling with the puffs of exploding Bofors shells which

173

moved west fast, stabbing out the course of half a dozen darting dark crosses. How *could* he have missed them? And why in God's name hadn't Pole told them? Keith could see his Hurricane slow-rolling above the sea front, ignoring the ack-ack, and saw, too, the scattered remains of his victim splashing into the sea.

'Buster Blue Section, they're coming out again east of Newhaven,' Keith transmitted.

The controller was chipping in now, as so often too late with very low flying raids: 'Fifteen plus bandits angels zero, course east, over Barnshy.'

They caught the tail runners about four miles out to sea off Newhaven harbour, and the 109s at once turned on them, using their superior climb to get above Keith's section. Keith caught a glimpse of the Pole, standing his Hurricane almost on end to get in a short burst at one of the Messerschmitts tight-turning above him.

For the next few seconds, Keith was busy trying to turn inside another enemy aircraft without blacking out. He got in a burst of tracer, made some strikes on the tailplane, but not mortal ones, followed the 109 right down to the sea, losing distance in the dive as always, and proving too slow for the fleeing fighter.

Oh God, for more power! The Merlin was labouring away at 9 lbs boost but the Hurricane just did not have the speed. Above him somebody was smoking badly. Dark and light wings. Roundels. A Hurricane, but he couldn't see the letter. It was smoking more than the emergency boost warranted and it was losing height fast. Keith ruddered his machine into a steep climbing turn, glimpsed a 109 hard on the Hurricane's

174

tail, identified the letter M on the Hurricane, and in a rush of anger and dismay saw that it was Farthing. And he was doomed. Nothing could save him now.

There were flames coming from the machine as Keith strived to get in a burst at the 109 at maximum range to distract the pilot. Then it went down—straight down, for a thousand feet. Farthing, in a last despairing cry for help, had left his transmitter on. Keith could imagine his small body jammed over the set in a futile effort to escape from the flames. His scream on its steady high note continued all the way down. Keith prayed for it to stop, for the boy's agony to end. It ceased at last when the Hurricane hit the water, which in a fury of white extinguished at once the searing fire and the awful sound.

The planes had fled. The 109s were dots far to the south, leaving as they had come, skimming the grey Channel. A single Hurricane was two miles to the west, climbing steeply. Another, Y-Yorker, was circling the area of combat like a soaring falcon—and, like this bird of prey, the machine suddenly swerved and dropped. Keith thought that the Pole might be wounded and now unconscious. Then, too late to call out, he saw his intention, his target in the sea, the white splash of the collapsed German parachute, the figure in the water beside it held up by his life-jacket and awaiting rescue.

There was to be no salvation for this Luftwaffe pilot, who had somehow contrived to get out safely from his burning machine at low level. Wrynkowski opened fire at 200 yards, churning the sea into a maelstrom of froth.

Keith transmitted, 'Blue One to Blue Two, cease firing and form up on me.' It was too late. Flying low over the sea, hood open, Keith saw the German pilot now mutilated beside his parachute, the stain from his body clouding the water red in a widening trail as he drifted on the waves.

What an op! What a bloody shambles! A cock-up, a waste. And he was responsible. As Section leader on the patrol, he should have spotted those 109s coming in, should have briefed the Pole more thoroughly beforehand, should never have allowed the inadequate Farthing out of his sight. But Farthing was also Winston-Greville's responsibility—and he had done a bunk before things got hot. What would be his excuse this time?

As he flew back over Brighton with the Pole, Keith's anger with himself and grief at the loss of Farthing, turned to anger against the wild Pole, against the handsome Fleet Air Arm pilot who never quite made it, against a system that left them to fight in planes that were too slow, underarmed, and always too few in numbers.

Back at Southdean, on the ground, he hurried over to Wrynkowski's machine. The Pole had a gleam of satisfaction in his grey eyes. 'You saw?' he kept asking. 'You saw? He thought he get away. But I fix him.' Then he shook his head and made a long face. 'But only one. It must be three, always three.'

'Lieutenant, we don't shoot helpless men in the water,' Keith said angrily. 'You are to obey the rules. And if you sight enemy planes, you must report to me . . .'

'Rules? What are these rules?' His eyes were flashing fire. 'They kill us, we kill them. There were no rules for my people—killed on the roads, women and children. Warsaw . . .'

They walked back to the club-house which served as pilots' ready room and squadron offices as well as bar and mess. 'In the R.A.F. we follow orders, lieutenant. We do as we're told, do you understand? Or there is a court martial and we're thrown out—see? No more flying. No more shooting down Huns.' He offered him a cigarette to indicate the end of the subject. 'Now we'll make our report and I shall say nothing.'

Keith threw his Mae West and helmet onto the Spy's desk. 'A cock-up. Farthing bought it off Newhaven. A flamer. Wrynkowski got a 109. Our naval hero dodged out of it. That's that little flap in essence.'

The Spy, as always looking cunningly Machiavellian, drew out a pad and pen and began writing, at the same time saying in a flat voice, 'Lieutenant Winston-Greville had trouble with his guns. It is being looked into now—by the C.O. Right, let's have this slowly . . .'

Combat reports, combat reports, combat reports. A dozen or more a day sometimes. Reports from every squadron, pouring in to Group and then Command. Did anyone bother to read them, did anyone have time to read them? Keith imagined them by the sackful going into a giant furnace at Bentley Priory to keep the massed gold braid warm in winter. All anyone really wanted to know was 'How many?' How many of theirs, how many of ours? The cricket season is still with us, and scores are reported daily—alongside a lot of lies about the imminent defeat of the Luftwaffe, the superior morale, the superior machines of the R.A.F. Not very much in the newspaper tomorrow about Pilot Officer Farthing being burnt to death at 350 m.p.h.

Keith looked out of the window as he reported to the Spy. 'About fifteen 109s. Red spinners. I saw no other identification except a red dolphin motif. They were going to attack Seaford . . .'

From where he was standing he could see the rolling South Downs, a clump of beech trees, distantly the soaring masts of Poling C.H. station like a whole city of cathedrals. Hurricanes were dispersed along the eastern perimeter of Southdean, including Winston-Greville's L-London, wing panels removed, the corporal armourer and two more airmen probing the gun bays. The C.O., in dirty Mae West and hatless, and Winston-Greville, in his spotless white overalls, were walking side by side across the grass deep in conversation.

Keith wondered what Rowbotham was saying, and told himself reprovingly that he had no business to be angry and exasperated when the C.O. had the double burden of leading the squadron in combat and coping with the never-ending human conflicts and problems. Mike had said only the previous day, 'Goddamit, why doesn't he fire the guy?' But Keith knew that it was not as simple as that. To have an officer posted away, especially an officer from another service who had volunteered for temporary transfer, was a time-consuming process that also required a lot of tact and explanation. And there was no proof of Winston-Greville's cowardice. He always gave the impression of being eager for ops. It was just that his machine had a jinx on it, and that he was not often seen around when events became really warm. No more than that.

Later in the day, Keith managed to speak to the C.O. alone for a moment. 'He just disappeared, sir, just like that, when we began mixing it. Left that poor sod Farthing with his tail unprotected.'

Rowbotham looked at him bleakly. His eyes were red-rimmed and, on top of his other problems, Keith guessed he was suffering from a major hangover. 'I know,' he said slowly. 'He had trouble with his guns.'

'The only trouble he had with his guns, sir,' Keith said angrily, 'is that he didn't hang around long enough to fire them.'

A rumour, emanating from the squadron armourers, was that all four starboard air lines to L-London's Brownings had been jammed with matchsticks, making them inoperable, and that there was to be an inquiry. Nothing was mentioned officially, and no one wanted to talk about the incident, but for the first time an atmosphere of distrust became apparent on this embattled little airfield in Sussex.

*

Keith received a letter from Jenny. Her neat, well-ordered handwriting was a reminder of a world of tenderness and understanding remote from life at Southdean where fear had dangerously lost its edge, so that, on every op, you had to remind yourself that one day your life might again become important. That envelope to 'Flying Officer K. Stewart D.F.C., R.A.F. Station Savile Farm . . .' and forwarded to his new address and now safely buttoned into his pocket for savouring later, was a day-long antidote to the corroding influence of life on this field and in the wretched little cheap bungalows, where they went to sleep off the beer and whisky and the day's quota of fear.

179

For Keith, oil was the ingredient that seemed most
to symbolize the squalor of their lives during these
mid-September days. By its very nature, oil figured in
every airman's life, but here with careless overfilling,
rapid turn-rounds and skimped daily services, it
seemed to spill everywhere and get on their clothes
and hands. By way of fitters' rags and hands, it got
into the cockpits, onto the controls, thence onto Mae
Wests and uniforms and gloves. It found its way onto
the deck-chairs where they sat in the sun between
ops, onto their playing cards as they gambled, onto
Stuffy's collar and the glasses and mugs from which
they drank too much. Washing facilities were limited,
the Gunk, the one remedy, in short supply. Keith
came to hate the oil, and even found it on the envelope of Jenny's letter when he drew it out to read
again in the privacy of his room.

'Darling Keith, I miss you most dreadfully.
Everybody talks about their ailments and their injuries here, and hardly at all about the war or anything that really matters. I think of you risking
your darling life every day for these women convalescing here and grumbling about their puny
aches and pains . . .'

On that same day, Keith also got a letter from Lady
Barrett. Yes, she had heard from Eileen at last, thank
goodness. She had been unwell and in a nursing
home, which was the reason why she had not written
earlier. (Or was it? Keith questioned.) She would be

out soon and would write again but would probably go straight back to the Admiralty.

Keith mentioned neither letter to Mike.

❋

They had been at Southdean a week and it felt like a year. All that they saw of the outside world was its panorama laid out below as remote and inaccessible as the surface of the moon. They saw moving vehicles, horses and carts bringing in the last of the harvest, people in the streets of the towns, staring up white-faced when they flew low. But it was a world seen from the travelling prison of their cockpits.

Newspapers told them nothing. 'Targets in the south-east . . .' 'A London hospital was severely damaged . . .' 'Our pilots scored their biggest success . . .' 'Resolution strengthened by German barbarity . . .'

Once Keith and Mike, borrowing the C.O.'s car, went out to the pub in Worthing. It was not a successful venture. The pub was almost empty, the locals elderly and unforthcoming, the beer warm and unsavoury. They drank a great deal and tried to recover their old ease of relationship which had brought them together into this service three years earlier.

Now there were too many constraints. Eileen was beyond consideration as a subject, and by association so was Rising Hall and the Barretts. They talked briefly of Tom and Moira, but neither had heard from them. Both were reluctant to talk about the immediate past because it included friends and fellow pilots who were dead or maimed. Because of its sour ring, they did not want to introduce the name of Winston-

181

Greville with whom they might be flying the next morning. This was limbo land.

So they talked shop, and drank too much and as a consequence became gloomy and morbid. It was dark when they left and they had difficulty finding their car. They heard the sound of women's voices in the dark, and recognized Winston-Greville's laugh. The lieutenant's white Daimler showed up clearly, and they stood back as it filled with several figures in long dresses. Winston-Greville was giving another of his parties, and as the car drove away they felt gloomier than ever.

'How on earth does he find them?' Keith mused as he drove the Hillman slowly and discreetly in the black-out along the coast road from Worthing.

'I guess he just lets it be known he's around, and they swarm like goddam bees,' Mike said bitterly.

'Only from the best places, of course.'

'Oh, sure. Great actor, our Arthur. Travelling showman, our gallant sailor boy.'

Keith said nothing for a moment, concentrating on the negotiation of a double bend on a moonless night with regulation shaded headlights. He was also puzzling over Mike's comment and his fuddled brain was not up to puzzling over anything. He stopped to light a cigarette. 'Actor? He wasn't acting when he did a bunk the other morning and left the poor sod, Halfpenny, to the wolves.'

'You know he's a phoney?' Mike said.

Keith agreed, and angrily suggested a few other names.

'No, seriously,' Mike pressed. 'I was going to keep this in case I ever saw them together, like you did.

Then spill the beans. The result might have been interesting.' He rolled an imaginary ball between his powerful hands, a nervous habit of his when he was tensed up. 'I did a bit of research that day we got our gongs. Prying, Edward G. Robinson might call it.'

He told Keith how he had gone to the London Library in St James's Square instead of the American Embassy, and although not a member, had been given advice by the genealogical specialist there over a 1934 copy of the annual, *Milton on the Peerage and Baronetage.* He pulled a scrap of paper out of his right breast pocket and read from it:

Winston-Greville of Kilcane. Since the death of Sir Arthur Winston-Greville, 6th Bart, which event occurred 28 Nov 1933, the succession to the baronetcy has not been established.

Lineage: John Winston-Greville of Arbtoin, Kilcane, Tipperary (whose will was proved 9 July 1727) son of . . .

Sir Richard Winston-Greville 3rd Bart married Florence Annie Marie, only child of Sir John Elliott Bart of . . . She d. 20 April 1910 having had issue:

1. Raymond Arthur 4th Bart
2. Charles Henry 5th Bart
3. Arthur 6th Bart b. 1863 m. 2 Oct 1916 Eva Gertrude d. of late Dr. Edmund Spencer . . . and d.s.p. (died *sine prole,* or without issue) 24 Oct 1931 since which date the baronetcy has remained dormant.

'So I thanked this nice guy and went on reading this crazy great fat dusty book and he went away. Then I

did some more Edward G. stuff and dug out a copy
of the same book, only 1936. And like some mesmer-
ized snake I looked up the same entry—and, Keith, I
guess you won't believe this, but it was not the same
entry, no sir. The "not" had disappeared. It was all cut
and dried. Eva Gertrude had had issue, if that's the
right word for procreation. She had had an Arthur
Winston-Greville, born 19 November 1919. Your
friend and my friend, gallant naval officer and pilot.
It seems he must have got busy with some phoney papers and maybe some real money, too, on this guy Milton of the Peerage.'

'You're mad,' Keith exclaimed. 'He wouldn't get
away with it.'

'He sure did. Until this bit of digging of mine. Gullible, those guys. Then I got busy calling up a few
numbers,' Mike continued. 'Drew what I expected—a
goddam blank. Various female remnants of the family
had never heard of him. Said they couldn't afford
Milton anyway.'

'And all those pictures he keeps?'

'Shot from the pages of society and sporting magazines—*Country Life, Tatler*. Nothing easier.'

Keith stopped the car again, distrusting his ability
to keep on the road at the same time as keeping his
mind on this extraordinary notion. 'But Mike, this is
crazy. He'd be bound to get rumbled. The Navy
would get him right at the start. References. Your Pop
had to write a letter, so did my adopted Pa.'

Mike had clearly thought it all out and had an answer to every question. 'Any good stationers in London. Like that place Truslove and something near
your father's tailors—Clifford Street. Get some headed

writing paper printed. Write a letter, ask for the reply to be sent to Sir's temporary London address where he'll be staying for a while—our Arthur's address, of course. There wouldn't be many questions. None at all, I guess, with that titled background in your class-crazy society.'

Keith was silent, taking it all in through his haze of alcohol and finding that he had no more questions to ask.

But Mike went on talking—murmuring rather, to himself. 'Say he had a bit of money anyway. Inherited some dough as well as plenty of fresh cheek to go with it. Saw the advantages of a title. Picked himself a swell white Daimler automobile. Charm, looks, title, goddam naval officer's uniform. Christ!' he exclaimed, 'he couldn't miss . . .'

Keith, only half listening, wound down the window and flicked his cigarette out into the dark. He could hear the uneven beat of German bombers overhead, probably heading for the Midlands or Liverpool. Two narrow yellow fingers of searchlights played fruit-lessly on the scattered cloud and there were cracks of heavy ack-ack from Portsmouth direction. They never hit anything but it kept the civilians happy.

'Pretty pathetic, really,' was Keith's final comment.

'Pathetic!' Mike exploded. 'Jeepers! You wouldn't find anything pathetic about a guy who seduced your Jenny—along with every other broad he picked up.'

He started. 'No, I only meant it must be pretty sad living a lie all your life.'

'Not if it gets you any woman you want. Anyway, I guess he really believes it by now.' The tone in which Mike spoke reflected the hard attitude he had as-

185

sumed since the revelation of Eileen's defection and the new intensification of the fighting. The spirited, waggish, happy-go-lucky Mike had become strained and bitter over recent weeks, talking little and flying like a hunter whose life depends on stalking and killing his prey.

*

The next morning dawned mistily, with a heavy dew on the grass. The early autumn sun would again soon clear both, but after several days of less intense pressure, no one was prepared for the onslaught that rapidly built up from the middle of the morning.

140 Squadron was brought to Readiness at 7 a.m. Mike made his way from the bungalow he shared with Range Powell, Kiwi Robinson and an A Flight flying officer, buying a newspaper from the boy who enterprisingly bicycled out from Lancing every morning. The scene at the B Flight dispersal was so familiar it had become timeless in his mind: the attitude of undisciplined relaxation, with the sprawled pilots doing nothing or occupying themselves in the way they preferred. At any moment a series of events would rapidly alter this picture of torpid inaction to furious activity, as if a switch had been thrown and the current sent flowing. And it was modern electronics that brought about this sudden change—a faint signal on the screen at Dover or Rye, Poling or Ventnor, a 'blip' recorded at Beachy Head's C.H.L. station, instant reports by R.A.F. and G.P.O. lines to Sector and Group, elaborated when height and strength and course were noted, a decision taking only seconds, and the despatch of the controllers' orders.

The Church Army van from Lancing had just arrived, and the ground crews were queueing for tea and cakes. Mike grabbed a deck-chair and stretched out, pretending to read the headlines of the *News Chronicle*, his mind on his alcoholic decision to tell Keith his discovery about Winston-Greville. He was pleased now that he had done so. If he were killed, the knowledge would not be lost. It would serve no purpose to tell Rowbotham. His answer would be a shrug of his bull-like shoulders. He could hear his deep, stabbing voice, 'I don't give a sod if he's President Roosevelt so long as he flies a kite O.K.'. Something like that.

The Navy lieutenant was talking to his fitter in the queue. They were laughing at something Winston-Greville had said, and other airmen nearby joined in. Mike watched him over the top of his newspaper, wondering what the truth of the man could be, his origins, his real upbringing, what had caused him to take up this bogus identity? His looks were certainly on his side, and he was an outstanding figure in any company. Had he really fooled Rowbotham as he had hoodwinked his way into Debrett, Milton and Burke? But Mike knew, as Keith knew, that Lieutenant Arthur Winston-Greville was yellow. They had both seen cowardice before, close to for weeks on end, before Rowbotham had taken command. Winston-Greville was only a hollow shell of a pilot, all show at formation, all splitarse at aerobatics, but in action a dangerous liability. Was Rowbotham all that gullible, all that blind?

But in the unlikely event of Winston-Greville being shot down and killed, Eileen would still be lost to Mike. Nothing could bring her back. The old Eileen had died with the end of innocence in 1940, along with freedom and frontiers and the lives of countless thousands in Poland and Norway, France and Belgium and Holland. She was one more casualty.

Mike dropped his eyes to the centre news page of the newspaper, reading 'Flying Fortresses for Britain'. Well, good for the old USA. Sure, great stuff. So 'the Committee to Defend America by Aiding the Allies, which was so successful in arousing opinion in favour of releasing fifty American destroyers to Great Britain, has started a new campaign . . .'

And at that moment the bell rang, the mosaic of leisure and relaxation momentarily frozen; then it was like a disorderly Olympic start. Mike threw down the *News Chronicle*. Yeah, good old F.D.R. Over here, we could do with some planes and pilots. A declaration of war would come in handy, too.

A plot just out to sea from Boulogne had built up into something really big. There was another developing over Calais as the powerful *Kampfgeschwaden* assembled, were joined by their numerous escort and set their compass course for England, a drill that was scarcely necessary as the undulating streak of white cliffs from beyond Dover in the east, and with a brief break, to Brighton in the west, was already visible through the mist.

At Bentley Priory, Air Chief Marshal 'Stuffy' Dowding suspected that this was going to be a hard day in which he might well again have to commit all his squadrons. His Chief of Staff agreed. Air Marshal Park at Uxbridge, Air Marshal Leigh-Mallory at Watnall, and Sir Marshall Brand at Rudloe Manor in Wiltshire made their dispositions and passed orders through their staff to the sector controllers. Telephones rang in watch offices, and at dispersals. And at Southdean, another 'Stuffy', an unprepossessing mongrel, followed the pilots out to their machines. Within seconds the sound of his barking was lost in the crash of engines, and he ran back, tail between his legs, in the blast of the slipstream. He hated scrambles.

Mike had Red Section, with the reassuring Bill Watson as his number two, then Polo Satterthwaite, pipe clamped between his teeth for take-off, and Winston-Greville—'my goddam Achilles' heel' Mike told himself, as number four. They took off cross-wind in loose formation, except the Navy Lieutenant who had tucked his wing tight behind Polo's and lifted off as if tied by a short length of string to his wingtip. Kiwi Robinson's section was already airborne, and A Flight with a contribution of four machines was gathering speed on the far side of the field. Twelve aircraft. A full squadron for once, thanks to new deliveries and 'Chiefy's' unremitting work.

As the volume of voices outside a cocktail party registers its size, so the state of the R/T when they became airborne indicated the extent and strength of the raids building up and coming across the Channel. It was going to be a busy morning all right, Mike recognized, a *very* busy morning. They were not quite comparable, but these days reminded him of the annual football game at Andover against Exeter, the raucous cheering as the 600-strong column made for the field, the agonizing sense of expectation. Days of innocence compared with this. But all the same . . .

Call-signs were thick in the air, messages succinct,

189

the formal regulation patter of peace-time abbreviated under the pressure of war. Eighteen squadrons already airborne, all to be directed. The new 11 Group policy was to work in pairs when possible, which made the controllers' task even more difficult.

'Sandbag leader. Patrol Matchstick angels one-five. Much trade for you.'

The dark shape of Brighton was already below them, the pattern of housing development working along the valleys behind the town and east and west along the coastline. Rowbotham took them north for five minutes to gain height, and they came back over the town at 12,000, still climbing but keeping emergency boost for the inevitable clash. Another squadron was coming up from the west, one or two of the machines with guns projecting from the wings. Four 20 mm Hispano cannon, the answer to a fighter pilot's dream. Lucky devils. 140 still had only one.

Like a blunt dagger aimed at the heart of Britain, the wedge of bombers came across the Channel at 14,000 feet, the sun behind them and reflecting glints like treacherous winks from the perspex of their cockpits. There were *Staffeln* of 109s close in on both sides, six altogether Mike reckoned, and, as always, there would be more above, as high as 32,000 to get above any Spitfires and ready to drop like darts onto the defenders. It seemed hardly credible that a sky which had known the aeroplane for a mere thirty years, and until last year had known only the occasional Imperial Airways or Air France airliner, could now be so crowded, day after day of this summer.

When the C.O. transmitted his brief order, which everyone understood and was itself hardly even necessary, it was a measure of how accustomed they had become to these odds-against challenges over the south coast. 'This is Sandbag Leader. Head on. Reform above. Watch your sodding tails.' No more.

A head-on attack had the advantage of breaking up the formation of the bombers and reducing the chances of suffering damage from co-ordinated enemy fire. With luck, you might also shoot down the formation leader who synchronized the attack with an exceptionally accurate bomb-aimer. The more skilful fighter pilots loved a head-on attack, the less experienced and less aggressive preferred taking their time from astern.

The starboard 109s were gaining height fast in order to swing back onto their tails as they went in. Mike recognized that they would be lucky to get in one short burst before mixing it with the fighters, and he pulled the plug for the extra speed he would need. Watson had followed suit, black smoke streaming from his exhausts. Like a good jockey, the Sergeant always managed to get the best out of his machine and was always faster, just as he seemed to react quicker than anyone else.

The nose of the bomber wedge was made up of Heinkel 111s, with twin-finned Dorniers behind, all trailing white vapour trails which made the calculation of vertical deflection easier. Mike allowed a half-ring, coming in at well above 350 m.p.h. but with his Hurricane rock-steady, the beautiful gun platform she always was. Watson was taking the starboard machine, Mike took the leader, saw yellow spinners, the perspex nose like a shooting gallery target, the single machine-gun the bull's-eye. It was already firing tracer, though still well out of range, in the hope of distracting him.

The frontal silhouette grew rapidly with the closing speed of nearly 600 m.p.h. Centre dot steady. Hold it! Hold it until your judgement tells you that you *will*, not maybe, crash head on. The old trial of nerves again. With the Heinkel's wingtips far outside the range bars, Mike at last squeezed the button momentarily, not even a full second burst.

The Heinkel lunged. It might have been his fire, or the pilot losing his nerve. It lunged up, and Mike threw all his strength into forcing his stick forward, the dark shape of the Heinkel filling the sky above him as he raced under with feet to spare. He was aware, too, of a sudden flash of light to his right, of his engine dead from temporary fuel starvation, the straps biting into his shoulders, of his body being strained to the uttermost.

But the mental demands were just as great, just as urgent, for this business of aerial combat marked the limit of human endeavour, and then the extra beyond—like the boost of his Merlin registering as soaring 9-plus on the red dial when he pulled up again, his vision fading into grey as he half blacked-out.

So big was this formation—this armada of bombers—that it had not completed its passage overhead when Mike had regained his altitude. Watson was right there beside him, like a good number two. 'Red One,' he transmitted, 'that's my sod.'

And Mike believed him. Bill Watson had blown up his machine on the first pass. A fading dark grey cloud among the fading white vapour trails marked the point of detonation of its fuel and bomb-load, the

192

aerial graves of its five men. The last of the wreckage, a single engineless wing, floated down at funeral speed but was already disappearing into the haze over the sea.

Mike himself had shot well, too. His Heinkel was losing height and flying due west. He guessed that he had killed several of the crew with that brief burst, and he could imagine the struggle for survival in the cockpit, with perhaps the rear gunner clearing the pilot's body from the controls. He had recently read an Intelligence summary which had stated that the ideal 'kill' was on a bomber before it dropped its bombs and which succeeded in getting back, and by crash-landing as its own base with dead and wounded on board, did the worst possible damage to morale.

But there was no time for reflection or self-congratulation, no time for anything except an electrifying swift response to the dogfight developing about them. While the bombers laboured to reform on their drive north, crossing over the South Downs and the Weald of Sussex, the two Hurricane squadrons struggled for survival against odds of four to one. It was the most relentless, the most protracted, the most fearsome engagement Mike had ever fought, and as he kicked rudder, broke violently, tightened a turn to bring the darting silhouette of a 109 into his sight, using every combat trick he had learned, he knew that this was a business for veterans only, that few of the weak or inexperienced on either side would survive. Only those with 'the highest factor of non-relaxation' (Rowbotham's coined phrase) would add to their score or come out alive.

Once an unidentified Hurricane soared past just

above Mike's head, inverted, hood closed, pouring smoke. Once he almost severed the shrouds of a parachute, and he caught a glimpse of a body hurtling past, tight-bunched, dead or wisely waiting to fall clear before pulling the rip cord. Once, he found himself so close alongside a German fighter they might have been practising formation. Both had their goggles up and they exchanged glances as impersonal as drivers at traffic lights awaiting the green.

Image piled upon image in the pace and fury of the 90-second struggle. A Hurricane with most of the canvas torn from its fuselage, its fin riddled, shot past fifty yards in front of Mike. He could see the 140 squadron letters RC but the rest had been torn away. It was losing height fast and in a straight line, and the Messerschmitt that had done the damage was closing in for another pass 500 yards astern.

Mike climbed, rolled off the top and came down behind the 109. To his astonishment, it tried no evasive action, and for the first time since the fighters had intervened, he found himself with a sitting target at his own speed.

A quarter-deflection stern shot, a two-second burst, and the 109 disintegrated before his eyes. It had happened to him only once before, and it was confirmation again of the effectiveness of eight machine-guns fired at the ideal harmonized range of 200 yards at an unarmoured antagonist. Small objects first peeled off, then larger. There was a small explosion, half a wing spiralled away, a dark object that might have been the pilot fell out from the distintegrating tangle. Then Mike saw nothing more as he raced past the scene of death and caught up the 109's own victim.

194

The sky above was empty, one sweep of a brush wiping it clear of detritus, the 109s making for home with red fuel warning lights blinking like a failing pulse rate. Some would inevitably drop into the Channel, victims of German optimism that took no account of having to fight a more distant enemy than an army in retreat, and had made provision for a range of a mere 400 miles.

The sorely-damaged Hurricane continued in a straight line, steadily losing height. 'Sandbag aircraft,' Mike transmitted, 'are you O.K.? This is Red One on your port side.'

Voices broke in on the R/T, distant messages of instruction and information on greater events, more acute crises. 'Mayfly leader, this is Acorn. Mayfly leader, pancake at Unicorn—over.' 'Blue Three to Escort Leader, I have a glycol leak and am pancaking at Pinetree.' A pause, and then seemingly more distant than ever, though only a hundred yards distant, a voice spoke, 'Sandbag Red One . . .' It faded out and came back again, ' . . . no aileron control . . . canopy jammed . . . rudder . . .'

'Sandbag aircraft, I will stay with you. Try trimtab. Land with rudder. You'll be O.K.' Mike accepted that the pilot's chances were not good, lacking aileron control, with doubtful steering and elevation, a failing radio and a canopy that prohibited bailing out. He called up Southdean and told them to stand by for a crash landing.

They were over Shoreham and down to 500 feet. More of the canvas had torn away, revealing the complex wooden ribwork below and proving once again the remarkable resistance of the Hawker aircraft to damage. He could see the silhouette of the pilot through the thick perspex, a man with small expectation of staying alive to deliver his combat report to the Spy.

'Wind the tab right back,' Mike ordered, 'tighten your straps and try your landing gear.'

There was no answer from the Hurricane but his message had got through, for, a few seconds later and to Mike's relief, first the undercarriage and then full flaps extended from the machine. They were only a mile from the field now, the shoreline on the left, tide out to reveal a narrow strip of sand, a group of khaki figures standing on the pebbles outside a sandbagged gun emplacement, tatty asbestos-roofed bungalows below. A Hurricane, wheels down, was circling, waiting for the cripple to touch down before landing. A green Very shot up from the front of the club-house. Mike could imagine Rowbotham firing it, watching the damaged Hurricane's descent with a set expression of concentration on his battered face. Was this to lead to another letter to next of kin or another pint too many. . . ?

The Hurricane was not losing height fast enough. It was still at 200 feet approaching the field's perimeter and then over the old windsock. 'Go round again!' Mike transmitted, repeating the order clearly in the hope that the pilot was still receiving. The machine travelled the length of Southdean at the same altitude, seemingly unable to climb or lose height, an uncertain skeleton of a machine with more of its canvas trailing like bunting from the tail. Then it made a flat, uneven turn through 90 degrees, and 90 degrees again, onto the downwind leg. Mike, circling over the sea, saw the less damaged starboard side for the first time, closing in to give moral support, and noting the full identification: RC–L.

The significance did not strike him at once. The Hurricane was already on its final approach, this time much lower, before Mike realized that he had just saved the life of Lieutenant Arthur Winston-Greville and was now, at this very moment, talking him down to safety. 'Cut your switches and turn off fuel cock,' he called when the Hurricane was over the perimeter fence, shadow and machine almost one. 'Pull the cut-out . . .' he repeated, and noted the Hurricane's propeller now only windmilling. The pilot was still having difficulty stalling, and the wheels did not touch down until half-way across the grass, bouncing awkwardly and still going too fast to stop, even if the brakes were working. But RC–L was only travelling at about 15 m.p.h. when it struck the hedge where it tipped forward without undue violence onto its nose.

By the time Mike had landed and taxied in, Chiefy, supervising a group of airmen in overalls, had got the Hurricane onto an even keel, and another pair were working on the jammed hood.

140's Navy lieutenant had come back safely once again, unlike Sergeant Pilot Willoughby D.F.M. of A Flight, and the lanky, quiet-spoken B. Flight commander, Kiwi Robinson, who had come 12,000 miles to defend the Mother Country, and was now buried ten feet beneath her soil within the shattered wreck of what was left of his Hurricane, in a newly-ploughed field just north of the village of Bolney.

7

THE LAST HEAD-ON

Keith was acting as duty pilot in the makeshift watch office at Southdean when he heard Mike's voice encouraging another pilot and talking him down to a safe landing. They were the last of 140 to return, and two were missing. Mike had overheard the report on Willoughby who crashed in flames. Another unidentified 140 Squadron machine had been seen to go down in a power dive: this could be either Winston-Greville or Kiwi Robinson. And, like Mike, it was not until the Hurricane had gone round again, revealing her other side, that Keith had had to accept that their Flight Commander was dead; and that, by a supreme example of black irony, Mike had saved the life of Winston-Greville.

It was 11.25 a.m., the sun was high, the last of the mist had cleared. A perfect autumn day. And still the Luftwaffe's pressure had not reached its zenith. Rowbotham, briefly on the telephone to Group, had learned that the Prime Minister was in the ops room with Park and that more plots than ever before were coming in. One massive formation of bombers, heading for London, was approaching Dungeness, 12 Group fighters were being scrambled, and 140 Squadron was ordered to be refuelled and rearmed in fifteen minutes.

Through the grief for the loss of his Flight Commander, and the confusion of feeling for the survival of Winston-Greville, Keith was also aware of an unprecedented revival of enthusiasm among the pilots and the ground crews. The exhilaration was unmistakeable. With the support of only one other Hurricane squadron, they had severely dented the massive raid heading for London, and word from Group to Rowbotham told of a 'big wing' assault on the demoralized crews from 12 Group, of the Dorniers and Heinkels and Junkers scattering and jettisoning their bombs over the Home Counties and suburbs. Few of the German bombers had got through to central London. This time Goering really was making the supreme, final effort. And the R.A.F. were holding him.

At the dispersal, Lieutenant Wrynkowski was seen joking with his crew and chivvying them along in his broken English while he polished and polished again his perspex with a soft cloth. 'It is goot to see ze Hun. It is bad not to see 'im.'

Drinking a pint mug of tea brewed by an L.A.C. armourer and fellow Yorkshireman, Polo Satterthwaite was heard to say, 'Aye, it's a champion day for Jerry-pranging.' Evil clouds of black smoke poured from his pipe, sparks falling unnoticed on his oil-streaked jersey.

Rowbotham had promoted Range Powell Flight Commander to succeed the New Zealander. 'Just watch your language in the air, Aussie,' he told him. 'Swearing wastes R/T time.'

'You bet your bloody life, cobber.'

199

'And you still call me "sir.".'

'You bloody well bet your bloody life—sir.'

140 Squadron was scrambled again at 1.50 p.m. This time Keith flew, and as he took off number three to Range Powell and raised his undercart, he felt relieved of the doubts of recent days when all their efforts seemed to have no effect on the Luftwaffe's assault and the chances of survival had seemed remote. They were winning and he was not going to be killed. The luck that had got him a share in his first Heinkel on his twenty-first birthday; the luck that had held—sometimes miraculously—in France, through the Dunkirk ops and ever since, was going to get him through this lot alive. But with the wisdom of hard experience, he knew that a mixture of superstition and practicality guides good fighters, that luck requires careful watching and constant support. 'All right,' he often imagined being told by some deity of fortune. 'All right, but you've got to do *your* bit.' And he would sharpen his responses by an imaginary last ultimate tightening of an imaginary screw, adjust his reflector sight just so, check his instruments, tighten his straps, and sweep the sky with his eyes, again and again. All this he did now, climbing fast east in the heat of the day, allowing himself only a momentary thought for Jenny Simpson, recovering somewhere in Norfolk.

A few minutes after 2 p.m., Keith saw the German bombers approaching the Kent coast from the Pas de Calais, an aerial armada some ten miles wide flying steadily and seemingly invincibly, like a shot from that doom-laden, prophetic H. G. Wells film, *The Shape of Things to Come*. Well, they had come. Here was the reality of annihilation from the air. 'The bomber will always get through,' they had said. But the R.A.F. had exploded that prophecy, had destroyed the myth of Nazi supremacy, symbolized by the stacks of smashed aircraft remains, bent and bullet-pierced black crosses and swastikas, that were growing all over south-east England.

This raid dwarfed the morning attack. It was the biggest ever mounted in the history of aerial warfare, and might have been fatally intimidating if it had crossed the Channel early in the battle. But after suffering wide fluctuations in morale, in losses and successes, in the availability of pilots and machines, every fighter squadron had been seized with new self-confidence. It was as if they had sensed the desperation of the enemy and were now relishing their survival, buoyed up by their ever-increasing squadron scores on the one hand and the new national acclaim they were enjoying on the other.

There might be three or four or six hundred aircraft heading for London and intent on its destruction, but the defences were repaired and intact, and from Northolt to Hornchurch, Duxford to Tangmere, from hard-pressed Biggin Hill to Middle Wallop in 10 Group, the Spitfires and Hurricanes gathered to do battle with the conviction that they would win.

Above the Kent hop fields and oast houses, the square miles of orchards and rolling countryside, the fighters tore into the huge formations like packs of terriers. 140 Squadron joined them at twenty-eight minutes past two o'clock. Amidst a cacophony of shouted orders and warnings on the R/T, Keith heard Rowbotham's steady voice. 'Tally-ho, Sandbag leader calling. Red Section, take those Dorniers three o'clock below. Blue and Green, follow me . . .'

The next half-hour was a confusion of the flashing images of air combat. There was the Dornier 17 jettisoning first its bombs and then its crew over Dartford; the symmetry of the spiral of smoke from a vertically cork-screwing-Spitfire; the trio of Heinkels turning tail and fleeing in a power dive so fast that they diminished out of Keith's sight before he could fire; the 109 shedding its wings in a vertical dive like a gannet plunging down to its prey; the 110 that shed its port engine after a two-second burst and went into a series of flick rolls so fast that the wing itself came off too—and the flash of satisfaction that Keith's score was in double figures . . .

The sky was a cobweb of vapour trails marking desperate evasions, determined attacks; the cordite smell filtered into the cockpit and beneath Keith's mask. There was a 20 mm shell hole in his port wing that had turned up the metal like a carelessly-opened can of beans, and Keith didn't care. There were the shock-wave patterns spreading out from a stick of bombs across Chislehurst Common, by contrast neatly punctured and symmetrical. There were five parachutes together like a white flower arrangement floating down, a complete Heinkel's crew on their leisurely way to a prisoner-of-war camp. And, by contrast, the single flaming parachute from a 109 with the suspended pilot dropping at an ever accelerating pace. And there was the clank of empty breech-blocks from Keith's eight machine-guns that told him his ammunition was exhausted, his battle over.

But it was not the end of that day of sweat and

endeavour. Mike and Keith flew together with six more of 140 Squadron, scrambling from Southdean just after 5 p.m. and climbing above newly-formed cloud over the Isle of Wight. Fighter-bomber 110s and 109s were reported but it was only a small raid, a ratty gesture of defiance after a catastrophic day for the Luftwaffe, and they saw nothing.

No one got drunk that night, as if the flow of adrenalin during the day had anesthetized them. Polo's head dropped during dinner, and he awoke at the sound of his own snores. They were too tired to rib him. Even the 'shop' talk was desultory. They had said what there was to be said to the Spy, who could be heard typing like a Browning machine-gun in his office. He would be there until 2 a.m. Keith and Mike tried playing darts and soon realized that they had exhausted their power of hitting anything more for one day. Rowbotham lay with a copy of the previous day's *Times* over his face like a grandfather at the seaside. The headlines read: 'BUCKINGHAM PALACE AGAIN BOMBED. THE KING AND QUEEN ON THEIR ESCAPE,' and the pint mug of beer at his side had not been touched.

Outside, the cloud had cleared and there was a half moon. Keith and Mike walked together down the track that led to the coast road and their bungalows, answering the sentry's salute and wishing him goodnight—two Flying Officer D.F.C.s and both limping slightly from accident or combat.

Mike said, 'I guess it must be ten light-years since we suffered that mutual fit of insanity.'

'You mean joined this lot?'

'Sure.'

'Have we been insane ever since?'

'Insaner—if that's possible. Especially me,' said Mike.

'You mean saving the Navy's life today?'

'Well that, I suppose. And getting engaged to Eileen. That was plumb crazy. The two things are linked.'

They walked past Mike's bungalow, watching the sea beyond the barbed wire pounding the pebble beach. Keith offered a cigarette and Mike lit them both.

Keith asked, 'If you'd known it was the Navy in that kite, would you have helped him back?'

'I'm not prepared to answer that.'

'Why not?'

'Because I don't know. In the balance, yes, I guess.'

Keith laughed, and paused at the broken gate to 'Sussex Glory'. 'On that reckoning, everything's in the balance. Since we went insane, I mean. Lots of balancing stuff. Very high wire stuff.'

Mike turned to walk back. 'Without a safety net.'

Was Mike recovering? Keith wondered. A lot would depend on the next few weeks—for him and everyone else for that matter.

Some very high flashes in the sky to the west over Portsmouth were followed seconds later by the beat of a bomber's engines and the faint crack of exploding shells.

As if catching a second wind, Keith felt restless and in no need of sleep. In his room, the black-out curtains were undrawn, the window open. He sat on the sill, looking out to sea, and lit another cigarette. It was quiet, no sound above the regular wash of waves. He thought again about this day of ordeal and jubilation, death and survival. Surely there would never be another like it. Surely this battle had to end. And one day, at last, they would be given leave. Generous leave. And he could lie night after night with Jenny again—Jenny with a mended leg and no plaster. Soon, for heaven's sake!

The murmur of a voice came to his ears. The ever-gambling Canadians were still at it? No, it came from the wrong direction, and it was near, very near, yet only a murmur. Then he realized it came from this bungalow, from the next room, on the opposite side to Wrynkowski's, Winston-Greville's. Talking in his sleep? It was not easy to pick out the words, and Keith had no special desire to do so. But the voice became louder, and the words were easily audible. 'No, not again. That's enough. Well, they always said it'd be like this.'

The accent was less grand in his sleep, perhaps the authentic voice of the real Winston-Greville, or whatever his real name was. It became faint again and Keith lost the words, and began to undress for bed. There was silence as he got into his pyjamas, and he lay still, his hands behind his head, staring out through the window at the square of moonlit sea and sky.

One more sunset gone. No, you're not allowed to say that. Then he thought of Jenny again, pretending this might make him feel less wide awake.

It did. He was in the half-world between uncon-sciousness and wakefulness when the voice began again, and he jumped with the shock. 'Go on, you bloody coward,' Winston-Greville was saying, roughly, as if in challenge to someone, and Keith, through his exasperation, could not help wondering at the irony of the words. The voice continued, more as a murmur, with only occasional words distinguishable, but the sound preventing Keith from going to sleep.

At last he got up, walked angrily to the door, along the short length of corridor and into the next room, ready to shake the man awake. There was no need for that. Winston-Greville was wide awake, a tall figure sitting at a table by the window, fully dressed in his uniform, the F.A.A. wings visible in the moonlight on his sleeve, his long black hair in a state of disorder.

Keith saw him turn, observed the light of the moon reflecting on a face that was pouring with sweat or tears, and heard his voice. 'Get out of here, Stewart. Get out. Get out, or I'll shoot you.'

Keith saw that he held a gun in his hand, Royal Navy issue revolver, undoubtedly loaded, and certainly about to be fired if Keith did not do something about it. He backed away to the door. 'What are you going to do with that, you fool?' he said shakily.

'What do you think, you jumped-up little bastard? I'm going to shoot you. And then me.' Winston-Greville laughed. It was on a high-pitched note, not the deep boom Keith had heard when he was with women or showing off to airmen.

Keith slid to one side of the door so that he would not be in silhouette against the faint light in the corridor. 'I shouldn't do that,' he said gravely. 'I shouldn't do either of those things. Very foolish.' He moved beside the bed and along the dark wall.

'Don't move. I can see you.'

But Keith was sure he was lying, or almost sure.

'I'm going to fire. I'm going to shoot you, Stewart.'

206

The voice was hysterical, high-pitched like the laugh. His hand would be shaking, too. Or so Keith hoped.

'Get out!' Winston-Greville shouted.

And then Keith jumped at the table, throwing it onto the man, who fell to the floor. At the same time, Keith shouted at the top of his voice, 'Polo! Come here.'

He was on top of Winston-Greville, and the man was not fighting back, not even struggling. Keith saw the revolver lying on the linoleum floor in the moonlight, and grasped it and threw it out through the open window.

The lieutenant was crying, a big man sobbing under him like the school bully worsted in a fight; and pathetic, not defiant. 'I can't stand it any longer. I've had too much. I'm no good at this. I'll be thrown out, and that'll be the end. They'll get me. Get me either way.'

There was a pause, and Keith could feel him making an effort to rise. But Polo and Wrynkowski were there, helping to hold him down. Not that there was need for two any more. He wasn't really struggling, only whimpering, 'Give me my gun! Give me my gun, will you . . . It's easier like that.'

The M.O. appeared later. They had got him onto the bed and were listening in mutual embarrassment to the hysterical confession and wishing that he would stop. 'I thought I'd be all right . . . good pilot . . . passed out well . . . not a bad shot . . . Oh God!'

The M.O. gave him an injection and within a minute, his big, too handsome head fell over to one side as if slapped, and he was asleep.

'Poor sod,' said the M.O., who was new to the squadron, new to the R.A.F. and very inexperienced in the ways and attitudes of pilots who have been fighting for weeks. 'I suppose today was too much for him. I'll get him away tomorrow.'

'Poor sod, my arse!' Polo commented on the way back to his room. It sounded like a comic's pay-off line in a northern music hall turn. He was wearing his oil-streaked polo-neck sweater, and before he turned into his room, Keith saw him stuff his pipe into his mouth like a ritual act of defiance against awkward sods who woke him up, and against the world in general. For some reason he did not understand, Keith felt strangely comforted by the expletive, the pipe, and the sweater, and went off to sleep almost as quickly as Lieutenant Winston-Greville had done.

*

Rowbotham was very bullish. 'You can't describe a naval officer as lacking in moral fibre,' he said. 'I mean, L.M.F. is a very dirty word and their Lordships wouldn't understand what it meant anyway.'

Keith said, 'Surely the M.O. can produce some sort of face-saver?'

'He's got him heavily sedated and an orderly with him. I don't want to fuss Group. They'll be up to their eyeballs in bumph today.' He picked up the telephone. 'I'll get through to Pompey direct. They can pack him into Haslar for a while,' he said, naming the big naval hospital at Portsmouth.

Keith had been describing the events of the previous evening to his C.O. 'Bloody rum show,' had been his comment. But the vagaries of life over the past violent weeks had made Rowbotham more imperturbable than ever. His resilience in the face of calamity, or in this case a mere awkward situation, continued to amaze Keith, and led him to realize again how fortunate they were to have his leadership.

Sobered by their losses of the previous day or simply discouraged by the low cloud over England, there was no report of enemy action during the morning. A strange Hurricane dropped in just as the Church Army van drove up, and there was a good deal of cursing among the ground crews when they heard that it contained brass and their break would therefore be interrupted. Then the word shot round—'the ace gen'—that it was not just brass but Air Marshal Park himself. Although the New Zealander was twenty-five years older than most of 140's pilots, he handled the Hurricane with perfect aplomb and as if driving a car, parking it by the club-house and crossing his hands to the awe-struck ground crew to indicate he had finished with his engine.

Rowbotham greeted his commander with a smart salute, and they walked together round Southdean's perimeter, the forty-eight-year-old Great War scout pilot in white flying overalls, with his strong face, grey moustache, shrewd grey eyes and characteristic Kiwi jaw, and the robust squadron commander who was still in the front line. They talked, Rowbotham recounted later, of the state of the battle, the quality of new pilots coming prematurely from operational training schools, and aircraft supply. There appeared to be no problems in supplies of Hurricanes any longer, and Keith Park was cautiously optimistic about the outcome of the battle. Yes, the eight-gun fighter would be superseded by the cannon machine, which was coming through in quantity now and they would soon be getting more. More power from the engine too. And there was something really wizard coming along—talk of top speed of over 400 straight and level.

He stayed for less than an hour, had an informal word with Chiefy and some of the pilots, paying special attention to those from overseas—Wrynkowski who stood strictly to attention throughout, and Mike. After he had taken off again, turning straight onto a northerly course for Uxbridge, Rowbotham explained that he made frequent visits to squadrons, and had chosen 140 today to hear in detail about the loss of his fellow New Zealander, and that he was intending to write a personal letter to his parents decribing the Flight Commander's career and the way he had died.

Then, before they could have lunch, the bell rang, the whole squadron was placed on Readiness, and five minutes later a single section of four was scrambled. Rowbotham led, and both Keith and Mike were included on the sortie, Keith as number two on the C.O.'s right, and Mike as number three, with Polo as four—a powerful foursome of the squadron's veterans who knew one another's special characteristics and qualities.

While taxi-ing out and before turning beside the windsock, now replaced by a standard R.A.F. issue one, they all briefly observed scurrying figures near the watch office. It might have been a group of airmen racing towards a N.A.A.F.I. van, or they might be simply ragging. Only Mike, on the port side of Rowbotham, saw the incident in slightly greater detail. During the take-off run, he gave a quick glance in the direction and witnessed the sight of a dozen or so airmen gathered as if frozen round Watson's T-Toc which was having a twenty-hour service, with its engine panels removed. The steps were no longer in position, and two more airmen were dragging a trolley-ac towards the machine.

The scene registered itself on Mike's mind only because of the number of airmen involved and the uncharacteristic attitude they had assumed for a routine operation of starting a Hurricane apparently for an engine test. Then Mike's eyes flicked back to Rowbotham's machine on his right. He opened the throttle slightly to keep up, and glanced at Polo on his left, who, for once, was taking off with his helmet on and his pipe no doubt in some pocket and burning a hole in it.

They were ordered to patrol off Selsey Bill at angels five. It sounded as if Sector were working on a hunch and that any raid would be small. The Luftwaffe, after serious losses of their twin-engine bombers over so many weeks, was increasingly using fighter-bomber techniques, and the Messerschmitt 110 with its speed of well above 300 m.p.h. was not always easy to intercept. They were above cloud at 5,000 feet, the sun blazing down in contrast to the dour Sussex coastline below, and casting racing shadows of their four aircraft, each with a faint halo, onto the glaring white upper surface of the cloud. There was nothing to be seen except a single distant aircraft inland and high above, and the R/T remained silent.

This is how it must have been in the Great War, Mike was thinking: endless tedium, your own engine the only sound. Also unchanged was the surprise element, the way in which the peace and beauty of the

211

sky could be transformed into fear, pain, death, with the speed of a machine-gun bullet. Mike looked about him, the routine never-ending search, then glanced at his fellow pilots, each so easily recognizable now with their hoods thrown back: Keith most distant and the tallest, back straight, head lifted as he scanned the sky; Polo on his left, much shorter, bow-backed like a scrum-half alertly awaiting the feed of the ball, and Rowbotham, another rugger figure, but prop-forward down for the scrum, and toughest of them all.

Then the C.O., with that smell for trouble that had so often saved them before, took them up another 2,000 feet.

The 110s and 109s—about thirty—detached themselves from the clouds below as if suddenly reborn after long interment and relishing their freedom in a wonderful burst of speed. The Hurricane pilots all saw them at the same time, and were too experienced to break radio silence needlessly. Rowbotham merely waggled his wings, and they followed him in the direction of the formation which was down-sun and had not yet seen them. The enemy must have crossed at nought feet to get under the R.D.F. and gained height and obscurity in the cloud when they had sighted and identified the English coast, intending to drop through cloud again near their target—perhaps Portsmouth dockyard or the Spitfire works at Southampton.

Sector control came through before they had completed their turn, and Rowbotham snapped back, 'We have them. They've turned west at angels four.'

Then the Hurricanes spread out, setting themselves up for a stern attack out of the sun. There were two great imponderables, Mike recognized at once: would they dive or would they fight; and for how much longer could they hope to remain unseen?

There must have been new pilots among the 109s, replacements as green as Mackay, and slack gunners among the 110 crews. They had still not been spotted at 850 yards, less than half a mile, and Mike was making the ridiculous calculation that if they each got one at the first pass that would leave only twenty-six, a mere six and a half to one. He was still wondering whether he had got the figure correctly when he saw, distantly ahead and above, a single machine, which upset his calculations. It was unlikely to be hostile under these circumstances; and, at second glance, Mike recognized the hunchback configuration of a Hurricane, diving, heading straight for the centre and foremost twin-engine Messerschmitt.

'Blue One—bogie ahead and above. One of ours, I think.'

Rowbotham came back, 'I've got it. Who the hell . . . ?'

The long, fast dive at full boost had brought the section of 140 Squadron almost within opening range, the German formation clearly distracted by the hostile machine coming straight at them.

Mike could see now that there was something wrong with the scene, like the unreal stage set on the ground. It wasn't right at all—a distortion of air battle. It was extraordinary that tracer fire was not coming up at them from the rear guns of the *Zerstören*, that there had been no attempt to turn on them; and, as well, the single Hurricane, belching smoke from excessive boost or engine damage, was without its engine panels or propeller boss, exposing its naked interior to the world.

Nor was it opening fire. By now they should be seeing the twinkle of Browning's gunports. But nothing. And still it came on, straight for the leading vic of 110s who were now firing all their formidable forward armament of cannon and machine-guns, tracer whipping round the Hurricane.

'Break—break for Christ's sake!' Mike shouted to himself; and then transmitted the same warning into a void. Before the words were out the Hurricane had struck the centre 110, blasting both machines into a smoke-shrouded ruin of pulverized alloy and steel.

For a moment nothing came out of the crushed mass of aircraft, which had broken up the entire formation, now swerving and banking to regain position. Then black objects, some small, some larger, fell away, no better than bits of a jig-saw puzzle, unrecognizable as pieces of aeroplanes that had collided at a combined speed of 700 m.p.h.

The disorder of the Germans increased 140's advantage, and they seized it with relish. The C.O. was first to score, blowing a 109 to shreds before Mike could open fire. When he did, on a 110 that did not even see him when he came in from below, he fired with the steady precision and accuracy of a young man with a good eye who had shot all his life—rabbits with a 410 when he was only eight, coyotes on a visit to California at ten, deer and bear in the Adirondacks from fourteen, Germans for almost a year now, and plenty of practice . . .

Of the first quarter-deflection burst, scarcely a .303 bullet failed to drill into the Messerschmitt, raking the belly from just forward of the wing root to the cross painted on the port side. The machine twitched at the impact but streamed on—no smoke, both engines O.K., when Mike lifted over, rolling and kicking rudder to evade the lines of fire that would inevitably follow him, then climbing at full boost, elated and bursting with self-confidence.

When he gained enough height, he spotted a 109 hard on his tail, disdainfully kicked the nippy Hurricane into a stall turn, saw him go by, and fell on the twin-engine machines again. They were jettisoning their bombs, diving for cloud. He saw Keith stopping the starboard engine of one of them. Another was consumed with fire, descending like a sycamore seed to its destruction. An upside-down 109 trailed glycol.

Mike took one of them from above this time—the same machine as before, he recognized, with a yellow F at each upper wingtip. No return fire. A sitting target, but a brief one for it was diving as fast as his Hurricane, black overboost smoke pouring from its straining Daimler-Benz engines.

Mike ran the dot from the nose to the tail-end of the cockpit, marking De Wilde strikes like a steady line of sparks struck from a thousand hammers. Checking his tail, he followed the 110 down for another five hundred feet, watching it turn over with the measured steadiness of an aerobatics contestant. It was upside down, wings level, when the cloud engulfed it.

Mike pulled his Hurricane into a sharp climbing turn, and, because it had happened so often before—though no one could explain why—he found the sky clear of any aircraft. Not one Messerschmitt. None of his three squadron members. Only a single fast-fading white cloud that marked some recent catastrophe.

The raid was scattered and must have gone home, utterly defeated in its purpose, but now beyond profitable pursuit. Mike transmitted for a fix and compass course for Southdean, settled himself into his cockpit again as he always did after combat, like a man in bed after making love, and when he had received his course, took off his helmet and with the hood open, allowed the wind to cool his sweating face and stream through his hair.

He was the last to land. Polo's tailplane, he could see, would need some patching, that was all. No one but Rowbotham could make a confirmed claim. The others would have to await reports from the Observer Corps or the Police. But it had been a highly successful morning to celebrate the visit from their Commander, and avenge the losses of yesterday.

Keith strolled over to Mike's J-Johnnie as he jumped down off the wing and gave the thumbs-up sign to his delighted fitter, Lofty Campbell.

Mike asked, 'Who is hell was that crazy loon in the half-cock Hurricane?'

Keith looked at him bleakly, one eyebrow raised. 'That was my fault.'

They walked in together, carrying parachutes and helmets.

'You're nuts, too. Come on, Keith, come clean.'

'It was your friend and my friend Arthur Winston-Greville. He of the oil-streaked screen, of the duff engine at the critical moment, of the matches in his Brownings.'

Mike stopped and stared at him, cigarette unlit between his lips. He took it out and said, 'You're kidding.'

'I'm not. Cross my heart. He held up Chiefy, marched him out to Bill Watson's kite, and when they tried to stop him, he fired one in the air and said he'd shoot him, and anyone else who didn't co-operate. So they brought up the trolley-ac . . .'

'Yeah, I saw, but . . . And how do *you* figure in this?'

'This morning I forgot all about that damn revolver I snatched from him last night.'

'What did you do with it, for chrissake?'

'I chucked it out of the window. *I* forgot. But he didn't. There was an orderly with him when he came round. He was allowed to go for a pee, ran out to that scruffy bit of overgrown garden, picked it up, and apparently went hell for leather for the dispersal. Just as the ambulance arrived, and just as we were scrambled.'

'Well, what d'you know?'

They sat down on deck-chairs, and Stuffy came up, wagging his stumpy tail for attention. Then the Spy joined them, sitting on the grass with his notebook.

'What's all this about?' Keith asked him. 'Are we all going mad?'

'No, only one of us,' replied Williams with a sly smile. 'And he's no longer with the living. And that's going to take some explaining to the Royal Navy. First it's L.M.F. Then a solo suicide effort that stops a raid. Tell that to Admiral Sir Dudley Pound.'

*

The outcome of a battle on land or at sea is usually known by those who fight and survive, not always at once but soon after the last shot is fired, the last man killed. Battles in the air are different. They are so fast, the impressions so fleeting, that the outcome of a combat in which conclusions can be drawn only from individual experiences, and even the identity of the casualties can be confused, for long remains in doubt. In the confusion of a running dogfight at speeds above 300 m.p.h., claims were duplicated, a bomber seen diving south with an engine on fire might survive, a fighter apparently unharmed diving into cloud might never pull out, its end in the Channel unwitnessed. German claims were sometimes exaggerated five times over, and R.A.F. figures of German losses were nearly always optimistic, too.

The Battle of Britain had no recognizable beginning, no single climax, no day on which Goering's pilots could say we have lost, nor Dowding's pilots claim we have won. German recognition that the Luftwaffe had not defeated Fighter Command came gradually, high in the autumn sky, when the massive bomber formations continued to face up to the furious attacks of a dozen squadrons of Hurricanes and Spitfires, at the same time when their leader was boasting to the world that the British Air Force was *kaput*. Disillusionment and dismay grew slowly but relentlessly amongst the German ground crews every time a dead or wounded crewman was lifted from a crash-landed Dornier in a French field; amongst the officers in high command when they learned that the date of the invasion—'Operational Seelöwe'—was once again postponed; amongst the crews of the German high speed launches and seaplanes every time *Seenotflugkommando* picked up a sodden, shaking 109 pilot from the Channel. It was cumulative, and finally deadly in its effect.

For the hard-pressed R.A.F. squadrons, intimations of success became perceptible only over a period of time, too, from the second half of September to the middle of October: in the fewer sightings of twin-engined bombers; in the longer periods—sometimes for a whole day—of being stood down; in the ample supply of aircraft; in the opportunities for practice flying for newly-posted pilots.

Recognition of victory was further delayed by new German tactics, by withdrawing altogether the bomber force from daylight attacks and switching them more and more to night bombing, and limiting day bombing to 110, and 109 fighters equipped with a single 250 kg bomb slung under their fuselage.

With the postponement on 12 October of the invasion until the next year, the R.A.F. had won the greatest and most decisive air battle in history—a struggle that had lasted longer than the Spanish Armada battle over 350 years earlier. But no one knew it at the time, even Dowding and his Group Commanders. And the rank and file of the R.A.F. were too preoccupied dealing with these new methods of attack, both of which proved very intractable, to comprehend the full meaning of what they had accomplished. The making of history is really a matter-of-fact business.

Two episodes brought home to 140 Squadron the continuing and devastating power of the Luftwaffe. Several airmen, whose homes in East London had been reduced to rubble in night bombing, returned from compassionate leave with accounts of the destruction of London's docks, of fires raging for days and nights on end, of whole streets devastated, warehouses blown up, the smoke from oil installations turning day into night and flames turning night into day. One of the airmen had lost both his parents. Sixty had been killed and hundreds injured by a single landmine. There had been panic, and looting, and thousands of people had brushed aside the police and wardens to seek shelter illegally in the underground stations.

Then, on 7 October, a Spitfire of 78 Squadron landed at Southdean, short of fuel and with several cannon holes in its fuselage. Keith and Mike were among several of 140 Squadron who talked to the pilot at the bar before lunch. He was a little Welsh Flying Officer, Taffy Jones. They had known him at Savile Farm, and now he was a highly-experienced pilot with four swastikas painted alongside the cockpit of his machine.

'It's the damn height, man,' he told them over a pint. 'And their speed. They come in sometimes fifty at a time, thirty-two thou, going Harry clappers, and—you know—we just can't get there. Come and go, like, while we're still pushing it up to twenty thou.'

Rowbotham said, 'They can't be doing much damage with one small bomb.'

'You tell that to Group,' the Welshman said. 'Very vexed in London they are. And a hundred a day of those kill a lot of people.'

They discussed the new tactics Park was using to counter this menace. These fighter-bombers were not going to win the war for Germany. They weren't going to pave the way for invasion either. But for the present the Luftwaffe controlled the higher skies over south-east England, and this was depressing and humiliating.

Mike asked, 'Where did you pick up those shells?'

'Well, that's it. I'll tell you . . .' And he did so, thirstily over another pint. Because the R.D.F. found difficulty in picking up these very high, very fast plots, and the Observer Corps could not see them even on a clear day, the 11 Group Spitfire squadrons had resorted to keeping a standing patrol during daylight hours over Kent, a sort of flying observer's post at around 28,000 feet. But it was an extremely hazardous business because these scouts could easily be bounced out of the sun and face overwhelming odds. Just this had happened to Taffy Jones that morning, and his number two had been shot down.

'The Spit, see, can't match the 109's dive,' he explained. 'Fifty against two of us, and a hell of a donny, I'll tell you.' The little dark Welshman studied the bottom of his empty mug mournfully. 'I can see no end to it, man.'

'Cheer up, Taffy. It's the end of that drink. Have another pint. We'll fix them in the end,' was Rowbotham's comment.

And so they did, but it took time. A few days later, both Keith and Mike were involved in an engagement that would help finish the menace of the high-flying fighter-bomber. It was the last big action in which they were involved in the long drawn out battle, and for this reason they remembered it in all its vivid detail long after the end of 1940.

It was late October, the long days when they could be scrambled at 5 a.m. or 10 p.m. were over, no longer did any pilot fly in shirt sleeves. After four months, the British Sector and Group controllers knew every German trick and could read the mind of the Luftwaffe High Command. It was not just an inspired guess that led Park and his Staff to calculate that a morning raid by some fifty 109s, half of them carrying bombs, would be followed forty-five minutes later—on the premise that the defenders would be refuelling and rearming—by a much bigger raid. Only two squadrons of Spitfires were scrambled to meet the first plots, and failed to make contact. But before they landed, Spitfires from Biggin Hill (like Savile Farm, now fully operational again), Hornchurch and other aerodromes were scrambled to 30,000 feet over southeast Kent, and four Hurricane squadrons took off and patrolled at their maximum effective altitude of 22,000. One of these was 140 Squadron, another the first all-Czech Hurricane Squadron.

The trap worked to perfection. A few minutes after mid-day, with a lot of high cirrus and five-tenths lower cloud, a scout Spitfire reported bandits high to the south and coming in fast over the coast. All the fifty-five Spitfires positioned themselves in the sun, dived through the top cover 109 fighters and pounced on the fighter-bombers.

Keith saw the fight above intermittently through the patchy cirrus and sensed victory in the biggest fighter battle of the war. He counted seven 109s screaming down in flames, two more crippled German machines were pounced on by the Czechs as they came down and blown up with impunity. Far below, scattered explosions in open farmland told of jettisoned bombs.

'Sandbag Leader calling B Flight, take that lot at three o'clock,' Rowbotham transmitted.

Inevitably, the dogfight was losing height as the 109s struggled to break free and dive back to the Pas de Calais across the Channel they now so hated and feared. For once, the R.A.F. were fighting with equal numbers and taking full advantage of their tactical superiority over their own land and close to their bases. The air was as full of whirling, diving, twisting, climbing planes as the ether with sharply spoken orders and urgent warnings. There were planes upside down, vertically climbing, jinking in frenzied evasion, diving to their own destruction or to the destruction of an enemy plane, turning so sharply that wingtips trailed streamers . . . Black cross, roundel, roundel, black cross, roundel, black cross.

Keith hurled his Hurricane after a vertically banking 109, got in a half-second burst, saw no hits, dived after another, lost it in cloud, climbed again at emergency boost, almost collided with a Spitfire, and caught up with another 109—caught it up so fast that he almost overshot it, steadied himself with the words of warning with which he so often instructed himself in combat, checked turn-and-bank and got in a long burst with half deflection.

The 109 made no attempt to evade, and afterwards Keith wondered if the pilot was already dead. Flames flicked from the engine exhaust, spread with awful speed engulfing the cockpit, consuming the whole fuselage. He had never been such a close eyewitness to a flamer, nor seen a fighter burn like this, and he prayed that the pilot had died earlier. It fell from

223

view below him, and he made no attempt to turn and watch it, instead kicking round his tail to check that he was not about to be jumped himself.

There was nothing in sight above or below except a crippled Spitfire, one wheel lowered, losing height over Faversham and heading for an awkward landing, and a lone 109 diving steeply to the south like a straggler from a hold-up. Keith gave chase, but it was too fast for him, and the last he saw of it was at 5,000 feet heading for Dover, where it received the full ack-ack treatment, its course marked by an excited trail of grey puffs.

Keith picked up Mike in the circuit. As usual after sustained combat, the American had taken off his helmet to let the cooling wind through his hair, and he grinned at Keith and gave the thumbs-up sign before turning onto the final approach with wheels and full flaps down.

So they had both scored! Eleven all. It was remarkable how their success ran in such close parallel. They had both been shot down once, too. But the days of high scoring were slipping away with the lengthening nights and the lack of bombers in the daylight sky.

After a late lunch, 140 was stood down. It was a cold, wet afternoon, and Keith proposed a trip to East Grinstead to see Buffer Davies at the burns hospital.

'It would seem the right thing to take Garbo,' Keith suggested. 'The sound of her exhaust might cheer up the old boy.'

Buffer Davies, their contemporary and old friend, had been shot down in flames on 4 July by a 109 escorting a Stuka raid on a Channel convoy. Keith had last seen him, upside down and losing height, the underside of his Hurricane torn open by cannon fire and with smoke pouring from his engine. He had later reported him as shot down and killed. But the lusty, happy-go-lucky ex-racing driver had always been a great survivor, and he had managed to get out, a cannon shell in his thigh and with terrible burns to his hands and face. He had been picked up unconscious from the sea, and had been under the care of the great burns healer, Archibald McIndoe, ever since.

'Are we brave enough?' Mike asked. 'We don't want a spot of bother with that motor,' he said in his ghastly parody of an English upper class accent which he sometimes affected when he was particularly pleased with life. It was many weeks since Keith had heard it and he was relieved at this further sign that he was getting over the loss of Eileen.

Rowbotham signed a chit to M.T. authorizing the petrol when Keith explained the mission of mercy, and he started up the huge engine. Garbo, which had proved as effective a survivor as its master through the two bombings of Savile Farm, was a 'special' built by Buffer in 1936 for racing at Brooklands, featuring a Bentley Speed Six engine in a cut-down truck chassis, bodied in aluminium with a pointed tail and two small bucket seats. Buffer had regularly driven it on the open road at 120 m.p.h.

Keith drove it as quietly and circumspectly as he could through the rain-sodden suburbs but could not help letting the great car have her head once or twice on the open road towards East Grinstead. They were exhilarated and soaking wet when they arrived.

'You'll find quite a change in Flying Officer Davies,' the matron warned them. 'He has had a lot of operations since you last saw him.'

They had both heard of the appalling disfigurement caused by facial burns and had already prepared themselves for the worst—or thought that they had until the double swing doors of the lounge swung open and a figure in a wheel-chair was pushed in by a nurse. For a moment Keith thought he was the patient awaited by the middle-aged couple on the other side of the room, and he looked away, anxious not to be caught staring.

When the familiar voice spoke, the old mock-cad's voice which Keith had always found so engaging, it was as if it came from a masked figure with a stocking pulled tight over the head, with slits for eyes and mouth; and to his own horror Keith audibly gasped.

'Well, ol' boys, decent of you to visit a feller in distress. Yes, it's ol' Buffer all right,' he laughed tinnily. 'Bit different now. Not such a wow with the ladies, eh? Lost that jolly seductive moustache.'

They both got up and hastened to relieve the nurse of her charge, pushing the wheel-chair close to the sofa where they had been sitting.

'It's grand to see you,' Keith managed to say. 'They *have* mucked you about a bit, haven't they?'

'Thirteen ops so far. Worth putting in the log book, what? Another low level sortie to the slab next week. They're trying to find me a jolly ol' nose to stick on.'

Mike had turned grey with the shock and did not speak until Buffer turned his white, creased mask of a face with the tiny pig eyes towards him and asked for news of the chaps.

'I guess there aren't many of the old bunch left,' Mike said shakily. 'Kiwi Robinson went for a burton last week. Polo's still around.' He laughed uncertainly. 'You know, Polo, if a Hun gets on his tail he just lights his goddam pipe and that fixes him. Chemical warfare.'

They talked shop and drank tea, Buffer through a straw helped by a nurse.

Then Keith asked, 'What about your popsies? Any of them come to see you?' The idea suddenly struck him as ludicrous and he wished he had not been so tactless.

'No, ol' boy. Course, I'm havin' to fight them off they're so crazy to see me. Thought I'd get my new face first. May take a bit of time.' Buffer's voice faded for the first time, losing its note of cheerful optimism. 'Yes, a bit of time yet.'

Mike chipped in quickly. 'We came in Garbo. I guess we thought you might like to hear the song of her exhaust. That's what you call it?'

There was no response in Buffer's face that he was pleased. It was the expressionless face by contrast with the old voice that was hardest to bear. And now the voice did express genuine pleasure. 'That's awfully decent of you, very spiffin'. How did the ol' girl go, eh?'

'Like a dream. I opened her up, just to clear the plugs and let her exercise herself,' Keith said.

'I'll come and watch you go off in her,' said Buffer. 'Nurse, will you take me to the front door?'

The rain had stopped and shafts of sunshine were playing on the drive. Keith wiped the aero screens and started up the Bentley engine. He pulled her up outside the front portico, the engine burbling at tick-over speed. The last they saw of Buffer was his figure in the wheel-chair just inside the open front door, his face like a crudely-formed effigy for some barbarous tribe, a deformed thumb raised above a deformed hand, the only recognition he could offer.

Then Mike blipped the throttle several times and took off as spectacularly as he dared with much flying gravel. They did not speak until they reached Redhill, where they were briefly held up at traffic lights. Raising his voice above the sound of the engine Mike simply said, 'My God, Keith.'

'I'd rather have the quick bullet than that,' Keith said. 'And Buffer of all people. What did we do to deserve such luck?' He still could not wipe his retina clear of that grotesque visage, the lipless mouth working like a ventriloquist's doll's.

*

For two successive days the poor weather kept the skies clear of the enemy. Then on the next fine day he did not come. Nor on the next day. The last mass assault by fighter-bombers, itself the last German tactical extemporization, had been tried, found wanting, and been severely mauled by the Command that had never accepted defeat. It was November. The daylight Battle of Britain was over. The threat of invasion had been destroyed, for that year anyway.

On 8 November a signal arrived for Mike, posting him on temporary detachment to Church Fenton, where 71 (Eagle) Squadron was working itself up to operational status on Brewster Buffaloes and Hurricanes. American pilots had crossed the Atlantic in such numbers that they had now been formed into one squadron. Almost every one of the handful of Americans who had fought through the battle were dead. Mike's experience would be priceless to these raw pilots, but he was not pleased to be leaving Savile Farm.

'Back to school to teach a bunch of rookies,' he grumbled as he packed his bags. 'I guess the war's over for us, Keith.'

Mike had never made a more inaccurate prediction in his life, and even Keith thought he was being over-optimistic, though he added, 'I hope you're right. Then I won't have to come back from leave.'

'How long have you got?'

'A week. Seven days. A lifetime.'

'Where're you going?' Mike asked.

'Where do you think, dim type?'

Mike secured his smart leather bags from Abercrombies and got up from his bed. 'Yeah, I guess I'll have to get me another girl. This celibate life doesn't suit me now we've got time to think.'

It was his first reference for weeks, if an indirect one, to his loss of Eileen.

'We may as well go up to London together,' Keith said. 'We could call in on Tom and Moira before our trains leave.'

It was black-out time when their taxi arrived, and the sirens were going. 'There's old Jerry, regular as clockwork,' said the driver philosophically as he shut the door on them.

8

ONE NIGHT'S TOLL

It was dark when they crossed Waterloo Bridge on foot and there was little traffic about. The raid had not developed and there were only one or two nuisance bombers about, mostly over the docks area. They could see several searchlights groping about the cloud base lethargically, as if unhopeful of finding their target, and the gunfire was intermittent. The office workers making for Waterloo hurried towards the station; a few stray bombers were far beneath notice.

Keith waved down a passing taxi with a shaded torch on Kingsway, and they were at Tom and Moira's bedsitter by seven o'clock.

Moira threw her arms round Keith's neck and kissed Mike on the cheek. 'How marvellous! Can you stay the night? You must. I've got some food. Tom, look who's here!'

Tom took off his spectacles as he emerged from the far end of the room where he had been bending over his desk. New spectacles; and a new sign of the strain reflected in his face, the pressure of overwork and lack of sleep. But he was as welcoming as Moira and looked them both up and down as if appraising them for damage. 'Grand to see you. How are you? Look at those flashy ribbons, Moira.'

They drank cider and, inevitably, talked about the Blitz. Tom was on the wards and had to help move patients to the hospital basement when there was an alert, and then stand by fire-watching over at the hospital laboratories. Four hours' sleep was a rare luxury, Moira told them, two more than usual. He was passionately, savagely bitter about the indiscriminate nature of the bombing. Keith had always regarded him as a man of peace, but like so many others, being in the front line had radically changed his views.

'My God, I hope you two have killed a lot of the bastards,' he said, long white fingers nervously fingering his glass. 'They hit University College Library the other night—a hundred thousand books up in smoke. Like those fires of books by Jewish writers in Munich—remember? Barbarians. But that's nothing. Come and see some of the wounded children we've got—blind, double amputees, broken backs and crippled for life.' He lit a cigarette with shaking hands, drawing on it deeply. Smoking was new too. He had always been against it. 'Or take those fifty geriatrics—all smashed to pieces when a land mine hit their ward.'

Mike said, 'Bad as that, is it? We're beginning to feel out of it now. A while back we were in the front line. Now I guess we're feeling guilty. We ought to be stopping the bastards. But it's the R.A.F.'s Achilles' heel.'

'Like the Navy not being able to fight dark in the Great War,' said Keith. 'But Jerry doesn't seem to mind. All he's got to do is cruise over London, shut his eyes and press the tit. Can't miss.'

'I'm going to get some supper,' Moira broke in. 'Tom, you'd better tell Keith.'

'Tell me what?'

Tom lit a second cigarette from the first. He was obviously reluctant to talk, and took a long drag on his cigarette and another drink before beginning. 'It's about Eileen.'

'Go on.'

'Well, you'll have to know some time,' and turning to Mike, added, 'I'm terribly sorry. I know how you felt about her. But she took up with some naval chap—an officer, I think. She's an officer herself now, you know.'

Keith said, 'Yes, I saw them together that night at the Savoy.'

'It seems unbelievable,' went on Tom. 'But she apparently got herself pregnant—Eileen of all people! And she had an abortion in a panic. Some back-street so-called posh clinic. Then septicaemia—it happens sometimes in those places. She got a message to me through a nurse, and I got our gyney man to get her out and into our place.'

'Is it dangerous?' Keith asked.

'Yes, very.'

'Is she going to die?'

'Fifty-fifty. Her parents came down to see her yesterday. They don't know the cause, of course. Not yet, anyway. I took them along myself to see her, made up some story about a minor injury turning septic, talked about overstrain, that sort of thing.'

Mike said breathlessly, 'When can I go and see her?'

'I think that would be a bad idea,' Tom said. 'Under the circumstances.'

A distant all-clear sounded its monotonous note, and was repeated raucously by the nearby Tottenham Court Road siren. Moira brought bowls of soup on a tray. 'Do you think we're going to have a quiet night for once, Keith?'

'I wish I knew,' he said abstractedly, still unable to take in the reality of what Tom had been saying. But Moira's question was answered after no more than two minutes of silence from the sirens by a renewal of the wailing, this time on the doom-laden undulating note. As they finished their soup and began on bread and pickles and cheddar cheese, they heard through their talk the deep pulsing sound of the first bombers. Tom's ears, canny now after weeks of bombing, recognized the nature of the attack before the first crumps of high explosive reached them in their fourth-floor room with windows and black-out curtains both closed.

'It's the real thing this time,' he said. 'I've got to push off.' He grabbed a tin helmet from the hook on the door and slung his gas-mask over his shoulder. 'Moira, you get down to the shelter. Take the blanket. I'll see you after the all-clear.'

Keith got up and said, 'I'm going to stay here till tomorrow, Mike. But I'll come to the station with you. And we'd better go before they prang it.'

Mike's train for Church Fenton was to leave in half an hour, if it was going to leave at all, with a change because of a blocked line, and the three of them followed Tom down into the dark street, where he ran off towards the Middlesex. Moira kissed them both good-bye, whispering earnestly in Keith's ear, 'I think *you* ought to see her.'

Then they saw her pause before making for the street shelter. 'Forgotten my torch,' she said, and ran inside again.

Keith and Mike walked up Tottenham Court Road and then cut through the narrower streets of the residential areas of Bloomsbury. There were a lot of bombers over this part of London now. The guns on Primrose Hill and in Regent's Park were firing rapidly, their muzzle flashes scoring the night above the skyline with a rippling splash of bright yellow, the heavy shells sounding a rustling noise. One, two, three, rapidly, four-five-six-seven almost simultaneously . . . Pause. Then again . . . The crump of their explosion thousands of feet above was a distant echo of the blasts that had sent them on their way, and in gaps in the cloud, which was now broken, they could sometimes see the winking sparkles of the bursts. The wild blitz orchestra sounded other notes: the light peppering sound of shell splinters on rooftops and roads, the thunderous crash of exploding bombs accompanied by the avalanche of collapsing buildings, and—as always—the uneven, unending droning chorus of the Heinkels and Dorniers high above.

'Take me back to good old Savile Farm,' Keith shouted. Farther up the road, towards Euston Station, a blinding flash silhouetted the intervening buildings and they felt for the first time the stirring of the air about them, the dying end of the blast which had toppled walls and roofs a quarter-mile away.

'That was a land-mine,' Mike said. 'I guess we're pretty stupid not to be in a shelter.'

Any doubts about the wisdom of taking cover were

decided for them by a warden on a bicycle. He got off when he saw them walking side by side on the pavement. 'There's a shelter down there,' he called out, pointing with his torch. 'Get into it.'

'But we've got a train to catch,' Keith protested.

'You'll be catching worse than trains if you don't get down there. Go on—hop it, quick. You ain't God almighty cos you're orficers . . .'

They ran down the street as ordered, identifying the brick shelter in the middle of the road by the 'S' sign.

Here was an unexpected and astonishing world, by contrast with the empty streets. It was packed with people, like some Topolski caricature of a cocktail party crush. The host—the shelter warden—was a figure of power and authority less concerned with the enjoyment than the discipline of his guests.

'Not much room left in 'ere,' he said. 'You'll just 'ave to muck in with the rest.'

The air was foul with the stench of bodies, and by the dim light they could see women and children and some elderly men lying or squatting or sitting on the ground. A bench running the length of the walls was tight-packed, hip to hip. Others had curled up on the concrete floor with a blanket and cushion. A family had brought in their fish and chips in newspapers and were eating them standing in a circle, silent in their ritual. There was a noisy group at the far end singing 'Roll out the Barrel' to a concertina, a couple tight-clutched together standing in the corner. A woman with long, lank hair hanging over her face, was changing a baby's nappy amid complaints from her neighbours. 'Shut up! Just shut up!' she was shouting in an ever-repeated litany.

235

Keith and Mike squeezed up into the corner close to the embracing couple, the only place where there seemed to be standing room.

'Oooh, look who we 'ave 'ere.' An elderly woman with few teeth looked up from the floor 'A couple of Brylcreem boys. You'll look after us, won't you, loves?'

Mike said, 'Sure we will, ma'am.' And a man on the bench, bald and sallow, in neck-tie and with a rumpled old jacket, hands on the cap on his knees, snapped, 'You ought to be up there dealing with them. All posh glamour, you lot, while we're being killed down 'ere.'

Mike turned away, exchanging bleak looks with Keith.

Another voice, half lost in ' . . . we'll 'ave a barrel of fun . . .' shouted, 'Cork it, Arthur. Them boys're doing a good job. They're The Few, Winnie said.'

The smell of sweat and the congealing fat of the fish and chips were making Keith feel sick. 'Let's get out,' he said.

The shelter warden stood in their way. 'You can't leave now,' he said, in a voice unaccustomed to being questioned yet on the brink of sounding craven.

'You try and stop us,' Mike said roughly. 'There's a guy in there telling us we ought to be getting airborne.' He pushed past the official and out into the cool, clean night air that smelt only faintly of cordite and smoke. The bombing was at its height, the noise cacophonous. From not far away but almost drowned by the crackle of flames, voices were shouting, the words inaudible but the note unarguably urgent.

In strange contrast to the violence and noise, a taxi

236

with flag up cruised along the street towards them, and they hailed it as if they had just emerged from Hatchetts.

'Euston,' Keith told the driver, who had a pipe clenched between his teeth and appeared oblivious to everything taking place about him. Keith could just see him nodding wordlessly as he climbed in.

It was a circuitous journey, involving many diversions, and it took them a quarter of an hour to get to Euston, where the great Doric portico reflected the flames of a fire in the Euston Road.

Mike got out and Keith paid off the driver. On an impulse, he said to him as they walked towards the barrier, 'I'm going to see Eileen tomorrow. Shall I give her a message?'

Mike dropped his bag and turned on him. 'Why can't I see her?' he demanded.

'Because they don't think it'll be good for her. I can see why, too. It's obviously touch and go and . . .'

Keith had never seen a man so crushed with anguish and grief.

Mike said, 'Will you let me know when you're through? Send me a telegram.'

'I'll try and telephone you later, in the evening. Six o'clock, so be near it.'

'Jesus, what a mess! What a mess of a life! What a goddam mess of a war!' He paused, and before walking off to the barrier, said, 'Tell her I love her, will you? Nothing absolutely nothing, makes any difference.'

Keith decided to take the tube back to Warren Street and walk from there.

He had heard that the stations were being used as shelters but was unprepared for the scene that met him below. There were hundreds of people lying or sitting on deck-chairs along the length of the platform, leaving only a few feet for passengers using the trains. Unlike the street shelter, this had a settled, secure air about it. A policeman and a shelter marshal were in charge, and the marshal was instructing a man to turn down the volume of his portable gramophone that was playing dance music. Picnics were being eaten from greaseproof paper packets, and half-undressed children added to the illusion that this was Margate beach in summer. Even an enterprising Walls ice cream man with a tray secured round his neck was picking his way among the bodies doing good late night business.

The Northern Line train ran into the station, and passengers got off and on, ignoring the packed platform. 'London Can Take It!' was the current poster claim; and down here at least, Keith saw, it was not empty propaganda.

It was all noise and confusion again when Keith emerged from the station into Tottenham Court Road. An ambulance raced past, one front wheel running unevenly on a puncture. There was a fire engine behind it, and a Wolseley police car, its bell ringing. The guns from the north-west were still pounding away as the bomber stream came in from the south and east. There were enough fires—an especially big one from the Oxford Street direction—to make a torch unnecessary.

The street where Tom and Moira had their room had its own fire, and as Keith hurried towards the

238

house, he saw that the blaze was close to it. He began running. It was not just close. It was consuming it, along with two houses on either side, old early Victorian houses with much tinder-dry wood that was providing the fuel for the blaze.

There was a single small A.F.S. appliance in the street, its hoses spread across the road and over the fresh-fallen rubble. They had got a single jet playing on the conflagration but it had no chance against these flames, and as Keith came near the jet died to a trickle. The hydrant had packed up, the mains severed somewhere in the complex tracery of London's streets.

A crowd held back by two Special Constables was on the far side of the street, anxious, upturned faces illuminated unevenly by the flames. Keith saw Tom among them and joined him.

'Any sign of Moira?' Keith asked, remembering how she had run back into the house as they left.

'No. They've taken out some bodies. But not hers. She went to the shelter, didn't she?'

'She was going to. She'll be all right. Moira's indestructible.'

Tom looked about him as if hoping to see her run down the street, her plump face glowing and happy. But there was only another fire engine in sight, a bigger appliance this time. The roof had already fallen in, and now two more floors crashed, sending out a cloud of sparks and a renewed blast of heat. The police were moving them away, shouting as men shout when seized by fear, raucously and with aimless gestures.

'Get away—go on, clear the street. Get to the shelters, you bloody fools.'

And then, as the crowd stumbled raggedly away,

Tom's dream of a moment before came partly true. Out of an alleyway Moira emerged, running, her face pink in the glare of the fire. She fell into Tom's arms. 'Oh, it's gone—our lovely room—oh, Tom!'

She was sobbing, and he patted her shoulder. 'It doesn't matter. You're safe, that's all that matters. We'll get another room.'

'But all your papers! And that lovely bed you bought. I heard in the shelter, and then I rushed to the hospital to try to find you. . . . '

Keith took them each by an arm and led them down the alley. 'Come on with me. I'm going to get you both a bed.'

They looked back for the last time. The water was coming through again, and the big engine had three jets on the blaze. But Niagara Falls could not save those houses now. The last floor fell in, and the firemen were stumbling back from a wall leaning over crazily towards the centre of the street.

All the taxis appeared to have gone home or been blown up. Keith saw a car edging its way along Oxford Street avoiding scattered rubble, and he raised his hand to stop it.

'Would you mind taking us to the Flying Club?' he asked the driver. 'These two have been bombed out and they need sleep.'

There was a big store blazing in Oxford Street with a dozen or more appliances outside, hoses intertwined like a pit of serpents and playing criss-crossing jets onto the fire. It looked as unprofitable an exercise as the one they had just left. Glass tinkled under the wheels of the car, and a barrier across the road was manned by police who sent them down through Soho.

Keith directed the driver to Pall Mall. He was an uncommunicative man, and as they felt shy at talking among themselves, the journey was undertaken in a strained silence which made them more than ever aware of the thunder of the raid. At the club Keith got out with his bag and thanked their driver. 'Where are you going now?' he asked him.

'I don't know.' He was a grave-featured man in a pin-striped business suit and there was a bowler hat on the seat beside him.

Keith paused momentarily. 'Can I direct you anywhere, sir?'

'No, not really, thank you, young man. You see, my wife was killed last night, and I don't know what to do.' He engaged the clutch of his Morris Oxford and drove off down Pall Mall.

There was only one member in the club lounge, and he was asleep. To Moira it was one more new world in a world gone mad. There was a lingering smell of good Havana cigar smoke. She stood looking about her in amazement, at the deep sofas, the tables stacked with magazines, the reading stands and the pictures on the walls of Western Front dog-fighting in the Great War, the airship R101 in flight, an Imperial Airways airliner at Croydon, a Spitfire in a dive. 'Well, it's all that I imagined it would be, but I still can't believe it.'

'You will when you wake up in the morning,' Keith said. 'Take a pew—or rather, take a sofa. We don't have beds at the Flying. I'll get some blankets.'

He rang a bell on the wall, and after a long interval a club servant appeared from the shelter in the basement. He did not look pleased at being brought up, and glanced in dismay at Moira who was making herself comfortable with cushions. 'Excuse me, sir, we don't have ladies in the club.'

'We do tonight,' said Keith brusquely. 'What is more, she requires some blankets. And so does my friend— and I require some too.'

The man muttered something about its being highly irregular, and Keith apologized but asked him to go.

The thick walls of the old building and the heavy velvet black-out curtains muffled the sound of the raid and seemed to insulate them from any threat from high explosive. Keith told the servant to build up the fire when he came back with half a dozen blankets, and they settled down for the night with a bottle of brandy. At midnight, as the all-clear sounded, Moira expressed herself as 'slightly squiffy' and was tucked up by Tom.

'It isn't as nice as our poor old bed, darling,' were her last words. 'But if one is going to be bombed out, this is a rather classy way of doing it . . .'

*

Keith saw Eileen the next morning. Tom took him along to her room while Moira registered as being bombed out and arranged for accommodation in a Rest Centre.

'About the same,' the sister told Tom in answer to his enquiry. 'Please don't stay more than five minutes.'

Keith's first impression after all these weeks was of Eileen's loveliness, made more delicate by the paleness of her face. Her fair, russet-touched hair was spread out over the pillow, and there was a serenity about her which seemed in odd contradiction to the

242

cause of her critical illness. At first she only turned her eyes towards them, then when she recognized them, she turned her head slowly on the pillow and smiled at Keith. She whispered something he could not hear and he bent down.

'Kiss me, Keith darling,' she said very softly. 'If you can forgive me.'

He did so, noting how cold her cheek was. He did not know what to say, and eventually said lamely, 'I'm sorry about this. Tom says you'll soon be better.'

Her eyes turned to Tom, challenging the lie, and Tom said, 'I'll drop in later,' and left.

Eileen turned her green eyes back to Keith and spoke again, but he had to put his ear close to her lips. 'How is Mike?' she asked. She paused as if searching for courage, or perhaps only for strength. 'Tell him I am sorry. Truly sorry. I can't ask him to forgive, but tell him that.'

'He's all right. Better now, anyway. He told me to tell you nothing makes any difference. He got a D.F.C. and now he's off to teach some other Americans.'

She raised a white hand from the bed as if to touch Keith's striped ribbon. 'You too,' she said, and smiled. Then the smile faded and she began to speak again, more quietly than ever. 'I can't explain why I did it, Keith, I don't understand. Not now. You know, I didn't even like him much.' She spoke slowly. 'Something about the Admiralty staff, everyone swamping me with compliments.' She smiled. 'Very different from Wycombe Abbey and that terrible place in Paris . . .'

'Try to forget about it. Shame and remorse won't help you to get better. And you need everything on your side.'

'Keith, I'm wasting their time. Terrible waste of time. So stupid . . . real people suffering, people bombed.' She turned her eyes towards him again. 'Am I going to die, Keith?'

He knew he had to be quick with his response, and uncompromisingly truthful, too. 'No, you won't die if you want to live very badly. But you might if you give up the struggle a little. So don't.' He kissed her again, and a voice from the door asked him to leave.

How little she knows, lying there on the threshold, Keith told himself as he left the Middlesex and stood in Mortimer Street waiting for a taxi. She might guess a little of Mike's torment, but not of how near it came to killing him. Nor anything of Winston-Greville, his breakdown under a pressure he should have been able to withstand, and his sudden, strange last minute redemption. She need never know. There was nothing to be gained by telling her, and it seemed unlikely that she would ever attempt to discover what happened to him, even if she lived. He prayed that he had said the right thing and that it was true and that she would fight to the utmost for her own survival.

He thought of the clear week with Jenny in Norfolk. How simple it would be after the complexities of life as he had experienced it recently. Simple and joyous. 'Liverpool Street,' he said to the driver. Shouted it, actually. The man looked startled.

❋

It did not turn out to be as simple or liberating as he had expected. While he drove Jenny about Norfolk, carried her down to the sand dunes at Overy Staithe and sat with her beneath a late autumn sun, watched the wildfowl, took her into cool, quiet, timeless churches and lay beside her every night in pubs and hotels from King's Lynn to Yarmouth—all the time his mind kept reverting to that night of bombing in London, just as if it were his first ever experience of war.

While he told Jenny several times how marvellous it was to be free from the sound of aircraft, to be on the ground and without a worry in the world for day after day, even while he told her how lovely she was (and that was more than several times), he felt the nagging beat of conscience.

Something had to be done. It was going on night after night. You could not detach yourself from the newspapers entirely, or the wireless news, even here in this countryside. Every night children were being killed and maimed, hearts and limbs broken, civilians burnt to death, as Moira so nearly had been. One bomb, and fifty old men torn to pieces.

This had nothing to do with dogfights at 15,000 feet, or even with the bombing of aerodromes and R.D.F. stations and factories that made Hurricanes. It was what Mike would call 'a different ball game altogether'. Something had to be done. And he was one of a comparatively small number of people who could do something about it.

High Command was of course doing what it could. The 'boffins', he knew, were desperately developing hush-hush weapons like airborne R.D.F. Rowbotham had once mentioned that this was going to enable pilots to be vectored onto a bomber in darkness until he was near enough to open fire. The Defiant, which had failed as a two-seat day fighter, was now being used as a night fighter, and most pilots had heard of the new twin-engined Bristol fighter just coming into production which would be able to carry the heavy airborne R.D.F.

But this remained in the future, and meanwhile neither Anti-Aircraft Command nor Fighter Command was even claiming more than a handful of German aircraft on the nights of these big raids on London and other cities. But Keith could fly Hurricanes at night, as they all could, and he was especially good at it, with exceptional night vision. Four-cannon Hurricanes were being used at night. Suddenly, Keith was filled with the need to take part in this nightly battle. It struck him as they were drinking a glass of beer outside a pub on a village green.

Jenny had already several times sensed his restlessness and rebuked him once in bed when he could not sleep after making love. 'For goodness sake, relax, darling,' she had said, and she had seized his hand.

'Oh, damn!' he exclaimed. 'This is supposed to be a holiday for you, too.'

She forced it out of him, and responded with her customary commonsense advice. 'A very good thing, too. It's much better than sitting around dispersals playing cards and drinking too much every night. Better to fly at night than that.' She paused and looked at him studying the bottom of his mug. 'And I know you're good at it and will be very successful.' Thank goodness, no 'do be carefuls' or even 'I'm sure you'll be all rights'.

'Perhaps I'll be your controller one night. That

would be fun! We can go halves on every Jerry you shoot down.'

He held her arm back to the car. She was walking much better now, and could even dispense with her stick for a few steps.

Half an hour later, finding that he was near Coltishall, he drove in and got a signal off to Rowbotham, and asked him to reply to Duxford.

He picked it up the next day. 'Posted to Netherton w.e.f. 21.11.40. Good luck. A bientôt. Squadron Leader Rowbotham.'

'I haven't got that word in my code book, sir,' said the signals corporal.

His leave ended on the twentieth, so that meant he could go direct to this new station and have his gear sent to him. Good for Bull Rowbotham!

The station adjutant was talking to Jenny when he got back to the car. 'This delightful lady refuses all offers of a drink in the mess,' he complained.

'Ah, she's a cripple, you see. I have to give up all my time to looking after her, sir,' said Keith, saluting smartly.

Later, they telephoned the Middlesex, as they had every day of the leave, always until now receiving the same answer: 'Still dangerously ill. No change.' This time, there was a faint note of optimism in the ward sister's report. And before they separated at Jenny's convalescent home near Ely, they rang again, and this time it seemed that the improvement had been sustained. 'Yes, I think we can say she is pulling round, although she has a long way to go and she's very weak.'

Keith squeezed Jenny's hand as they held the receiver between their ears, and exchanged glances of relief.

'I'll get onto Church Fenton right away,' said Keith.

There were people coming and going all the time in the hall, and they had to have one of their formal goodbyes. 'This is it, then. Fly well, darling . . .'

＊

Netherton was a big, bleak bomber station in Lincolnshire, built during the rearmament drive in the mid-1930s. Everything about it was dour, from the police at the main gate to the massive camouflaged hangars, from the dark Wellingtons dispersed in nearby woods to the black water tower on its skeleton structure.

The character of the station was different from a fighter aerodrome, steadier, more disciplined and formal, the crews who always flew together tending to keep together on the ground, too, and further subdivided between officers and N.C.O.s. It was not unfriendly, and there was no doubt of its efficiency. From the beginning of his career, Keith had been conscious of the efficiency of this junior service of his, and took pride in it. Here at Netherton, two or three times a week, the 'Wimpey' crews would go to their briefing and later make their way by lorry out to the big low-slung, twin-engined bombers which had been serviced and bombed-up by the ground crews all day.

Then, with immaculate regularity, they would tap out a letter on their downward recognition light, and on the O.K. from an Aldis light from the watch office, they would thunder down the long concrete runway, lift off and climb like an old man going upstairs, and set course—for factories, steel plants, the railway sidings at Hamm, and other German military targets. Long, cold, perilous journeys. Once or twice a week, one or perhaps more would not return, and others would be tractor-towed into one of the hangars to be patched up from ack-ack or fighter damage.

It was a ponderous, slowed-down version of the activities on a fighter station, played out fatalistically by night instead of swiftly by day.

On the far side of the aerodrome, scattered about two prefabricated low buildings and a pair of blister hangars, were the black Hurricanes of 77 Night Fighter Squadron, not yet operational and being worked up rapidly by an officer who looked as different from the heavy, withdrawn Wing Commander of the Wellington Squadron as his nippy Hurricanes were from the ponderous Wimpeys.

Squadron Leader Harry Dibbs was a wiry, restless man with a little ginger moustache and dancing blue eyes. He had been a flight commander in 10 Group, a less involved command during the Battle of Britain, but had contrived to shoot down two Dorniers in a raid on the Bristol area, and had caught a high-flying photo-recce Junkers 88 the next morning, for which he had earned a D.F.C.

Flight commanders and pilots, commissioned and noncommissioned, were all enthusiastic volunteers, like Keith anxious to continue flying operationally in spite of the absence of daylight raiders: a volatile, noisy bunch whose mess behaviour sometimes puzzled or even outraged the steady Wimpey boys. The station Commander looked as if he would have preferred them elsewhere, and had once told Squadron Leader Dibbs just that.

To his surprise, Keith found himself the top-scoring pilot and treated with some deference. Apart from being a good runner at school, he had not experienced much praise in his twenty-two years and certainly had never thought that he deserved any. Now, with his twelve victories, spanning the period from November 1939 (shared with Mike), the fall of France and the Battle of Britain, and the D.F.C. ribbon as visual proof of his quality, for the first time in his life he found himself receiving interested glances, in public and even on R.A.F. stations. This was both comforting and dismaying, in about equal proportion. With fellow pilots, he conformed to the 'anti-line-shooting' style, which covered up the smallest threat of boasting with a sort of throw-away modesty. It could sound patronizing, but it was a useful camouflage, a good leveller.

Technical talk was something altogether different. It was as intense and detailed as that of a top football team, with the stakes a great deal higher. With all the horseplay, seeming lightheartedness, 'boozing and wenching', for which they were renowned, Fighter Command's pilots were 100 per cent professional. Or the successful ones were. Those who weren't were mostly dead by November 1940. You could not do anything about the balance of luck, but you could do a lot about your degree of skill.

Night fighting demanded a different technique from fighting in daylight, and the Mk IIC Hurricane with its four Hispano 20 mm cannon and more power in its now 2-stage supercharge engine, was an even more potent weapon of destruction. Keith could remember countless occasions when a single 20 mm cannon, with its 600 rounds per minute rate of fire and explosive charge would have destroyed an enemy plane which he had only damaged. He remembered trying to work out the number of .303 bullet holes in a crashed Dornier 17 he had at last managed to shoot down with the help of a Spitfire, and he had lost count after 200. A dozen shell strikes might well have blown the bomber to pieces.

Now with no more effort—the same touch of the electric button on the stick—he had ten times the destructive power. 'It's heady stuff,' he had exclaimed to his C.O. down at the stop butts where he had tried out the feel of the cannon and had his guns harmonized at 300 yards.

'The trouble is,' Dibbs had commented, 'that when we could see the buggers we had pea-shooters. Now we've got real bangers we can't see the buggers.'

Sitting on the wing of Keith's black Hurricane while the armourers worked on the Hispanos, they fell again into shop talk: best stern approach, best action to take if you lost your bandit, best way of conditioning your eyes and avoiding the glare over a burning city. . . .

77 Squadron went operational at the beginning of December. At Netherton they were well placed not only to defend the bomber base itself but also Manchester, Liverpool, Sheffield, Hull and the other big industrial northern cities. Most had balloon barrages, and ack-ack had priority up to 12,000 feet. Above that, the night fighters were free to range at will. Dibbs and the two flight commanders worked out patrol lines for the different targets when they became known, with 500-feet zones for each machine: ideally, twelve planes between 12,000 and 18,000 feet, but in practice it was more likely to be nine or ten.

They had their first briefing on the same evening when the Wellingtons were going out, and they shared a late tea with the bomber crews. The Wimpeys' Wing Commander came over to Dibbs before they went their separate ways, one to face night fighters and drop bombs on Germany, the other to fight German bombers over Britain.

'Glad to see they're making honest men of you at last, Harry,' said the Winco.

'You'd better watch it in the circuit,' Dibbs replied as he finished his bacon and eggs. 'My types are a trigger-happy bunch. And you can't tell a Wimpey from a Dornier on a night like this.'

'My tail gunners are trigger happy too, Harry.'

The men laughed, and Keith wondered what it was like to fly eight hours at a stretch, most of the way over an icy winter sea or hostile land. As boring and dangerous as trench warfare.

Later that evening, Keith had to accept that the life of a night fighter pilot could be boring, too, as they sat about in the Readiness hut down at the dispersal wearing their 'dimmer' glasses to accustom their eyes to the darkness. No darts, no shove ha'penny, no reading. Just talking—girls, news, jokes, anecdotes, and back again to shop.

The telephone rang soon after ten o'clock. There were signs that one of the plots crossing the south coast might be heading north, away from London. This brought them to Immediate Readiness, and Dibbs told them to put on their gear, an elaborate procedure compared with those hot days of August: inner padded flying suit, outer Sidcot, Irvin, trousers as well as coat, Mae West—by now beginning to look like that busty film star—silk gloves, woolen gloves, gauntlets, wool-lined flying boots.

Three minutes later the telephone rang again. Plots heading for Manchester area, a big stream.

'Patrol L—Q,' said Dibbs. 'O.K. chaps, let's go.'

They had been practising this for a month. The scramble could never match the speed of day fighters, but the C.O. was off within three minutes, and the others followed rapidly in succession down the wide concrete runway, glim-lights to guide them on the left.

Keith signalled chocks away and taxied out fast behind the red and green wingtip lights and the small tail light of the plane in front of him, watched it swing into wind and at once open full throttle, flames (baffled to protect the pilot's eyes) squirting back from the Merlin's exhausts.

Keith thrust his own throttle lever forward, kept eyes half on the dimmed instrument panel and half-looking through the screen, with the glim-lights passing ever more rapidly until he felt his Hurricane lose contact, when they disappeared at once below.

He could feel the sharp night air flooding into the cockpit and shut the hood even before he raised his undercarriage. For a moment he saw no horizon at all, and recalled those early solo night flights on Tutors when the panic had to be firmly suppressed and he had broken out in sweat. 'It's always bloody there, you bloody fool,' Randall used to shout at him down the tube, referring to the elusive horizon on a moonless night.

Now Keith dropped his eyes to the artificial horizon, checked his rate of climb instrument to its right, reduced boost and brought the pitch back. It would come. And so it did, a diffuse horizontal strip—not a line—dividing dark grey against marginally darker grey, his own wings matching the miniature wings against the horizon line in the centre of his instrument panel.

At 2,000 feet it was better, almost a line now, and it conformed geometrically with a glowing dot that moved from right to left, a train on the Lincoln-Tuxford line. He made a steady rate two turn to the right, setting his compass on 245 degrees. Control was feeding in what information it had, but it was very sketchy compared with the R.D.F. plots over the Channel. This was Observer Corps gen. Good men, and women, every one of them, and doing their best. But it was mainly aural stuff unless the searchlights were lucky.

The searchlights south of Manchester were already probing, and Keith cursed them. They were regarded as a worse enemy than the ack-ack fire, spoiling their night vision.

'Kingcup leader, calling Kingcup leader, I have trade for you. Angels twelve, ten miles north of Coalking, course 345 . . .'

Half an hour later, from his patrol altitude of a freezing 14,000 feet, Keith saw the first incendiaries take root and then flower like supernaturally fast-growing plants in Manchester, and saw the first lines of sparks marking a stick of high explosive bombs. He was due south of the city, banking right and left and straining his eyes for a sign of passing shadow below. What tricks the eyes and imagination could play, too! Especially in scattered cloud from which an object that could be a plane might emerge and turn at once to a fragment of detached cloud, or to nothing.

Once, he saw the cross-shape of a plane just below, silhouetted against the glow of a growing fire, but even before he could react he recognized the Hurricane's wing shape. It was Sergeant Maudling patrolling the zone below him, caught momentarily in his own private, lonely world.

A few minutes later, he heard another of 77 transmitting for a fix. Keith knew well that feeling of being utterly lost, the hopelessness, the certainty that you would never again see a recognizable landmark, or a light even; only the phosphorescent glow of your own instruments on which your life depends.

According to the controller there were plenty of bombers still streaming in, and this was confirmed by the continuous fury of the ack-ack and the sweeping lines of the searchlights. One of these pinpointed a Heinkel 111, and a dozen more swung onto it like greedy fingers seizing a morsel. It was as if the bomber had been frozen in space for its photograph, its mystery unveiled. And then the guns began, sighting and firing rapidly, thankful for a target they could see at last and filling the bright cone with bursts.

Keith felt tempted to risk the ack-ack and go in, but the 111, twisting and turning like a fish on the line, broke out of the illumination, and in spite of the frantic probing to and fro of the beams, was not seen again.

A swift passing glow at his own level caught Keith's eye. He was not seeing well after watching the searchlight display, and almost lost it, but turned parallel with what he calculated to be its course. It was there again, just ahead, a faint exhaust glow, and another close to it. Twin engines. And it must be a hostile.

Quickly Keith climbed in an effort to catch the machine's silhouette against the pulsing glow of the bombed city ahead. Yes, there it was. A Dornier 17. He could see the shape of the whole machine for a second, the thin fuselage, twin fins, and he put his nose down, bringing his dimmed reflector sight onto the target and aiming at the fuselage forward.

But if he kept the machine in silhouette, he had to turn up his rheostat, and if he did that it blinded his sensitive eyes and he could no longer see his target. He had heard of this dilemma from experienced night fighter pilots, and there was no real answer except to fire blind, and 'hose' his cannon, or drop back and hope to pick up the bomber from below. He chose the second course, lost the shape entirely and was seen by the rear gunner who opened fire. The muzzle flashes of the machine-gun gave him something to shoot at, and he pressed the button, kicking very gently left and right, then stick forward and back—a long burst, the flash from his own cannon utterly blinding him.

Keith pulled up into a climbing turn, expecting to see flames from his victim. He saw nothing, nothing at all, no horizon, no stars, no cloud, and no Dornier going down. Only the pulsing pattern of lights, some small and some frighteningly large, of a great city on fire below.

Feeling frustrated, Keith got his machine back on a straight and level course, and continued the fruitless patrol. So he was going to save lives. Take vengeance on these murdering bombers. 'Like hell!' he shouted angrily into his mask.

Back at the dispersal, he found that two other pilots had had a similar experience. It took a miracle to sight a hostile, and then luck at a 100:1 to shoot at it successfully.

Dibbs agreed that it was a chancy business. 'Not hit and miss, just miss and miss,' he commented as he stripped off his Irvin jacket and hung it up. 'We're waiting for science to catch up. But we'll get one of the buggers in the end. And every time we open fire, we give some Jerry the squitters and maybe put him off his target.'

One night a pilot officer flew into the balloons, and another of 77 was killed in a landing accident. Looking at the remains of the plane the next day, Dibbs and Keith found a hole in the tailplane that was not crash damage. It was clear that the machine had been hit by ack-ack splinters, its rudder or elevator controls probably severed.

On another night, towards the middle of December, Keith on a liaison exercise with the Observer Corps, found himself in the circuit as the Wellingtons were beginning to land after a raid. He had plenty of fuel and was ordered to stand by and keep a good look out. He was circling two miles west of the aerodrome at 2,000 feet, and he could just make out the shape of the Wellingtons at the end of their landing run as they slowed and taxied off.

The R/T talk was businesslike and there seemed to be no trouble as permission to land was given in rapid succession: 'Blackbush four-zero, O.K. to pancake . . .'

Then there was a yellow glow above the final approach line, which grew at once like a bonfire that has petrol thrown onto it. A second later it was as rapidly doused, leaving only a faint glow. The glims were switched off, too, and the controller's voice called urgently, 'All Blackbush aircraft keep clear of base, I repeat . . . there is a bandit in the circuit. . . .'

It was not the first time an intruder had reached this far north to hover about the airfields and pounce on weary bomber crews in the circuit.

Keith had already opened up to full throttle and raced towards Netherton, telling control to warn the defences against mistaken identity. The remains of the Wellington smouldered in a field a quarter-mile short of the perimeter track.

Keith's guess was that the German pilot would not hang about after his success. That would be pushing his luck, and he would know that the bombers would be dispersed to other bases if they had enough fuel. He would fly south, was Keith's calculation, but not due south. He might make for the safety of the sea. Keith steered 120 degrees, and prayed for a return of the luck that had eluded him recently.

In five minutes he was at the coast, suddenly excited and reassured when he received news of an Observer Corps sighting and then a report from another bomber base that a hostile had crossed very low. Keith hit the coast at Friskney Flats. Mud or sand, the tide far out, and there was a flutter of moonlight distantly on the sea where there was a break in the clouds. The moonlight spread as he left the flat land behind, and there in front of him was his midnight gift, a Junkers 88.

For some reason which Keith did not fully understand, at the sight of the enemy he felt a tense nervousness which he thought he had thrown off for ever after the many combats of the last months. Something to do with the shock of witnessing the explosive end of the heavy bomber and six of his fellow aircrew? Just when they thought they were back to safety. Perhaps. These speculations came later. For the present he was not even conscious of the heat, low down here when he was dressed for high altitudes, or of the sweat in which he was bathed. The Junkers was a fast and difficult target and needed all his concentration. And, no, he was not going to let it get away.

With this more powerful Merlin, he had no difficulty in outpacing his protagonist. He kept 500 feet above it and out on its port side where he could see it sharply silhouetted against the sea, its moonlight shadow pursuing it just astern and rippling over the waves.

Keith was not seen by the rear gunner until he was about to open fire at 300 yards range, the 88's wingtips just inside the range bars. He was attacking from 10 degrees astern and had his thumb over the button when the gunner opened up, using no tracer but firing with great accuracy—German gunners always were uncomfortably accurate. At the same time, the pilot began kicking right-left rudder, the big twin-engined plane slewing from side to side to disturb his deflection calculations.

Keith closed in, steadied the sight, checked bank and turn, fired a short burst. He saw no hits. The 88 was opening up to its maximum speed, the exhausts from its radial engines glowing red, and Keith pulled the plug for full emergency boost, climbed over the bomber, ruddered steeply and came in on a starboard attack. This time, his target was jinking vertically, too, and moving to and fro within Keith's reflector sight so rapidly that it proved impossible to keep the centre dot steady. He fired a long burst, closing right in and taking a rough average in the hope that some of his shells would strike home.

Again he saw no strikes, and he had little time now. They were travelling at close to 300 m.p.h., and every mile reduced Keith's chances and increased proportionately the bomber's chances of escape. Only when he turned back did he see that he had hit the 88. Its starboard engine was smoking. But it was also climbing steeply. Keith had failed to see the cloud ahead, and the Junkers was making for it, already almost lost in its shadow; and as Keith pursued it furiously it was swallowed up.

The cloud was patchy and scattered, and for some five minutes the Junkers and the Hurricane played a deadly game of flickering hide-and-seek in and out of the clouds and their shadows, but always driving farther and farther south-east and out to sea. But once, when Keith was hard on its tail, the bomber turned as sharply as any fighter, and the nose gunner got in a burst before Keith could throw him off, and the sky was empty when he looked around again. For a further few minutes Keith flew on the bomber's original course and gained altitude to broaden his area of vision.

What a fool! He couldn't even keep it in sight, let alone shoot it down!

The trail of black smoke still pouring from its starboard engine gave the Junkers's position away. It was far to the north, back at sea level and travelling as fast as ever. Keith pressed the button for a fuel reading and switched the cock to reserve. Unless he wanted a

North Sea winter swim, this would be his last pass. He came down on it from well above, dodging clouds on the way that offered him temporary concealment.

Confident that they had thrown him off, the Ju.88 crew did not appear to see him this time. There was no return fire, no evasion. He gave his target half a ring, and gave a long closing burst aimed at the bomber's nose. It was a classic stern attack, without interference, the target symmetrical all the way. The four big Hispanos fired perfectly, the shells coming in on their Deuser pattern at 300 yards, half high-explosive, half armour-piercing. At this range Keith held his Hurricane and used up every round, while his machine shuddered as if in ecstasy at this killing, and the heady-scented cordite filtered back into the cockpit.

The Junkers went straight in, its dive as swift, steady and deadly as Keith's long last burst. He saw the great white splash in the moonlight. The water fell back, closed in, and within ten seconds it was sealed over, just as if nothing had ever happened out here in these grey wastes. No wreckage came up. Just nothing.

Keith climbed slowly, at economic revs, full lean mixture, and transmitted for a fix and course home. '. . . ten, nine, eight, seven . . .'

Now he was aware of the heat and his sweat. Now he knew from his shaking hands the strain he had been enduring through that long combat. He was experiencing that familiar and contradictory sensation of disturbed contentment. Never, not even in those hot August days of killing, was he able to put his mind completely at rest after successful combat. He had long ago succeeded in thrusting aside any feeling that might lead to hesitation in firing to kill. But his boyhood repugnance at killing game on the big Leicestershire shoots and at Rising Hall, was there in the record. History now, but indelible. Mike would have got that 88, if not on the first pass then on the second. He had never known misgivings. And his eyes were like an eagle's.

The cloud had cleared over Lincolnshire and the moon was like a flood of celebration after the black doings of the darkness. Landmarks he knew by day were all there below, diffuse but recognizable. The small town of Horncastle on the starboard side, the branch railway line leading up to it from the south, a glittering river, a faint spread of light from a late night car on the main road; and then the city of Lincoln itself, the Norman towers of its cathedral the highest point for many miles around of this flat countryside.

Keith checked his fuel for the last time. Zero in the reserve. 'Kingcup Red One,' he called up Netherton. 'Out of fuel and pancaking. Glims please . . .'

The lights came on at once. Keith corrected his course a few degrees, throttled back and selected his undercarriage down and full flaps. The red light remained steadily on, and he tried again, using violence. The emergency release did not operate either. Somewhere a hydraulic line had been severed by the 88's fire.

There was no time for a circuit. Scarcely time to call control. The flarepath came up to meet him, and Keith switched on his R/T momentarily—'Emergency landing . . .' That was all he had time for before he switched off what few drops of fuel he might have left in his tanks, allowed for a higher stalling speed because his flaps were not working either, and turned slightly to avoid the runway. No risk of sparks from grass, and there was plenty of it between the runways at Netherton.

Keith's Hurricane touched heavily, bounced once, came down again, slewed right and left on the dew-sodden grass, and came to a standstill with its nose 90 degrees off course.

The crash wagon was beside him as he began to unstrap himself and climb down, and the ambulance was there a few seconds later, dimmed headlights illuminating the crash-landed Hurricane lying at the end of the long deep scar it had made.

'Are you O.K., sir?'

'Just hot, thanks,' Keith said, and began unzipping his jacket and giving up almost at once in case his shaking hands let him down. 'Anyone got a cigarette?' A corporal lit it for him, so that was all right. But he would feel better for a drink, too.

'You know a Wimpey pranged, sir? They got it landing.'

'Yes, I saw it. I got him, too. Just. An 88.'

Dibbs had arrived now in his car. 'Any luck?'

'You could call it that, sir,' said Keith. There was a cool wind blowing over the field and he no longer felt the need to take off his Irvin.

On the drive back to the mess they passed the big station ambulance returning from the scene of the Wellington crash. Six British corpses, and four Germans tangled in the shattered skeleton of their Junkers at the bottom of the sea. One night's toll.

'That's wizard,' Dibbs was saying. 'Zero's a depressing squadron score. Now we can put up one on the board.'

*

'One' remained 77 Squadron's score all through that long winter of bombing. Night after night the squadron, or sections, were scrambled to intercept bomber streams. Often, not even a sighting was made. It was too much to expect from one pair of eyes, unsupported by any navigational aid. One or two pilots on other night fighter squadrons blessed with exceptional luck, an anticipatory instinct, and good night vision, were working up modest scores. But for all their enthusiasm and skill as pilots, only Keith had scored at the end of February 1941, and frustration led to falling morale. Harry Dibbs swore and flew every night when there was the hint of a raid, unless the weather was impossible. But he shared Keith's relief when a signal arrived early in March with the information that the squadron was to be posted to the Middle East and converted back to day fighting. Twin-engined Beaufighters with A.I. (Air Interception) were to take over. Science had come to their aid at last. Keith and two others on temporary attachment were posted back to their squadrons.

That night Keith telephoned Jenny at Bentley Priory where she was on an advanced controllers' course. 'Darling, I have a piece of paper in my hand. A note from my C.O. to say I have forty-eight hours of freedom. Yes, forty-eight. What generosity! And, guess what, I'm going to share it with you.'

She did not understand at first. The line was very

bad and the operator kept chipping in. 'Share what, Keith?' she kept asking.

'A bed, of course,' he shouted, and then the operator cut him off.

But by sheer tenacity, he arranged things as he wanted them. Two days and nights in London. Jenny's flat in Half Moon Street was undamaged, and together they removed the dust covers, let in the spring air from Green Park, pretended they were married and the war was over, and lunched at the Ritz and saw a revue with Edith Evans, Joyce Grenfell and Bernard Miles. But the illusion of peace was difficult to sustain. There were too many tragic gaps in the offices, the shops and blocks of flats in the West End for that. And though the bombing which had been continuous all through the autumn and winter had died down, there were still raids, and the sound of sirens penetrated into the snug little comfortable flat off Piccadilly during the night while they talked and made love.

Keith ordered Jenny out of uniform and admired her pre-war suits which she claimed were horribly out of fashion. 'I only wish I had some civvies,' Keith said. 'I'd do anything to get out of this lot.' They made a striking pair together, Jenny with her dark good looks and the hair she managed to keep so delightfully and illegally long, and Keith, tall and straight-backed, forage cap at an angle leaving much of his corn-coloured hair exposed, promoted to Flight Lieutenant now, an unmistakable 'one of the few' with his top button undone. Heads turned wherever they went, and Keith hated it.

'Let's just stay in and go out in the black-out,' he said to Jenny. 'Then we can make love all through the day, too.'

He left her at Piccadilly tube station on a Saturday afternoon. Even their loose interpretation of the rules and etiquette for R.A.F. officers forbade them from kissing in public. They had said good-bye properly in Half Moon Street, and now with the crowds swirling round, they saluted rather self-consciously, and Jenny turned and ran for the escalators and was lost in the crowds before she reached them.

9

TWO O'CLOCK ABOVE

The Breda-Tilborg road was dead straight for mile after mile, and now empty of traffic, as if the Germans had swept Holland clear of all its cars and lorries as well as its pride, leaving only a few peasants with their bicycles and an occasional horse-drawn cart. Not a gun had been fired at them, even when crossing the coast. No hostile gesture of any kind. Holland appeared to be living in a vacuum.

Then Flynn spotted a dark splash far ahead on the road and waggled his wings and pointed to draw Mike's attention. They were keeping radio silence on this mission. The stain rapidly took shape as a collection of vehicles, and Mike and Flynn spread out, keeping the road between them, and glanced yet again in their rear-view mirror.

Mike kept a quarter-mile to the left of the vehicles, skimming at nought feet over the black Dutch soil of a ploughed field. Yes, German all right. What else? There were half-track trucks with heavy artillery in tow, open and closed trucks, *Personenkraftwagen,* and little open *Kraftwagen,* fifty or more vehicles, all stationary, with their crews sitting or lying on the grass verge.

'Jeez, it's the Wehrmacht having a picnic!' Mike exclaimed into his mask. 'Like a goddam Sunday club outing with their buses.'

And it seemed as friendly, too, for he could see a number of the soldiers rising to their feet, looking in his direction, and waving. Yes, *waving*! What sort of celebration was this? Had peace broken out since they had left England forty minutes ago?

Fascinated by these signs of friendliness, Mike banked in a steep turn to port through 180 degrees, while Flynn followed suit in the opposite direction. Mike came straight at the convoy this time. The temptation to open fire was almost irresistible. What a target! But orders on this op were to avoid all hostile action. So he punched the override to his cine-camera, which normally operated only when the guns were fired, and photographed the massed vehicles.

For the fraction of a second, Mike saw the scene as a stationary set-piece, the soldiers on their feet, most with their helmets removed, all in long field greatcoats and clutching fat sandwiches. It was the German army's lunch break, and they were delighted to exchange fraternal greetings with the wonderful Luftwaffe. Mike could see the grins on their faces, one of them holding out an enormous sausage in mock offering. That would make a good shot when his film was processed!

Then they were over and past, the flat fields ahead again, and Mike set his compass on 275 degrees. It was time to go home. The Spy would not believe them, of course: the combined fantasies of an American drunk and an English poet. Rowbotham would say it was time they went on rest—a cosy little posting to Training Command in Scotland. And then Mike would say, 'Take a look at this, then!' And hand over the film.

Their Spitfires carried normal markings, roundels prominent on the sides of fuselages, and their machine's configuration was quite different from the 109's. Only arrogance, the steel-hard conviction that no enemy would dare to penetrate the borders of the new Greater German Reich in daylight, had led those munching soldiers to assume they were being greeted and entertained by the German Air Force. It boded well for future surprise attacks. But it was humiliating, too.

Now there was a village ahead. Mike could not see it on the map on his knee, and circled it at very low level, with Flynn behind him. A church, a large building beside it. A little dusty square, trim Dutch houses, humble but cared for, with window boxes and carefully-dug gardens awaiting the spring. A cart in the square, the driver striving to hold his alarmed horse. Another sleepy scene until, on their second circuit, suddenly the place woke up. The villagers poured from their houses, some carrying babies, others holding children's hands or waving shawls. A man picked up his bicycle and waved that jubilantly. From nowhere there suddenly appeared an illegal Dutch flag with two girls waving it.

There was no doubt that they had been recognized here, and that there was real cause for the welcome. Mike made one more low run at slow speed, scraping the rooftops and with his hood open and mask off, smiling and waving back. Then he resumed their old westerly course for the long trip back, and firmly reminded himself that there was a war on.

In four minutes they were at the coast again—all sand-dunes and sand-banks. He saw one gun post, apparently unmanned.

Mike and Flynn were completing the Wing's first reconnaissance over enemy-occupied Europe on a fine, December day in 1940. Since the end of massed daylight attacks in the late autumn, R.A.F. Fighter Command had been building up its strength until the new C.-in-C., Sholto Douglas, felt the time had come to test the German defences before reversing roles and putting the R.A.F. on the offensive. Air power was all that Britain had for months and perhaps years ahead to take the fight onto enemy soil, and Sholto Douglas obviously had no intention of leaving all the hitting to Bomber Command.

Half-way across the Channel, Mike began climbing, and at 5,000 feet they could see the coastline of southeast England, the white cliffs from Dover round to Foreness and the mouth of the Thames Estuary. He broke radio silence to call up Eastington, to warn of their imminent return. Their I.F.F. (Identification Friend or Foe) was supposed to tell everyone that they were not 109s on a tip and run raid, but there were usually some itchy-finger naval gunners or bored army gunners ready to loose off a few rounds in their direction.

Mike began weaving as they approached the coast, still, after a month with them, glorying in the handling and the power of the Spitfire.

*

270

It had been an eventful and in some ways a confusing winter for Mike. He identified himself so closely with England and the English cause that the agony of the bombing ordeal outraged and affected him just as strongly as it had Keith and the other pilots of 140 Squadron. He had done some night flying from Church Fenton from time to time in the hope of picking off the odd bomber but with no more success than most other single-seat fighter pilots, and he had been too busy during the day to do more than put in a token effort. He had enjoyed his time with the first Eagle Squadron and had fought off successfully any tendency to get a swelled head as a result of the hero-worshipping of his rookie fellow Americans.

Mike had heard from his father of the relief he and most of his friends felt about the re-election of Roosevelt—an old family friend—as President, from his mother, stoically not mentioning any anxieties she felt for him, from his own friends saying that Lend-Lease was not enough and that it was time the USA came to Britain's support militarily.

And Eileen? Well, there had been the wave of relief on hearing Keith's news, reinforced a month later when he had heard—again from Keith—that she was convalescing. But he thought of her now only as a warm and comforting but fading memory: not as a figure in his future life (for what that was worth).

With the approach of Christmas, the exciting news of the crippling of the Italian fleet at Taranto and the crushing defeat of the Italians in North Africa, helped Mike feel in good shape all round. Eastington was a great base to be stationed at, right in the front line, only a few minutes' flying from the Pas de Calais. And, like all 140 pilots he loved the Spitfire now that he had got used to its sensitive ways, its narrow undercarriage and its tricky handling when landing and taking off in strong cross-winds.

Rowbotham was in boisterous, bullish form on the evening after the recce trip. He sought out Mike when he spotted him in a corner of the mess reading a book. He took it from him, glancing at the title.

'You can't understand that, Yank. *For Whom the Bell Tolls!*' he exclaimed. 'It's going to toll for us all— every intrepid aviator.'

'Nothing like improving the mind, sir,' Mike said.

'Don't give me that rot. Retards it. Retards promotion, too. Stupidity, booze and a fund of dirty stories. That's the way to get on in the Raf. Look at me.'

He took Mike to the bar to confirm his aphorism with reality, but had no stories. Instead, he told him he had been to Uxbridge to see Leigh-Mallory, the new Commander of 11 Group. 'Your little jaunt today was by way of a curtain-raiser. We're crossing the Channel in Wing strength from now on. "Leaning forward into France", is how Air House defines it. Sweeps, Circuses, Rhubarbs.'

Mike raised an eyebrow quizzically. These were new code names to him.

'Never heard of a Rhubarb?' said Rowbotham, nodding to the barman for another round. 'That's what you've been doing today. Only hitting the Hun. Not sharing lunch with him. Or so Spy tells me.'

'And?'

'A Sweep's what it sounds like. Just fighters trying to raise 109s to shoot down. And sometimes we'll be

272

taking a few bombers with us, then it'll be called a Circus.'

*

140 Squadron was celebrating a successful Sweep on the night Keith rejoined them, three months later. It had been a perfect Spring day and two Spitfire Wings had gone in east of Calais at 23,000 feet and flown south over St Omer and St Pol to Amiens and out again at Le Tréport. On the last overland leg, they had met the inevitable 109s and had fought a savage battle all the way to the coast. Without loss to themselves, they had bagged three—one of them being credited to Flynn Marston. The C.O. decided that warranted a party.

Mike saw Keith standing at the door blinking in the bright light after the black-out just as the party was reaching its climax, with fire extinguishers replacing soda syphons as prime weapons. At first there had been three warring factions representing the three squadrons, but anarchy had long since taken over, and it was every man for himself. Flynn was out of it, having drunk himself unconscious. He was stretched out along the bar. Rowbotham was down to shirt and trousers rugger-tackling anyone still on their legs. When he recognized Keith at the door, he let out a yell that drowned all the other sounds.

'Golden boy's back!' he shouted. 'Our wizard ace of the night. Let's have 'em off.'

Keith turned and ran down the corridor but he did not stand a chance. By the time Mike had caught him up, his trousers were hanging from a chandelier and he was lying on the ground, his head well soaked in beer.

'Things don't seem to have changed much,' he said, attempting to dry his hair on his handkerchief. 'What's all this in aid of?'

'Flynn pranged a Jerry today. So the C.O. made him write a song. And, gee, it was awful. "Flynn" and "getting some in", and "Marston" rhyming with "a Hun passed on . . ." So he had to drink three pints in a row. And it went on from there.'

Mike recovered Keith's trousers and insisted on a walk in the black-out to clear his head. There was no moon but it was a clear starlit night, and down at the dispersal the Spitfires in their blast pens were like thoroughbreds in their stalls after a hard day.

'You like them O.K.?' Keith asked.

'You can talk to them, and they'll do anything, even before you ask 'em. Stand on end, flick roll you out of any trouble, as split-arse as the Gauntlet and nearly twice the speed.' Mike patted the projecting cannon from the wing of his own machine. 'These help, too.'

Keith tried the cockpit for size and noted how small and restricted it was after the Hurricane, itself ungenerous in its dimensions. He had to set the seat right down in order to give his head an inch clearance with the canopy shut.

'Today was unusual,' Mike said, sounding a warning note. 'We don't often get away without any losses. Things are in the Huns' favour now. They're hard to shoot down and they bail out into their own territory.'

Mike had got a bottle of Bourbon from a friend at the American Embassy in London, and they drank some of it and talked late into the night in Mike's room, pleased at the prospect of flying together again.

They flew together all through that spring and summer, with only one leave period and a few weekends in London. They flew on Sweeps and Circuses, did half a dozen Rhubarbs together, relishing the low level, their freedom to seek out 'targets of opportunity', beating up trains and barges, power stations and factories, and (foolhardy this) Luftwaffe bases. While Germany suddenly swung about and launched a vast attack on Russia, intervened in Greece and threw out the Allies, captured Crete and cancelled out all the British gains in North Africa; while Churchill and Roosevelt conferred about war strategy, much of central London was burned in a gigantic fire raid, and bomber command answered in kind on Nuremburg, 140 Squadron participated in shipping strikes and escorted British convoys, scrambled after German tip-and-run raiders at nought feet and strived to reach the very high-flying German photo-recce machines.

Rowbotham was shot down but managed to bring his crippled Spitfire back across the Channel to crash-land near Dungeness, breaking his nose again and making himself look more bullish than ever. Bill Watson took his score to twelve, was given a bar to his D.F.M. and again refused a commission. Garçon Rideau accepted, however, and the shy, serious French-Canadian was given a ferocious first night party in the Officers' Mess. Four pilots were lost, but the 'old contemptibles' (as they called themselves) of 140 survived, and Keith began to feel that if he once stopped flying he would drop to the ground like a Spitfire that has lost its wings. He missed the ruggedness of the old

Hurricane, which had been taken out of front-line fighter service in Britain, and the Spitfire could not match it as a steady gun platform. But the Spit's speed in the climb, its acceleration, its aileron response, made it a fighter pilot's dream. Keith loved the little machine, volunteered to fly engine tests, and searched for any excuse to get airborne.

Then, late in September 1941, Keith and Mike, Polo and Range Powell, all received posting orders, Keith and Mike as instructor at an Operational Training Unit in Scotland, Polo as an instructor in Rhodesia, and Range Powell to command an Australian Buffalo squadron being worked up in Singapore.

They were in the Spy's office when the news arrived. Keith read his through. It was like a police summons. 'My God,' he sighed, 'the end of an era.' He was being only half facetious. Once, he remembered, a million flying hours ago, he had longed for a break from the strain—just one day's dud weather would do. Since then, with the pressure eased, the act of flying operationally had become a drug to which he was addicted

'The end of the goddam world!' said Mike. 'I came here to fight not teach spotty creeps to fly. I'll resign my commission,' he told the Spy, who looked at him bleakly. 'I'll transfer to one of the Eagle Squadrons. With my experience, they sure won't turn me down.'

Polo asked, 'Where's bluddy Rhodesia? I'll bet it's more than a mile or two from Bradford', while Range released a string of obscenities which none of them could have matched.

The Spy waited for the protests to exhaust themselves, and then glanced at each of them in turn from under his hedge-like eyebrows. 'You know you'll all do exactly as you're told so you may as well come quietly, as the Bishop said to . . .'

'Oh, stuff it, Spy. Polo, shove your pipe down his throat.'

Then the telephone rang, and the Spy nodded as he listened to the voice at the other end of the line, switched to the scrambler, and began to take notes.

'Your life on ops is not yet over,' he announced when he put down the red scrambler phone. 'It's off to La Belle France again this afternoon. Blenheims to St Artoise. A P.R.U. picture shows these new Focke-Wulf fighters there and our lords and masters say we are to prang them. Airborne 14.00. Rendezvous with the bombers angels twelve Dover 14.15.'

True to form, the Spy gave the impression that the Circus was some Machiavellian plot in which he was secretly and deeply involved. Keith could no more imagine life at an O.T.U. than squadron life without Willy Williams, who had been plotting and conspiring since the first day of the war.

Their outrage did not diminish after leaving the Spy's office, but the need to prepare for the afternoon's operation took priority, and they went down to the dispersal where the C.O. had the latest met. report and they could work out their course on their maps, and check their kit and their planes. Mike's was unserviceable and he was allotted the spare, X-X-ray, which was also the squadron veteran with ack-ack splinter patches all over the wings and fuselage. His fitter, Lofty Campbell, had his head inside the V-12 engine when Mike arrived to set up his parachute and helmet in the cockpit. 'I thought you'd fancy a new set of plugs,' he said in his rich Scottish voice. 'You never ken with these ol' machines.'

'I'd fancy a new engine,' said Mike. 'And airframe.'

Half an hour before they were due to take off, those on the operation assembled in the Spy's office again to turn out their pockets and collect their money and escape gear—500 francs in various denominations in a waterproof bag, the little compass to augment the button compasses they all wore and knew to be unreliable, and the day's code card. They also strapped on their broad webbing belts with gun holster, but Mike and Keith had their own armament arrangements, Keith keeping his .38 Smith and Wesson secured inside his right flying boot, where it would not obstruct any hasty exit from the narrow cockpit. Mike preferred to keep his own little .25 Browning strapped to his braces, in the small of his back now, comfortable and out of sight.

It was a cool day with broken cloud, and most of the pilots put on everything they had against the cold at high altitude. They would be away for nearly two hours and they all knew how cold you could get at 20,000 feet-plus. A stiff northerly wind would slow their return flight.

Keith and Mike smoked a last cigarette outside before going to their Spitfires. As well as an old machine, Mike had a new pilot flying as his number two, a Sergeant Pilot called Geoff Rawson who looked green but who was putting a brave face on it. Mike called him over and told him again to stick to him if they met any trouble. 'No goddam one-man wars from you,' he told him, but with an encouraging smile. 'It's your business to look after me first, and your own tail a close second. Don't use the R/T unless it's real urgent. Then use it fast. O.K.?'

The sergeant nodded and said, 'Right, sir. Understood.' Keith noticed that he was so young that he had not even learned how to smoke professionally. Still, it was better than last year when they had been coming in to the heat of the Battle of Britain with their pathetic twenty hours on single-seaters. . . .

'Let's get weaving.' Rowbotham came barging out of his office. 'I'll be pressing the tit—' he glanced at his watch—'in just three minutes from now.'

Some eager pilot or his fitter had already started an engine, the slipstream sending up a cloud of dust from his pen. The other two Spitfire squadrons on the far side of the field were also bursting into life. The station commander's car was outside the Watch Office, and there were figures visible inside ready to deal with any crisis at the wing take-off. The fire crew in their thick teddy-bear fireproof suits were standing by, like the ground crews beside their charges. The windsock stood out stiffly, like the R.A.F. flag, pointing south towards their target. Eastington was once again ready to function, to despatch safely thirty-six Spitfires over enemy-held land.

Keith walked fast towards his C-Charlie, his mind on the briefing, on the critical minutiae of the operation ahead: the turning points marked on his map, the worst ack-ack zones marked with red chalk cross-hatching, the photograph of St Artoise they had just been studying, the code words of the day. Then, like a physical punch, the truth struck him that this was probably his last operation with 140. The future was a dull grey prairie of repetitive routine, lit only by the pleasure of a week's leave and seeing Jenny first.

Keith climbed up onto the port wing and dropped into the little cockpit. His rigger helped him tighten the straps, inserted the pin, and handed him his helmet and gauntlets. 'Good luck, sir.' The words were part of the invariable routine—like the closing of the little hinged door, the last wipe with the spotless cloth over the perspex and the armoured screen, Keith's cockpit drill, swift but never perfunctory, the exchange of glances with the engine fitter standing beside the trolley-ac, and the brief answering nod from Keith. Then the crash of the Merlin as he pressed the starter button, the chocks away sign and the magneto check as he taxied out.

They could take off in fours line abreast from Eastington's new wide tarmac runway, and Keith led his section off the moment he saw Rowbotham getting airborne and the little ballerina-like undercarriage tucking into his wings. The circuit was already full, with the other two Spitfire squadrons forming up on the Wing Commander Flying, identifiable by the extra wide white band just forward of the tail.

Five minutes later they were breaking through the scattered cloud and into the clear glaring sunshine above. A second wing was coming in from the west, at this distance looking like a swarm of migrant birds. At precisely a quarter past two, the Blenheim squadron appeared from the north, twelve twin-engine machines, faster than the old Hampdens and Battles, but still not fast enough and still under-armed. They would need the protection of every Spitfire airborne if they were to survive.

Still not a word had been spoken on the R/T, giving the impression that this complex massing of almost a hundred aircraft was no more than a spectacle in silent mime. They would be showing on the German R.D.F. screens but it was an invariable rule to keep radio silence until the enemy coast was crossed, unless some emergency arose.

The Eastington Wing climbed another 3,000 feet above the Blenheims to give top cover, and they proceeded out over battered Dover and its massive castle of earlier wars. Two M.T.B.s were entering the harbour. A single car made its way towards Deal on the coast road.

Weaving gently in order not to overshoot the bombers, they were soon across the Channel, over Gris Nez, and the flat, featureless farming land of the Pas de Calais. The ack-ack was concentrating on the bombers. The light grey dots left drifting stains behind. They might appear innocuous to the uninitiated, but when they had the measure of you and you could see the little yellow hearts, caught the whiff of high explosive and felt the turbulent shock and the patter of splinters on your frail fuselage—then this heavy ack-ack was an alarming experience, especially after you had witnessed a direct hit.

Now the Blenheims were weaving sharply, ruddering and dropping and climbing again, and they all passed through this first patch safely. St Artoise was just north-east of Albert on the Somme, where Keith's father and his adopted father had both been wounded on the first day of the 1916 push. Keith never flew over this part of France, which had been so devastated and was the scene of such dreadful bloodshed just twenty-five years ago, without thinking of those two men among the thousands who had gone over the top at dawn on that 1st July—these two mercifully to survive. And now here they were about to add another small ration of high explosive to tear up the French soil again and kill a few more people. . . .

The wing leaders were talking on the R/T and exchanging notes with the bombers as they forged south into the sun. 'Where're the buggers this afternoon, Johnny?' 'Search me. Gone to Russia?' 'Charlie, I think we want to turn about two degrees to starboard. That curve in the river down there ought to be on our port side.' 'Yeah—the wind's stronger here. Rowboat leader'—addressing the Blenheims' squadron commander—'everything hunky-dory?' 'Rowboat leader, here. Yes, no flap. Whoops—spoke too soon.'

Keith saw the first ack-ack bursts, smack among the bombers in the disconcerting way the Germans had of getting straight onto the target. Almost at once, one of the Blenheims pulled out of the loose formation, streaming smoke.

'Rowboat leader, I've had this engine.'

'So I can see. Hard cheese. D'you want to go back?'

'Rowboat leader, I've lost most of the aileron, too.'

A section of Spitfires was deputed to give the stricken Blenheim close escort. Keith considered its chances of making it slim. The bomber was losing height as it disappeared to the north, and its long black smoke trail would attract the eye of every gunner and any German fighter in the sky.

'This is Rowboat leader, close in now. Target dead ahead.'

There were fields, woods, a curving railway line leading towards Arras to the north, a village strung out along a narrow road, and then the hangars and scattered buildings of St Artoise, camouflaged fuel tanks, a black water tower, the three camouflaged wide runways, and the blast pens spread far and wide. It might have been any station on the English side of the Channel, except that the little single-engine fighters carried black crosses on their wings. Not that Keith could see these. Even with his very sharp eyes, he could not recognize the aircraft themselves from this height.

The ack-ack was becoming very fierce, bursting among the Spitfires, even reaching up to the top cover. But the main concentration was aimed at the Blenheims, which suddenly looked a pitiably small force for dealing with such a large and hostile target. And on this last run-up they could take no evasive action.

Still no fighters appeared. The bombs went cascading down, and before they burst along an uneven line of pens, the bombers were taking violent evasive action. Then the 109s came down like lapwings, from the south-west and, inevitably, straight out of the sun.

Rowbotham was quick, as always. 'Sandbag aircraft—here they come. Two o'clock above . . .'

The timing was classic, too. Just as the guns were losing the range, and they were at their farthest point from base. Like the 109s over London fourteen months ago, the fuel consideration would always be with them, a restraint in this type of close action, when there should be no restraint.

283

The 109s must have been doing over 400 m.p.h. as they went through the top cover Spitfires, hoping to get among the Blenheims before anyone could touch them. They probably would, too, Keith calculated. He pushed his stick hard forward (no hesitation now with the new carburettors), broke through the gate with his throttle, and took his section down in pursuit.

There were at least three Staffeln of 109s—no sign of the new Focke-Wulfs—and they seemed to slide vertically into the distance, lost against the patchwork of the landscape below. For a few seconds, Keith lost all touch with them. Then, with his own A.S.I. showing far above the 400-mark, he caught sight of one, then two more, then many many more, pulling out of their dives astern of the Blenheims, banking, weaving, setting themselves up steadily for their run-in.

'Rowboat leader calling, close right up. Here they come.'

There were no flippant calls on the R/T now that battle was joined. The 11 bombers were in vics, wing-tip to wing-tip. Keith dragged himself out of his flat-out dive, blacked-out, hauled back on the stick, and had one of the 109s in his sight. 500 yards, nearer 600. The tracer from the bombers' rear guns arched away below. Several Spits were closer to the 109s. He could see Rowbotham hard on the tail of one, disregarding the Blenheims' fire, and on Keith's starboard side, a little above and in a steep turn, was old X-X-ray—Mike in customary form, mixing it early and sharp with a bandit.

Keith, missing his chance of a first pass, pulled up for height: altitude, the first formula for success, for survival, in any dogfight. You had to shoot, too. And watch out. And—oh, many other qualities had to be tested. But superior height in air combat was as priceless an advantage as a soldier commanding a ridge, a naval commander possessing longer-ranging guns. . . .

A sharp aileron turn, almost onto his back as he caught sight of a stray 109, yellow spinner, vivid identification badge on his fuselage, and only 300 yards away. He was climbing fast, but Keith had the speed. A too hastily-calculated deflection, and his burst went wide. He pulled in tighter, blacked-out again in a very sharp climbing turn, and lost him. . . . Bad show! What the hell was the matter with him?

For a fleeting second when he could see again but with his wingtips still making streamers, there all about him, above and below, was the whole three-dimensional panorama of mass air combat as he had known it for eighteen months now: this boiling cauldron of movement in the sky, stirred by the giant hand of some insane cook, faster and faster. The reactions demanded were too swift for the eye, among the spread of angled wings, of fleeting fuselages, the sparkle of gunports, the answering sparkle of De Wilde strikes, of perspex canopies momentarily reflecting the sun.

Here, by any normal reckoning, there should have been mass hysteria. But there were men in these whirling machines who had developed a special discipline, others who were bold and imprudent but had the habit of luck on their side, others who placed a higher value on their life and had become practised at preserving it. Most of these were winners, sharp-eyed in protection as well as destruction. Not all. A Flight

Commander who had been through the Battle of Britain succumbed to a long burst aimed at his blind spot and was killed instantly with half a dozen machine-gun bullets and a cannon shell in his body. A young Feldwebel who had come out top at shooting during his final training and was expected to amass a high score in action—he was caught in the Blenheims' cross-fire, his 109 caught fire, and he died slowly and in agony on the long fall, for his hood was jammed by a single .303 bullet.

But death struck mostly at those who had never gained or had now lost the fine edge of self-confidence, or, by the smallest failing in character, had allowed themselves too much; at those who were experienced but not quite experienced enough to throw off an antagonist of exceptional experience and tenacity; at a Leutnant called Wolfgang Müller (born Mainz October 1920—his twenty-first birthday next week) who had been rebuked by his Hauptmann shortly before being scrambled for wearing dirty boots. He was still stinging at this supposed injustice just before he had opened fire, and was dead with an a.p. 20 mm cannon shell through his head eight seconds later.

The bomber formation had been broken up. Keith saw the crew fall from one, and blossoming parachutes seconds later. Another was on fire. 'Rowboat leader calling—form up on me. I am firing a red flare—now.'

Far below a Spitfire with one wing was falling like a sycamore seed. No smoke, and, Keith prayed, no pilot.

Then he got his chance. It happened like that sometimes. An undeserved chance. Perhaps it was already damaged, its pilot wounded. But the 109 came past so slowly, a shade to the right and below, that Keith ruddered hard, did a quick aileron turn, and was behind and underneath in two seconds. Then, after a quick glance at his turn-and-bank, he opened fire at 150 yards, cannon and machine-guns, and the fighter broke up before his eyes, shedding pieces like an ovcrloaded scrap lorry on a corner. But from out of the racing ruin, a crouching figure emerged and, with relief because no one deserved to die after such bad luck, a parachute opened, the figure jerked from horizontal to swinging vertical, and fell from sight.

Keith glanced round defensively, and into his rear view mirror. The attacks were falling off as the remaining Blenheims approached Arras and a barrage of ack-ack. A 109 glided past a half mile distant, trailing white smoke. Keith was about to turn after it when it blew up. Then another machine floated down, quite gently, from the fighting above him. It was in an inverted glide. A Spitfire, and one of 140's. He saw the letters RC and ruddered to get alongside. Then the angle of descent steepened and it began to bank towards the south, shutting him off from sight of the side fuselage. . . .

But he saw the letter just in time—before it turned over again and dropped ever faster, and before Keith had to turn sharply as tracer zipped past his port wingtip. It was X-X-ray. There was no doubt of it. No doubt whatever.

It was bound to happen. It had to happen, Keith kept telling himself as if the agony of inevitability might be a comfort instead of a turn of the knife.

Mike should have gone in August last year when he was flying like a demented animal, hurling himself into fatal situations and coming out, day after hot, sweat-and-oil begrimed day. When Keith knew that by Mike's calculation any injury was better than the pain in his heart and death would be a comfort.

And now, when things had stabilized and he was almost back to his old form, now on his last op, on the way home from his last op, Mike had bought it. Surely he had. Surely no one had got out of that Spit. By now he had an almost unerring eye for a fatally damaged plane in which the pilot was dying or would soon be dead. They would post him 'Missing'. But it was really worse than that: 'Missing Believed Killed'. Six feet deep in a French field with hot, oil-streaked alloy for a coffin.

Keith had been shocked into carelessness once or twice before. Back in May 1940 when hawk-eyed Sergeant Henry had gone down slumped over his stick, the blood on the inside of his canopy streaming like rain on a car's windscreen. Back in July, and on a third occasion—but only briefly—when they had got Buffer Davies . . . Now, as he formed up with two more of his original section and turned west to avoid St Omer, he was a sitting target for any hostile. Stunned.

Gone for a burton, old Mike! He was tempted to call up and tell Rowbotham. Then he decided to hug the dreadful truth to himself for fifteen more minutes. Would it be easier on the ground? No, it would not.

'Sandbag Red Two, don't lag,' he transmitted, glad of the excuse to snap.

They left the Blenheims in mid-Channel, losing

height while the bombers turned north-west, seven of them in a brave formation with Spits from Tangmere continuing to give them close cover. Another lagged behind and far below, perhaps to drop into the drink, but with four more Spitfires in close attendance.

Dover harbour below, the two long moles, the M.T.B.s, tied up now, the scarred town, shelled as well as bombed, the castle, and soaring higher than ever for this new war, the aerial towers of the C.H. station. It was just as they had seen it on the way out. The shadows of the towers had swung round a few degrees, the cloud had thinned a shade, the car on the road to Deal had presumably arrived at its destination.

No, very little had changed. Except that Mike Browning was dead.

10

ST ARTOISE CIRCUS

Mike, with his healthy disrespect for superstition, had experienced at lunch a premonition about the Circus to St Artoise. He had crossly stamped it out and then drunk another cup of coffee very quickly to wash away any remains of such dangerous nonsense. He re-membered it with a sense more of disappointment than anger when he was hit. A belief, long held, had been shattered as sharply as the perspex on his star-board side by a 7.9 mm bullet. Shells and bullets had followed the first hit, and he knew this was it. The goddam it—the end he had long deserved.

The 109 passed within a few feet of this wingtip, flaunting its mottled underside as a savage will ex-pose its posterior in mockery. X-X-ray's old engine had been turned into a chaos of crankshafts and cam-shafts, pistons and plugs, by an exceptionally accurate burst of cannon and machine-gun fire from a quarter-deflection stern attack which Mike should have spot-ted three seconds earlier, and his number two earlier still but he had his eyes on Mike instead of his at-tacker. (The boy was shot down and killed three min-utes later, which he deserved in the savage justice of dog-fighting. . . .)

290

Mike had heard of pilots' reluctance to get out in the hope of some miraculous recovery. Over England, he might have stayed a fraction of a second. Here it was best to be gone, fast, with an imminent roasting as the only alternative.

So off with helmet—unclipped, thank God. Grab code card. Back with the hood, the suction power taking him by surprise. He had given only a preliminary kick but was at once drawn clear, missing the tailplane, over and over, dropping the code card as he grabbed for the D-ring. (It was picked up the next day by a farmer who saw it lying in the stubble and halted his oxen. He puzzled over 'Margate—Dubloon' and 'Canterbury—Honeybee' and dropped it again, where it was later ploughed into the good loam.)

Mike failed to find the ripcord first time, then decided to fall for a while. Delayed drop. Get away from the mêlée. Free of any anxiety about being shot at and more likely to reach the ground unseen as well as alive.

He free-fell for 6,000 feet, enjoying the sensation, panicked when he saw how fast the ground was coming up to meet him, and as a result pulled the ripcord hard enough to hurt the inside of his hand.

The sudden deceleration jarred his body, and by the time he had looked around and taken his bearing, he was at barely 1,000 feet. Below was a large triangular-shaped wood which he was going to miss, thanks to the strong north wind. A winding river of modest breadth, a bridge over it to the west. A single small farmhouse with outbuildings. A distant railway line running east-west. A nearer main road. A scattering of house and a church to the south. But nothing moving anywhere and no sign of life, not even stock in the fields. A dead land.

Mike took mental photographs and prepared for the landing. He came down on grass a few yards from an unkempt hedge. The landing was soft and easy, and he struck the quick-release box hard just before his feet made contact and at once ran after his billowing 'chute, fought with it briefly, deflated it and rolled it up. There was a ditch beside the hedge, damp and with stretches of stagnant water. He burrowed out a shallow hole, placed his Mae West in it and then jammed the bundle into it and covered them both with mud and twigs. Some time, long after he had gone (he hoped), someone would find that 'chute and it would be like the discovery of the Koh-i-Noor diamond, the material for countless Frenchwomen's unobtainable blouses, dresses and petticoats.

Then he sat down close by in the shelter of the hedge and took the target map out of his boot. It was not a difficult task to locate his position. They had been about three minutes on the homeward leg when the 109s had struck and the fighting had not caused them to divert more than a few miles either way from their course. The river was the Conche, the railway from St Pol to Arras. The village to the south was probably Laonne. He made a small cross at his likely position on the map. He was nearer to Eastington than Paris. But there was the small matter of twenty-one miles of sea to take into consideration.

They had been briefed on evasion, even practised it among the Kent fields and woodlands, feeling rather foolish as if discovered playing kids' games. The drill was straightforward for an operation which, to be successful, depended on quick thinking, rapid extemporization, nerve and luck. It was to avoid being picked up by German or French authorities, seek out a likely sympathizer, and ask for the nearest contact.

For some months now, a 'line' had been operating across Occupied France, into Vichy France, and then over the frontier into Spain. It was frequently broken, people disappeared without a word, but after a while the gap was filled and a steady trickle of R.A.F. aircrew were returned—only a small proportion of the total who were shot down, but each one a recovered, valuable, trained airman.

Mike, ever the optimist, rated his chances of success as high, and totted up the factors on his side:

The nights were still reasonably warm.

He knew where he was and where he wanted to go.

He was unhurt, fit, had hard rations for forty-eight hours, benzedrine, compasses, maps, and a knife.

He had 500 French francs.

He had a gun.

He took a Horlicks tablet and began walking. Just like that. He had no need of a compass at this stage. It was still only ten past three—less than an hour since he had left England—and all he had to do was walk towards the sun for the time being, keep on the alert and with map at the ready.

The first indication that anything lived around this part of the Pas de Calais was the sound of an engine, an engine with an irregular beat, probably air-cooled. As it became louder, Mike dropped into the ditch, noticing for the first time that a narrow dirt road ran on the far side of the hedge; and the vehicle was driving along it, slowly, at the speed you would expect of searching men.

He caught a blurred glimpse of its outline as it passed, a sloping-fronted open vehicle with a spare wheel on the bonnet—a *Kraftwagen,* the ubiquitous German small personnel carrier based on the 'people's car'—the Volkswagen. It passed by, and even at its slow pace, raised a chalky dust cloud which seeped through the hedge.

Five minutes later, crossing a road leading to the village, Mike saw another distant vehicle, and then a third. So the area was by no means dead. But its inhabitants seemed to be exclusively German—the Wehrmacht in search of downed enemy aircrew, an essential operation after an air battle in which there had been enemy losses.

The next sound was a great deal more sinister. It was the sound of a light aero engine, flying low. Mike was working his way along the lee of another hedge, and the moment he heard it he threw himself to the ground again, face down. The sound rapidly increased in volume. He felt it pass directly overhead, thought he even felt a breath of the machine's slipstream. It had faded far into the distance before he dared to look up. The little shape in the sky confirmed his guess that it was a Fieseler Storch, an army spotter and communications machine that looked like a crane-fly and could land and take off in little more space than that insect required.

Mike's early hopes of half an hour before began to fade. He still had not seen a Frenchman, let alone anyone who looked as if they might help him. The remains of his Spitfire had no doubt been discovered, and the Luftwaffe would have reported that several bombers had been downed, too.

'If I'm going to get out of this mess,' Mike told himself as he sat up, still half in the hedge and ears alert for further hostile sounds, 'I'd better lie low until dark. And then get the hell out—and fast.' Clothing was his first need—it always was with evaders, then papers, then mobility. . . .

Mike spent the greater part of that first evening right there in the hedge, fearful of moving, alert for the earliest sound of more searching vehicles. Once he heard voices, too distant to identify the language, but probably German because of the volume and their authoritative ring. He began to feel cold for the first time, in spite of his Irvin jacket and wool-lined boots. He also began to feel lonely for the first time, and this, too, surprised him: they had not been told about loneliness at evasion lectures. And he had been shot down only five hours ago, and was barely a mile from where he had landed! With the loneliness there came another unpredicted response: that of being a trespasser; an alien of foreign soil, no permission given.

He was glad to be able to move when darkness had settled. He ran for a while to get his circulation moving again. It was a clear night with the stars offering enough light to keep him from walking into trees. There would be a moon later, he knew, rising at about 1 a.m. He crossed several newly-ploughed fields, which made heavy-going, and many meadows, which were fast and trouble-free. Once a dog barked nearby, and he saw a momentary light and heard a voice shouting, 'Tais-toi, Albert!' and wondered what breed of dog Albert was.

The rising of the moon was a comfort, and provided cheer, like a dimmed room suddenly floodlit. But an hour and four miles later, he felt the melancholy creeping back, and he chided himself. Fear and loneliness? What sort of D.F.C. fighter pilot was that, for Pete's sake? This was crazy, and he tried running across the next field until his old hip injury began to play up, and he was struck with a sudden fear that it might prevent him from walking at all, that he would have to give himself up in the morning. This led to more violent self-criticism until he forced himself to sit down by a deep ditch he was about to cross and begin an argument with himself.

'Do you want to get out of this goddam country? Right. Or would you prefer the comforting security of a prison-of-war camp? Plenty of buddies. The war can't last for ever . . .

And ended on a firm note of resolve. 'O.K., so this is a game, and you don't like being beaten, do you?' He thought of Rowbotham in his situation, and that gave him courage.

Then he got up and jumped the ditch, without a twinge from his hip, regarding the gap as a symbolic demarcation line between timidity and resolve . . .

Mike met his first Frenchman after crossing a bridge over the Somme at first light. He was an old man on a bicycle with fat tyres, a hen in a wired box on the rear carrier.

Mike said, 'Bonjour, monsieur. S'il vous plaît . . .'

The Frenchman slowed, looked at him briefly with watery eyes, and turned away.

'Mais, monsieur—' Mike ran after him, and then gave up. The man did not look round, nor did he pedal any faster. It was as if he had had Mike pointed out to him and had not be bothered to credit his existence: lost in the half light with his chicken on a dusty road flanked by poplars.

Mike realized that he could have shot him, stripped him of his clothes, thrown him in the ditch, taken his bicycle and hen and made twenty-five miles in two hours before hiding the bicycle. . . . But even as the speculation crossed his mind, he knew that he could never have done it. Not an old French peasant with watery eyes.

He cut across another field, found a haystack, and lay down to await full daylight. He ate two more Horlicks tablets and some chocolate concentrate and wished he had something to drink. He thought briefly of Keith having a few drinks on his behalf last night in the bar. He hoped Rowbotham might join him and they might have said they'd miss old Yank. It never crossed his mind that they would think he had bought it. . . .

He awoke with the sun directly in his eyes, and the sound of a distant woman's voice in his ears. He had not earlier noticed the cottage a hundred yards away close to a wood. A middle-aged woman in a black dress was feeding her hens, calling them in turn—'Eh, petite Emilie, comment vas-tu ce matin . . . et Suzanne? . . .' A soft litany of love answered by clucking.

Mike walked over to her and said, 'Bonjour, madame, je suis aviateur du R.A.F.'

She looked up. She had a full, round, cheerful face with a high colour in her cheeks and black hair tied tightly behind her head. Stocky rather than overweight. And apparently not surprised to see him. 'Bonjour. Ah,, vous êtes Anglais . . . ?'

Mike decided not to complicate the situation by going into his American nationality. Yes, he was hungry. He would like a cup of coffee and understood that it was substitute. No real coffee in France now, except on the black market in Paris 'sans doute'. She spoke the word Paris as a term of abuse.

Mike could follow her without difficulty. His French, like his German, was not bad for an American, but also like most Americans, his accent was execrable and he was often not understood.

He drank the coffee and ate bread and raspberry jam with many pips in it on the porch of the little single-floor house. He felt like a nephew who had dropped in on his aunt in the country for a chat and refreshment, and tried to put this idiot notion into words. She did not at first understand but pressed him to explain, and when she recognized what he was saying, she burst into peals of laughter, slapping her thighs and wiping the tears from her eyes with the sleeve of her black dress. 'Ah, très drôle!'

She knew nothing about 'the line' but said, yes, she would make enquiries when she went into the market later in the morning. Yes, she would be very discreet.

'Now I will leave you. If you are hungry there are eggs and bread. My husband will probably not be seen until the evening. But if he comes back— sometimes he returns for yet more wine—you can explain that you are my guest.' She tapped her head with a finger like a very old carrot. 'He is not very good up there, you know.'

She left Mike in a little lean-to shed into which she placed a bale of straw. 'Dormez bien, mon petit. Mon neveu!' And she was still laughing as she mounted her ancient bicycle and pedalled off to the market.

The woman was unable to provide Mike with any useful contact. She explained later that she had made several enquiries but all her friends had told her to have nothing to do with him, that it was very dangerous, that the Germans would shoot her for certain.

'Cela m'est égal!' she told Mike. 'Restez ici aussi longtemps que vous voulez. Mais vous désirez sans doute poursuivre votre voyage.'

Mike asked her for clothes and she was equally obliging, and overwhelmed at the idea that he was giving her his Irvin jacket. 'Madam, il ne me sert plus. Avec ça, on voit tout-de-suite que je suis aviateur.'

She stroked the fur lining with her raddled fingers and put the leather to her nose. As Mike knew, it now smelt more of oil than leather, and when he explained this to her, she burst into more peals of laughter. In return, she brought out from a wardrobe a shiny suit in vivid blue, clearly her husband's best and perhaps only suit, purchased many years ago with much heart searching and bargaining over the price.

Mike shook his head. No, he could not take that. What would her husband wear? She explained that he wore it only once a year—for the regimental reunion. And as evidence, Mike saw the three campaign medals and the victory medal. He unpinned them gravely and handed them to her. She threw them perfunctorily into an open drawer. 'He only gets so drunk there that he has to be carried home,' she said as if referring to the indiscretions of a dog.

Before leaving, she gave him a baguette and a hunk of hard cheese and a litre bottle of *vin du pays*. He cut through the threads securing the shoe of his flying boots—designed to look like walking shoes—with the wool-lined uppers. He presented them to her, and she held them against her black-stockinged calves. 'That will be very comfortable in the winter.'

It was dark when he left. 'Bonne chance, aviateur. A bientôt. . . .'

He never saw her husband but he carried away with him on the vivid blue suit he wore over his uniform the pungent smell of that little dwelling—a compound of strong cigarette smoke, garlic and country sweat. He supposed the old man was still at the local café with his cronies . . .

*

Under the clock above the Restaurant Vincennes in the cathedral square at Rouen. 11 a.m. Those were his instructions. A young man had referred him to the proprietor of a *Boulangerie* who had told him to call on the Curé after six o'clock. The Curé had rustled up a bicycle and given him a huge glass of calvados which had made it almost impossible to mount the great machine ten minutes later. He had made it clear he was not 'in the line' but a man called Charles in Rouen might be able to help with an identity card and instructions. He should look up at the clock every five minutes exactly and light a cigarette at the same time. 'Here is a packet. I hope you smoke, young man.'

Mike had thanked him, not least for the cigarettes which were becoming a real need as he had not the confidence to go into a shop.

There was a long hill down into Rouen, and he was anxious about the bicycle's brakes as well as the likelihood of a checkpoint. Rough *pavé*, over the Boulevard de Verdun with its tramlines, past the Musée de la Ferronuerie and the big Lycée on the left. Very few people about. For a moment he confused the spectacular Eglise St Ouen with the cathedral, then pedalled and rattled on in his terrible blue suit to the cathedral. Here he found the little square without difficulty and had identified the restaurant half an hour before the appointed time.

Mike had known France well before the war, and now in spite of the defeat and the occupation there was little surface evidence of a great change. There were a few German soldiers off duty and looking into the shop windows, several German military vehicles parked at the far end of the square, and only a scattering of French Peugeots and Citroëns, several with a huge gas container secured to the roof. The women looked austerely dressed, it was true, without stockings, and many with head-scarves rather than hats. But their shopping bags appeared full, the shops were apparently doing good business, and a collection of stalls on the other side of the square were selling fresh fruit and vegetables.

Mike noticed a young, shabby, stooping figure leaning against a lamp post. He was still there when he lit another cigarette and glanced up at the clock, making a show of it this time.

'Vous avez du feu, monsieur?'

Mike took out a box of matches and struck one. 'J'attends un camarade qui s'appelle Charles,' Mike said as he blew out the match.

'34 Rue Jeanne d'Arc,' the young man said. He turned away at once, adding, 'A six heures.'

*

They took away almost everything he had—the bicycle, to be returned to the Curé, his maps, his emergency food pack, his shoes and knife (both 'trop Anglais') and gave him in exchange an oil-stained pair of dungarees, blue shirt coarser than the one he was wearing, underclothes, an old French-made pen-knife, a notebook, a railwayman's dinner box, timetable, union card and identity card: the photograph for the last would be ready tomorrow morning.

'Maintenant, s'il vous plaît, donnez-moi votre uniforme et votre arme.'

He was a hard-faced man with a dead cigarette stuck to his lower lip. They were not exactly hostile, but their cool and impersonal style bordered on it. He had heard that they were politically motivated rather than purely humanitarian or patriotic, enthusiasts for the anti-German cause only since Russia had been attacked. Mike thought wistfully of the laughing peasant's wife. 'I will give you my uniform. I have no firearms,' he said, raising his arms as an invitation to be frisked. It was not accepted.

They were in the attic of the house in the Rue Jeanne d'Arc, seven of them in all, two of them young women. One of the women took Mike down a steep flight of stairs and showed him a lavatory without a lock, and smelling as only French lavatories can smell. Here he took off his uniform with the Smithers of Cork Street label on the collar. It had seen a lot of service since its first fitting at Sir Richard Barrett's tailors back in '37: oil-stained and patched at the el-

bows, but undeserving of this end, doubtless in the
fire of some communist household in Rouen.

He wondered if he should tear the silk escape map
from the lining or keep the compass buttons. He decided against doing so, reasoning that there was nothing to be gained by revealing R.A.F. security details
to these people. His Browning was different. He was
prepared to take the risk of being searched if he was
captured and of its being found. Better still, he would
use it to escape. Without the little .25 tight against the
small of his back he would feel lost and unsafe. Rapidly he transferred the braces from his uniform trousers to the Frenchman's, together with the strapped
attachment holding the gun.

The smell of the stale garlic on the suit, of oil on the
dungarees combined with the stench of the lavatory
made him thankful to return to the attic in his new
guise, complete with beret. They nodded acknowledgement and one of the girls who took the bundle of
his uniform actually smiled and offered him a glass of
wine which they were all drinking round the table.

He was Jean-Claud Duhamel, aged nineteen, a
third-year fireman apprentice on the railway. Exempt
from conscript labour for he was vital to French transport and therefore to the German war machine. Address: 37 Rue de Buffon, where he lived with his parents.

They handed him a complete dossier: family,
school, friends, three more addresses, girlfriend even—
all typed out but the sheet was to be burnt the next
morning without fail, when he would have learned by
heart the details of his new identity. Mike reflected
sardonically that even if he was questioned by a non

French-speaking German his accent would give him away within seconds.

The next morning at 5.30 he would clock in at the Gare d'Orleans, and proceed to platform 3 where the driver and fireman of the 6.20 train to Le Mans would be awaiting him. If he was stopped by *flics* just show his papers and say nothing. 'You betcha!' exclaimed Mike, and the girl who had taken his uniform and spoke a little English said, ' "Betcha"—comment dire "Betcha" en Français?'

They all became less grim as the wine began to flow. They ate bread and cheese and the other girl went downstairs to make some ersatz coffee while the first girl unpicked Mike's wings and D.F.C. ribbon. 'You must be brave,' she said in French. 'How many Germans have you killed?'

Mike said, uncomfortably, 'Oh a few, I guess.'

She persisted, and the others were silent, looking at him keenly for the first time. He thought back to the bombers that he had blown up, a Stuka gunner collapsed over his weapon, of 109s dropping like flaming meteors, and said, without doing any serious arithmetic, 'Oh, about twenty, thirty maybe.'

The man who appeared to be in command—bald, thirtyish, a weasel's face with three days' growth of beard—said, 'This is why we get you back. To continue the good work of Boche-killing. When it is a hundred we send you a Croix de Guerre, eh?' His laugh was like pebbles rattling in a tin.

Later, they gave him a camp bed and blankets and told him he would be woken in the morning. The girl with his uniform lingered behind, perhaps waiting to be seduced, but Mike wanted none of it. She kissed his wings and ribbon and slipped them down her dress. She had unpicked the entire lining of the uniform jacket, and he guessed that she was going to save that from the incinerator, as well as the silk map of northern Europe, which she held up in wondering triumph. Frugal lot, the French. He waited until she had gone and then slipped out of the smelly dungarees and horrible smooth blue suit, tucking the gun under his pillow: his friend, and about all he could call his own.

*

It was still dark when he crossed the Seine by the Pont Boïeldieu. He had been stopped almost at once by a gendarme who searched his meal box. His union card and papers got him through and he even dared to say, 'Merci, monsieur.'

He could just make out the massive front of the station across the Place Carnot, and hurried towards it, his metal-heeled French shoes making an appalling noise—or so it seemed—on the *pavé*. As an operative, did one enter a railroad station by the front, like a passenger? Or from the side, like a servant calling at a house in England? Mike marched boldly up the steps, showed his papers again, and attempted to appear decisive as he searched for evidence of Platform Three. Old-fashioned gas lamps, turned down, gave only a flickering light, but he could see a number of early passengers in small groups with their luggage, and a party of German soldiers, silent and mournful in their long coats with kitbags stacked beside them. Mike saw the sign 'Voie 3' and turned towards it.

*

They reached Le Mans at 10.30 that morning, after a circuitous journey involving many stops. The fireman and his driver were as unforthcoming as the underground men in the Rue Jeanne d'Arc, nodding a welcome when he first arrived but taking little further notice of him. Once, to show willing, and enter into the part, Mike had indicated that perhaps he should shovel some coal, but his offer was brushed aside, and he had contented himself with watching them exercise their skills in the heat of the cab, and gazing at the delightful French scenery which was rolling by. It was a typical massive black French locomotive of the kind they often attacked on Rhubarbs, and he reflected on the irony if they were to be blown up by Spitfires from 140 Squadron.

There was a hot meal in the canteen at Le Mans. It was almost as stifling as on the footplate, and the air was thick with steam and pipe and cigarette smoke. The crews ate greedily, heads deep in their tin plates, and then pushing them away to light up and drink massively of the wine, and talk. Beyond a glance or two, no one took any notice of him, and he had the impression that everyone in the hut knew what he was, just one more evader from the R.A.F. passing down the line, to be ignored and carried on his way as quickly as possible.

Soon after he had finished, and was emulating the others by drinking wine and lighting a cigarette, a burly man tapped him on the shoulder, and nodded his head towards the door. Mike followed him out, and with another young man of his own age, followed him across the tracks to another locomotive.

On the next leg of the journey, not a single word was said to him, and he began to feel not just lonely but as if he no longer existed, that perhaps old X-X-ray had taken him down with her after all and his afterlife was to be a never-ending procession about the land on which he had crashed—past rivers like the Sarthe and Loire, through choking tunnels and out into the October sunshine again, over bridges, and then the shriek of brakes as they slowed for one more small town.

At Tours, they crossed the Loire and slowly circled the ancient city to pull in at the big terminus. The burly driver turned to Mike for the first time, and said in rapid French, 'We shall shortly cross the frontier into Vichy France and your papers will be examined closely. Say nothing unless it is necessary.' He held out his hand to examine the papers, swearing at their cleanness and rubbing his coal- and oil-stained fingers over them before handing them back.

German officials were working their way through the carriages, and when they climbed down from the first one, the three of them left the footplate and stood with their papers steady. A man looking like Conrad Veidt, a caricature of German officialdom at its most arrogant, took Mike's and glanced from the newly-taken photograph to his coal dust-stained face. He went through them slowly, page by page. He wore black gloves, and Mike with his experienced eye was delighted to notice that he had not cleaned his buttons that morning. But it was only passing encouragement. The others had climbed back onto the footplate, their interrogators walking on, and Conrad Veidt was starting all over again with his papers. To affect casualness he lit a cigarette and the official snapped, 'Éteignez!'

He read even more slowly after that. Then he suddenly thrust them back at Mike and turned and marched off without a word.

At Poitiers, a town Mike knew well from his pre-war travels, his crew was replaced, and late in the afternoon he was taken to a canteen with a dormitory attached in which he was told he would be spending the night.

So far his journey down the line had been more uneventful than he could have hoped, and on his first day he had travelled half across France. Apart from the check at Tours, he had seen no sign of suspicion or hostility. The dirt and the heat were the only trials he had had to bear.

They had a goods train the following day, full of empty wine barrels, and worked slowly south again, soon entering a country of endless vineyards and châteaux. In the late autumn sun, picking was at its height, and Mike could see men and women in broad straw hats working along the lines with their baskets.

'At the next station you will get out,' the engine driver told him. It was almost the only occasion he had spoken but Mike did not care. It seemed an excellent place to leave the locomotive. 'You must take the road to the east, walk for about five kilometres and you will see a château on your left. It is called Château Epernette. Go there.'

It was no more than a wayside halt with a wooden platform. Only a mangy dog lying in the shade of the shelter on the platform saw him descend from the footplate. Mike glanced back at the driver and fireman and was relieved to see them give a perfunctory wave. 'Bonne chance!' said the burly driver who was wiping his hands on some waste.

Mike took off the dungarees in the shelter, rolled them up tightly and tucked them under his arm. Then he removed his horrible blue shiny jacket because of the heat, and began walking along the dusty road. A signpost pointed west to Librourne. He was in the heart of Bordeaux, near the town of St-Emilion, where the soil was so precious that there were almost no flowers and everything was sacrificed to Bacchus and profit. Vines, some still heavy with grapes that would soon become the 1941 vintage of some of the finest wine in the world, grew hard up to the road, and empty and full baskets lay at the end of the rows. From this rolling green sea of vines there arose old grey spires and towers that could have been here when this land belonged to England.

Two of these towers belonged to Château Epernette, set back half a kilometre from the road up a poplar-lined drive. A dog barked as he approached and two girls of about four and six years watched him solemnly from a small patch of lawn. A woman appeared at the door when he was a dozen yards from it, a tall, young woman of great beauty in a long dress with her fair hair drawn up tightly at the back. She looked at Mike expressionlessly and demanded sharply who he was.

'Je suis Jean-Claud Duhamel, originaire de Rouen,' Mike replied smartly, standing still under the hot sun, awaiting rejection or welcome.

'Ah, oui.' Then she began speaking in perfect English with scarcely a trace of accent. 'And where were you shot down?'

'Not far from Arras, ma'am.'

'Two or three days ago?'

'Sure thing.'

'It must have been an expensive raid.' She smiled and indicated that he should come in out of the sun. 'I have a squadron leader here already. Perhaps you know him? His name is Dick Anderson? His brother was shot down at the same time.'

It was wonderfully cool in the long parquet hall that ran right through the centre of the château, with a distant sight of another small lawn, geraniums, late shrub roses in bloom. The smell of French floor polish was quite different from English or American— sharper, more pungent. There were water colours on the wall which Mike guessed were painted by this woman, who now introduced herself.

'My name is Liversidge. Marie-Ann Liversidge. Not very French you will say. My husband is English, you see. Or perhaps was English. I do not know. The Germans have taken him away and I have heard nothing from him.' They walked slowly side by side towards the brilliant rectangle of light in the rear garden. 'That is one reason why I am helping.' She turned her strong face towards Mike, and then ran her eyes up and down his dusty, shiny blue suit. 'That is truly dreadful,' she said, smiling. 'You must choose something different from my husband's wardrobe.' She laughed, looking at his face. 'And perhaps a wash?'

Later, he was shown into Mr Liversidge's dressing-room and selected from a cupboard one of many finely tailored English tweed suits.

310

Mike met Squadron Leader Anderson over an aperitif in the drawing-room. They remembered one another from Eldergrove during their initial flying training. He was a heavily-built, dark man, with a pencil-thin R.A.F.-style moustache and slicked down black hair. Mike had read somewhere that he had won a D.F.C. bombing bridges in May '40 and earned a D.S.O. later. A valuable catch for the Germans, a serious loss for the R.A.F.

'Well, Dick, I guess you can say we let you down.'

'Hell, no. But that was some donny, eh! Nothing more you could do. And at least we were on target.'

Madame Liversidge had left them alone to exchange reminiscences—these two young men in her husband's good English tweed suits that were too big for the American and too small for the squadron leader.

Mike asked, 'Any of your crew get away with it?'

'I'm afraid they both went for a burton. Never saw them brolly-hop, anyway. We were very low and a bit pushed for time.' Anderson had come through the same line at Rouen twenty-four hours after Mike but had come down in a heavy lorry packed with drainage pipes. 'They had to prop me up after eight hours in one of them,' Anderson added wryly.

Then they had dinner with Madame—a delicious meal accompanied by a fresh 1937 St-Emilion so delicate that Mike knew someone more knowledgeable than he should be drinking it. They played three-handed bridge over coffee, Madame Liversidge suggesting that it was time the Germans spared her another pilot for a fourth. She went to bed early, and Dick and Mike discussed admiringly this remarkable and remarkably courageous woman. They turned off the light and went out through the heavy black-out curtains onto the lawn. It was a clear, cool night, and they were engulfed by the heady scent of grapes.

'It's beautiful O.K., but I guess I'd go nuts living here,' said Mike.

'I thought I'd go nuts after less than a day. I asked if we could go out and help with the picking, but Madame said it was too risky. The servants are O.K., she says. And almost certainly most of her workers, but they would talk and the word would get around.'

Mike asked, 'How long are we going to be stuck here?'

'No way of telling.' Dick Anderson laughed and offered Mike a cigarette. 'But the cuisine's O.K. And she's a grand lady to have around.'

'I'd do my nut if I was her. If I ever get out of here, I'll go back to Hun-pasting with relish.' And then he remembered, for the first time. 'Hey, Dick, d'you know I was on my last op? The first almost two years ago—the last three days ago. How d'you like that?'

*

They shot crap, played pontoon, read and improved their French, played with the two little girls, and talked. The servants moved discreetly about them, sometimes enquiring if there was anything they required. There was no whisky or gin in the house, but Pernod, strange syrup drinks that Mike found disgusting, and an abundance of brandy—and the vineyard's own wine with every meal.

Madame Liversidge was often out for lunch, but always there at dinner time, and always she began the conversation, 'Not tomorrow, I'm afraid. But soon I

312

hope,' spoken with a mournful expression on her face. They had been told that there was rarely more than twenty-four hours' notice of when they could move on, sometimes less. The line seemed to have got jammed somewhere; which probably meant that the Gestapo had struck and some wretched, brave body was being tortured.

Mike and Dick began to get slack and livery with the rich food and lack of exercise, so with Madame's permission they took to running in shorts late at night round the vineyards. She also discovered some boxing gloves in the attic, and they had a few bouts every day, to the delight of the girls.

The picking was over, the days were becoming shorter and colder. A light mist hung over the shallow valleys about the château in the early mornings, and the sun had to exert itself to find the heat to dispel it. Sunbathing was less of a pleasure, and they became fretful and snappy with one another.

Mike said late one evening, not meaning a word of it, 'Jeez, I'm going to give myself up soon. I really *am* going nuts—d'you know that?'

The following morning it was pouring with rain, and Madame came down late to breakfast. 'At last!' she said, smiling at them from the door. 'After lunch today you will take a walk together to where I tell you.'

'That's great, Madame,' said Mike, getting up from the table. 'I guess we'll need umbrellas.'

It was still raining at lunchtime. 'At three o'clock a Peugeot van will stop at the end of my drive. You will get in the back—there will be things to conceal you. You will be driven to near the frontier. I do not know

313

where—we only hear what we need to know. But I think you may be in Spain tonight.'

They were given old raincoats, and with the berets they had been given in Rouen, they looked like any pair of penurious peasants of the Gironde. They kissed the children and Madame on both cheeks. The servants, too, were in the hall when they left. 'Adieu et bonne chance, messieurs!' they called out.

'We can't thank you enough,' said Dick to Madame, now shaking her hand. 'We'll pray for your safety, and for your husband's.'

The van was late. At 3.15 it had still not appeared. Mike did not mind getting wet, but as the minutes passed he became increasingly anxious, and he had to accept that he was terribly strung up now that the climax had arrived.

'Here it comes,' said Dick. 'A bit late on its E.T.A.'

A small dark shape emerged from a distant cloud of spray. The van was going at a good speed, and in less than a minute was beside them. A man with a mournful moustache was at the wheel.

'Montez vite!' he said. There was a pile of empty sacks in the back. Nothing else and nothing to conceal them. Dick was over the side, and Mike had one foot on the rear mudguard, when a large man in a long brown coat emerged from the vines flanking the road. He walked so slowly you could call it sauntering towards the van.

'Eh bien, messieurs . . .' he began. His voice was scarcely audible above the sound of the ticking-over Peugeot engine. Mike turned and saw his pale face, streaming with rain for he wore no hat, and his overcoat was dark with dampness. Mike stood quite still, one arm resting on the Peugeot's tailboard and watched the gendarme, wearing a shiny cape and pointing a James Cagney tommy-gun at him, emerging from the vineyard. Out of the corner of his eye, Mike could see two more, one on the other side of the road and the third walking towards the front of the van.

'Descendez,' the man with the gentle voice said to the driver, at the same time opening the door and grabbing his collar. In a movement requiring great strength he lifted him and threw him into the road as if dashing a small animal to death. One of the *flics* kicked him in the stomach and ordered him to get up.

They were all handcuffed and were standing at the road-side like peasants waiting for a bus to market when a car and a big Citroën van arrived. The rain was coming down harder than ever and the windscreen-wipers were making little impression. With agony in his heart, Mike watched the car skid-turn into the drive and race up to the château. Two more orphaned children to join the army of them in France and Belgium, Poland and Holland and Norway. What a God-awful, ghastly war!

The inside of the Citroën smelt of death, too; death in the bars over the two small windows, death in the steel sides, the wooden benches upon which they sat, each manacled to a gendarme, whose cape dripped water noisily onto the death floor. The Frenchman who had been driving the Peugeot had been sick before being half dragged into the van, and was being sick again between his knees. There were two surprises about the gendarme to whom he was handcuffed: he had taken his pillbox hat off to reveal car-

315

roty hair, and he had a jaunty expression on his face.
He took no notice of the vomiting.

Dick Anderson said, 'We'll get out of this O.K.—the
bloody bastards.' And his guard told him to shut up.

They drove for miles in silence. The Frenchman
was not sick any more but he coughed from time to
time and was obviously still in pain. Mike guessed
they were being taken to Bordeaux. He could see only
a blurred image of the passing scenery but after an
hour and a half the number of houses as well as the
traffic appeared to increase, and they stopped more
frequently. *Pavé* shook the body of the Citroën and a
tramcar rattled past in the opposite direction. Mike
saw a spread of grey water through the grey sweeping
rain. That would be the Gironde, and on the other
side of the tramcars were more numerous and he
caught a glimpse of a gendarme in a black cape like
their captors' giving them priority at a crossroads.

The Citroën drew up roughly. Mike briefly saw the
plainclothes man's head glancing through the glass
panel from the driving compartment and then disap-
pear as he stepped down onto the pavement. They
were taken out through the door at the back, the man
with the melancholy moustache first, looking very
pale and not glancing at them as he was led away.
Dick's guard descended the step onto the road clumsily, pulling on the handcuff so that he caused Dick to
miss his step and half fall, dragging his guard down
with him. They shouted at one another angrily, cursing in their own language and Mike thought Dick was
going to punch him.

The rest of the day was a time of waiting in the
Gendarmerie: waiting on a bench in a passage to see

316

an official, waiting in a bare room, waiting in another smaller room, dim-lit with one high barred window to tell them that night had fallen. They were given nothing to eat or drink, and when they were allowed to the urinal the guard stood beside them. Always their guard. And waiting. And no talking.

Neither had a watch but Mike knew it must be past midnight when they were taken into a less austere room and were confronted by an evidently senior official who spoke to them in French. They had been perfunctorily frisked earlier but now this official—to keep his hand in? to show he meant business? to impress his subordinates by his thoroughness?—ordered Dick to raise his arms, his gendarme's handcuffed arm conforming willy-nilly as if they were at ballet school.

Then it was Mike's turn. The chief was fat and bald and, of course, smelt of garlic. He also looked tired and harassed. 'Now what are you hiding, hein?' he said in French. 'Guns, knives? The Gestapo will not love me if I send you to them armed to the teeth ("armé aux dents").'

'The Gestapo have no business with us,' Mike said sharply. 'We are prisoners of war. The army, yes. The Gestapo, no.'

The fat white hands were running up the inside of his legs like a tailor's fitter measuring for trousers. Then the outside, caressingly, slowly. There were some coins in one pocket, the old French pen-knife in the other. The official held up the knife in front of the gendarme's face. 'You say you searched him, and you leave him with this? You must be mad. You will be reported. We have our orders—you know that.

These men have knowledge of all the traitors to Vichy who are on the escape line.'

Then chest and inside of his jacket, down the back, a hand each side as if Mike and he were lovers, the hands running over his hips and down the back of the legs again just missing the .25.

'Good. Now you will each sign this form.' The papers were on the edge of the desk, facing them, a badly-duplicated sheet of cheap foolscap paper, headed with the name, address and telephone number of the Gendarmerie.

'There is no necessity to read it,' the official snapped at Mike.

Mike muttered in English, 'My Pop told me never, but never, to sign any goddam paper without understanding it.' He read the first lines of legalistic verbiage, and then: 'j'étais en civile au moment qu'on m'a arrêté . . .'

The official was becoming fretful, wringing his hands and pacing up and down. 'Signez!' he shouted suddenly, and pointed a stubby finger at the bottom line. They *had* been in civilian clothes when evading capture . . . Hell, he would have to sign in the end, as Dick had. But just to be difficult he claimed to be left-handed, which meant finding the keys to the handcuffs, unlocking them, and a minute's theatrical massaging of his wrist before taking the pen from the irate official and clumsily writing his name.

They were then each put into a single common cell with unclean brown blankets on a wooden bunk without springs. Mike was given a bowl of soup and some bread and cheese which he ate wearily, for the first time contemplating the future with real anxiety. The Gestapo. An ugly word for an ugly bunch of murderers and torturers. And the official had meant it, of that he was sure. But they had committed no crime. To evade capture, in or out of uniform, was not against the Haig Convention or the Rules of War. Perhaps they were going to be forced to disclose the identity of all who had passed them down the line? But hadn't this line been blown already?

Mike wondered how much—if any—he would be able to take before they extracted everything they wanted to know. He threw the blankets onto the stone floor, folded his ridiculously large jacket into a pillow and was asleep in seconds.

*

After the interminable waiting of the previous day, events moved swiftly in the morning, as if the two signatures had released all impediments. Moreover, there was no more roughness from the Gendarmerie; on the contrary, there was even a hint of concern and sympathy now that it was generally known that they were to be handed over.

They were allowed to talk to one another, and when the gendarmes slipped on handcuffs for the journey, one of them apologized to Dick; who said in English to Mike, 'I've always heard, old boy, that the toughest jailer is kind on the morning of execution.'

They were given a car, too, instead of the rattly van, a big black front-wheel-drive Citroën with tip-up seats in the back, which swallowed the worst *pavé* without a jolt. And this was as well for they drove so fast it was as if they were being pursued.

319

Gestapo headquarters were in the Rue George V. Mike read the name on the blue-and-white sign as they drew up outside and drew Dick's attention to it. 'Poor show,' he commented. 'They ought to change it to Rue Adolf Hitler.'

*

The airfield was on the west side of the city, an old civilian 'drome with dusty grassy runways, a large watch office, and a sad, peeling sign, reading 'Aero Club du Sud-Ouest'. Outside the single hangar stood several ancient Air France biplanes, gaping orifices where there had once been radial engines. It could not be an important Luftwaffe base although there was a massive Focke-Wulf 200 parked on the far side. Their plane was obviously the Junkers 52 standing beside the watch office, its three engines already turning over, the three-man crew standing nearby out of the slipstream and smoking.

There were five of them in the big Mercedes besides the driver: a Gestapo officer who sat in front, presenting his close-cropped back of head, rolls of neck fat, and the tight white collar which emphasized them. This officer—chinless, fragment of moustache, pig's eyes behind thick spectacles—might have been David Low's model for his cartoons of the dreaded Gestapo chief himself, Himmler. Even his voice as he told them they were to be taken at once to Gestapo headquarters in Paris was an echo of Himmler's.

They had been only an hour in the Rue George V, much of that time occupied in washing, changing and shaving, as if being spruced up for the honour of presentation to the Gauleiters of Paris. They had also been given an excellent breakfast, with plenty of German sausage; no French coffee-and-croissant non-sense. The treatment had been coldly polite, as it was when the car stopped beside the Junkers and they got out, awkwardly because of the handcuffs—shiny, flamboyant handcuffs unlike the plain black of the French kind.

Mike had never seen a 52 in the air, to his regret because he had heard what fat, vulnerable targets they were. It was well known as the workhouse of the Luftwaffe, and propaganda photographs of numbers of them dropping paratroops and supplies and being loaded with guns and motor-cycle and side-car combinations had appeared in newspapers and magazines throughout the world. An ugly, awkward-looking machine with its third engine like a boil on a nose, the heavy fixed undercarriage, and the all-corrugated metal skin from which its nickname 'Iron Annie' was derived. And now, what might well be their last flight was to be in this shuddering black and grey beast towards which they now walked, observed curiously by the ground crew.

One of the mechanics drew a short ladder from a shelf under the door and hooked it into place. The Gestapo officer was more than ever like Himmler now that he had on his ridiculously tall peaked hat with the comic opera skull-and-crossbones beneath the eagle, and outside holster for his Luger. He stood by the door and nodded to their armed guards, who were all in black uniform, too, with shining boots—bully-boy boots with hard toe-caps for kicking Jews in the testicles.

Dick went in first and Mike followed, casting his eyes quickly over the plane's interior: a small door at

321

the rear, leading to store and lavatory, he guessed. Flip-up seats facing inwards and running longitudinally almost the full length of the cabin, which he calculated as about twenty feet. Fixed windows. Three trap-doors in the floor leading probably to luggage space. Wireless and operator's table at the far end outside the cabin.

They sat down in pairs facing one another, the machine vibrating with the tick over, exhaust fumes filtering in through the open door. Mike winked at Dick and studied the interior more carefully. The cockpit doors were a curious feature. They were little more than four feet hight, reminding him of Alice in Wonderland's shrunk door, awkward to pass through and necessary, he surmised, for structural strength. Above in the roof a blanked-off circle indicated the gun position when the machine was armed, and on the starboard side was the big cargo door, split horizontally and hinged top and bottom. Ugly maybe, but a cleverly-designed machine and with an unsurpassed reputation for reliability. Just look at those vertical glass-tube gas gauges above each engine!

The officer had settled himself stiffly on one of the seats forward. He had taken off his hat and was mopping his forehead although the temperature was not unduly high and the slipstream was stirring the air. Mike guessed that he was not looking forward to this journey, and was reassured by the thought. Perhaps their guards would be sick, too. Then, with much stamping of heavy boots, a Luftwaffe Hauptmann marched down the aisle, ostentatiously wielding a Schmeisser machine-pistol. And it seemed highly unlikely that he was going to be airsick. He was followed by the crew—pilot, co-pilot and a third man lacking goggles and helmet who sat down in front of the wireless and folded out first a small table and then his maps.

The pilot meanwhile had opened the double doors and bent down to pass through to the cabin. Mike caught a glimpse of two wooden wheels and instruments, triple throttle and mixture controls, a V windscreen beyond. The mechanic who had started the engine and run them up made way for the pilot and walked past them, through the door, which he secured behind him. The co-pilot shut the cockpit doors, and within less than a minute the chocks had been signalled away and the big tri-motor edged forward and taxied fast and bumpily towards the end of the runway.

With the long slots on the trailing edge of the wings, the take-off run of the Junkers was very short, and they were soon banking steeply over the city with the River Garonne winding through it and down towards its wide, island-studded estuary. They steadied on a north-easterly heading, but were flying just below scattered cumulus and bumping about a lot.

It was the ghastly sub-Himmler who decided Mike's course of action. Within a few minutes of the plane's settling on course for Paris, this officer had turned pale and now rose shakily from his seat and with handkerchief to his mouth, hastened unsteadily down the aisle towards the rear. When he re-emerged through the door he was wiping his face and his creased neck with his handkerchief, pince-nez in his other hand, all dignity cast away.

Mike began his act, assisted by a faint feeling of

genuine nausea as a result of the Gestapo officer's performance. First he dropped his head onto his right hand, elbows on knees. He remained in this position for perhaps a minute, drew a handkerchief from his pocket and held it over his mouth and turned his head towards his guard, who disregarded Mike until he pulled hard on the handcuffs and pointed towards the rear of the cabin. The guard shook his head and Mike called out in English, 'I'm going to be sick, goddam it,' and made as if he was about to do just that.

The Gestapo officer was too preoccupied with his own lamentable condition even to notice what was going on, but the Hauptmann must have got up from his seat at the forward end for Mike saw his legs and boots close below his head. He was shouting something to the guard which Mike did not understand, but he felt the handcuffs being unlocked and heard the Hauptmann shouting at him to be quick.

The Hauptmann followed close behind, the Schmeisser much in evidence, and posted himself close to the door and near the Gestapo officer while Mike made much of staggering, clutching the door handle and lurching in, slamming the door behind him.

He was in an ill-lit area, chest parachutes piled in the corner and a crate lying unsecured at the far side. The little lavatory door was on the starboard side and Mike swung it open, suddenly swift and purposeful in his movements.

Back at Savile Farm he had practised this in the privacy of his room many times, always with the feeling that George Brent would be scornful of his clumsiness. Now, with both hands behind his back, he unbuckled the strap securing the little Browning to his braces and slipped it into his right jacket pocket, gambling on his guard handcuffing his left wrist as before. He dropped the strap into the deep pan, gave himself another minute, and then, feeling quite steady and clear in his intentions, let himself out of this dim area and opened the door into the cabin, wiping his face at the same time just as the Gestapo officer had done.

He was glad of his decision not to rush things when he saw the Hauptmann standing no more than a yard away, the Schmeisser, and cold grey eyes, aimed straight at him. Dick was looking up curiously and the Gestapo officer brushed past to return hastily to the lavatory. Mike made his way to his old seat, sitting down on his guard's right and offering his left wrist. He noticed that they were flying in cloud now, that they were bumping more than ever. 320 or so miles Bordeaux to Paris. Cruising speed 110 m.p.h. They had been airborne about half an hour. Time was slipping by and was not to be wasted.

The Hauptmann with the heavy boots had not returned to his old seat, no doubt calculating that there might be more visits to the rear compartment, and settling himself on the last flip-up seat by the door, the pistol across his knees. Mike measured the distance between them—just over three paces, say ten feet. He repeated in his mind the sequence and approximate timing, slipped his right hand into the voluminous pocket of his jacket.

The butt of the Browning was still warm from its recent proximity to the small of his back, and he slipped his hand round it, finding it as comforting as the hand of a mother to an uneasy child. He counted three slowly, a particularly violent lurch of the Junkers coinciding with the last number, and sunlight streaming into the cockpit as the Junkers emerged from the cloud.

Now he leapt to his feet, dragging his guard with him. 3/8ths of a second. Shouted at Dick—'Grab him.' Nil time. Drew the .25, squeezed the rear of the butt to release the safety-catch, and fired at the Hauptmann at precisely four feet range. 5/8ths of a second, and long enough for the Hauptmann to seize his Schmeisser. He had it in his hands but 5/8ths was not long enough by perhaps 1/8th to aim and fire. By this time Mike had done both, and as fast as his index finger could pull the light, beautifully balanced trigger, fired again, hitting the German in the chest with the first shot, and in the stomach, as he rose, with the second.

Mike, with too much to do, did not wait to see the Hauptmann collapse. He heard the crash of the Schmeisser on the metal floor but was now pressing the Browning into the stomach of his guard, just below the fancy belt with all the gleaming brass. An idiot belt for an idiot who, shaken by the sudden activity, had not even begun to get his left hand to the Luger holster.

'Schlüssel. Schnell!' Mike yelled. Behind him he heard above the roar of the engines the tussle between Dick and his guard. Nothing was to be gained by doubting the outcome, and he kept his eyes on his guard's shaking hand as he inserted the key.

Dick was shouting, 'The Wop. Look out . . . !' There was a shot, this time a deeper-noted, more authoritative sound, and Mike swung around to see the Wireless Operator staggering down the centre aisle, his hands over a face that was pouring blood.

Five seconds. Maybe six. Not more. The handcuffs were off, he had his guard's Luger. Dick had knocked out his guard but was still handcuffed to him. The Hauptmann was sprawled half under the flip-up seats, and there was a lot of blood around him, too.

The Wireless Operator still had some life in him. He was kneeling now.

Behind him the twin doors had opened and the co-pilot was peering through into the cabin, a strange sight doubled up like that, his face set in an expression of total non-comprehension—at what he saw.

The Wireless Operator, who should not have lasted this long, now lay quite still, his head on one of the trap-doors, his knees in an attitude of prayer, his blood flooding out over the metal floor—'Blut und Eisen'—'Blood and Iron'—'. . . sie macht sich nur durch Blut und Eisen'.

Dick Anderson, still linked to his guard, was unimpressed. He had grasped the Schmeisser from the blood-streaked floor, and while the co-pilot was still staring at the scene of mayhem, fired a two-second burst of stunning accuracy which threw him back into the cockpit by the pulverizing weight of metal that tore into his chest and stomach.

The pilot was stunned by the reappearance backwards of his second pilot, and was also having to exert all his strength to hold the plane steady against the weight on the second wheel of the man's torn, blood-streaming body.

Nor was it the end of violence in this ride above the

lovely Poitou countryside at angel goddam nine. Now it was Dick searching the pockets of his guard for the key to his handcuffs. Now it was Mike heading for the cockpit. Luger in one hand, Browning with four unspent bullets in the other—Jesus Christ, an embarras de goddam richesse of goddam ironmongery.

He was bending down to get through the door. The pilot was using a booted leg to try to kick his co-pilot off the second wheel and was losing control at the same time. The Junkers was going into a steep dive, the B.M.W. engines already rising to a scream. And then, just as he was almost through, Mike felt the touch on his right shoulder, a red hot poker's caress, no more. But it was enough to spin him round and send him falling into the cockpit so that he could see, far away down the aisle, Herr pseudo-Himmler, with a very purposeful Luger in his other hand being fired with great accuracy down the tilting aisle.

EPILOGUE

That meeting in Hornberg in the Black Forest. At Uxbridge on the day they joined the R.A.F. At Savile Farm when they had both been posted to 140 Squadron. Again and again after the whirling fury of combat, a brief wave, thumbs up, formating alongside one another. Always the reunion. Mike talked about 'the goddam flying fates', and that is what their meetings were.

For this reason, after the first impact of shock and relief and delight, their confrontation at the front door of Rising Hall seemed as natural and inevitable a reunion as all the earlier coincidences which they had shared since they had first met in Germany back in 1937.

Stokes would normally have opened the front door, of course, but the Barretts' was not a formal household and it was natural for Keith to answer the bell as he was passing it, first switching off the light and using the torch that always hung beside the great iron-studded oak front door. Darkness had long since fallen and it was a black night, and he aimed the torch on the ground in front of the unseen figure in the now customary manner in the black-out.

329

'Good evening . . .'

'Hi, Keith.'

Keith raised the beam of the torch up the long service greatcoat to a smiling mouth, far-apart brown
eyes, a wrinkled forehead, tousled hair.

'You're ruining my night vision,' Mike said. 'Permission to pancake?'

Keith shut the door behind them and switched on
the hall light. 'You're supposed to be dead.'

'Thanks, kid.'

Keith glanced down at the empty right sleeve and
the bulge across Mike's chest. 'So they only winged
you.'

'That came later. How's Eileen?'

'My God, Mike, there's so much to talk about!'

Spontaneously, but awkwardly because of Mike's
injury, they suddenly shook hands, and as he helped
Mike off with his coat, Keith told him that she was
here, at Rising Hall, recovering from a breakdown
which had followed her long critical illness, which
had been further intensified by the news of Mike's almost certain death. 'But she's O.K. Better every day,
and we're all trying to pump up her self-esteem and
self-confidence. That's the quack's recipe . . .'

'All?'

'Her parents, who still know nothing of her affair.
And Jenny who's on leave here. And. Oh my Lord,
prepare yourself for a shock. They'll have to. Your
parents.'

'Here? Jeepers . . . !'

Ralph and Suzy Browning had wangled a berth on
the *Louis Pasteur* from Halifax in order to learn at
first hand about the fate of their son. Staying at the

Embassy in London, they had gathered what news they could from the Air Ministry, including the fact that Keith was on leave at Rising Hall. The Barretts had at once invited them to come as guests.

'Go in there and have a wash,' said Keith. 'I'd better go ahead and warn them. We dine in five minutes. Hungry?'

'What d'you think, kid?'

Dinner was postponed half an hour and Mike and his parents were left to greet one another privately in the library while Sir Richard and Lady Barrett, Jenny and Keith, drank another glass of sherry.

'It really is incredible,' Keith said at one point. 'There wasn't one of us gave him a chance. No 'chute. No news from the underground. Nothing from Gib. Not even a phone call here.'

Jenny, smart in an all-black long dress with just a single string of pearls and Keith's new engagement ring, broke in from her chair: 'He told me he had cabled from Gib, and telephoned, but . . .'

Keith laughed. 'All right, darling. We know what you're going to say.' He turned to Sir Richard. 'Father, we must recognize that we now live in the twentieth century, and telephones need not be hidden in remote corners under stairs where no one can hear them.'

Lady Barrett said, 'I am now going to put down my famous foot, Richard. Yes, we shall have a proper telephone in a place where we can all hear it. I am constantly using it. I have just done so this minute, and to useful purpose.'

'What do you mean by that, dear?' Sir Richard Barrett glanced again at the grandfather clock, hating any break in his routine.

'To ask Dr Samson whether it would be all right for Eileen to see Mike tonight. And he said, "Yes, do her all the good in the world." '

Mike came down late to the delayed dinner. Keith knew that he would be shocked by the sight of Eileen, pale and thin but as lovely as ever; and by her remoteness, the way she seemed unable to concentrate on anything for long; and by her physical weakness. Mike made no comment when he sat down at the table between his mother, on Constance Barrett's left, and Jenny, but gave Keith a confidential wink. Keith knew it would be O.K. but it was nice to have the confirmation.

'Now let the boy *eat*,' ordered Lady Barrett. 'The poor soul looks tired out and half-starved.' A description that was so patently inaccurate that everyone at the table laughed.

Mike began the story of his escape when the maid brought in the cheese, limited now to a small segment of cheddar tactfully divided into seven equal slivers.

'I guess I'll skip the detail at dinner about conditions in that Junkers,' he said after covering the tragic circumstances of their arrest. 'It wasn't too nice, though, and I thought we were both going to be added to the casualty list. He winged me lightly again, but I think Herr Himmler's general state of queasiness caused him to be a mite slow after that. Anyhow, he was too late to avoid a colossal kick very low in the stomach delivered by Dick. Away went his pince-nez, and that was the end of the shooting. There was only the pilot left, and he was unarmed and still very, very busy, with me giving a hand—a left hand.'

The pilot and the guards had been offered the alternative of bailing out over France or being arrested when they reached Gibraltar. They decided to leave, and Dick took over the controls of the Junkers 52, which had already been turned through 180 degrees. They gave them chest chutes from the store and allowed them to jump over the Pyrenees, where it would take a day or two to find a telephone.

'We used another chute to cover up the bodies, and the shrouds to secure Herr Himmler. We sure weren't going to let *him* go. A bit of reverse interrogation was called for in his case.'

Keith asked, 'What sort of reception did you get at Gib? Busy?'

'Yeah, I guess you can call it that. Dick and I decided to come in low and slow. We stuck a white flag on a stick through port and starboard sliding windows in the cockpit, and Dick rocked the wings till I thought they'd come off. In the end we had an escort of a dozen Hurris and a pair of Gladiators, all slavering away and watching for an excuse to put us into the drink. Then, after we landed and a trip to the doc, a crazy series of parties, broken by Intelligence investigations and a funeral for the guys we'd shot.'

Mike smiled at his mother, who butttered him another biscuit and, because she was holding his one good arm, put it in his mouth.

Sir Richard Barrett, at the other end of the table, grunted and congratulated Mike. 'A credit to your country, my boy,' he said, and momentarily glowed pink with embarrassment. Then, on firmer ground, suggested to his wife that the ladies shouldn't leave the table tonight. 'Damned irregular, dear. But everything's been put out with this young fellow's turning up out of the blue. I'll put the news on and we can have our port and coffee in here.'

He pushed back his chair and walked towards the double doors leading to the drawing-room, a stocky, greying figure with his slight Great War limp. Stokes had built up a blazing log fire, the heat from which reached them thirty feet away. The wireless was on the Chippendale table beside the fireplace, like some totem to the new religion of war news. To miss the nine o'clock news when the world was being torn apart was near sacrilegious.

The conversation at the table died away with the ringing sound of Big Ben's bell . . . 'Here is the nine o'clock news and this is Alvar Liddell reading it. President Roosevelt has just announced Japanese air attacks on American bases in the Hawaiian Islands: the Japanese envoys in Washington are now at the State Department . . .'

Later, with no trace of self-consciousness this time, Sir Richard Barrett stood and raised his glass. 'To our new Allies.' He nodded first to Suzy Browning, then to her husband and finally to Mike, who rose in his turn and sipped his port—which was rare and pale and soft, better than Fonseca '27.

Wings of Victory, a novel about two RAF pilots who fly missions high above France and Germany during the last crucial days of the war is spiced with their engaging relationships with two beautiful and provocative women on the ground. Here is a stirring look at the action in WINGS OF VICTORY which will be published by Dell in September, 1981.

This was the moment—the very second—when the fighters liked to come in; and with predictable precision the warning cry came from—who else?—Milt Scheller: "Bandits, boss, four o'clock high!"

"Chee-rist!" shouted another voice; and Mike at once threw over his switch, "Medway Leader—shut that mouth." Then: "Buster!" for full emergency boost, and finally, "Medway aircraft, take them as they go down and wait till you can count the rivets before you press the tit."

They did not need the advice, and Mike knew it. 10th Eagle knew exactly what to do, and there was not a squadron on either side with higher shooting standards than these Americans. But he also knew that they liked a few encouraging words of incitement, like a cavalry regiment's bugle call or a mariner's drum rifle before combat.

They were Messerchmitt 109Fs, faster than the 109s Mike had fought against so often in the Battle of Britain, with a strutless tail and retractable tailwheel, which gave a smoother configuration. They might be faster than the earlier mark, but so was his Spitfire V with the clipped wings, especially when they were low down like this. There was little or nothing to choose between them.

There were at least forty 109s, probably three *Jagdeswaden* from Schipol, hardened by experience like 10 Squadron, tough antagonists every one of them. They came down like plummeting lapwings, aileroning over onto their backs and streaking after the fleeing Beaufighters.

Mike turned his section to meet them and when the Germans went through without firing, threw his Spitfire into a vertical dive that quickly built up past the 400 m.p.h. mark on his A.S.I., the rev counter needle spinning as swiftly round the dial.

As Admiral Lord Nelson claimed that the word *Frigate* would be engraved upon his heart, Mike knew that the shape of a 109 would be etched upon the retina of his eye for all time—that arrowlike, villainous-looking, lethal little fighter that had killed so many of his friends. He hated the 109s with a cold, controlled fury and fought them with the knowledge that both his antagonist and his weapons were as good as he and his Spitfire were, and that therefore only consuming concentration would result in the destruction of his foe and his own survival. Once, long ago, it had not been like this, when the fury was white-hot, and he knew that he had not deserved to survive then.

Not now. Now he reduced the angle of his dive, with the mottled sea coming up fast to meet him, half rolled onto his back, and chose his target, the third from the left of a *Schwarm* of four, hoping the pilot was the leader.

Little high-set tail, arrogant black cross on the fuselage, radio aerial just aft of the cockpit, the black dot in the cockpit—the pilot's head....What was going on in that head? He really thought he could get at that Beaufighter skimming the sea a mile ahead and below before the Spits could get at him? When a glance in his mirror would show Mike at 800 yards and fast catching up. And this was one of the feared Schipol *Jagdeswaden.*

Then, the sight bars told Mike that the range was 600 yards and it was worth a short 10-degree deflection shot. The whole *Schwarm* began to jink evasively, with that incredibly fast up-and-down motion that made shooting so difficult. But the German made no attempt to turn into the attack, and Mike let him pulsate for several more seconds, the gap closing fast as the 109 lost some speed.

It was nearer five degrees when Mike squeezed the cannon button with his thumb, and the shells—high explosive, armor piercing, tracer, in that order—linked the two racing machines.

Mike had had his first gun at six, and had been shooting ever since—quail, coyotes, roe deer and stags, buck rabbit and elegant pheasant; and, more recently, German airmen, how many he would never know.

Mike added one to his score now, at 0825 precisely on this 28th day of September, 1942. He was twenty-year-old Hauptmann Hans Flecker from Ingolstadt in Bayern, and he experienced no alarm nor pain beyond the searing, instantaneous heat blast that utterly destroyed his chest after the 20 mm. A.P. shell thrust through the armor plate behind his seat as if it did not exist. His 109F continued its flight with dead hands and feet on the controls, little damaged and as if nothing had happened.

Mike did not see it crash, but two of his section watched the fighter steepen its dive as if seeking concealment in its shame, and go straight in, the spume falling back like a shroud.